HEART

OF

ARSON

"THE PHOENIX QUEEN"

BY CARAMIA, SAMI

<u>*Prologue*</u>

(Maria's POV)

My first love was fire. As a child, I would spend hours watching the flames of a candle flicker, dancing around like a passionate ballerina, desperate to use its career to gain social status. I often studied its movements, as if there was a pattern that could tell a story. When I got older and was forced to watch the enemies of my father burn, I learned the fire had variations. Sometimes it was the elegant dancer I knew well, other times it was a powerful force, which wouldn't stop consuming until it reached every crevice of its destination.

I know this isn't a story I can tell in its entirety from my own perspective. My bias makes me unable to contain my deep displeasure that sometimes I was wrong. I fear even more that I may have been right, but was born into a world where I was destined to never belong. Regardless, if I can contribute one last thing to the world, it will be my story as is, even if the version of that story is beyond my control.

I come in defense of the child version of me, where I suppose the story really began, or at least bearing the factors that would determine its outcome. The first thing I can remember before being reborn in a sense, was the night I realized my father's tyranny did not exclude his own family. The night I realized that just because I am a part of the Fiamma bloodline, doesn't mean I am immune to fire.

It was the night he charged my mother with treason.

There were rumors, I thought were fairy tales considering my age at the time, that the Fiamma bloodline was once immune to fire. Legend has it they were pyrotechnics right after the fall of the old world. Gifts the gods must have granted them back when they were nothing, their ability to survive strong heat waves and volcanic eruptions being impressive even to the divine forces that sought to send humanity into extinction.

I always loved the story of the first Fiamma, Firenze.

As the myth goes, she was a fierce individual who sacrificed her humanity to save her family as the world caught ablaze. The gods respected her sacrifice, blessing the InFiamma bloodline, but not until the remaining Fiammas who were deemed unworthy burst into flames.

Firenze couldn't bear to remain in her homeland knowing her sacrifice was for nothing. The ghosts of those who perished looming over her shoulders in the place they passed. She soon founded InFiamma, her fire-wielding skills both feared and respected by those who came together to form the kingdom that stands to this day.

The Fiammas presumably lost their powers a few generations later with Blaze "The Burnt" and his questionable ego, which briefly left the Fiamma name vulnerable. It was Ash Fiamma, son of Blaze, who was named "The Great" and restored the Fiamma honor.

This was the story that ran through my mind the night I heard my mother's screams as she was hauled from our wing. We were the only two inhabitants of the west wing, something I thought was a privilege before I realized it was a cage, like we were my father's pets. I left my chambers to see her dragged from the room right before the stairs. The room that would be boarded up and covered with wallpaper shortly after her death.

I made eye contact with one of the guards, my father's best friend, Thoman. He pointed with a finger harshly to my chambers, signaling me to go back inside immediately. No affection or worry on his face, just blank monotone composure. My mother looked back at me, begging them to take me instead. I didn't understand what was happening, but because of that, I thought it was my fault.

So, I hovered my much smaller hand over an open flame, holding my own sacrifice inspired by Firenze's story as my mother's screams could be heard throughout the castle, even while she was on the pyre acres away. Whether it was to beg the shadows to take me instead of my mother, or as a bargain to make me invincible to fire itself, I no longer remember. It is the flaw with my account of how this all came to be.

What I know for certain is that the outcome did not save her, but granted me a set of scars up to my elbow, as well as a valuable gift, the ability to see the dead.

It was that night I met my ancestor Brando, brother to Blaze "The Burnt" and ruler of InFiamma centuries ago. I knew of him from history books, as he was labeled "The Odd" for the very gift I now possessed. When Brando saw ghosts, he was called crazy. When Firenze did, she was powerful. I did not want to test where I'd fall on the line of sanity, so I kept my mouth shut.

Brando taught me to master blending into the shadows, to find the hollow indents behind tapestries, to make myself scarce in a court that would soon grow to hate their mad king, and take their hate out on me as well. He was the companion in my isolation.

Being alone from such a young age, save for my best friend who was gone by the time I became queen, and my cousin who had his own duties even younger, I both knew exactly who I was and not at all. I feared the fire in a way that made me consumed with it all while hugging the shadows, for so long the only intimacy I would allow.

Truth was, I didn't know who I was at my fundamental core until Arabella Marella told me herself. Us two were complete opposites, destructive towards each other's nature. However, there's a moment when the lava hits the water, where it's content in being extinguished, the raging waters brought to a soft steam.

I don't have any regrets. I would do it over again a million times or until the sun takes the earth, I really don't care. Since I have an indefinite amount of time to kill, I might as well confess the sins of my reign.

Chapter 1

Maria Fiamma would be more content watching the entirety of her father's kingdom burst into flames before she was forced to take on the burden, yet her father was the one whose ashes lit her reign ablaze.

Her ability to see ghosts did not help the matter at hand. Especially considering the apparitions who walked with her through the halls during her late night stroll were the last victims of her father, King Elias.

Elias Fiamma burnt everyone at the stake. At first, only the fiercest of enemies, but as his madness inclined, even the most common of crimes would be punishable by pyre. It got to the point that there would be mass burning parties for the accused. Crimes from legitimate treason, which was rarer than the other end of the spectrum, to missing a court event by five minutes. It was those victims that found their way into the halls the night before Maria's coronation.

She ignored apparitions well, though amongst themselves they all knew she had the sight. It didn't stop her from apathetically staring past the burned figures with missing eyelids as they glared at the heir with an intensity that wasn't just directed at her, but her entire bloodline. They did not speak, did not yell at her, but they didn't need to for Maria to know why they were looming.

The living, the dead, it really made no difference. They all hated her equally. When you're the spitting image of the man who murdered millions in the kingdom, that'll happen.

Maria had dark eyes, with a rough shaggy haircut and sharp features. Her tall height was the only thing her mother's genetics thought was worth putting up a fight. Other than that, she could have been mistaken for King Elias' twin brother, if he was to have walked straight out of some classic romance.

Maria couldn't help that either. Her mother made gorgeous dresses, sure, but being isolated for so long had Maria develop a disdain for being uncomfortable in the name of adhering to social norms. The most effort she'd ever muster is when her childhood confidant made her wear a homemade black corset over her white flowy shirt. Maria could've sworn her ribs would puncture her lung. Therefore, if any court members were awake at this hour, they wouldn't be surprised to see Maria strolling about in said white flowy shirt and brown pants, sword at her hilt.

They would, however, be very surprised to see her whirl around, yelling at thin air.

"I'm not the one who killed you, so maybe get your fucking ugly faces on elsewhere. Go find peace or something," she spat once the numbers became too much. It was at the point where there were at least fifty in the grand foyer, the most she'd ever seen in one spot at once. The max before was around eight, and even that was excessive.

They just remained still, staring at her, smelling like leather and ash, eyeballs unmoving. Ghosts didn't need to appear the way they died; they were doing it on purpose. Maria knew this, so if the ghosts were full of spite, they had met their match with her. She simply pulled a vial of lotion from a small satchel connected to the hilt of her sword, before applying it while she stuck her middle finger up.

As she lathered her own scars in the scent of patchouli, that is where the focus of the ghost's eyes went. It made Maria feel more self conscious, which caused her to express more rage.

Before she could throw her lotion into the swarm, a voice sounded behind her, making all other apparitions disappear.

"Maria," Brando, her ancestor and personal apparition as she liked to refer to him, spoke with a sternness in his voice.

"Fuck them," Maria murmured, putting the lotion away regardless.

"No," he said taking a step forward, "Not 'fuck them', they will not find peace unless there is change.

Especially since your father found peace, leaving his victims to out-suffer him.”

Maria considered it of course, but didn’t actually think her father found peace. Especially considering he burned himself alive, in an ironic twist of fate, in order to engage in war with the gods, to rule over them too. How could he not have a special purgatory? Maria never asked. She never asked why she couldn’t see her mother's ghost either. She did not want to know the answer.

“He’s dead, shouldn’t they be satisfied? Or do they want me to off myself as well?” Maria scoffed as she strode past Brando, heading back to her solo, semi-abandoned west wing.

“I need you to be serious. Your coronation is no joke, and you’re lucky retired commander Thoman and your cousin Cienfuegos are still alive to ensure you even have a shot of ruling this kingdom,” Brando expressed as he followed after Maria. She pulled a joint from her pocket and put it to her lips, lighting it with a match.

“I should just go fuck off into the woods and live like the feral animal everyone in this kingdom has treated me as,” Maria stated, her voice laced with irritation.

Brando, although never with ill manners or disdain, matched her irritation. “Take whichever mistress your father hasn’t touched yet to bed to relieve some steam for all I care. Just make sure come tomorrow you are able to make coherent speeches and logical decisions."

Maria knew he was right. If she left it all behind, it would leave Cienfuegos vulnerable. He was her closest friend, even after he was forced to run the military district at age sixteen, just three hours after becoming an orphan. If he could take on the responsibility and still have the stamina seven years later to keep her alive, she could return the energy. So she strode to bed, begrudgingly preparing for her future as Queen Maria Fiamma.

Brando knew she would. He saw her future already all those years ago, when he was first brought to her. Because of that, he also knew that she would be going to bed without anyone to love for the last time. He could only pray that once the gods saw that love, who Maria could be if she was given a chance, they wouldn't take her away.

'♥♥♥'

Luckily, it wasn't public knowledge that Maria treated her coronation like a colonoscopy. That she spent the days leading up to it drinking non stop, and groggily approached the event with disdain.

InFiamma's rulers, by custom, never did the extravagant servitude compared to kingdoms like Cadence, whose rulers were physically bathed by their serfs. Maria was given her breakfast, curtains flung open, then left alone to ponder her future.

It gave Maria a chance to talk to Brando before leaving her room for the last time, a mere child of the Mad King.

"You won't be able to see me, but I'll be there. Just remember not to break your neck when the crown is put on. It weighs a ton," Brando said from the corner of the room, sipping a coffee that no one prepared for him.

Maria tried the thousand question game with him the first few weeks of his appearance, but he never budged. The only explanation for the random obtaining of objects was, *"I lived through life, I deserve my simple pleasures."*

As he put down his coffee, crossing his legs in satirized elegance, Maria cracked a smile out of nervousness. "Comforting."

He replied with the most warmth Maria has ever seen him express, "Have some tea by the window and clear your mind. All will be well." Warmth, but not happiness, as a hidden sadness lingered behind his dark eyes.

"I'm fine, you know. I'm not going to bolt. I have nowhere to go anyways," Maria expressed, moving her shaggy, nearly curly hair from her face.

"I know you aren't going anywhere, but the road ahead is long and complicated. The players you meet today will be definitive forces in the game of your reign. Assess them well."

Maria glanced at her sword that laid against the red velvet armchair by the fireplace. Per tradition, InFiamma rulers could take one object from their past into their reign, an object that best defines their spirit. You ask anyone in the castle, they'd tell you the loner child that roamed the halls had a sharp edge that kept everyone 13 feet away.

It is why Maria wasn't in a position to seek friends out in the crowd, especially since her cousin Cienfuegos was stuck in Inferniana, the military city.

"Pray tell, Odd One, who are these key players?" Maria insisted as she took a bite out of the toast her servants made for her. It made her a bit uneasy, seeing as the only time she'd eat regularly would be when the castle slept. The delivery of food only started when her father died.

"I do not grant the details, but as you already know almost every territory and continental kingdom will be in attendance. Except Eminence, and Inferniana, of course…"

Maria rolled her eyes at the mention of her aunt's kingdom, ruled by her mother's sister, Lucille. After her mother's death, Lucille declared InFiamma as a whole her enemy, and due to Maria's identical resemblance to Elias, she left Maria to live with what was presumably her ilk.

Never giving another thought to her niece, who was to become queen.

"Yes, yes, I know who RSVP'd but *who* from Cadence, *who* from Withelle—"

"Think closer to home. Think… of rekindling," Brando replied, swirling around his coffee using his pinky. He did that whenever he wanted to give an answer to the weird things he hinted at, but wouldn't, or couldn't, get into detail.

Maria considered where there was estrangement. She was a huge history person, spending most her life reading up on those who ruled before her, like Brando himself, who did decently in his reign.

The only place she could think of was a deteriorating island territory that politically branched away from InFiamma before Brando's rule. It was ruled semi-democratically, the head councilmen being a Marella. The Marellas were a house that created most of the plumbing, fishing, sewage, and even on occasion, electrical resources for InFiamma.

If it wasn't for them, the mainland wouldn't have any modern industrialization since the Secondary Dark Ages centuries ago.

Before Maria could question it further, Brando was gone in the blink of an eye, obviously avoiding the conversation. It left her staring behind where he sat, at the armor she was set to wear at her coronation.

She slid out of bed and gazed into the mirror. She didn't quite understand the purpose of the person that greeted her in the reflection, face sharp, guarded by her typical thick black hair.

Now, with a kingdom on her back, she doubted she would have the time to do that soul searching. It was a shame she gained so many burdens, just as she gained freedom from her father. She allowed herself the final moments of contemplation as she sat on the windowsill just outside of her chambers.

'♥♥♥'

Arabella Marella arrived at InFiamma's kingdom with her father, Aquilla, and little sister, Margaret. Some people from home found Arabella's face off-putting, claiming she was a demonic sea spirit with her lithe figure and huge round eyes. Her fierce waves of emotions added to her disarming nature.

Margaret was a more classic beauty, a girl just of twelve. Margaret never had trouble making friends, fitting into gossip groups with ease. It made Arabella even more mortified at the fact that she was constantly in, or the subject of, said gossip back home. Never a mere spectator.

It was a factor into the reason Arabella practically threw her family onto the ship to come go the mainland, the second the council decided it was wise to do so. The Island gained their independence at the cost of losing all resources the mainland provided, being choked off from gaining those resources themselves. Now, with all the hardships the people of the Island faced, it was time to rejoin InFiamma for said resources, a risk that one never would have tried with Elias on the throne.

"Desperate times, desperate measures," Aquilla said to Arabella when the news broke of King Elias' death.

Arabella always felt robbed of her nobility, of being a part of a court that wasn't constantly suffering from natural disasters and a heroin epidemic. Instead she longed for InFiamma's traditions of bonfires and autumnal festivities. She had a habit of idealizing life in InFiamma long before her arrival was possible.

As they arrived on the castle grounds, the dead patches of grass where bodies once burned looked an awful lot like plots for her to plant her garden of luxury.

The footmen anticipated their arrival, as well as everyone else from all surrounding courts. It was customary for everyone to show up the same day of the coronation. It was a general rule actually, to prevent one party from scheming faster than another.

Therefore, they made great haste retrieving luggage and bringing it to the respective rooms. Arabella's father and little sister followed the footman while she was far too immersed in the architecture, leaving her behind to gawk at the ceiling.

There was a grand painting on the ceiling that looked as if heaven and hell of an ancient religion became one in the same. The polished wood was carefully sculpted into swirly designs and human anatomy. Once she snapped out of it after admiring every engraving the room had to provide, she realized she was abandoned.

Guests by the dozens began flooding in as there was a surge of arrivals. So, Arabella slipped down the first corridor she saw. She remembered from her father's discussions with the council that her family would be staying on the fourth floor of the east wing. Arabella, terrible at directions, assumed that was where she was heading. Unfortunately, she desperately needed a compass, as she clearly had no idea what east meant.

Arabella's heart began to palpitate when she realized the deeper she went—into what was actually the west wing—the more desolate and abandoned it looked. The wallpaper peeled as Arabella ran her hands along the wall, causing her to sharply pull back in fear she would get charged with the damages.

She focused on the stairs and how they went from a mahogany wood to caved in stone the higher she climbed. Arabella assumed the change was due to any recent renovations in the castle stopping abruptly. It felt like she was entering a tower guarded by a dragon, that no other person would dare enter. For a moment, her illusion of InFiamma, the way it appeared in her dreams, was fractured. Her hands began to sweat, and she felt something brew in her stomach that she pinpointed as homesickness.

She noted that multiple windows were broken open on her left, vines infiltrating the interior of the stairwell and wrapping its ivy around the railings. It was when she got to the top of the stairs that things began looking slightly neater. A tad more lived in at least. She allowed herself a sigh of relief, releasing some tension. Maybe the floor she lived on would be habitable.

Regardless, she was just about to turn around when she saw a woman with black hair leaning against a pillar looking out a window, into the thick forest where the trees reached the heavens. Her face looked tired and worn from stress as she was sipping a cup of tea, too deep in thought to even notice Arabella peering behind the corner.

It wasn't until she attempted to slide back that she ended up tripping against a loose risen stone, straight into the woman's point of view. Arabella stumbled again when attempting to stand up straight, her foot getting caught on the bottom of her dress. The woman stared at her, cup of tea still in her mouth. Her dark eyes were fixated on Arabella, looking her up and down as she smoothed her dress out.

Arabella avoided eye contact, but noted the women's casual attire, and build that hinted at hard labor. "Sorry, I'm lost," Arabella said, waving her hand slightly, a pathetic attempt at an introduction.

"Yeah, I gathered that," the woman said as she stared blankly at Arabella's clothing, causing Arabella to fidget with the hems of her sleeves. The woman took pity on her though, speaking up again to ask, "What's your name?"

Arabella responded, "Arabella Marella," blushing with anxiety. Her experience with having a name that rhymes always set her up to be the subject of schoolyard taunts. The woman sipped her tea once more as she redirected her gaze to the forest outside.

"Down the way you came, the wing directly across."

The woman had no time to introduce herself in return before Arabella turned heel and ran out of embarrassment. Arabella didn't question how the woman knew where her family was staying. She assumed it was a servant on their personal time.

Which could have been true if the woman hadn't muttered under her breath, "I'm Maria Fiamma, by the way."

With that, Maria returned to her room, once again left to consider the armor she was born to wear before preparing herself for her coronation. The festivities were only a few hours away.

Chapter 2

Despite the sun shining just hours before, thunder began to crack around the castle. The cobblestone walls outside were drenched with the rain. The forest, despite the thick tall trees, swayed ever so slightly as the wind pounded into them. Stable boys could hardly be seen in the storm as they gathered the animals into shelter. The storm was projected to get worse.

Most everyone was in the great hall awaiting Maria's arrival, idly chatting amongst themselves, indulging in speculation. Would Maria burn her enemies like her father? Would she take after her graceful mother, whose memory was wiped from the castle the day she was murdered?

Speculation went rampant on whether she would take dozens to her bed the second the festivities were through, just as her father did. It was as if two thirds of the people waiting in that hall weren't the same people that watched Maria grow up in the castle. She was virtually hated by all of them because of who she came from. The face she wore served as her father's proxy as the teachers made her cry, as if she could change the laws. As if she could un-burn her math teacher's lover at 8 years old.

As she sat in the empty kitchens, listening to drinking glasses clink together while hanging upside down, the window cracked open, beckoning the storm. Maria wanted nothing more than to be one of the mice feasting on the crumbs under the cabinet. If she too were a mouse, maybe she could run into the forest and live in some ragged tree that fell from a storm centuries ago, ready to host life once more.

Again, Maria didn't care for the throne. She did when she was younger, a reckless teen who was ready to live the life she was denied until her father publicly designated her his heir, after the doctor confirmed the likeness of the king producing children at his age would be lower than possible. Before then, when Maria was thirteen, she built her entire reign in her head, her cousin Cienfuegos at her side, and her best friend that would eventually become her first love, Abigail, her consort.

Maria once wanted that power, and wanted everyone to know she would hold it. She'd let every authority figure know when the tables were turned, her reign would be hers, and no one else's. She had mentally scripted what she'd say on her coronation day over and over again.

Her words failed her now that it was time. She could feel her inner teenager particularly betrayed by the lack of ability to communicate those feelings she could no longer identify. It was like there was a distant echo in her armor, right where her heart should be.

Even she didn't know the answer to the questions the public anticipated. She knew nothing at all as she peeled herself from the floor of that kitchen, into the hallway where the royal guard waited for her.

Maria was greeted first by her father's best friend, the same man that dragged her mother to her execution. Behind him were two rows of a dozen soldiers each, ready to lead the way. They gave each other a hesitant look before Thoman gestured his head towards the hall that would lead Maria to her coronation.

'♥♥♥'

Maria tried not to see red as she entered the great hall. The last time she was there was when her father died. He went to her chambers himself, the only time he did so since her mother died.

"Come with me to the throne room, it is almost time!" he exclaimed erratically, his hair disheveled.

It was like Maria was looking into a mirror of madness, seeing someone that could've been her if she lost all her wits. She was in a position where she hardly left her rooms, lest she got in the middle of one of his moments. Him coming by himself, no guards, no consorts or mistresses, was troubling. It was then she knew only one of them would survive the day.

He brought her to the empty throne room, a negative omen considering towards the end of his life there was a new party every day, or an orgy more like. He climbed up the steps of the dais to sit on his throne.

Maria noticed his throne was wet, but wasn't too concerned in the moment considering he was always spilling alcohol everywhere, all the time. The liquid being all over himself told her he either had a rough night, or pissed himself. None of which would be shocking.

"I am going to war, son? Daughter? I forget what you are," he threw out nonchalantly, considering the left-over memories of the person he used to be, and family he used to have. The nonsensical comment almost made Maria laugh, but she wouldn't dare when he was in this erratic state that only came on in the last two years.

"Anyways, I have decided to challenge God for his throne. As my heir, you must rule this kingdom until I return," he insisted with a tone of urgency, taking a lighter out of his pocket. Objects like a lighter fell under items that shouldn't exist anymore. Elias looked his daughter in the eyes, gave a small smile, and lit it.

The royal guard entered, Thoman at the lead, getting ready to deliver news on the war plans being set to wipe out Eminence's resources. They were there to see Elias drop the lighter onto his lap, to see how quickly he went up in flames. As he tossed the lighter to the side. Everyone in the room could have sworn he was laughing instead of screaming as he burned himself alive.

Maria walked under the man-made sword arch that led straight towards the dais. It was both for show, and protection. Through that tunnel she saw the throne in the back center of the stage, a fire pit on the side of the stage, and across from that on the adjacent side, a variety of tasks she'd have to complete involving fire to entertain her people.

True to the coronation tradition, inspired by Firenze Fiamma's power-granting sacrifice making it so the upcoming ruler must take an unconcealed object with them to their coronation, Maria tightly grasped her sword as she climbed the stairs to the dais platform. Out of instinct, and nervousness, she held it firm against her hip.

She reached the top of the steps, her armor slightly glistening in the light as she scanned the crowd. She was greeted with wary faces. Some she recognized as long standing houses at court, some emissaries from foreign courts such as Withelle, hard to miss with their bohemian attire. One face in particular caught her eye, the eerie looking woman that stumbled into her wing earlier that day, who was looking at her with her already large eyes bulging with surprise.

An amused smirk crossed Maria's face. To be fair, Maria didn't need guards considering she was feared like some mythic beast, locked away for everyone's safety. It was true she was lethally skilled when it came to using swords, daggers, and even most hand-to-hand combat, but she never had to use it against anyone except the one occasion regarding her father.

Nevertheless, Maria wasn't interested in a meet and greet. She just wanted to get the ceremony over with.

If the heir did not have a regent or authority figure to give over the crown, a stand in would be used. The person who stepped up from the shadows to bestow the honor had everyone trembling, gasps murmuring throughout the crowd.

"You son of a- I thought you weren't coming," Maria beamed, her body language turning more relaxed.

"If I told you I was coming, it could've gotten into the wrong hands. I can only do the ceremony though. I can't leave the military district for long," her cousin Cienfuegos replied, arms spread wide with a huge smile on his face.

Despite their cheerful attitude towards each other, the crowd remained cautious. Cienfuegos was the second most feared, most powerful person in InFiamma. His presence alone secured Maria's reign with the backing of Inferniana, the military district. Any ideas of a coup would be dismissed quickly.

Cienfuegos grabbed Maria's crown, a skeletal looking accessory made of gold and garnet. She took a knee as they proceeded, both of them familiar with how the ceremony went.

"This crown is a symbol of loyalty, of the people, of your divinity. Treat them well and they shall do the same. Treat them ill and you may meet hell's flames," Cienfuegos recited. Maria made a face that almost caused both of them to erupt into laughter. "Swear that you will perform your duties as ruler of this kingdom to the best of your ability, with good intentions and good faith."

"I swear," Maria replied as he placed the truly heavy, as Brando warned, crown on her head. She was sure he was watching from somewhere in the back, or from some rafter in the ceiling. Even though they could communicate, that didn't mean Maria monitored his every movement.

Cienfuegos extended an arm, assisting Maria up. There were more tasks she had to complete though. Rituals that were ridiculously dangerous and useless for anything other than posturing.

The one she was hesitant the most about was the trial of fire, a mock ceremony similar to the Firenze legend she performed as a child that granted her those scars. Most rituals were based on Firenze, which her experience proved to be both an advantage and disadvantage.

The test was that Maria had to hover her hand over the flames until the chanting was done, as a symbol of strength, and a promise of a blessed reign. Rumor had it, back then her father couldn't dish what he regularly served, as he lifted his hand before the chanting ended. Maria made her way to the firepit left of the stage as the officiant began.

Maria dipped her hand just over the flame with ease, her eyes showing a clear sign of the dissociation she long ago mastered. She remained there until Cienfuegos nudged her.

"I've got places to be, show off," Cienfuegos muttered.

Maria lifted her hand from the flames. They were already calloused and scarred, so any potential harm wasn't noticeable compared to her youth. The crowd was murmuring at the nonchalant display, words like *Pyro*, and *Firenze reincarnate*, raging through the crowd. Maria, despite being no novice, still took a minute to regain socially acceptable consciousness when coming out of her dissociation.

She rolled her wrists, squared her shoulders, and did her best to prepare for Cienfuegos' choice of trial, where the fun actually began. They never made it there though, because as Maria strolled for her cousin, a loud bang sounded in between them.

The world stopped for everyone in the building. There were lists of contraband that shouldn't exist anymore given The Accords, made around the beginning of InFiamma, honored both by them and all surrounding kingdoms.

A firearm was most definitely amongst that list of contraband. Most people had never seen one in person for well over a hundred years, factoring into why there was such a delayed reaction after it was fired off.

There was rustling in the silence, then a yelp. The culprit, a ragged looking man no doubt from Eminence, was pinned to the ground by Aquilla Marella. The gun was kicked from the man's hand, and one of the guardsmen arrived at the scene within seconds to help apprehend him.

Maria took in the scent of the room after the gun was fired off. She knew of gunpowder, but not of its pungent smell. The history books never mentioned that in all her years of reading in the corner of her room.

Cienfuegos jumped off the stage, his axe handed to him by another military companion, the infantry doctor and son of Thoman, Jessie. He had the man pulled to the ground, axe against the man's throat in seconds before he shoved towards Maria.

"What would you like to do with him?" Cienfuegos asked Maria, gritting through his teeth as he pressed the blade tighter to the man's neck.

Maria looked around, first to Thoman who was directly to the right of the stage. He looked at her with a stare that read "*Make him your next trial.*" She looked back to Cienfuegos, whose eyes practically begged to be the one to do the man in on command. She then scanned the room over the faces of her people, all holding their breath. She knew they were waiting for the command for a pyre to be readied. In fact, their faces read very little hope that Elias' tyranny had ended, rather took on new forms.

Then, there were the actual victims of King Elias, appearing to her once more in their charred form, standing shoulder to shoulder with the unsuspecting guests.

Indeed, a pin drop would have been an atomic sound with how deafening it was, her eyes searching for Brando to indicate something, *anything*. Her eyes instead landed on the big-eyed woman she met hours before, who was the first person to grace her presence not as a subject or political diplomat, but a complete stranger.

In that rip in time, where it seemed to be frozen completely, Maria pondered who she would have been if she wasn't a royal, but a lonely traveler in a pub, playing a guitar, locking eyes with that of a beautiful tavern wench after a drunken brawl. She would have, in that world, done just what she did next as she considered the scars on her hands.

"Let him go. He's not worth it," she decided hesitantly, but firmly, as the room erupted into gasps.

"He had a weapon," Thoman spat out as he approached the man in Cienfuegos' arms.

"And he will be thoroughly questioned by my cousin here back in Inferniana, but if you want my father's opinions you should collect his scattered ashes and ask him," Maria spoke with an authority she did not recognize.

The murmuring resumed even more intense than before, as a voice amongst the crowd declared:

"All hail Maria, the Phoenix Queen!"

The ghosts crowding the room changed forms from the state they were in when they died, to who they were when they lived. Maria nearly couldn't tell who in the entire great hall was actually alive. It wasn't until the dead turned around in bulk to exit, whole families that once perished by fire looking as though they were on their way to a carnival for some fun, that Maria Fiamma realized it would be the last time their souls would walk through the castle.

Chapter 3

The assailant made sure to exhibit little gratification for the mercy as he cursed at Maria during his exit. He was shoved into a military carriage along with Cienfuegos and Jessie. Their goodbyes were brief due to the sensitive nature of the situation, as well as the fact that it was still pouring outside.

Maria knew Cienfuegos would have a field day questioning the man. Figuring out if it was a personal issue, or one that threatened war. God, Maria did not have the energy for a war.

Socialites and court bachelorettes flocked to Maria as the celebratory party began. She still wasn't quite all there, everything feeling a tad mentally hazy, on top of the sensory overload issue she was facing.

She was, however, doing well enough to entertain with as much amusement as she would when she first started the night. The women were beautiful, and the men were making pretty promises of military alliances amongst funding for projects Elias would've hated, but offered no appeal to Maria, either.

The way everyone praised her at the drop of a dime made her nostalgic for those early days in her life when she wanted to be loved and accepted by her people. She was being regarded as some hero that was different from her father. What kept her levelheaded was remembering something bad about each person who greeted her, from her childhood teacher's curt bows and congratulations, to the few other people her age at court who excluded her from everything, now planning V.I.P parties. The only person she cared about, that was alive, already left for what Maria anticipated was an equally long time.

Thoman, who barely said goodbye to his son, was the one that proposed Maria reconvened in the council room to examine the firearm. Maria obliged, both so she could leave the exhausting spectacle, and to geek out over the forbidden artifact in private. She bid everyone a general farewell, but encouraged them to get shitfaced enough to leave her alone for the next week while she could find someone to keep the nobles booked and busy.

Maria sat enthusiastically in a secured office just before the council chambers. Chewing on her rubber hair band, she intently examined the firearm. The handle looked like bone white porcelain, but didn't feel it, engraved with tan swirly designs. She wasn't familiar with the particular model, but appraised it to be from the mid to late 19th century. The intricacy of the design, and shape of the handle gave it away, as well as the simplicity of its functions.

Maria had seen firearms before, a privilege only those with royal status were permitted to know about. There was a secure location in the archives dedicated to the blueprints of such weapons, and how they worked. She only had a moment with the weapon before there was a knock at the door.

"Aquilla Marella from the Island would like a word," a guard spoke. Maria nodded her head in permission. She remembered Aquilla had the man down in seconds after the shot was fired, keeping the man on the ground from trying to get in another. In Maria's personal presence, he looked less determined and, if anything, stressed and nervous.

His posture was straight, and while that would usually give off confidence, his back was stiff like a board. His jaw was clenched down tight as he tried to give a polite smile.

"Your Majesty, the Island needs InFiamma's support desperately with the consistent storms and hurricanes that have plagued us. We lack the resources to rebuild after these disasters hit. We currently have three sections of the Island destroyed by Hurricane Pearl, and dozens of families displaced. I believe, in exchange, we can provide InFiamma with ideas for architecture and industrialization that are still compliant with The Accords," he explained, listing all his hopes for their political merger.

The Marellas were the first noble family in the court of InFiamma. Their people mastered the water that overtook a majority of what the land used to be before it was hit with the natural disasters that consumed humanity long, long ago. The Fiammas mastered the flame; their original homeland in the west being consumed by volcanic lava and fires, as well as solar flares.

The conflicting natures should have influenced the two houses against each other. Yet, the Fiammas were strong when the Marellas were passive. The Marellas were the voice of reason when the Fiammas needed softness. They worked fairly well, until the Island tried to become independent from InFiamma, in Ares Fiamma's time. Their independence was shortly won until they realized they lacked the key resources to carry on, now pleading to rejoin the kingdom of InFiamma.

Although Aquilla still had a clear strain on his face, as if expecting rejection, Maria surprised him when she granted him his wish to be a part of her personal council.

"Anyone willing to take down an assassin for me, before I even have a chance to prove myself worthy of saving, is bound to be of great counsel," Maria said with a light chuckle, and a tad of awkwardness, as she solidified his title as councilman.

She was spinning a ring on her finger to calm her anxiety, something no one else would have noticed, except Arabella, who was hyper-observant in the shadows. Arabella slipped into the room behind her father while no one was looking, except Maria, who knew Arabella thought she was slick. Maria would have to keep her eyes on the woman, who seemed to rival even Maria's own abilities with the way she moved through the shadows.

Nearing the end of the conversation, as they reconvened in the hallway Arabella found herself lingering behind Maria to overhear when the first council meeting would be held. When Maria bowed to take her leave from Aquilla, she nearly stumbled into Arabella, slightly towering over her.

Their eyes met, cheeks beginning to blush with the close proximity. Maria assumed that Arabella would scurry away again out of shyness, which was cute, but Maria couldn't get caught up with cute. She would smother cute.

Arabella, despite her calm flowy composure, practically had lightning bolts forming above her head as she said, "You could have mentioned you were the QUEEN," as she reprimanded Maria with dramatic hand gestures.

Aquilla lifted his eyebrows in amusement, and took his dismissal, allowing his daughter privacy in scolding the queen. He knew better than to ask questions. This took Maria aback, as she had never been scolded before by anyone in a lower station than her, beyond personal attacks.

Her cheeks turned a dark red. "I would have if you didn't flee like an injured dove, flailing your wings as you retreated," Maria mocked, flapping her arms with a smirk.

Arabella, being the nervous type, felt her heart leap into her throat, just as her younger sister Margaret burst into the hallway talking a mile a minute about a lord with many lands inviting their father to go hunting. She decided that was a good time to withdraw.

The guards beyond the study suggested it would be a good time for Maria to retire for the evening to prepare for the long years of duty ahead. She was more than happy to be saved by the graces of the guards, who displayed trust in her abilities as queen due to her mercy of the evening. The entire court felt gratitude that they were no longer ruled by Elias' paranoia.

Nevertheless, despite the praise and a day of achievements, Maria dismissed the guards, assigning them to the east wing to ward off any retaliation attacks from sympathizers in the castle. She only bothered to grab her cloak and dagger before setting off for the woods to think.

Maria crossed paths with various people on her way through the castle. She locked eyes with a few familiar faces from her father's council, those that were there that one day when she stepped over the line. The disapproving looks at the merciful daughter to the ruthless king they blindly followed were enough to make her shiver with anxiety.

One of the children of Withelle slipped their way up to Maria, wearing the tiara of their intuitives, the Oracles. The people of Withelle were incredibly passive and spiritual. They only came to events like such out of respect, usually delivering a prophecy to the upcoming ruler regarding their reign. Most Oracles were children, like the one who approached her.

The child cleared her throat before she began, "The Fae of the Fates spoke: The end of an Autumn rain, brings back what you've lost, takes away what you gained. Use those who are gone to aid in your reign. Ask, if the spark is started by arson, is it still a Twin Flame?"

Maria looked down at the child who was grinning, clearly excited that they were the chosen one to deliver the prophecy. "Thanks kid. Any other advice?"

"Just one thing," the child contemplated, her escort's eyes going wide, signaling for her to be quiet, but she was too deep in thought to pay any notice. "When your fate has aligned…when the cycle has been broken and started anew, and the wound bleeds red by the hands of blue…know you did all you could do."

"Morbid," Maria replied as she contemplated both rhymes. "Mind sending me a transcript of that?" she asked, cracking a grin, not letting herself internalize yet another fairytale too much. After all, her father's prophecy was something along the lines of 'great fame by great flames.'

The child smiled back, happy the prophecy had Maria amused. "It is already in the mail, on its way, Your Majesty."

That made sense, as her father had an elegantly designed poster of his prophecy on it. It contains a weird artistry that was ancient, that only those in Withelle could provide. The child's escorts tried to conceal their relief as they guided her away to the rest of their court.

Maria hardly took the Withelle ways to heart, but they were attuned with something that made them right in mysterious ways.

Chapter 4

When one becomes a ruler, the first order of business is typically to rule. With that comes the first council meeting held at dawn's first light the day following the coronation.

Most rulers barely take it seriously, either drunk or incredibly hungover from the previous day's festivities. Maria, on the other hand, went to bed after her stroll through the wet woods in its pitch black darkness, using the light from her tower's window as a beacon home.

She tried to find her sleep as early as possible, but not before requesting Arabella Marella also sit in on the council meeting to gain perspectives from someone else other than people two generations above her. She had about two hours of sleep, but was luckily as lucid as she was used to being.

They gathered in a mahogany room with gold accents, and a firepit that was so large it threatened the tapestry above. Maria sat at the head of the table, wearing a more practical crown of gold compared to the one from her coronation, studying that tapestry of silent fortitude. The tapestry was recently replaced with one depicting a queen sitting with a melancholy expression, gripping a scepter, which Maria too could understand. Beside the queen in the tapestry, similar virtues laid out, serving as a reminder that those even in the old world, the oldest world presumably, knew of such struggle.

Maria was thankful that the meeting started off with enough to talk about, and that those topics weren't of a threatening concern. The failed assassin did indeed hail from the northeast region, the kingdom Eminence, too small to consider a threat as of now. However, the motions were put into place to secure the border for the rest of the year, when they would reevaluate the threat.

Aquilla spoke of how the island territory was in desperate need of disaster relief from a recent storm that destroyed many community buildings. Elias' old supporters sneered just at the sight of the Marellas' presence, nevermind their participation and requests. It was inevitably up to Maria though, who decided to grant aid in exchange for seafood trade in the season for such.

It didn't get hot until Maria, in all her straightforward nature, asked the question, "It has been less than twelve hours since my coronation, but how is my reign being perceived in court?"

The council froze, considering their next words. Maria rolled her eyes, "Just be honest. You won't lose a tongue."

While her tone showed not a care for the perception either way, inside a flame was flickering rapidly, her pride hanging on a rope bridge just above.

Thoman, her father's most loyal supporter replied, "To be frank Your Majesty, there are concerns, despite the mercy you've shown at your coronation. They're regarding your past behavior, some of which have taken place in these very chambers."

Maria knew what he was alluding to. The day that Maria found out her dearest friend, and lover, was gone. Her entire family ashes mixed with pyre wood, serving as a reminder that Maria was not untouchable.

For the first time ever, Maria did not retaliate for her father's attention.

No, she marched right into his council meeting in the midst of him planning his great war that never came, and tore the place to pieces. This wasn't about the court's perception. It was about Thoman's, and the rest of the growing wrinkly faces around the table, just barely containing their grunts of agreement.

It was windy throughout the entire territory, causing most of the castle's residents to be in their own suites, making it easy for Maria to fly through corridors on her war path. Although the lights around the castle were dim, flickering from the oncoming storm, anyone could see the rare tears streaming down Maria's face, along with her jaw clenched so tight it threatened to break.

When she reached the council room, she kicked in the door with a swift motion, strolling right up to her father's chair. He was in the middle of a battle strategy using vintage chess pieces, marching into both the north and southeast territories, separate kingdoms independent from InFiamma.

"May I help you, child?" he asked, not looking away from his board, having no regard for Maria's clear distress.

It was what threw her over the edge. She originally planned to violate him verbally, maybe threaten to make his life harder by misbehaving at court, now that she was his sole heir and a bit more protected.

His disregard, however, unlocked an unfounded level of rage. Maria spat in his face from an already up-close position, a disadvantage after his pause turned into a right hook, cracking Maria's cheek from her right, then her left, until she was stumbling back with blood spewing from her mouth. If there was one thing true about Maria's character, it was that she simply didn't know when to quit once her rage activated.

Rage she did, as she got up from where the last hook knocked her on the floor, and charged at her father while dodging another one of his hits. Elias was a muscular man, built in the way where he could lift up a small horse if he put his energy into it. Maria was quite tall considering she was sixteen at the time, but she was just barely beginning to gain muscle. Nonetheless, her body was quite agile, so it was no unmatched opponent.

She hit him in the sweet spot the jaw provided, not needing her rings to be an assist, as she put her entire body weight into the blow. He went down with the same pace a lion takes down a zebra, being the one truly at a disadvantage as he laid sprawled out. His love-scorned daughter got on top of him, delivering hit after hit, until Thoman, in his less lethargic days, pried her off enough for her father to get up.

"Where is she!?" Maria screamed, blood following the words out of her mouth.

"Check the clearing, I'm sure one of the ash piles will provide some sort of identification," he said with a sly smirk, mirroring Maria by spitting his own blood as well.

He confirmed that Maria was too late to save Abigail, and somewhere her love, first love, met the same fate her mother did. It was enough to drive anyone insane, but Maria chose the path right then and there to operate out of spite. Spite, and solitude, so she would never feel the crippling rip of grief ever again.

Maria marched to the table, knocking every piece off of the board. She then stomped around the room ripping tapestries, breaking tables with a kick of her steel toe boots. Her grand finale, taking a chair to the royal portrait of her father, knocking it off the mantle and into the fire. Her father took a step towards her, but paused at her manic expression.

"Go ahead, father. Burn me. Burn me like you burned my mother. Like you burned my lover. Like you burn anyone unfortunate enough to know you. Rest assured I've

been preparing. I may not be fireproof, but I have the tolerance to take you down with me."

There was a beat of silence as they stared at each other, wondering who would make their move next. When it was clear Elias would not, Maria left the room. Despite dreading what she might find, she had to see it for herself, especially with Abigail's ghost nowhere to be found. It was after sifting through dirt and ashes for hours that Elias' claim was validated. Abigail's necklace was buried in ash next to her father's pocket watch.

Brando was there already, his silence not the result of having nothing to say, but rather knowing it was for the best to let the events run their course.

"Yes, that. I understand the concern, but rest assured I do not intend to care about anything that passionately again, except for this kingdom and the people in this room." A truth.

Lord Thoman studied her for a moment, considering. "Very well, Your Majesty. We understand your father, although necessary in strength, was messy and provoked much… irritation."

Maria was sure that wouldn't be the end of that, but it would have to suffice so they could talk about something of substance regarding the kingdom itself.

"Talk to me then. What are we looking at regarding the immediate territory?"

"I propose expanding public services and buildings within the villages. The better supported your communities are, the better they will return their benefits back to the kingdom" Arabella spoke up for the first time throughout the entire meeting.

Up until then, she'd just been listening in the background. Even Maria nearly forgot she was there during the memories of her father.

"Return back in what way?" the court's emissary asked thoughtfully. He was the most respectable towards the Marellas but that wasn't saying much. Maria could tell by observing Aquilla's reactions that the two men must've met while Aquilla was running the Island. The room was laced with tension.

Maria studied Arabella, who looked to her for approval to continue. Maria nodded, confirmation to go on.

"On the Island, although it has been proven we need InFiamma's resources, we have excelled in cultivating a culture where we give each other as much as we take, which expands the community's ability to work together and grow. For example, our public libraries and education curriculum have given us a spike in architects in the recent generations, who invented a beautiful solution to the current public health problem that InFiamma's main territory faces amongst the common folks—"

"Please spare me-" Thoman interrupted.

Both Aquilla and Maria insisted at the same time, "Let her finish," causing Thoman's face to turn red with embarrassment. Maria shot him a look, knowing full and well his leash would always be held by the most ruthless one in the room. She hoped he wouldn't make her prove herself on that front. Maria feared she wouldn't have the stomach to see those ruthless needs through, or wouldn't want to stop.

Thoman kept his mouth shut as Arabella went on. Clearly, she had a passion for expanding the public's resources. Maria agreed to have the semi-decent library expanded into a larger one, with critical texts moved once the renovations were finished.

She also agreed to have architecture students come study in InFiamma, offering a fully-funded internship as guests of court. She left that task to Arabella, finding the right candidates with the right ideas.

They discussed the old world, many of its inventions forgotten intentionally due to them producing harmful results, causing the world to collapse in the process. That is why The Accords, agreed upon even by rival kingdoms, states any new inventions concerning the public must be reviewed at a summit. The next summit wasn't for a few years, but Maria was someone who liked to be prepared well in advance when it came to reinventing history.

"So, it is settled. Aquilla, you're assigned to carry out the disaster relief trade. You have control of the ports indefinitely. Arabella, whoever impresses you the most, send their portfolio to me. You are assigned to public health indefinitely. Lord Thoman, you are now Ser Thoman and commander of the left legion. Apply that sneer to our enemies and they may shit themselves, lord knows you could use the air and excitement," which earned an uncontainable, though not without attempted restraint, smirk from the otherwise irritated man.

Thoman used to be the head commander of the military before he was pulled to be captain of the royal guard by Elias himself. The two never went long without being in each other's presence. His title, restored to a lesser degree, granted him the power that rivaled everyone except Cienfuegos and Maria herself.

In Maria's opinion, if he kept her alive thus far, he was the only man for the job. If there's any issues after that, it was her cousin's job to take care of. He could deal with the grouchy bastard.

"Everyone else, focus on our borders. I also want a report on what our armies look like, as well. In fact, Thoman, switch places with my cousin for a few weeks so you can get reacquainted with things. Other than that, you are all dismissed.”

Thoman even gave Maria a semi-attempted-gracious bow as she exited the council room. She barely noticed though, stealing a sideward glance in Arabella’s direction as she did so.

Brando appeared to her as she walked down the hall to her private wing. He knew she couldn’t acknowledge him, so he simply said, “Well done, Maria. You satisfied both parties in your first meeting and gained critical respect. Your reign will be prosperous for years to come,” he ominously stated with unfocused eyes.

<u>*Chapter 5*</u>

"I still have no idea how you managed to get on the council as well," Aquilla told his daughter as they settled into their chambers. "Nevertheless, I'm proud of you. You did well."

Arabella gave her father a smile as she sketched a few drawings next to her court notes, consisting of some portraits she did in the meeting. One was of the queen, who Arabella had to admit was much more attractive than she anticipated.

Arabella was pondering over Maria's visually pleasing self when her little sister snatched the sketch from her hands.

"Arabella has a crush!" Margaret screeched, running around the living area. Arabella wouldn't be surprised if her neighbors throughout the entire east side of the castle heard her.

"Shut up please," Arabella groaned over her sister's theatrics. She swore her sister was never quiet, and would kill to have a bit of peace where Margaret was concerned.

Unfortunately, Arabella was stuck listening to her sister as she had nothing to do other than schedule in future council obligations. Mainly, her source of fun was doing household chores, as she wanted their living space to mirror how impeccable it was in her dreams. Even then, as she'd wash the walls or brush out the carpet, her mind still wandered to what could be. Visualizing a distant version of herself in the future. That was until a letter was delivered at the door for Arabella, inviting her to the Museum of InFiamma.

"Arabella,

If you are feeling cooped up or generally curious, I would like you to join me on my trip this evening to InFiamma's private museum. They have a collection of ancient architecture I think you may be interested in. No pressure. I'll wait at the stables until noon. Try not to get lost again. I should have attached a compass, but I fear it would be too heavy for the envelope.
~Maria"

Arabella wasted no time jumping from her seat, rushing to get ready despite it only being the early afternoon. She already planned to indulge in the library to read up on the mainland's customs, outside of what her education provided on the Island. She understood even with the Island's own education on the surrounding kingdoms, she was likely taught things with a bias in mind.

She wanted to clear herself of all opinions when looking at the InFiamma side of things, while still keeping her knowledge from home. Through that analysis, she thought it could be the best way to make positive change while speaking to both parties, now that she was something of an appointed diplomat.

The museum would be even better, she thought. It combined not just written history, but physical artifacts as well. To see how the world was hundreds of years ago when everything reset, the beginning of the Age of Aquarius and the wars that followed… The invitation was a high honor.

Arabella would eventually start a conversation with the queen on why the museum's materials would be better shared with the public, making sure everyone is on the same page of what the history was. However, before potentially offending the queen and bossing her around, which she was destined to do regardless, she needed to learn the queen's personality in order to find the right language to use.

Arabella dressed in a shimmery, indicolite blue dress, with white ribbons going up the bodice. The ribbons tied off with a small bow at the top of her breasts. The bottom of the dress was circular and flowy, delayed in following her movements.

For her makeup, she tried to indulge in many of the popular makeup trends in InFiamma tradition, because that she did know. InFiamma's makeup usually consisted of a bare face since foundation was too easily melted in the fire's heat. Since many of InFiamma's traditions were fire based, even before the tyranny of Elias, it just wasn't practical.

Aside from that, glowing liquid highlighter and sharp eyeliner was always encouraged. While some people opted for the gold highlight, Arabella knew her strengths, and went for a more iridescent glow.

After spending two hours getting ready and fighting Margaret for her comments on "trying too hard", she gave her father a side hug before leaving. She found Maria relatively quickly, the stables being located in the southeast of the castle.

"You didn't get lost. Good job," Maria teased subtly.

"Hard to get lost when the person I'm meeting is pushing six feet and has so much hair," Arabella teased back.

Maria brushed her hair to the side in a jokingly pretentious manner. "The ladies would kill for this hair."

Arabella rolled her eyes, secretly noting that's not the only thing the ladies would kill for where Maria was concerned.

'♥♥♥'

While Maria would've preferred plain horseback riding, just a saddle and the wind, she didn't know how Arabella would have fared riding. Therefore, from the stables they took the royal carriage to the main village, the Heart of InFiamma.

The two women talked about their mutual appreciation for history, Arabella even inserting some Island history Maria did not know. This surprised Maria. She considered herself somewhat of a historian after a life in isolated silence, only her history books to keep her company.

Apparently, when the Island went independent, they had a period of enlightenment where the curriculum in schools was less mandated and more focused on life skills and the arts. From that, the practicality of architecture came into fruition.

Inside the Heart of InFiamma, Arabella watched out the window as they drove to the core, where all the political information was typically stored when outside the castle itself.

The streets were lined with merchants selling glass art and crochet materials, amongst more practical things such as pottery and heavy duty leather shoes. Arabella observed, mouth open with surprise. Maria watched Arabella's expression softly.

People took note of the royal carriage, trying to glance in to see their new ruler whom they've yet to place outside of the public portrait. Maria sunk back further into her seat, bringing her knuckles to her lips in order to inconspicuously shield herself.

"Don't you want to see your people?" Arabella asked. Maria shook her head while remaining silent.

Arabella also sat back in her seat, allowing herself to watch the scenery go from a village town to an official place of business.

Stone buildings turned to marble, people wearing finer clothes and more concerned with getting to their destination. The driver opened Maria's door first once they stopped, but it was Maria herself who opened Arabella's.

Maria extended her hand for Arabella to take as she shimmied out of the carriage, minding her dress. Maria was wearing her typical flowy shirt and brown dress pants tailored to her figure.

An older woman greeted the two outside of the museum. Her hair was brown with gray highlights in it, and she wore it in a messy bun. She looked like one's stereotypical archivist librarian.

"Your Majesty," the woman bowed, which made Maria blush.

"Stop. It's still just Maria," Maria replied, waving the woman off. "This is Ember, professor of archives at InFiamma College down the road," Maria explained.

"I'm Arabella. Nice to meet you," she curtseyed, assuming it was the custom. Ember's lip twitched up as she looked at Maria, who was also smiling.

"Nice to meet you, Arabella," she bowed her head in return. "Follow me please."

"I didn't know InFiamma had a college. I thought everyone went to Cadence," Arabella whispered to Maria as they walked down the hall of the museum's entrance. She cringed when her voice echoed, definitely heard by Ember.

"Well, yes, but we offer some college programs as well. I had a personalized study, so I was with Ember here once I turned seventeen. I was here studying three weeks a year," Maria explained. Arabella wondered what Maria's education looked like other than those three weeks, if she had a semi-normal one.

"Now, if I wanted to do anything artistic for the sake of creating art, instead of preserving it, I'd go to Cadence. If I wanted to study medicine or agriculture, or even herbalism, I'd go to Withelle. To study marine biology, I suppose we'd typically send those guys to you, back in the day," Maria finished explaining as they arrived at large double doors.

A set of footsteps approached quickly from behind, padding up to Ember.

"Mom, there's been an incident with one of the major documents at the northern campus," a young woman blushed.

The woman was slightly older than Maria, and obviously Ember's daughter. Not only had she called her "mom," but her mousy brown eyes and curly hair placed in a bun looked just like Ember's. The resemblance was uncanny.

Ember's face turned as red as fire as she glanced at Maria. "Here's your final exam, I guess. You've been here enough to know the tour."

Maria nodded her head, and gave a smile to Ember's daughter whose eyes went wide once she realized who she barged in on. Ember dragged her daughter away, who was only able to give Maria a little wave.

Once Ember was gone, Maria spoke. "Want to see something totally off limits to the public?"

'♥♥♥'

Behind four bolted doors, that required three sets of puzzles keeping the wooden gears locked, was a gigantic room filled with a variety of foreign looking materials.

"Welcome to the world at the start of the Age of Aquarius," Maria whispered. Arabella nearly fainted. She grabbed Maria's arm on instinct as her head spun, Maria grasping under to support her should she actually faint.

First, there was a large paper poster of different logos explaining various digital platforms from the time. From social media apps where there were only photos being shared, to forums discussing whether aliens were a threat.

"Aliens?!" Arabella squeaked.

"There's no alien threat, it's just an example," Maria chuckled as she took Arabella's sleeve, dragging her to the next artifact.

There was a large table that held various burial methods, from sarcophagi to coffins, including urns and Viking boats. Arabella read the descriptions for each. "On my island, we do something similar to the Vikings, that's so interesting," Arabella explained.

"Lately though, there've been mostly casualties by storms hitting the Island, and well…" she trailed off.

"That's awful," Maria said before an idea flashed into her head. "Here, let's look at this."

All the way across the giant room there was another huge poster that represented a map, showing what the continents looked like before the flooding. At the bottom was a scale from what hurricanes typically looked like, to what they were when things got bad.

"Oh yes, I know about this. Even the deserts in the northern American continent were hit by tropical storms and hurricanes, until finally—"

"They got beaches?" Maria finished.

Arabella cut Maria a side eye before replying, "yeah."

Arabella's mother was always on the water when she was younger. She was a stubborn woman who refused to leave anyone behind, costing her own life when a category four hit the island. Her body was never found.

"Where is the information on architecture located?" Arabella asked to change the conversation.

Maria tilted her head to the door about five feet away. "Behind the adjacent door."

The doorknob was metal and cool to the touch. The inside had Arabella running about, looking at each table with wonder in her eyes. One table had a rather large diorama of a giant reddish bridge. The next table, a building called Burj Khalifa that was allegedly twice the size of the previous record holder for the tallest building, the Empire State. When she saw just how tall it was in reference to a tiny toy human, she took a seat on the ground and put her hand over her beating heart.

"I knew of these buildings but there were no replicas or dioramas… all just theory using sketches and blueprints," Arabella explained. She patted for her notebook, hidden in the deep pocket of her dress. She began taking notes frantically.

"Woah there sweetie, make sure it's legible," Maria chuckled, but Arabella waved her away. "You know, I'm okay with letting the interns in here as well to devise plans. On one condition that is," Maria smirked.

Arabella's eyes went into shock. "What's the condition?"

Maria gestured for Arabella to follow her over to a set of dioramas that had very peculiar designs. "You want me," Arabella cocked her head, "to build you a shiny bean?"

Maria dropped to the floor in a fit of laughter. "No, I want the green building next to it with the gold accents. Granted, not a tall one, make it wide, but that style has always been my favorite," Maria explained as she gestured around the building, highlighting her favorite features.

"I'm pretty sure we can make that work, granted you provide the resources," Arabella nodded, appreciating its gothic style.

"Excellent," Maria quipped happily. "When you mentioned public buildings, what for?"

"When I sent the letters yesterday, I requested that they come prepared to expand a community center that doubles as a new library, and recreational center," Arabella explained as they began their exit from the diorama room.

Before she left, she caught her eye on a series of dioramas against the wall from which they came, making it so she didn't initially see them.

"Are those automobiles?" Arabella asked with her head tilted.

"Close, they are airplanes," Maria explained. "Like UFOs but for humans," she teased.

Arabella slapped Maria's arm with her long sleeve.

Maria faked an "ouch" noise before revealing, "When I was younger and first heard of them, I swore every slow twinkling star was a flying machine in the distance. A part of the world that survived and didn't give up their way of life."

Arabella could swear she saw the vision behind Maria's eyes like a motion picture, a world that somehow fit everything in the museum. Likely more, as there was so much information lost once the elements took over. She imagined a quarter of the land went underwater just from rainfall alone.

On top of that, it had been centuries since that series of events occurred in human history. To most people, it was so far irrelevant that some barely paid attention in their classes when it was taught. Arabella couldn't fathom how humanity was proven to have such vastly different phases of existence. And yet some people just cared about the now.

Maria, on the other hand, knew her privilege intimately. She knew about the rise and fall of worlds because she had private instructors and the key to the city's secrets, even if her childhood was depressing. Her father, on the rare occasion in her very early childhood, served some use when he let her into the council meetings at eight years old. It was after her mother's death, when he taught her the importance of The Accords with the other nations. He kept that educational momentum until she was thirteen.

When leaving the area that held all of the forbidden knowledge and contraband, they entered the main area that Maria was initially expected to show Arabella. It provided the names and taglines of the rulers who came before her.

"Let's do a rundown quickly in case Ember quizzes you," Maria suggested with a half serious tone.

There was a giant stone wall that was carved with depictions of suns, stars, and black holes. There were many old world religions with sun gods, but InFiamma didn't pull from those as much as they remembered the devastating solar flares that knocked out most of technology a few centuries ago. On the same wall, the names of every relevant Fiamma were carved.

Firenze Fiamma "The Pyro"- Founder of InFiamma

Cyrus Fiamma- "The Tinker"

Unknown Sibling "The Forgotten" & Ares Fiamma (Spare to Heir)- "The Commander"

Blaze "The Burnt" & Brando Fiamma (Spare to Heir)- "The Odd"

Ash Fiamma- "The Great"

Elias Fiamma "The Mad"

Maria Fiamma "The Phoenix Queen"

Maria's throat bobbed at her name being freshly etched in on the stone, so soon into her reign. To her, the tag line was even worse. Elias' Fiamma wasn't added until his death; though he never cared for the village, or archives anyways. Maria hated her tagline for how it framed her entire life. It sounded as if she was some noble survivor in the House Fiamma, not someone who was actively treated as her father's accomplice.

"Are you offended that your father was labeled mad?" Arabella inquired. In waiting for a response, she fidgeted with her thumbs inside of her sleeve.

Maria didn't keep her waiting. In fact, she replied rather immediately. "No, I guess I'm just a sucker for the truth."

"Was it hard? Well, let me rephrase it. I can see it was hard. I'm just trying to piece together which part was hard for you," Arabella replied, inquiring not for a hidden motive, but genuine curiosity.

"All of it, truthfully," Maria shrugged as she moved on to the various other exhibits. The secondary exit, where they were leaving from, housed the hall of portraits. Everyone, except for Ares Fiamma's unknown sibling, had one. While Maria got curious and tried everything to get information on Ares' sibling, nothing existed. Otherwise, each person's portrait shared some sort of resemblance to Maria, even if it wasn't physical. Brando Fiamma looked most like Maria, in the way his eyes looked tired.

Arabella didn't question anything else. They barely spoke again until Maria said her goodbyes to Ember, who was dealing with the fact that someone used packaging tape to fix one of the oldest InFiamma documents. Maria made sure to put in the appointments for the interns to see the dioramas in the restricted section, which had Ember giving a knowing raised brow to both women.

When they climbed back into the carriage, unprompted, Maria gave answers to some of the questions Arabella had been repressing. Maria could see Arabella was nearly bursting at the seams with inquiries, but was too polite to bring them up.

"I mainly studied at home by myself. I was in charge of my own education outside of wars and strategy, and also math. I was not willingly going to do math," Maria smiled and then continued. "My teachers weren't very fond of me because of my father's actions, so I was always getting into trouble when I was younger. On the rare occasion I was intermingled with the court children. At fourteen I branched away from everyone else in educational and social matters."

"That's really sad—" Arabella fixed to say, but Maria cut her off.

"No, let's not do all that. It never would have been worth it forming attachments to those friendships anyways," Maria trailed off for a moment before snapping back into the conversation. "Most court kids my age left to study in Cadence, which you likely already figured."

"How come they never come home with the knowledge they gained from the arts, expanding

InFiamma's own artistic path?" Arabella inquired, lightly pressing her head against the window.

"Would you want to?" was Maria's simple reply.

They went over a bump in the road, banging Arabella's head off the window. "Ouch," both her and Maria said in unison. It did force Arabella to lift her head to see some people in an alleyway holding something over a fire.

"What about homelessness? What do you plan to do about that?" Arabella asked with her notepad already in hand.

Maria looked over at her with a confused expression. "There is no homelessness in InFiamma."

Arabella explained what she saw in the alleyway, and Maria chuckled. "That was an InFiamma ritual. They're probably burning something of a loved one's. It's a common ritual, but the most popular one is Firenze's, which I don't recommend doing."

Arabella was going to question why, but Maria switched the conversation. "I honestly didn't think I was going to live this long given my home situation, so until my father's abrupt death, I wasn't planning that far ahead," Maria confessed. "However, when I was younger and more opinionated on the topic, I suppose my first logical decision would be to make sure our homeland resources were secured, should my father ever cause InFiamma to be placed under sanctions.”

“Do you think the man with that contraband was declaring war?” inquired Arabella as she played with the hem of her sleeve.

Maria noted Arabella’s nervousness. She never typically had it in her to lie when it came to sparing the feelings of others, she also wanted to show hope in the situation as well.

“I can’t rule it out. I know my father’s personal enemies and why they’d want to sow chaos in my kingdom, using my rise to the throne as the event to set it off. However, I can’t become paranoid. I can only continue my trade negotiations with integrity, and plan for the worst in case it happens,” Maria expressed rather humbly.

Arabella nodded, sending her mind down a rabbit hole of various resources that need to be squared away, both in reserves and for trading purposes. She feared what a war would do to Gloucester, her island and home, which was just barely gaining those very resources that could be cut off.

Withelle held most medicines, and because of that they always tended to stay neutral in political affairs. Cadence was the one to worry about, because although their neutrality was forced by their people, they could withhold an abundance of necessary goods, not just art.

Withelle's trades worked on a bartering system. In exchange for medicine and herbs, along with more minor trades, InFiamma provided them protection on their borders. Withelle needed that compensation for their lack of military discipline. They haven't defended themselves since a war that happened generations ago, and due to their pacifism as a group of people, everyone was on board leaving them be.

Cadence, on the other hand, had their hands tied by their people constantly rebelling against the lavish ways of the wealthy. They did not have the funds nor personal resources to hold off their rebellions and fight an enemy kingdom.

They could, however, soothe their unrest by taking resources from InFiamma, and giving it to their own people. That would give them time to scheme in their own sinister ways, allying with whoever could provide them with assistance when they decide to take their people's resources away once more. Cadence's main motivation would be taking the land that would be left decimated from war as their own, for luxury living and splendor.

The Island was now a factor, re-allied with InFiamma. However, their combat techniques were so heavily water based, the use of tritons and spears wouldn't make a difference.

"Would you make the people from the Island come here if a war did start? You know, to fight?" Arabella mused, but Maria could feel the tension in the question.

"No," Maria confided. "In fact, I would send a lot of our defenseless citizens to the Island if you could spare the room, with resources to help ward off any invasive threats. I intend to have your father plan that for me."

Arabella admitted that was the smartest choice, especially if other kingdoms were showing their hand with special grade contraband. That was another thing Arabella needed to address.

"There were technological worlds, burials, and outlines for what the world used to be in that museum, but you did not show me the weapons. Do we have contraband like the one used against you at your coronation?"

Maria gave Arabella a look. Even those beautiful big eyes could not get her to slip such classified information to someone she just met, even if they were now an official confidant. Thoman knew that answer, showed her the day before, and Maria would pray to every god—the Sun God, the God of War, Thoth, and Hermes—if it meant some rationality could be placed in the senses of her enemies. She did not want to unleash her father's plans. His weapons that should have been destroyed hundreds of years ago.

Arabella took the hint and spent the rest of the ride appreciating the smells of the village as her window was slightly propped open. She smelt garlic, curry, patchouli, and a variety of mixed scents she swore carried the heart of the ocean with them. It was as if she was being lulled by the city around her, the ambiance around her like the sound of music. Sleep inevitably took her.

Maria stayed tucked into herself the remainder of the trip. She did not look outside of the window much, keeping her face hidden from people curious over such an official mode of transportation. Most people walked in InFiamma, or rode horses, even taking a few underground routes to get around.

Maria was exhausted though, barely sleeping since her coronation. Then again, she barely slept even before then. She went from tired and withdrawn to tired and busy, which was a lot on her battered soul. Refraining from lashing out on anyone had been proven to be incredibly hard, yet she managed to keep her temper and antisocial tendencies at bay.

Most gratefully, Maria felt blessed that she didn't have to completely mask herself in front of Arabella, who she observed was drooling a bit on the window. Maria was able to joke and be a bit less formal without feeling like Arabella was going to cry. After all, Miss Marella had some kick to her tone at times as well.

Arabella woke as they arrived at the castle. The carriage bumped over gravelly roads as they pulled into the stables. It smelt like horses and pine distinctly, Arabella noted, as she sleepily said her formal goodbyes to Maria. Maria dismissed Arabella for a day of naps and architectural planning.

It was only a mere thirty minutes before Maria herself was groggily heading to her chambers. She curled into a ball in her own large bed, trying to calm herself despite her harshly rising heartbeat.

Maria felt as though she wasn't able to retain much anymore. She had a hard time being able to distinguish the next second from the last. The amount of social intake she had today scared her, even if she would never admit it.

Although Maria couldn't remember every detail, she knew she had fun with Arabella. She remembered those bright eyes looking into her own, and knew that she did not want to lose the feeling of enjoyment she had in her chest. It was a feeling that combated the nausea and anxiety under the surface. And because she didn't want to lose that, with her luck, she surely would.

Chapter 6

At the end of July, Maria was forced to actually speak to her court.

"My dad never spoke to anyone outside of hunting and mistresses, which was the same thing in two different fonts," Maria grounded out as she threw her pillow over her face.

Thoman picked up a pitcher of ice water, freshly served to her by the long list of servants who finally began acknowledging her existence. With a flick of his wrist, he dumped the contents, ice cubes and all, on his queen's face.

Maria made a tight grunting noise before removing the pillow from her head. "Oh. I didn't know you wanted to die. That's crazy," she mused with an intentional dry calmness.

"You already let it be known to your court that you don't have the balls. Cute though."

Maria sat up fully, cutting Thoman a sharp stare. "Tell me, did you enjoy all those years you had to throw water on my father to get him out of his drunken sleep? Reliving the glory days of being in a perpetual limbo?"

Thoman brushed off the disrespect. "You have to be in the great hall in two hours to decide on the August ritual. Get dressed."

As Thoman went to exit Maria's chambers, she yelled after him. "Bring that Marella girl to me, since you have so much time on your hands!"

Arabella arrived at Maria's chamber doors with not a clue as to why she was summoned. Thoman surely did not say why she was needed, walking in absolute silence behind her accompanied by three guards. She was lounging in her own chambers within the east wing when he knocked firmly on the door. "You're summoned by the queen," he said ruggedly, and then led her to the west wing.

Arabella tried asking, or rather, began asking why she was needed. Thoman just gave a sigh louder than the volume she was speaking, encouraging her to quickly shut up.

Before she could internalize it in a way that would manifest a one sided rivalry between her and Thoman, Arabella was in front of Maria's door. After knocking three times, Thoman abandoned her there. Maria answered on the third knock, as she could practically hear Thoman's heavy breathing from a mile away.

Arabella was greeted by Maria wearing dark leather pants and a black sports bra, clearly in the middle of getting ready for the event soon to come. Arabella had already prepared hours before, wearing a dress like a pale blue rose. Maria was in the middle of inserting a studded earring, her mismatched key earring already in the other ear.

She slightly towered over Arabella, looking down at her through her eyelashes as she greeted her with a relatively warm yet awkward tone.

"I need your help. You're my age, I think? Well, I assumed. Anyways, I need someone to choose a fancy event for August. Please give me ideas that don't suck," Maria pleaded as she gestured for Arabella to enter her room while she sorted through her shirts.

"I am twenty-one, so just about two years off, which is why you hired me," Arabella began, obeying as she entered Maria's room.

Arabella was instantly hit with the smell of sandalwood and patchouli. She observed the red, orange, and accented gold tones throughout the decent sized chambers. Maria, without looking up from her clothes, gestured to Arabella to take a seat on the four poster bed.

"When coming to the mainland from the Island, I was most excited for your bonfire night tradition. I would like to see that," Arabella expressed in a hopeful tone.

Maria tensed at the mention of fire, but not enough for Arabella to notice. She subtly observed Arabella's light expression. Poor woman was nervously kicking her feet while sitting on the bed for an answer, and Maria couldn't say no. Especially when Maria had no ideas on what else to do.

"Okay. Nice," Maria said blankly, grabbing a white button up shirt. Arabella watched as Maria applied it to her body, observing the way Maria's core muscles rippled with the movement. Arabella's cheeks began to heat, and the rest of her body followed suit. When Maria cut Arabella a look, she snapped her eyes away. They sat in silence for about forty seconds before Arabella got up and dismissed herself, unsure if that was the right move.

"I should go," Arabella said, nervously looking around various places in the room. The distraction caused her to bump straight into the wall on her way out. She bolted from the room as casually as she could muster, so she wasn't able to see the way Maria humorously scoffed, going back to her dresser with a smirk.

'♥♥♥'

Naturally, Arabella was the first to arrive for the announcement in the great hall, where Maria's coronation was not that long ago. The fire pit and various decorations were removed since then, leaving just Maria's throne on the dais. It looked cold and unused.

Some guards tried following Maria around the event, but she politely shrugged them off, telling them to protect someone like the Marellas instead. That new assignment was a duty they took seriously, forming an inconspicuous circle around Arabella, Margaret, and Aquilla. Arabella found it a bit suffocating, but Aquilla made good conversation with the guards.

Maria waltzed up to the foot of the stage like she wasn't their ruler, instead casual without a care in the world. Cheers erupted as she climbed up the stairs. Once settled into her new throne, Maria lifted her hand in hopes it would quiet them. Luckily, it did.

"I know that it has been a long time since there were regular festivities around here. At least ones you could bring your children to."

A few people coughed at that. Maria couldn't read if it was to hold back a laugh, or if it was due to discomfort. Nevertheless, she continued. "I've decided, with help from my council, to resume Firenight on the thirtieth of August. It will both be the first event of my reign, and hope for a new beginning for all of us, where everyone can get some air." ***Without being the ones burning***, Maria thought after she finished.

Everyone expressed their excitement from gasps to hollers. Maria allowed her shoulders to sag with relief, just barely. She contemplated the room as they celebrated, the people she hardly recognized, and that hardly recognized her. Maria assumed their cheers would be replaced with complaints about her the second she left the hall.

Most court children her age were out in the world at the moment, wandering the spiritual woods of Withelle learning herbalism. Painting, dancing, thriving in Cadence all on their daddy's dime. Not her. She was forced to control the parents and bloodlines who remained at their roots. Maria understood how easy one could go mad in the position, ever standing still on their throne while the world spins outside.

"I would also like to take this time to talk about what I've been doing since my coronation," Maria began as the crowd fell silent. "I've come to some amazing trade of resources with the Island territory, something that will be beneficial to both parties as we merge into one."

People glanced at the Marellas who gave Maria smiles. Aquilla then put an arm around his daughter's shoulders, a silent encouragement for the work she too had planned.

"In that light of transparency, I think it's only fair to hear suggestions from the people in this room. Yes, you can talk about what events you want, whatever you feel should be heard. You each can give me one thing," and with that, Maria gestured Arabella up to the dais.

"Can you help me keep track of all this, since I've already decided you're the organized one?"

Arabella's eyes slightly lit up as she nodded, retrieving a clipboard.

People lined up to give their suggestions, and Maria listened. Everything from balls and festivals, to tangible complaints of repairs in the castle. Safety walking the grounds at night, and education reform for the court children that could be conducted in their own home territory. Maria took down them all, promising that the top priorities would be discussed at future council meetings.

Maria then invited Arabella to follow her to the stables, and then the servant side of the castle, to hear the plight of those whose opinions were often overlooked. She didn't realize how out of hand her father's reign was, and what it did to those who lived in the castle with less freedom than she assumed.

It was deduced that they needed a serious pay increase, as some of them were barely alive. They also needed better access to hygienics and more established boundaries between the living quarters, as some people were too close to the sick in the medical pit. Some worried about what would happen if a sickness broke out. Some healers with their credentials from Withelle agreed, claiming they could sense it.

Brushing off the hippy nonsense, Maria assured them she'd obtain every tool she'd need to address their concerns. She tasked Arabella with finding out where the castle blueprint was, letting her know her best bet was asking Thoman. Maria decided to renovate a new space for the medical wing just to make things simpler, but needed to see a full scale to be sure.

Maria felt bad for holding her, but planned to give her something soon to make up for it. "I apologize for dragging you with me. You never asked for this," Maria began, but Arabella cut in.

"Don't. I am happy to be a part of something useful. My hometown never suited my talents."

"Talents?"

"I will have this kingdom thriving, entertained, and sanitized by your next birthday," Arabella responded with a chuckle. Maria knew she was joking, she had to be. Maria's birthday was August 14th, two weeks away.

Arabella knew this of course, indulging in everything that has to do with the queen since her coronation. She got her main source of information from a woman her age living adjacent to her, Payje, who was allegedly the most notorious court gossip.

Payje knew everything, saw it all firsthand with Maria being shunned by their peers. Along with being exiled by teachers, adults, everyone but the librarian who took pity on her as she studied history in the pits of the bookstacks. Some say she'd occasionally whisper to herself as she read, her loneliness being mistaken for an oddity.

It didn't change the way Arabella respected her. Whatever the people saw was a grotesque misjudgment to the person who listened to everyone's suggestions all day. Or so Arabella presumed. Nothing malicious in Maria's personality was hinted at as she escorted Arabella back to the east wing.

"Wouldn't want you getting confused again, little dove," Maria recited as she gestured the flapping wings once more, hastily exiting before Arabella could step on her foot, or throw back another remark.

Chapter 7

Thoman had his own suggestion once he heard of Maria's impromptu charity. He planned to beat the scrap from her bones for it, proposing she reinstated public training.

This wasn't Maria's first time picking up a sword nor her first time wielding it professionally. Her father, despite his neglect and insanity, was perfect for just that. Elias didn't really care what Maria did in her spare time, as long as it was away from him and out of earshot.

Maria's main instructor was the weapons master at court, who took Cienfuegos and her under his wing when they were young. Maria practiced twice a week with him. Once to stay sane, the other to become deadly should a coup ever take place against her father. Elias gave the Fiamma name more than enough cause for extinction.

While it used to be customary for a ruler's combat training to be public, it was never something Maria witnessed. Long before she reached a certain age of awareness, her father stopped being active in anything other than fucking mistresses and hunting birds. His only true productive activity was planning a theoretical war he'd never follow through with.

When it came to Maria, there was an array of people watching her during her training. From a few council members, to noble families, to stable boys. She would have been lying if she said that she wasn't slightly flexing her muscles when the ladies at court showed up. It got old after a while, as Maria and Thoman were going at it for hours, or so it felt like.

Maria remained specifically aware of the big-eyed clumsy mess, Arabella, who brought a notebook with her so she could pretend she wasn't watching, determined to set herself apart from the other women at court. Yet, Arabella was feeling the same flush in her cheeks as them regardless when Maria slid backwards, perfectly dodging a hit. The dirt in the pit flew upward at the traction, heightening the smell of horses, but surprisingly no one seemed to care.

It wasn't until the crowd gasped that Arabella snapped her focus upwards, watching as blood splattered from Maria's mouth. Maria looked up and gave a small grin to Arabella before sweeping Thoman's feet from under him.

"You're getting old, Ser. Perhaps I should get a nurse to assist you back to your chambers… or a hospital bed," Maria said smugly, but half worried about whether she hurt her councilman. It was too fresh to be disrespecting the relationship itself.

"Foolish girl, if I'm so old, why did I nearly knock your tooth from its root?" he grumbled, as he peeled himself off the dirt floor.

Maria and Thoman were still far from wrapping up their sparring when a figure emerged from the armory. It was Cienfuegos, who was nearly indistinguishable to Maria, the only exception being his dark complexion. They both stood with a similar arrogance with swords on their hips. Once Maria spotted him, they both gave a knowing smirk.

"My turn," Cienfuegos volunteered, unsheathing his blade. They met at the center of the pit, neither saying a word as they engaged in combat.

There were whispers from the crowd, the name of the merciless general Cienfuegos ringing throughout. As if there was a fire, the court gossip, Payje began flapping around circles to relay the gossip to her few peers, as well as whatever willing audience would listen.

While Maria was fierce in nature, Cienfuegos was a natural warrior. The two were nearly equally matched, until he kicked the back of Maria's kneecaps, then pinned her to the ground. Maria's sword instructor watched from the back of the stables and tried not to chuckle, as if they were two children tussling in a sandbox.

While any other ruler would be pissed after being bested, Maria began hysterically laughing. Cienfuegos extended a hand to aid Maria up, which she took with a firm grasp, pulling Cienfuegos down with her.

"Mature, Maria," he whined in reply. Arabella was stunned at the casualness, considering they were both powerful people joking around in front of their wealthy subjects. Maria showed little care for the opinions of her audience as she warmly embraced Cienfuegos. "Welcome home, Cousin."

'♥♥♥'

The crowd cheered as their session came to an end, and Maria began undoing her iron sleeves. There was a clasp caught on the back forearm that made it hard to unlatch with just one hand. She was nearly ready to give up, content to live her life with a chained forearm before Arabella slipped through the crowd.

Arabella grazed her long fingers over the jammed latch and popped it open. She lingered for a moment as she slowly pulled the armor from Maria's forearm. As the metal slid down, their eyes slowly met.

It was the first time Arabella was able to see the freckles at the bridge of Maria's nose. She never noticed them before, and yet in the end of summer sun, they were clear as day. When the light hit Maria's dark eyes, turning them a honey color, a breath caught in Arabella's throat.

Arabella turned to leave, but Maria caught her wrist with the hand now free of armor, gently pulling Arabella's side into her chest. In the dirt pit, shoulder to chest, was Maria and Arabella in a private, silent hold that lasted a millisecond.

"Thank you, m'lady" Maria said a tad hoarse before bowing her head in return.

Their fingers grazed as Maria's hold released. When Maria turned away towards the stables, Arabella could've sworn she saw Maria rub her scarred fingers together, before straining her hand outward in nervous angst.

Cienfuegos was waiting for Maria at one of the posts, watching the interaction from afar. He raised his eyebrows at Maria in a knowing manner, inspiring Maria to lightly kick dust at him.

'♥♥♥'

Cienfuegos lounged in a similar fashion that Brando often did as he drank his coffee in Maria's chambers. "Tell me about the woman who was *assisting* you," he inquired dramatically.

Maria rolled her eyes, lighting a cigar. "Her name is Arabella Marella. She's working on a public building for the neighboring village, as well as assisting me on a few projects."

To anyone else, Maria would've sounded indifferent. Cienfuegos, however, knew Maria for as long as both of them have been alive. He immediately clocked the way the tips of Maria's ears turned a shade of red.

"Uh huh," Cienfuegos rolled his eyes back. "Well, she's hot. If you won't, I will," he said smugly. Maria shot a lethal side eye, which served as an admission of guilt.

"We both need to leave her alone. She's too sweet. Plus, I have my suspicions of your love life if you want to talk about that," Maria explained, taking a hit of her cigar.

"You act like either of us are ruffians. I can be sweet too," he pouted.

"Speak for yourself," Maria protested, furrowing her brow.

Cienfuegos stole her cigar from her hands, taking it as his own. "For the love of the Sun, Maria, it's okay to get laid."

Maria kicked her feet up onto the ottoman, leaning back with her eyes closed. "I fully intend to, later, actually."

"Oh cool, just not with someone you could potentially fall in love with," he teased, resting back as well.

"Always a pleasure to have your company, cousin," was Maria's only reply. Internally, she pondered the topic of conversation. She vowed before her coronation to never fall in love again. Have sex though? Yes. She wasn't unrealistic. However, she wasn't itching to feel the impending doom that loomed in her chest, the potential of loss and falling into the unknown.

"I'll be staying on and off until the end of the year, recruiting, council meetings, et cetera," Cienfuegos announced, in which Maria muttered her approval. Thoman already left to trade with Cienfuegos' command, getting into the new way of doing things since his position of legion commander was revoked.

The both of them slipped off into a power nap. Despite being separated for years they would always be at home with each other, comfortable enough to let their guard down. Overall, Maria was rather pleased he could still knock her on her ass. After all, it meant there was strength where she needed it most.

Chapter 8

Maria once again could not fall asleep. Just as she did the night of her coronation, she peeled herself from her bed to face the ghosts in the castle as they roamed around her. She felt as though they made misery comfortable. She often found herself wishing she could just be one of them already. Unperceivable, not responsible.

The kingdom already made such progress in the little time she'd been queen. The interns would be coming soon enough. The people in the Heart of InFiamma had been made aware of the steps being taken to benefit them. No one opposed, but she could still feel the uncertainty everyone had for her.

Elizabeth, a frequent apparition in the castle, appeared before Maria. "So sad little Regina, why so?" she teased. Elizabeth had dark black hair, eerily pale skin, and an alarming energy to her. She wore her typical luxurious red and tan gown. It made her look like an expensive curtain.

"When you killed for power, why did you want it? It's exhausting," Maria stated. She found herself sweating despite the incoming autumn air beginning to chill the night. Even with her unbuttoned shirt, she still felt constricted.

"I wanted something that only power could grant me, the ability to… carry out my methods," Elizabeth hesitated. She was a beautiful woman, around thirty-five, who had a gash in her neck she showed off like a designer necklace. She didn't have to flaunt it, but she did as a statement to the rare perceptive people that may be watching.

Maria knew what she meant though. Elizabeth needed power to keep the people silent as she slit the throats of young women to use as skin care, aiming to stay young forever. It wasn't power she wanted, it was youth. That desire for youthful immortality kept her tethered to the castle, destined to watch her potential victims grow up to wrinkle and be wise. She would never be granted that youth, or that wisdom.

"Always a pleasure, maniac," Maria taunted Elizabeth. Maria had an expression that was deeper than her usual resting agitated face, more tense and contorted with stress. Elizabeth made a gesture that would have been a stroke of the cheek, if she was able to actually touch Maria.

"You'll get frown lines," Elizabeth affectionately tutted before disappearing.

Maria had no clue what she wanted that could be used as motivation. She supposed, if she wasn't a coward in her youth, she would have run away and avoided her reign altogether.

When she dreams of escape, she tells herself to retreat into the forest until she eventually discovers the ruins of a city, built with the same sky scrapers she showed Arabella. But even that wouldn't satisfy her. Because she would be alone with those godly buildings, still feeling so small.

"Hello, I was just looking for you actually," Arabella said with a genuine smile. She had a folder in her hands containing the layout of the castle, per Maria's request. "I got them from Thoman as he was on his way out."

A light breeze came from somewhere Maria couldn't source. Arabella felt it too as it moved her dark hair. "Thank you," was all Maria could think to say, mesmerized by the way Arabella's hair fell down her shoulders.

"Maria," Brando spoke from behind her. She ignored him, mentally waving him off. Arabella's chest began to rise, as if she was giggling.

"Maria," he repeated, but Maria crooked her neck, as if to get him out of her head. Arabella's giggle sounds turned to hard coughing, blood slowly dripping from her nose.

"Maria!" Brando bellowed inches from her face. Maria turned her head to face him as he said, "There were too many of your father's victims in the castle during your coronation, too much death in the air. I told you what would occur if that ever happened."

Arabella fainted. Maria dropped down to swoop her into her arms, processing the situation in seconds. It was to be a nightmare come true as many, many people died.

"It started a plague," Maria said in aggravated disbelief, cradling Arabella in her arms.

Chapter 9

Maria ran through the castle cradling Arabella, who had blood falling lightly down her left cheek. Brando was at her side, invisible to Arabella in her arms, but giving support as best he could.

"Arabella is doing great. She's staying semi-lucid. She might make it," Brando encouraged as Maria arrived at the medical wing off of the servant quarters. It was already filled with patients with similar symptoms. Aquilla was one, his eyes watering as he threw up into a trash can.

"I'm sorry Your Majesty, but half the court is here already," a young medical nurse, barely old enough to be out of training, spoke with genuine sincerity. She was wearing a white mask and all white uniform, splattered in blood and fluid. Maria could hardly make out the girl's dirty blonde hair and brown eyes.

Maria assessed the scene, and Aquilla, who was actively being tended to. She told the young nurse, "I'm taking her to my chambers. Let her father, Aquilla Marella, know. I will be having my personal medics aid her. Send them up please."

Although Maria said it with near inaudible haste, the nurse was quick on her feet to Aquilla, then to the head nurse to have medics sent to the west wing immediately.

Maria wasn't worried about her own health with the sickness. Being around the dead and receiving their energy in microdoses for nearly two decades, she was immune to diseases such as this. Her gift acted like a vaccine. Unfortunately, it was a plague no ordinary vaccine could be made for.

Maria acknowledged that the very servants she talked to with Arabella would likely be next to be hit with the plague, if not already dying in their rooms. While she could have evacuated them, turned around and saved dozens, she instead looked to the solo being in her arms. Maria knew she needed to choose her people in this. To get onto the medical floor and try to save as many people as possible. The color drained from Arabella's face and blood pooled from her nose. Maria made her decision then, and chose Arabella.

Arabella let out a sob, and grasped onto Maria's semi-opened shirt as she was carried up to the west wing. She was laid delicately on Maria's bed as Maria tended to her with a wet cloth. Arabella started heaving, and that was when Maria snapped.

"Do whatever you have to, take whoever you have to instead. Make sure she doesn't die," Maria spat to what Arabella perceived as thin air. She balanced in and out of consciousness while her body entered a state of paralysis.

Arabella couldn't see it was Brando who Maria barked at, on the other end of the conversation. She could, however, hear a faint whisper in her ear that sounded like, *"hush, she can hear you."*

"I don't care," Maria seethed as she applied a wet compress to Arabella's temple. Brando took in Maria's frantic state while she tended to Arabella. It was behavior he had never seen come from her before, leading him to cave to her request, despite the cost.

"Consider it done."

Maria stayed put, wiping Arabella's face from the sweat and blood that coated it. She didn't move until the entirety of her personal medical team arrived; the great perk of being a queen.

"I'm fine, but ensure she survives please while I find my cousin," Maria began, but sure enough Cienfuegos walked in hazily. He wore gray sweatpants and a black bathrobe, like he had a hangover and the flu at once.

"I'm okay for now. They retrieved me from the den," he mustered out before coughing harshly, luckily no blood detected.

Maria sighed in relief. She supposed he too wouldn't be all that ill, being the bringer of death in every battle for the past seven years. When it came down to it, it was only the innocent who would die for the crimes of Maria's father, one last time. She almost let herself believe the people she saw finding peace were then finding their forgiveness, but of course they'd leave behind a plague, a vengeance.

"Even the main medical team is dropping. A lot of people are about to die," Cienfuegos said to Maria. Her personal team remained silent with grief.

"I'm going to help them," Maria offered before Cienfuegos grabbed her arm weakly. "Like hell you are."

"I'm not impacted, as you can see. Everyone who was going to fall ill has already. I must check on the rest of my council," she demanded in return, pacing from her chambers.

'♥♥♥'

The medical unit caught Maria up to speed on the specific ailments the people were faced with, and how to go about assisting. Originally, the professionals left working in the medical wing refused to let Maria near the sick, but gave in after she demanded to be of help.

The illness was classified to those unbeknownst to the aspects of the soul, as an upper respiratory issue. The people had an electrolyte deficiency, as well as a projection of anemic symptoms after all the blood loss. They were given hydration bags as a start, and so that is where Maria was assisting, refilling and inserting IVs after a twenty minute crash course demonstration.

Maria ran around giving chest compressions to those who she already knew were gone. Once the soul gave up there was no coming back. She fetched water, gave out blankets, and overall did not sleep for about twelve hours. Those factors led her to believe she was suffering from exhaustion when she stumbled upon a little girl screaming. The little girl was yelling directly at Aquilla as he slowly recovered, the first to do so.

"Dad, why won't you look at me?!" the girl sobbed as she panicked mere inches from his face. Aquilla was unaware of the commotion in front of him. Maria looked at the scene with confusion. It wasn't as if what she learned from Aquilla the past few days hinted to him being a negligent parent, so Maria approached.

"Aquilla, are you alright?" Maria asked him as he drank water from a cup, his hands shaking slightly. The girl still sobbed, but stopped screaming when she made eye contact with Maria. It sent a shiver down Maria's spine, which was a bad sign.

"I'm better. The nurses say I will make it now that the worst is over," he replied, examining the room of bodies covered with sheets before him. A frown formed on his lips. Maria knew that she had to have these bodies removed before the sickness resumed.

"How is Arabella?" he asked, taking another sip.

"She is okay, recovering as well. My nurses recently updated me," Maria replied, still looking at the shaking little girl. Maria checked in on Arabella multiple times, grateful that she seemed healthy as she slept off the illness.

"And what of Margaret, my youngest? I had a nurse send for her," Aquilla resumed, the scent of death in the air heightening. Maria froze as the little girl screamed once more, "Dad, I'm right here!"

Maria's heart thudded in her chest. She knew Arabella had a younger sister, saw the child at her coronation, but didn't think once to check in on her after seeing Aquilla clearly incapable of doing so himself.

"I'll go look for her right now," Maria replied hastily. Before she could bolt, Aquilla grabbed her hand. "Thank you, Your Majesty."

Maria patted his hand, replying with sorrow, "Please, just call me Maria."

Maria then retreated to the east wing, smelling even more death, seeing blood stains streaking the floors before she entered the Marella's suite. While Maria did not see the little girl follow her, she assumed Margaret was the presence of sorrow she felt.

"You can see me. Why is everyone ignoring me?" Margaret frustratingly asked as Maria slid through the chambers, inspecting around for evidence of the child.

"I'm afraid to answer that before I know for sure. Were you sick? Do you remember being ill, Margaret?" Maria asked softly as she opened the bathroom door, examining the blood splattered on the ground.

"No, I don't remember anything since we got here, as in InFiamma," Margaret explained as she continued following Maria at her heels. Maria entered one bedroom, presumably Aquilla's, and Margaret was nowhere to be seen other than the apparition behind her.

"Why are you going through our rooms? I'm right here," the girl sneered as her energy increased.

"I'm looking for something. Hush," Maria insisted, waving the girl off. Maria hoped Margaret wouldn't be around when she found what she was looking for.

Maria entered the next room, Arabella's. It was an alluring blue, which was fitting for Arabella considering she was constantly wearing blue tones. While Gloucester, Cadence, and Eminence all associated their territories with blue tones, they had wildly varying shades that were quite distinctive. It stemmed from those territories being native to the continent, but with the specific blue around her, Maria could tell the decor was intentional to mirror the Island.

Maria investigated the decently sized room, from the pearl jewelry on the nightstand, to the court notes spread out on Arabella's bed. Maria examined those as well out of instinctual curiosity, noticing a series of sketches and words on the notepad.

One sketch was of a building, another of a bridge, and then there was one of Maria sitting with her elbows on the table, showing off her profile view. Maria knew it was from the first council meeting, but with the way Arabella studied Maria long enough to get her curved nose just right, it made Maria blush. Margaret let out a giggle, as well as some kissy noises.

"Mature," Maria snapped, which made Margaret chuckle a bit more. Maria instantly felt bad, considering when she opened the last door, her suspicions that Margaret would indeed never grow up or mature were proven to be true.

Margaret let out a blood-curdling scream as she saw her own body lying on the floor, covered in her own blood. Margaret choked to death on the blood from what Maria could assess. "I'm so sorry—" Maria began before Margaret cut her off.

"No, No You're playing tricks. I want my sister!" Margaret screamed before vanishing into thin air. It would be a long while before the young girl was seen again.

After a personal investigation, it was revealed the nurse who greeted Maria at the beginning of the epidemic, and who was tasked to retrieve Margaret, died before she could reach the top of the east wing.

The nurse became ill, and running around didn't help her case. She fainted on the stairs and did not wake again. She looked to be around the same age as Margaret herself as Maria recalled their encounter, watching the surviving nurses mourn their friend.

It was Maria who broke the news to Aquilla, feeling partially responsible. He said no words, just screamed and screamed until Maria heard the rip in his vocal cords. She then had to break the news to Arabella.

Maria stood outside her own bedroom door, scratching at the peeling wallpaper before she worked up the courage to enter her own room. To the right, the fire was going strong. Arabella was sitting up and drinking soup while engaging in conversation with Cienfuegos.

"I think tridents would make a sick weapon," Cienfuegos praised before he caught the glimpse of fear in his cousin's eyes. He slowly rose from his seat.

"Cousin, may I have a minute with Arabella alone?"
Maria managed to say while swallowing her words.
Cienfuegos met Arabella's eyes. "I guess I will see you
around, Bella."

As he strode out, he stole one last look at his cousin.
Maria let out a sigh. She took a seat on the bed before
running her hands down her face. "I'm so sorry, sweetie,"
Maria began in probably the softest voice she'd ever used.

Arabella nodded, her voice hoarse from recovery as
she said, not as a question, but a statement, "Who died."

Maria played with the furs on her bed, tangling them
in between her fingers as she avoided Arabella's eyes.
Arabella wouldn't have it. Arabella shot her hand out to
grab Maria's chin, forcing Maria's eyes to focus on her own.

"Your sister. I'm sorry."

At first, Arabella said nothing. She leaned back
against her plush, propped up pillows and put her hands in
her lap. Maria refused to speak first, wanting to give her all
the time she needed. It reminded Maria of something she'd
forgotten after her mother died. How she did not say a word
for days, and how no one asked her to.

Tears welled in Arabella's eyes, and Maria silently
held her hand. "I'm feeling better. I should see my dad,"
Arabella chirped in a forced manner.

"Of course," Maria replied, holding out a stiff arm to assist Arabella up from the bed. She shakily took it, letting Maria slowly escort her to the medical unit where Aquilla was being discharged as they arrived.

Aquilla ran as fast as he could to his remaining daughter, taking her into his arms. Maria slowly stepped back, allowing them their moment. They spent a long while allowing their tears to flow in silence.

"Thank you, Maria," Aquilla said with his strained, half audible voice when they were finally ready to break away, but he was met with open air. Maria already retreated to the council room, grabbing Cienfuegos on the way. Once again, the InFiamma people were to be burned in masses.

Chapter 10

"A burnt child loves the fire" ~ Oscar Wilde

The damage was done by the second week of August, thirteen days after the plague began. The court that previously held three thousand people was reduced to one thousand. Some whole households were obliterated. Most houses lost crucial members of their homes, such as ones that financially supported the rest through their exclusive stations.

The military district remained on lockdown and untouched, but the main village was hit due to people trying to escape the castle at the last minute, during the initial breakout. There weren't many punishments to be dealt, as all known defectors perished alongside two thousand people in the city.

There wasn't nearly enough room on the castle grounds to combine funerals between the castle and village. There was also a factor of the cost and danger of transporting bodies, which made it impossible. Regardless, Maria put Inferniana on supplying the village with what they needed to gain their health once more.

Within the council only Maria, Aquilla, Arabella, Cienfuegos, and Thoman lived through the outbreak. Three of Elias' original members, who sat in on Maria's first meeting, were too old to break their fevers, and were amongst the first to die.

Overall, it was one of the worst devastations to hit InFiamma since the year of the plagues hundreds of years ago, when the ice caps melted and released millions of centuries old viruses.

The day mourning was to begin, those remaining four council members waited for Maria outdoors. They stood upon a wooden stage, built at the end of the rows holding the countless covered bodies. Everyone wore black medical masks to control the stench of the deceased, adorned with a pocket to insert whatever scent one preferred.

Maria tensed when the sea of people waiting for her turned in her direction. Their eyes widened as she arrived on the scene, ready to give her memorial speech before the bodies were to be burned. She wore all black as well, but not her casual pants and dress shirt. She wore something she never thought she'd have the heart to, her father's all black armor. It was passed down by all the greatest InFiamma commanders, starting with Ares Fiamma.

Maria planned to give it to Cienfuegos, with him being the rightful commander. He surely didn't want it though, pleased to keep the standard armor he'd been wearing since forever, taking the time to have it fitted over the years. At twenty-three, it looked like a welding experiment. Maria didn't want to acknowledge that in her own way, she needed to wear it for herself with what she was about to do.

The armor was like wearing a witch hat to a court battle, where you're accused of being a witch. Yet, it was the only thing that seemed comfortable and consistent.

Whispers broke out amongst the crowd as she made her way down the dirt path, looking only at the ground as she arrived at the podium. When she finally looked up, she met eyes with Thoman who had an eerily emotional look in his eyes. Maria couldn't stomach looking at Arabella, it felt like sacrilege to do so.

Once she was front and center before the crowd of grievers, she gave the lengthy speech she spent the night writing with her cousin at her side.

"There was a time not too long ago that our kingdom's holy symbol, fire, took many people to their deaths. I know I cannot be the only one grappling with the multiple levels of grief saturating today," nods in agreement from the audience, some grunts cursing Elias Fiamma.

Maria proceeded, *"Truth is, as a child, I would watch the fire in my rooms, whether it be a candle or my grand fireplace, and I would imagine the flames dancing in an ensemble. I looked at the fire with… such wonder. Such admiration. Maybe that is something I had in common with my father, until I realized even I wasn't safe from death by the flames. I too carry the scars, unfortunately in a literal sense, from the sins committed by those before me,"* Maria gestured to her right arm, the one that carried the burns from the night she tried to sacrifice anything, to prevent what would inevitably change her life.

"There was a saying in a book I read in the back of the library when no one cared to know me, when I was just Elias 2.0. It talked about children burned by fire, as I was. "A burned child fears the fire", or "A burned child loves the fire", I no longer remember which version was the original, as I no longer know which version is true.

I do not know if I find it a dishonor to burn these bodies, despite the necessity, due to this court's recent history. Or if I find it a great comfort knowing they too will dance with the flames somewhere on the Sun, waiting for us to join them.

I am your ruler, I'm not supposed to admit fear, but I don't know which child I will be when I light that pyre and am forced to take on my father's role officially, for better or worse. I do promise that I will try to restore the fire in a way worth celebrating, a way of honor, as I hope to restore my family's honor as well." Maria finished, letting out a huff of air.

Cienfuegos joined her side, lighting the first torch, slowly handing it to his cousin with tears in his eyes. Maria hesitantly took it with unsteady hands, allowing her knees to bend as she descended the stairs, lighting the first mount of bodies.

First, everyone from the council lit a pyre for people they knew or were unidentified. Arabella and Aquilla lit the pyre that Margaret was resting on together, hands locking as they laid her to rest. While they had reservations for giving Margaret an InFiamma burial, the risk to get to the sea was too great. Then, the rest of the court lit a match, saying their own goodbyes in groups, lighting their families into rest as well.

Maria held out from leaving before all the piles were lit. It was a miracle she lasted that long, as when she finally left the clearing, she immediately began throwing up. She was so disoriented, she didn't even realize she was being followed by Thoman. He placed a firm hand on her shoulder, causing her to whirl around to face him.

"I never said I was sorry. For looking you in the eye that day when I dragged your mother away," he confessed as his hand stayed in place. Maria did not brush it off.

"Why," she breathed out with a near sob. "Why would you do it?"

"Your mother would have traded places with you if it was an option, as I recall. That is why I do not feel bad about it in the slightest. I was firm with you because if I wasn't, if you followed us, you would be dead as well. I did

101

it because I was told to, and for that yes, I'm a sick coward," Thoman replied with gut wrenching honesty.

"Why would you allow him to have that power? You've known each other your whole lives. Why didn't you stop him?!" Maria screamed.

"I loved him. He was my family," Thoman professed. "You're right. I knew him my whole life. I loved him in the purest way humans could love, even if his actions weren't pure. My son is the only good thing I've done. I see him and Cienfuegos and I see myself and your dad, and I can only feel pride that they are nothing like him and I."

Maria let out a long sigh. She and Thoman sat in silence for a beat.

"I was the one who found you, after you passed out from the pain. If you remember at all, I was there in the hospital wing when you woke up because I carried you there," Thoman gestured to Maria's arms. "I had a gut feeling to check on you as soon as your father was done. The first time I ever disobeyed him was when he told me to leave you be, as he went to try and make another heir to replace you."

Maria winced. "That comment wasn't necessary," she replied.

"Apologies. For all of it, truly."

Maria reflected his stance, grasping his shoulder in return with her firm armor. "I'll cope."

Thoman nodded. "Take it however you want, you could never be your father, even if you tried. You could burn me right now on a pyre, you'd never be him."

"I could be so much worse, I fear," Maria professed.

"Maybe, but your motivations aren't his. I see you're motivated by-"

Arabella rounded the corner of the west wing's side entrance, where the two were speaking. Her eyes were bloodshot as they met Maria's.

"It's something more passionate," Thoman finished, leaving it at that as he bowed to both women, taking his exit.

"I'm sorry, Your Majesty," Arabella said in a strained voice, still healing. She recovered relatively early in the breakout, but the illness did a number on her throat. Aquilla could still barely speak both from the throwing up, and his screaming.

"I think it's cool for you to call me Maria, Arabella," Maria replied with a brow raise. She dug into a secret pocket in the side of the armor where she stored a cigarette.

Typically, it could be used for a pocket knife or poison. The cigarette could kill her too, so she supposed it was fitting.

"Well, Maria, I see there were perks to wearing your father's skin today," Arabella replied, motioning to Maria's appearance.

"What does that mean?" Maria asked without hostility, rather genuine curiosity.

"I just don't know if it was the best idea," Arabella pushed, leaning against the outer stone wall.

"I don't care," Maria waved the comment off with a gesture, leaning next to Arabella.

"You should. Even though everyone at court took it as you changing the course of history, the people in the villages might presume you're rewriting it."

Maria scoffed at that, "I literally described how my father has hurt me."

"So poor you and your trauma while people burn their loved ones?" Arabella protested, slightly raising her voice.

Maria's eyes lit ablaze, a deadly grin spreading across her face. "Were they burned, I don't know, alive? No? Oh. Okay."

Maria took a sharp inhale of her cigarette, holding the smoke in her lungs as Arabella continued. "So again, we all need to think of your pain and how ours could be worse?"

Maria let out a laugh the same time she let out the smoke. "Is this how normal people grieve? It's fucking weird."

Arabella turned to the side, removing one of her outdoor shoes, throwing it at Maria's chest from the short distance between them. "Are you intentionally trying to make me mad?" Maria questioned rather calmly, which made Arabella develop goosebumps. Arabella didn't reply as she stormed off, damning everything she dreamed of when arriving at InFiamma's court.

"Damn," was all Maria muttered to herself as she picked up the shoe Arabella left behind. She smiled at how it was like a story she read, containing some common girl losing her shoe that somehow snowballed into her marrying a prince with a foot fetish.

It was then Maria felt a tinge of insecurity at the fact she was not a graceful, lover boy prince. She then realized that Arabella may not even like women, specifically women like Maria.

Maria was even more appalled that she was putting herself in a position where those thoughts could slip through, after what happened to the last person she loved. What it cost.

She put out her cigarette as she entered the side of her wing, Arabella's shoe in hand. She focused on that instead of the cloud of smoke behind her, as big as the castle itself. The ashes were carrying away two-thirds of her court. This time, those who turned to dust would find peace in the wind that carried them away. Almost all, except Margaret Marella.

Chapter 11

The sound of Arabella's foot slapping on the stone took up most of the noise in the otherwise quiet castle. She was too busy drowning in her emotions to register the cool floor beneath her. She did know enough to smell the smoke around her. It was a heavy smell despite the source being a few acres away.

Even though Arabella enjoyed being around Maria, and would even dare consider her a friend, the storm swirling above her head threatened to take out anyone within proximity. Truth was, she simply did not care when she got like this. As far as she was concerned, it was the person's fault for being in the line of fire.

"Too much happening, the world is suffocating," Arabella thought as she exited the west wing, heading to the east. She could hardly breathe in her black babydoll style dress as she pulled at the white collar.

She planned to retreat to her family's chambers, avoid her sister's room at all costs, and take a bath. Those were the intentions, but as she entered the living area of the suite, she heard rustling coming from her own bedroom.

Arabella froze, her shoeless foot curling into the light blue carpet. She slowly made a circle as she walked around the embroidered ivory furniture. She intentionally followed the settled spots in the floorboards, staying as silent as possible.

When she reached her bedroom, which was second in the hallway, nuzzled between both her father and sister's, she slowly grasped the white doorknob. Careful to prevent the knob from turning to avoid warning the intruder of her presence, she swung the door open as fast as possible.

Arabella's adrenaline picked up as her heart thundered fiercely in her chest. That was just before she realized it wasn't some criminal or spy. In fact, she almost wished it was. It would've made infinitely more sense than the sight before her. On Arabella's bed was her sister Margaret, flipping through duplicates of her court notes.

Even just a month ago Arabella would have yelled at her sister for going through her things. This time, she just remained frozen. Margaret spoke first, quite casually after realizing her sister was not going to freak out on her.

"When are you going to tell the queen you have a crush on her? Although, I don't think I approve. She's kinda mean. She told me I was dead as some sick prank. Even dad played along!" Margaret complained, gesturing at Arabella's sketch of Maria. It was once again buried in her notes from the council meeting. Under stacks of self-imposed projects, because all Arabella had done for the past two weeks was work until she fell asleep.

Arabella did not say a word. Did not breathe. She simply turned heel, and walked right out of her room, exiting her suite. Her legs moved on their own, pacing out of the castle and as far into the forest as her legs would take her.

'♥♥♥'

There were always rumors that the castle was haunted by King Elias' victims. It was a fun way to ignore the wind during storms, as getting attacked by a hand that will always go through you is a lot better than your house being destroyed by a tree with you in it.

While everyone acknowledged that fun, there were still eerie elements to the dark corners of the castle. Those eerie feelings manifested into a horrifying truth for twenty unlucky individuals that gained the sight, through bargain or fate, after surviving the plague.

Thoman met with Maria once again later that evening, letting her know the recent development that had been making medical cases for days. The after-effects were being categorized as a long term illness too risky to keep around others, lest the sickness resumes by those allegedly carrying the virus around.

"There's word of a place out of the kingdom where we usually take people with this specific ailment. There's been one plague like this before, with the same hallucinogenic outcomes shown this time around," Thoman explained, sitting next to Maria in their one-on-one meeting within the council room.

"The Odd ruler Brando made this step-by-step plan when he was alive, considering he was affected first hand, and one of the people deemed disturbed," Thoman continued while Maria played with a coin on the table. She knew this of course. Knew that the plan was giving a mercy of resources and a boat, but no real tangible place to go but west, where other continents still burn.

"I know. He didn't want to execute the innocent, or make them live in confinement for something they couldn't control," Maria responded. Brando was ironically at the end of the table listening in. He already saw this coming, warned Maria. Now, he wanted to see if his plans still helped save those affected innocents generations later.

"Dropping them to live in the middle of nowhere on a destroyed continent too hazardous to occupy isn't exactly a mercy," Thoman scoffed. "Nevertheless, they are being talked to and transferred as we speak. Their families are mainly dead, but the few whose loved ones survived are being bribed for their silence."

"Well, Serfuckface, I'll have you know that they did just fine before the crown cut their resources off, with my nephew's blessing," Brando retaliated, as if Thoman could hear him. He couldn't though, and so Maria had to hide her laugh under the surface.

"Sound's good. Thank you. You should get settled in after your visit to Inferniana," Maria stood, scooting her chair.

"I'd like to bring Cienfuegos back soon, and regularly trade posts with him," Thoman offered, slowly standing as well. He was old to Maria, about fifty, which honestly wasn't that old. However, as much as she liked to make fun of him, he was still in fine shape. Especially so upon returning from the military district. "I'd like that as well," Maria granted, taking her leave.

Maria then caught up with her cousin before he left to go back to Inferniana. They enjoyed their usual vodka and cigars despite the circumstances. They also got into a total of two wrestling matches, and Maria dared Cienfuegos to steal all of Thoman's socks. After all, he wouldn't need to deal with the repercussions from that.

As Cienfuegos was leaving, Maria gave him a big hug. "I will be visiting you this time around. I still can't believe I've never visited in all these years you've had command."

"You better. If it wasn't for Jessie, I'd be so lonely," Cienfuegos said, trying to brush it off as a fake pout, but it was genuine.

"I promise," Maria swore as she let her cousin go to his carriage. She had the entire day with him, technically weeks although the plague was a real buzzkill. In truth, proximity was all she begged for after the past seven years being apart.

Maria looked up to the setting sun and took in the August air. The sunsets in August were always so beautiful in InFiamma, the weather always switching between sunny summer days and monsoon season. It felt as temperamental as she was most of her life.

She admired the forest as she headed into its foliage, noticing some trees slightly yellowing. A lot of the trees, such as the giant pines remained the same, but some of the white oaks gave hints that autumn was on its way.

As much as Maria loved her fall strolls due to it being her favorite season, she decided to take in the greenery one last time. It was the last allowance she gave herself to ponder the Withelle girl's prophecy.

'♥♥♥'

Arabella couldn't tell how long she walked through the forest. She followed the star constellation of Orion's belt and kept going until her legs gave out. Luckily, in an odd circular patch within the forest, surrounded by tall bushes and trees, was a big boulder for her to sit on.

It was windy and the air smelt of rain, a promise that a storm was soon to arrive despite the clear skies just twenty minutes prior. Arabella cared not, as she'd rather sleep drenched in the woods than in a castle with, well, whatever it was she saw.

She stayed on that boulder listening to the sounds of the trees swaying, and some running water nearby. Breathing so frantic, she could only just make out the twigs snapping, light humming, right as it was creeping behind her. As the branches that shielded her from the view of the path parted, a tall towering figure appeared between them causing Arabella to yelp, falling off the boulder.

The tall figure staggered back a step as Arabella shot to her feet, meeting eyes with Maria for the second time that day. Maria, used to her isolation and frankly unflattering attitude, didn't think before she blurted, "You're really weird."

Maria didn't mean it like that, more as a deflection of her embarrassment that she too was in the middle of the woods alone, ever mistaken as a monster like it was her personal signature. Less than a month after her coronation she was constantly reminded that maybe she wasn't safe from the perceptions of others. Arabella surely reminded her that type of love was conditional, as it should be.

"I'm not the only one in the woods alone right now," Arabella rebutted, chest still heaving. She was clutching her collar, pulling it from her neck.

"You're having a panic attack," Maria observed, looking down her nose at Arabella's neck. "Besides, you're the only one who looks like you've seen a ghost," Maria jested as Arabella tensed, hard. Maria's eyes darkened once she realized.

"Did you? See a ghost, Arabella?" Maria prayed Arabella would give a snide remark about how such things were folly, and that she was more sane than anyone ever. She did not.

"I don't know what that was. I saw my sister. She said she talked to you and that my dad ignored her... I've lost it. The stress has caused me to lose my mind."

Maria exhaled as if she was holding her breath and just got the worst, most inconvenient news possible. It made Arabella's lip curl at the lack of sensitivity.

"They won't harm you, they cannot touch you," Maria replied, ignoring Arabella's sneer, leaning into a more relaxed pose.

"How come no one else has brought them to attention at court? Hundreds have died," Arabella said with a horrified tone, taking a seat once more on the boulder.

Maria considered the question. "Because, up until now I'm the only one who has been able to see them. Before that, my ancestor Brando, which is why they called him 'The Odd'. Thought it would be better to keep it to myself," she began to toss a stone she picked up off the forest floor in her hand.

"Especially considering those who have recently developed the sight are being shipped away as we speak to keep them from being labeled as insane."

Arabella took a step back with fright. She nearly stumbled on a smaller rock in the raised moss, but Maria reached for her before she could fall. Maria grasped her shoulder, slipping upwards to cup her hand behind Arabella's ear. She still remained an arms length distance away.

"Listen sweetie, nothing is going to happen to you. I do need you to be silent about this because I only have so much privilege, even as queen," Maria absent mindedly soothed her thumb over Arabella's neck. Arabella betrayed her beating heart, slightly melting into the touch.

"I'm scared. I still don't understand how I can see them now…" Arabella contemplated, eyes bewildered as they clouded like the sky above. Maria released her and took a step back to give her some space.

"I know, but they cannot harm you. The way I began seeing them was an unintentional familial sacrifice. Your sister died and now you can see ghosts, just like Firenze Fiamma could. Like I can," Maria replied, crossing her arms, which came off as apathetic, but she was truly just desensitized to it.

"Why was there a sacrifice, and why was the price my sister, the punishment… this?" Arabella's head spun as she sat back on the boulder from before.

Maria considered telling the truth, but a feeling deep in her stomach made her do something she didn't usually do. Lie. "I don't know, fate is weird, and the plague in itself was spiritual in nature. I'll explain on the way back to the castle," Maria gestured to the path she was on, extending a hand.

Arabella's head spun as she pulled her knees to her chest. "I don't think I can go back tonight, just leave me here."

Maria evaluated the options to get Arabella off that rock. Eventually she came to an easy conclusion, one she hesitated due to the amount of trust she had in herself. "Come stay with me tonight, they won't bother you in my room."

"What if I see Margaret? Is it even really her or are they demonic?" asked Arabella as she shook, thunder sounding from miles away.

"The odds of seeing her consistently at this stage are slim. If she told you about our conversation, chances are she just regained consciousness after weeks," Maria explained as she hauled Arabella up, scooping her into a bridal style hold as she began their retreat from the forest.

"There are three classifications: first is the Tortured. Those that cannot move on until they are put to rest. My father's victims were haunting me at the beginning of my coronation, but found peace. No longer around now, thank God," Maria explained, still cradling Arabella, who would protest if the information being relayed wasn't so pressing.

"There are Everymans, who can't find peace because something is holding them to the earth. They can't let go of some person or possession. There's a ghost named Elizabeth in the castle with her death wound cauterized across her neck. She was a serial killer who used to slit throats and use the blood as cosmetics. Nice lady otherwise though. Can't move on because of her possessions and ego, and again, she can't hurt you," Maria continued.

"Lastly, there is the Servient. They are advisors, soldiers of fate. I don't know much other than that. They're secretive beings so don't ask me. All I know is my ancestor, the first person I could see and an advisor of sorts, is one of them," she finished as the lightning picked up, somewhat still in the distance.

Arabella pondered what to do with that information.

"Have you seen your parents?" she asked, wondering how Maria's parents must have commented on their daughter's reign.

"No, they either found peace, or never wanted to see me. The rules are pretty simple. Die missing somebody or something, or with an obligation, and that attachment keeps you where you died. They cannot leave the castle either, so if you hear something rustling in the woods, odds are it is a monster," the last sentence had Maria smirking at her own joke as she tilted her head to meet Arabella's eyes, already rolling to the back of her head. Arabella kicked her feet to be let down.

For the rest of the walk, they mainly engaged in small talk. Maria hardly made eye contact, and Arabella rambled about where she was from on the Island. Maria was listening to every word attentively, barely remembering the ocean herself. She found the imagery fascinating. It wasn't until a drop of rain fell on Maria's temple did she let out a sigh.

"Do you not like the rain?" Arabella asked as it slowly started to pick up.

"It's not that, it's just annoying when it pelts on my face," Maria replied in irritation, sliding her fingers up Arabella's forearm, and tugging her to the right.

"The castle is just a few minutes away," Maria said while trotting through the branches. Arabella looked up at her, watching the raindrops fall off Maria's nose as the rain intensified.

"When we get there, I hope you intend to explain further the state your court is in." Arabella said with an edge, not a malicious one though.

"No need to rid yourself of your other shoe. I am happy to oblige, m'lady," Maria said in an intentionally mocking voice, which had Arabella's nose wrinkling.

'♥♥♥'

"Do you miss your mother?" Arabella asked, sitting by the fire, running her fingers through her hair.

"No," Maria replied with little give in her voice. Arabella was under the impression she had overstepped as she watched Maria's pupils narrow while looking in the flame, her breath as strong as a dragon.

"Apologies, Your Majesty," Arabella said in an attempt to correct her intrusion. Maria waved her off. Arabella, however, still felt guilty for overstepping more than once that day. Her eyes glossed over due to the fire being so close. Maria noticed it through her peripheral vision, relaxing a bit at the sight.

Maria knew Arabella was curious, but she wasn't at all offended by that curiosity. When it comes to her mother, it would always be a sore topic. However, she couldn't leave the girl sulking into her knees.

"I don't really remember my mother, she died when I was six years old," Maria opened up, hoping that would suffice. It didn't.

"Surely you felt her absence, I still feel my mother's absence often. She died in a storm," Arabella stated, picking up her own stick, poking at the fire.

"Not really. She spoke very little to me. The only parental influence, and half of my genetics I have to go off of, is my father's," Maria replied, putting the stick down, tilting her head back and closing her eyes.

For a moment Maria and Arabella sat in comfortable silence while the storm raged outside. The howling became a loud whistle as thunder clashed overhead.

"You should get some rest," Maria suggested, offering Arabella her bed as she closed her eyes. "I will tend to the fire."

When Maria awoke just at dawn break, her head was in the lap of a sleeping Arabella, who never left her side that night. Maria noticed that Arabella's gown was coated in mud, still damp from the drizzle they walked through. She laid out a big shirt for Arabella to wear instead as she sent a request for breakfast.

Chapter 12

"The next time there's a sleepover, let me know so I'm not searching for you at four in the morning," Aquilla reprimanded his adult daughter.

"Sorry dad. There was a storm and we just got cozy I guess," Arabella lied, quite well considering she usually was a bad liar. With the emotional stress the knowledge of her curse would cause her father, she felt the stakes were too high to get caught in the fib.

At the mention of the word "cozy", Thoman was looking at Maria with a side eye, and raised brow. Maria ignored him, but gulped when Aquilla gave her the same look when Arabella wasn't looking.

Thoman, despite his shared sentiment with Aquilla, spared Maria by speaking up. "Would you like to tell me where all my socks are, Maria?"

This had everyone's attention. Maria clamped her lips down but failed to contain her laugh. "Uh, ask Cienfuegos maybe, I don't know."

"More pressing matters," Arabella cleared her throat, cheeks red from embarrassment after what Maria could tell was caused by her own silent glances.

"The interns from the island will be here soon, their itinerary has been sent and I have approved it. They will be staying in the village until the building's completion. Then, Maria will go down there to meet them for the unveiling," Arabella explained, showing layouts from her work the past three and a half weeks.

"Sounds good. Any other matters? This meeting feels too light," Maria joked half-heartedly.

"Well, the Eminence assassin was interrogated by me personally. Cienfuegos had his fun before I got there, but my son informed me the man didn't speak prior to our interaction. I got out of him that Eminence is planning something bigger, so we need to be on alert," Thoman warned as he too examined his personal notes.

"Where is he now?" Maria engaged, writing her notes in a code so even if their notes were stolen, they couldn't be deciphered.

"Exterminated. I didn't want to bring it up, but now I know it is important more than ever to let you know their motives. He told us 'Abigail isn't going to be the last loved one of the queen's to go.' He was killed immediately following the threat, by me personally."

Maria paled, her jaw slacking a tad. Thoman's eyes turned into worry, but he wouldn't do her the dishonor of catering to her feelings when he was partially responsible

123

for them, at least as an accomplice. He was the one who tied Abigail's father's hands to the pyre as he screamed for his daughter.

"I want double scouts inconspicuously patrolling the borders to the east. Cover it with a false slip that it is a new training measure. I want the Marella's suite guarded heavier than the weight of gravity on the sun. Same for anyone you deem important, Thoman," Maria began spouting demands with a cool tone in her voice, nearly evil.

Thoman's most precious of loved ones wouldn't be in harm's way anytime soon though, his son being Cienfuegos' closest person, living in the military district. Those two were practically inseparable, even sharing a room together.

By the time she was done speaking, everyone had three pages of handwritten notes, from the castle's safety, to the interns in the village. Thoman was giddy with the adrenaline he was long deprived of, but Aquilla was silent.

"Arabella, I think it is best if you stay in our chambers unless there is a meeting. At least for the next few days as we prepare for the bonfire," he finally proposed to his daughter, tenderly.

Before Arabella could object, which she was definitely gearing up to do, Maria said, "Excellent idea. I'll have some watercolors and various things sent to your room to keep you occupied."

Arabella's mouth dropped open, "Like hell-"

"That's an order. I wasn't asking," Maria insisted, beginning to zone out. Thoman knew it was time for her to leave the meeting. As much as Maria was compared to the tough members of her lineage, Thoman watched Maria grow up, and knew her better than she knew herself. "We will discuss further tomorrow?" he said in an oddly casual tone.

"Very well. Everyone's dismissed," Maria rushed out, taking long strides to her room.

Arabella wasn't going to let it go, though. To have her newfound authority turn into something that simultaneously takes away her freedom, all before she could attend an event, was unacceptable. She would not stand for it.

She ran after Maria, cornering her halfway up the west wing stairs. She roughly placed her forearm against Maria's chest, feeling her breasts through the large fitting shirt as she backed Maria into the wall. Maria put her hand on Arabella's hip, steadying them on the unbalanced stairs.

"You don't get to tell me what to do and lock me away like a child in time out," Arabella protested in Maria's face.

Maria used her free hand to grip Arabella's chin. "You forget yourself. Go to your rooms, play with popsicle sticks and build this kingdom a museum to envy the gods, paint a canary, I don't give a fuck. You will stay in those rooms or so God help me—"

"What? What will you do if I leave?" Arabella pressed on stubbornly, calling Maria's bluff. If all else failed, Maria would understand fully that Arabella could take care of herself.

"This is not the island where your biggest threat is the occasional tweaker. This is a security threat," Maria explained calmly.

"And I am a grown woman who won't accept being coddled like I can't decide on my own wellbeing," Arabella pressed forward.

Maria hated that her first thought was, *'I wouldn't find this so attractive if I didn't view you as an equal, you rat.'*

Before Maria could find a variation of that sentiment to express, Aquilla was behind Arabella pulling her away from Maria.

"That is the QUEEN, in case you forgot. Enough of the entitlement. You were raised better, and with all respect to Maria-" Aquilla paused, glancing at Maria sympathetically before resuming, "If you leave our suite, there's no punishment worse than the one I'll give you. A one-way fare home."

Maria nodded, bowing her leave but made sure to give a mocking gesture at Arabella before continuing on to her rooms. Arabella stayed firm in her position, tears welling in her eyes from the embarrassment and what it did to her ego. After a beat, she stormed off to her chambers, where her three-day isolation took place.

'♥♥♥'

To be fair, Maria did send Arabella a trove of crafts, and that did include watercolor and popsicle sticks. Arabella listened to her orders, only because her father watched her like a hawk. His dark hair grew a new gray strand a day since Margaret's death, and Arabella did not make it easier with her strange behavior. She was constantly jolting at noises, paranoid that a ghost would be wandering about her suite.

"You may get the mail when it comes today, but that's the only time I want to hear of your fingers on that doorknob while I'm away," Aquilla demanded as he gathered his coat and satchel, readying himself for a hunting day trip with Maria and Thoman. "I'll be sure to tell Maria you are sorry while I'm out, and by the time you see her again, you better say it yourself, Miss Marella."

With that, he was gone. She knew he would really know if she left, the neighbor across the way being an elderly lady with nothing better to do than look out her peep hole. So, she retreated into her room, making a bridge out of those stupid sticks, trying to construct one that uses manual gears to rise and fall.

Her day, and weekend as a whole really, didn't get interesting until the mail courier knocked at the door. That in itself was mundane, but to be sure it wasn't a threat she stored a dagger sheathed up her sleeve. It was all she needed to open the door safely and retrieve the mail from the ten-year-old paperboy.

"Thank you, Oliver," Arabella drawled as she flipped through Island correspondences. In the mail were a few leftover condolences for Margaret from people Arabella never liked, and some court schedules Arabella herself made to keep people occupied with meals and low scale entertainment. Nothing noteworthy at all. Until…

"Oh! Arabella! I've been wondering when I'd be seeing you," said her neighbor, Payje, who lived diagonally from her. She was a tall blonde girl who had a talent for spreading gossip, yet was never malicious and always nice. Arabella always thought it was fake if she was being truthful.

"Hello, Payje," was all Arabella said, giving a little wave, readying to close the door.

"Wait! There's a party tonight in the library with the returning court members our age! Please come, everyone is going," Payje begged, desperately trying to sell the vision.

Arabella bought that dream, as she was insufferably bored with how dry the court was. If people her age were returning, and there was to be a party, how could she not go? All she wanted was to climb the social ladder, and she couldn't do that from her room.

"I can't..."

"You have to! Oh my, your sister always said how you wanted to be young and alive for once and how you never shut up about your anticipated social life here. This is your chance!" Payje gave a devious look in a way Arabella did not want to understand.

True, that was her biggest hope before all life was drained from her.

"Fine."

Payje squealed. "Meet me downstairs at midnight!"

Arabella's elderly neighbor opened her door, watching the interaction with squinted eyes. Arabella lifted her hand holding the letters. "Just getting the mail," she lied, retreating into her rooms officially.

Chapter 13

Maria didn't smoke marijuana often, but when she did, she became her soul's potential. Her usual state was either wound up, or angry. Spiteful, or vengeful. She knew as much as any, although most would never admit, that her childhood gave her toxic survival tactics that destroyed her ability to come into her own being. When she had that aid, rare considering the current climate of everything, she had the ability to wind down and simply be.

She should have known better than to smoke it at a secret gathering with the few nobles her age. An old peer and classmate of hers, Johnny, imported it from Withelle, so he must have forgiven her for the time she bit him when they were seven, because he offered his resources. She knew he wasn't planning any ill games, and was likely just kissing ass, but she brought her dagger to be sure.

She completely forgot it was in the holster under her shirt, until Johnny and the others attending the gathering brought in a group of women. Their corsets were a size too tight for emphasis. *Beautiful, glorious emphasis*, Maria thought as one was straddled over her while she laid back, joint hanging from her mouth.

The woman unbuttoned Maria's shirt, leaving it just closed enough to conceal her nipples, as she dipped her fingers into the shirt and began stroking Maria's sides.

The woman spotted the dagger from the now looseness of Maria's shirt, and unsheathed it from its holster. Maria knew she was being irresponsible for allowing herself in the position she was currently in. She was too far away from reality to care though, especially as the woman ran the blade lightly down Maria's chest causing her to arch slightly, cupping the woman's breast in her hand.

The woman had the same hair color as Arabella, but the eye color of Maria's first love, one genetically rare in the kingdom of InFiamma. It was like absinthe and peridot, a pond surrounded by trees. Maria was most focused on the woman's hips, the way they were full, and the way they waved back and forth as she started moving on Maria. The woman brought her head down to kiss the red trail she made with the dagger on Maria's body.

Things got heated as the woman, name still unknown, began giving Maria love bites on her neck. This earned a moan from Maria. A moan the fates placed at the tip of her tongue, as she accidentally moaned a name she did know.

"Arabella."

The woman paused as Maria's eyes went wide with embarrassment. She lightly pushed the woman off and sat there for a minute, like one does when waking up early in the morning, trying to make their mind become one with their body.

"Why the fuck did I say that?" Maria asked herself.

"I have to go," she announced to no one in particular, as everyone was in sexual entanglements of their own. Johnny shot up, trying to coerce Maria to stay, but she simply waved him off, not really comprehending anything around her.

Maria found her way into the library, where the main homecoming party for her former peers was taking place. Her shirt was still messy, but secured more than it was a moment ago as she fidgeted with the buttons. It was due to a cruel, twisted, sick fate that she ran into Arabella herself, dressed in a little black dress that hugged her body deliciously. Maria almost fell to her knees.

'♥♥♥'

Aquilla was fast asleep by the time Arabella snuck out of their shared suite. She made it seem like she was going to pull an all-nighter with a building idea she needed to meticulously calculate. She'd lie later and say it didn't work out without admitting she was wrong of course. That would be a dead giveaway.

Wearing the smallest piece of black fabric imaginable, she slid out the door holding her high heels as she padded downstairs to meet Payje, who was also wearing very little. She was in a two-piece pink glittery outfit, her hair in some stylish nest looking thing. They gave each other a silent laugh before winding down the south wing where the library was located.

Arabella saw the ghostly woman Elizabeth, with the gash in her neck. Elizabeth was reading a book in solitude as the people beside her could not sense her presence. Arabella did her best to ignore her, not wanting any apparitions to know of her new gift.

There were way more young people than Arabella had ever seen at one time in the kingdom. In one section was a group of women, about Arabella's age, drinking wine and gossiping. In another section, there were women dressed as if they came directly from Cadence, looking like royal ballerinas. Payje must have forgotten she came with Arabella because she left her standing in the center of the library in favor of reuniting with the first group of women.

There were some older 20-somethings smoking joints in the corner, definitely ruining the quality of the materials within the library. Some people were making out, panting like sweaty athletes after practice. It was the weirdest mix of every social medium, all in one place. The exact cliche Arabella was envisioning when she traveled to InFiamma's court.

In the far back of the library, Arabella could make out a tall individual wearing a loosely buttoned maroon shirt and denim pants, hair bound in a thick low ponytail, holding a murderous expression. "Oh no," Arabella said out loud when she realized it was Maria.

A squeal from Payje sounded from in between the two women. The sound hit one of Arabella's nerves, making her question if the invite was a set up. Arabella couldn't have known, but Payje had been pairing the two together since Maria's coronation.

Payje didn't know Arabella wasn't supposed to be there though, but it was the least of Payje's initial worries. She didn't expect Maria to run off into that separate room, either. All she knew prior was that Maria was going to be there for once, and that Arabella had been cooped up for days. When Payje made her ecstatic feelings known, Arabella took it as an offense, adding onto her already furious feelings.

Maria strutted for Arabella, alcohol in one hand, other hand pointing at the floor as if to demand Arabella meet her halfway. Arabella reluctantly obliged, her tight dress feeling a lot tighter.

"You are in so much trouble," Maria whispered in Arabella's ear.

"I'm sorry, I just wanted to have somewhat of a normal life after the past few weeks. I came to InFiamma hoping to have a better social life, but that has been taken from me," Arabella expressed candidly, because it was either expressing passiveness or undiluted rage.

If she started yelling at Maria, she wasn't sure if she'd be able to stop. With all the people around, it would be more of a negative reflection on herself. Maria could see through the façade Arabella was putting on though, right down to the anger that was boiling inside. Maria too knew that she was in the wrong on some level, so she gave Arabella a stiff nod.

"You don't leave my side tonight. Period," Maria said once again in Arabella's ear, head still in the crook of her neck. "And don't take anything from Johnny, he's a creep for feminine girls."

"I take it you're safe then?" Arabella mustered out.

Maria folded her arms, giving Arabella a bored head tilt. "I can be feminine; I just don't like it." She then dragged Arabella to the keg station. Naturally, Maria engaged in various drinking games, blending in with the people already there.

Arabella fell into the group easily, which surprised Maria. In a perfect world, Arabella would have gotten bored and retreated back to her rooms, giving Maria an excuse to do the same. She wasn't necessarily enjoying the socialization with Cienfuegos gone, but needed to get a read on how InFiammans her age were perceiving her reign.

Maria wasn't thrilled to be around them all again. Even the ones that now included her, such as Johnny, were complacent in Maria's torment at times. In Johnny's case it was more so his father, a councilman reject. When Maria bit Johnny that one time, his father acted as if an amputation was needed. Payje's father was more decent. He was an English teacher who used to look at Maria with a hopelessness and pity that still bothers her to this day.

Those were kids who stayed, clearly not minding Elias' reign as much as the ones who left, such as Viktorie. She went to Cadence to do something with her life, far away from the castle plagued by Elias' cruelty. The king's eyes didn't stick solely to the mistresses trained for the job, and no woman wanted to be around when they turned old enough to gain the misfortune of his attention. Anything was better than that, even if that something was prancing on a stage while her family stayed behind to fight in Elias' wars.

Since the party was somewhat of a business meeting to her, Maria tried to keep her drinking to a minimum. That was until the woman she was just making out with came over to join them. That's when she began pounding back various types of alcohol, nearly throwing up what she consumed thus far when the woman asked Arabella her name. Maria avoided any eye contact with both of them.

When Arabella answered with an unknowing smile, the woman gave Maria a sideward glance. Maria's fifth drink was finished in a matter of seconds, encouraging her to move onto the next. Maria grabbed Arabella by the hand and dragged her along.

"She was nice, why can't I stay there and chat with her?" Arabella groaned as she slumped into dead weight to make it harder for Maria to drag her.

"Whiskey," was all Maria replied. If Cienfuegos was there, he'd have Maria in her rooms with electrolytes to keep the hangover at bay. He especially wouldn't let her drink whiskey; the worst alcohol Maria could ingest. It always got her obliterated within minutes.

Arabella learned that soon enough. Maria began giggling like a maniac as she stumbled through the library, still dragging Arabella around by the hand. Women by the dozens began flirting with Maria while she lounged at a study carrel.

"I want to go. I'm not having fun," Arabella eventually said after hours of watching people fawn over their queen, making her feel an overwhelming pang of jealousy. One of the sultry women invited Maria to indulge in whatever was going on between a circle of people and a bottle.

Maria tilted her head to the side, meeting Arabella's pouting eyes. "Okay, let me walk you to your room," Maria offered with no hesitation. She abandoned the group of people without so much as a goodbye, which left more than one person glowering at Arabella.

To Arabella, the best part of the night was the walk up the east wing. Maria was spinning Arabella in circles and doing a terrible waltz as they approached the Marella suite. Maria still had her right senses about her to whisper.

"You look so beautiful Arabella," Maria commented softly, taking in her black dress and the way it cut low.

"What?" Arabella whispered back, blinking in surprise, blushing feverously.

"So beautiful," Maria insisted as she began stretching her arms, after the soreness from doing a pull up contest for gelatin shots set in. Arabella would have felt the compliment to be genuine if Maria hadn't stumbled down the hallway, landing on her hands right after.

Arabella let out a long sigh, knowing she couldn't let Maria walk back to the west wing by herself. Moreso, she didn't want to as she feared what would happen if the threat was real and already in the castle. She also couldn't go with her, because if she wasn't in her room when her father woke, she was done for. Despite being twenty-one, she felt more restricted than Margaret ever was at twelve.

138

Maybe that was because Margaret didn't come home drunk and scared at sixteen because she nearly died when out with a group of friends she didn't trust. No one believed Arabella when she said someone tried to drag her into the shadows, to the point where she no longer believed herself. Only her father took her seriously, ready to hunt every shadow like he himself was the sun.

Maria was sitting on the floor when Arabella crouched down to meet her eyes, cupping Maria's cheeks in her hands. "Would you like to sleep with me tonight?"

Maria never looked so innocent in her life, the way she almost squeaked as she replied in a cracked voice, "Huh?"

"You're too drunk to walk to the west wing. I'd like you to stay with me. Just promise when my dad asks what happened you'll tell him you came here to talk or something," Arabella pleaded, smoothing her thumb over Maria's freckles.

Maria nodded, head still in Arabella's hands. Maria could've sworn her heart was too. With that, Maria stood up and watched Arabella use the key she stashed below her right breast to unlock the door, snuggled somewhere in her bra this entire time. As they walked in, it was completely dark until a light flicked on.

Sitting in an armchair, wearing blue and gray flannel pajama pants, was Aquilla. He was smoking a cigar and holding a cup of oat milk in his hand. He first looked to Maria, the taller of the two, who gave him a wide smile. "Hi Aquilla," she waved. Aquilla gave her a genuine smile that crinkled his eyes, then focused on his daughter.

"I can explain!" Arabella said before feeling incredibly uncomfortable, remembering she was wearing a dress that barely covered her body. Her father was a rather lenient person in that department, more willing to break the hands of others than reprimand her, but even he sighed in annoyance.

"She was good the whole night, she didn't leave my side," Maria swore, putting her arm around Arabella, leaning down to put her head on Arabella's shoulder. "We'll talk in the morning," Aquilla told his daughter, letting Arabella and Maria retreat to the bedroom.

When inside Arabella's room, Maria flopped onto a small couch, definitely too small to sleep on with her height. Yet she curled into a ball, holding onto herself. Arabella began peeling off her clothes as she told Maria, "You can sleep on the bed, I don't mind."

Maria rolled over to tell Arabella it was okay, but ended up falling onto the floor once she saw Arabella topless. She used the foot of Arabella's bed to peel herself up, putting her head on the footboard as if counting for hide-

and-seek. "Sorry," she muttered, concealing her dark red cheeks.

"I don't care if you see my boobs, we both have them," Arabella sighed, throwing on a giant oversized t-shirt.

Maria didn't move, she just remained isolated in the hole she created for herself. Arabella strolled over to assist Maria in getting dressed, assuming she was too drunk.

When she went to grasp the front of Maria's shirt, she felt that Maria clearly had exceptional core strength. Maria grasped her hand to pause her. Arabella analyzed how her dark eyes were significantly lighter now, like a puppy begging for food, yearning for something. "I'm fine, go to bed I'll only hog the blankets. I'm very selfish," Maria said softly.

Arabella tried for the past month to keep things professional with the queen. Standing before her topless a moment ago, she had to rationalize that she must be misreading Maria's compliments and glances. She told herself that surely Maria would never look at her with the same sensual affections she too possessed. Arabella wouldn't act on anything with the queen in her current state, and to have some sort of confirmation or confession that she too felt the same way…that would take a level of courage and clarity Arabella was not ready to possess.

"Stupid girl with your stupid unattainable crushes," Arabella thought as she let sleep consume her.

'♥♥♥'

In the morning, after an awkward breakfast with Aquilla glancing between the two, he excused Arabella's behavior and allowed her lockdown to be lifted. That is, as long as she stays armed with a weapon of her choosing.

Maria apologized profusely for getting that drunk but both Aquilla and Arabella brushed it off, finding it humorous. Maria and Arabella then spent the day in Arabella's bedroom looking over the blueprints she got from Thoman regarding the castle's layout.

While nibbling on toast Arabella stated, "There's a misprint, there's no room next to yours by the stairs."

Maria was lying flat on her stomach as she leaned over, peaking at the document. "No there is, it has been boarded up," Maria responded with a yawn.

"Why? It looks huge." The room on the blueprint was about two times the size of Maria's chambers, making the other room about the same size as the Marella suite combined. While most hallways held around five suites, the top floor of the west wing only held Maria's rather small room that looked like a studio apartment at best.

"It was my mother's. They boarded it up the night she died," Maria explained as she folded her arms and put her head into them.

Arabella considered why the room would be sealed all together, instead of given to Maria or, knowing Elias, one of his mistresses. "What if everything we need to know regarding Eminence is in correspondence between Lady Odette, and Eminence's Queen Lucille? What if your mom wrote to her sister regarding tactical plans that could give you leverage?"

Maria considered it before she replied, "We will look into it when it's needed."

"Okay," Arabella moved on. "What about this huge one, right off of the library? I didn't see anything to give it away last night."

Maria darted her eyes back to the parchment map. "That- I haven't seen that one before." The two women locked eyes, both with concern, then flickered to excitement. "Let's go look," Arabella proposed, Maria cracked a grin.

As they jumped up from Maria's bed, Brando appeared in front of them. "No," was all he said, putting a hand out as if to block the path. Arabella flew back onto the bed from fright, but Maria just crossed her arms. "Brando, say hi first, I have guests."

Arabella looked at Brando, observing his features similar to Maria's, but looked even more tired if possible. "Hello, Arabella. Nice to finally meet you."

"Finally?" Arabella croaked out. Brando ignored her fear as he pressed on. "That room is off limits. You are not to enter."

Maria looked at him with a raised brow and a shit-eating grin. "Okay. I'm sending for Cienfuegos if it's that good."

"Let's go to your room first, I want to look at the quality of the boarded wall while you get ready," Arabella suggested, slightly weary of Brando still.

"Sounds good," Maria smiled as they gathered the court papers they were working on, placing them neatly in Arabella's safe hidden behind her full body mirror. There were frantic voices coming from outside Arabella's bedroom, so after exchanging yet another curious glance, they went to investigate.

"Her chambers are completely trashed, the wall outside cracked as if they were trying to go through it," Thoman explained to Aquilla with his face turning red. He locked eyes with Maria and sighed with relief.

"You are lucky to be alive, girl," Thoman ground out. "Your rooms have been destroyed and whoever did it was looking for something important. Worst of all, the damage was so cataclysmic that it means they couldn't have been alone."

Maria paused at his words. "I've lived in that wing for my entire life without security, and there's been no threat that I couldn't survive by hiding in my own rooms."

Thoman cocked his head. "You think you weren't protected?" Out of everything Maria had accused Thoman of, he looked most distressed by that claim. The near betrayal of Maria's sentiment showed in the whites of his eyes.

"There were never any guards around, of course I wasn't," Maria squinted, calculating how to go about that conversation.

Thoman straightened. "Just because our guards weren't seen, doesn't mean they weren't there."

Maria thought his eyes unfocused, but that was the opposite. He was focusing on the energy behind Maria and Arabella. Brando's eyes widened as he realized Thoman could, at the very least, sense him.

"Follow me," Maria commanded Thoman as she left Arabella's chambers, asking Aquilla to summon Cienfuegos back to the castle as she exited. Arabella followed, and since she already knew everything, Maria didn't see it as an issue. If anything, she felt her stomach hollow out when she noted her subconscious desire for Arabella to be with her.

"I've always known you were an odd kid like Brando. In some ways, I too could sometimes sense something looming over your shoulder. I could even moments ago, it's incredibly creepy," Thoman explained as they headed towards the west wing. He was sure to divulge all of this out of earshot from any court members.

"There's no denying your father went mad, but I don't think it was a sickness, like syphilis. He would always be in a dark corner whispering. It had been going on since your mother died, actually. Whenever he'd finish that whispering, he'd tell me there was a threat to his heir," Thoman explained, and Maria tensed at the revelation. She prayed it didn't mean what she thought it did.

"Fifteen assassination attempts were planned to take your life throughout the years. Every single one was figured out before they could even reach the steps to your wing," Thoman explained as they began climbing those first steps. Maria ran her fingers through her hair as she sighed deeply.

"When I demanded you have at least a protective companion in your isolation, he told me you already did. I figured around that time, about thirteen years old, you had Cienfuegos or that Abigail girl. I always assumed your father was so careless to assume it was enough. It wasn't until I myself heard a whisper as I was waking up this morning, in some middle state of consciousness, that I truly understood."

They reached the top of the west wing, greeted with broken splintered wood throughout. There were holes in the wall, but they weren't made by trivial hammers or by fists, but rather some military grade breaching tool. It was intentional in the way the holes lined up. They weren't trying to enter Maria's room through the walls, or even reach Maria herself. They were trying to find Odette Fiamma's chambers.

"What did the voice say," Arabella asked, already piecing together the intruder's intentions.

Thoman swallowed hard, he too understood what this meant. "I was hardly awake, ready to chalk it down to a bad dream, but my intuition knew otherwise. I swear they said, "Enemies are here. Eminence is in the west wing."

<u>Chapter 14</u>

The military district, widely known as Inferniana, was at the edge of InFiamma's habited territory. Beyond InFiamma's populous no one cared for the barren land. Therefore, the military district wasn't quite on the southern border, but was placed at the relevant line of civilization, crammed up against the eastern border as well.

To get to the main village, the Heart of InFiamma, it is a few hours horse ride. It was double that time to get to the castle. So, the village was typically a midpoint catered to recuperating the men going to the castle's barracks.

Cienfuegos didn't allow himself the scenic route like he usually did, appreciating his own culture through foods and revelries. He stopped at the fortress just outside the outer wall made specifically for emergency instances like the one he was presented with. Jessie came with him this time, riding on an opalescent white horse beside him.

Neither hesitated to leap off their horses once they reached the castle. They flew off their saddles, hardly taking the time to hand the reins to the stable boys in the pit before running to the west wing.

Once there, they were greeted by Maria taking a hammer to the wall where her mother's rooms were sealed. While a hammer shouldn't have done more than whatever tools the perpetrators used, no one questioned Maria as darkness and rage shone through her eyes. Thoman was by her side, letting her do all the work knowing she needed it more than he did. After all, Thoman dropped a series of informative bombs on her less than a day ago which brought up too many childhood memories.

Maria didn't see her cousin enter, she only saw red. When she laid her hand against the wall in an effort to put her weight into her hits she ended up smashing her pinky and ring finger. She let out a scream and slew of profanities as she threw the hammer at the wall behind her, creating an adjacent dent in what was luckily stone. It was then she saw her cousin standing on the top step of the staircase, clasping his hands in front of him.

Jessie, being a doctor, rushed to Maria. She did not protest when he took her hand in his. Looking down at what she'd done there was no denying her pinky was damaged. "I have to put a splint on," Jessie informed her.

"Go find some broken wood in my room. Lord knows there's an abundance of it," Maria absently replied. Jessie obeyed, not making eye contact with his father.

Jessie loved his father, and Thoman loved him, but a relationship between parents takes more than just being loved. After Jessie's parents divorced, it became clear that Thoman and Jessie's mother were out of love for quite some time. Learning of the arrangement that held his parent's union together did damage that fell on Thoman more than Jessie's mother.

Jessie slipped into Maria's room, found a shard of wood polished enough to not cause splinters, and ripped some already shredded fabric from her four-poster bed. He made quick work of binding her hand as Cienfuegos resumed working the area that was needed to finish demolishing the wall. They just needed to focus on one spot large enough for someone to enter. That was where Eminence was sloppy, as it looked like they rushed to find a weak spot that didn't exist.

It took another four hours for the group to break through the wall while Maria tried her hardest to hotbox her now destroyed room, despite there being holes in her door which she fixed using a sheet. It wasn't just the physical pain of her hand that she was trying to drown out. When Cienfuegos called for her, she exited her room accompanied by an alarming amount of smoke.

"I don't know what's in there, but I can feel it," Thoman said groggily, taking a step back. "It does not like me at all."

Maria stepped towards the hole while cradling her hand. She could feel the looming darkness enveloping her, as if the shadows longed for her presence after all these months she'd lived in the light. It was so familiar. How she nearly forgot how much it weighed, she'll never know. As she took a breath in, even the air felt thicker, probably due to the mildew smell that occupied the abandoned space.

Maria did not proceed though. She was afraid if she stepped back into that darkness, nothing, not even her cousin could pull her back out of it.

"There's no point in going in there tonight. The power likely was cut to conserve energy flow in the castle anyways, so trying to find correspondences in the dark is futile," Maria rationalized as she retreated to her chambers.

"I want you to guard it tonight, I'll go in alone in the morning," Maria told Cienfuegos as she played with the hinges on her door, whatever was left of it. "Thoman, go watch Arabella and Aquilla's suite for me," was the last thing she said before shutting herself in her room, her door nothing but an outline of wood and a pathetic sheet to shield her from the outside.

'♥♥♥'

At dawn the castle loomed blue, surrounded by thick clouds in the sky, which was the new normal in the kingdom with the ongoing monsoon season. It smelt like rain and evergreen forest anywhere you went. Some people even began burning their fall incense.

Maria was given a pumpkin coffee from Thoman as he woke her to get the task of the day over with. She sipped on its hot contents as she once again stared into the entryway of her mother's chambers.

"I can still feel that damned presence," Thoman muttered, keeping to the wall.

Cienfuegos traded with Maria, taking a nap in her chambers after being up for 48 hours straight due to dealing with previous business. He knew she wouldn't let anyone in during this, not even him. Thoman knew this as well, and along with the tension he felt in that room he thought it better to sit out what he couldn't fight with his bare hands.

Maria didn't send for Arabella again, leaving her in ignorance. Whatever feelings she had regarding Arabella's company and soothing nature was numbed and overridden by everything else.

The entryway to Odette Fiamma's chambers was a small walk in, met with a wall adorned with a portrait of Odette herself, along with a breakfast buffet that held a vase of dead dried flowers. Pink roses, to be exact. Maria assumed that was the mildew smell from last night, which was luckily a bit more aired out now.

The suite itself began on either side. To the left was her bedroom and dressing room, on the right, her living area. The latter was where Maria began.

The living area had only stained glass windows, making it so no one could see in or out. It was intricate depictions of roses and religious battles that ended with the death of a martyr. Maria flipped through desks and drawers with her intact hand, finding small things like invites to courtly events and embroidered pieces.

She figured that anything of personal importance would be stored in a personal place, not just in the open where people could sneak in throughout the night.

Maria was sure to feel out the floorboards on her way to the bedroom, in case there were hollowed out spots. This distracted her from the fact that the suite did not reflect that of a mother. Not a trace of Maria's existence remained, until she entered the bedroom.

There were large bay windows spanning to the ceiling, cracked, with ivy that crawled up the castle's exterior which now infiltrated the rooms. It spread throughout the walls, reflecting just how abandoned the place was.

The aesthetic of the room was rose gold and white, her mother's favorites. She was a fashion designer with her infinite spare time, which Maria imagined was a great distraction from having Elias as a husband. Her last piece was left still in progress on a mannequin. It was designed to be somewhat of a rib cage, mixed with a bird cage around a corset. Left never to be finished.

Hanging from that cage was a toy soldier that vaguely called to Maria's memories. She remembered it being her favorite as a kid, playing war games with Cienfuegos. She wanted to be a knight more than she ever wanted to rule as a queen. Back then, Cienfuegos chose the bard as he always wanted to be a poet and travel the world; write about places no human would ever set foot again. Places where the continent was assumed to still be burning. The toy soldier hung onto the cage that guarded the heart.

Maria analyzed the toy, playing with it between her fingers which were much larger now than they were twenty years ago, which made the proportions feel unnatural. *"**Life is so weird when the filters of nostalgia are lifted, and you're left with a tin knight as hollow as adulthood feels**,"* she thought to herself.

As Maria's mind wandered to a different life, a voice creaked behind her. "It's been so long since you've visited me."

Maria froze, her pupils dilating was the only tell to her shock. She turned her head only enough for a few wispy strands of hair to fall into her line of vision, eyes narrowing as she saw the wisp looking woman before her.

She was so pale, and as tall as Maria, about 180 cm. Maria never saw an apparition appear in a nearly translucent state like the one before her, which made her think she was

154

letting her internal struggles get the best of her mental state. It wasn't until the woman spoke again, moving forward in a fluid motion that Maria knew it was worse than madness. It was a nightmare come true.

"Oh, Elias. You have finally come for me."

Maria stumbled back until her legs slammed into the footboard of her mother's bed. She still did not initially speak as her heart rate climbed to dangerous rates.

Maria sat down on the bed and ran her fingers through her hair. "I'm not Elias. I'm Maria," was all she could eventually say, becoming uneasily pale. She put her arms in a hold around her own waist, half holding herself, half preparing to be sick.

Odette Fiamma did not move, or breathe due to the lack of necessity, as she eventually said in a raspy voice, "Maria is six years old."

Maria's chest rose harshly with every sharp inhale, desperate to breathe. "I'm twenty-three," was all Maria could manage to reply. She tilted her head with consideration as she explained, "You're dead, and I can't explain how you're here right now without the concept of time passing. I also don't feel like explaining how I can see you—" Maria began, but was cut off by her mother.

"You don't feel like it? You tell me you're my daughter seventeen years later—who looks nothing like me by the way, how disappointing—and it's just too much to take a second to explain that?" her mother quipped.

Maria looked up at her mom through her lashes, holding an irritated expression as her mouth opened slightly. "Well, what's the last thing you remember?"

Odette stared on unimpressed, ignoring the question altogether before musing, "Why am I here?"

"How the hell should I know?" Maria asked as she stood from the bed, resuming her search for anything on Eminence once more. Maria wanted to be out of there as soon as possible, but she knew finishing with her mother wouldn't delay the harsh truth that Brando had been withholding something like this. That conversation was going to be a war in itself.

"That's how you speak to your dead mother?" Odette scoffed loudly, like all the audacity in the world was turned onto her. Her body language was even more dramatic.

"Apologies, Mrs. Fiamma," Maria said to her mother disingenuously. She returned to digging through her mother's nightstand.

"What *are* you looking for?" her mother drawled. "And why is it so important that your disrespect becomes so rife?"

Maria blew at the strains of hair that kept falling in her face, so she took one of her mother's scrunchies and used it to fasten her thick hair into a ponytail. She was planning on just ignoring her mother, having no idea what to say to her anyways. Odette Fiamma spoke again, tipping Maria over the edge.

"Did you ask to use my things?"

"Did you ask for the guards to take me instead of you the night you died? Yeah, that's crazy. I think you did." Maria snapped, yet did so with incredibly calm body language.

"I did NOT," Odette protested with offense, stepping towards her daughter.

"I was there, we made eye contact," Maria paused what she was doing before facing her mother. "What is the last thing you remember? You don't get to demand answers but evade my questions."

"I'm queen. I can do what I want," Odette crossed her arms, looking down her nose at Maria.

"No, I'm the queen. If every ghost could claim their rulership, we would be forced to participate in democracy," Maria replied, eyeing a pack of cigarettes on her mother's coffee table, taking it upon herself to indulge.

Odette watched as Maria inhaled a puff of smoke, and held it. Maria looked around the room and was impressed that there was barely any smoke damage when it came to the colors of the walls. Maria kept the smoke in her lungs for a beat, until her mother spoke.

"I wasn't telling them to kill you, I didn't think I was going to die. Also, stop smoking. It's disgusting. Even I was trying to quit towards the end."

Maria let out the cloud of smoke, the smell of nicotine filling the bedroom as a few ashes fell to the carpet. Odette reached for her ashtray, but could not pick it up. Shock filled her features when she summoned her own from sheer will.

She couldn't hand it to Maria either. Summoned objects and physical objects are not able to be exchanged, although replication is fine. Maria learned that when she tried to snatch Brando's coffee once.

"I- well I asked them to exile you," Odette eventually said once the shock waivered.

"Oh, nice. That's so much better," Maria said with a monotone voice, taking another inhale.

"I thought the original plan, your father's original decision, would be to exile me to the cottage I'd frequently go to with you every weekend. I didn't know that plan was to change until I was in the middle of the burning party as the guest of honor," Odette explained with clouded eyes.

"The last thing I remember was seeing you. You were unconscious with burns up your arm. I did not leave you until a man appeared, who told me you would be safe now, and he would watch over you. I felt ready then, and that's the last I was."

Maria's eyes glossed over as she looked her mom in hers, peering for the truth and seeing it was already spoken. She began fidgeting with the cigarette. "I'm in trouble, mom," Maria said as she put the cigarette in the ashtray. Maria then sat down in an armchair and began.

Maria then explained it all. From what happened to her, and how she was able to see ghosts, and why she bears the scars she does. All the way to her father's death, her coronation, and the impending war if she doesn't find leverage. Maria also explained how up until then, her mother's rooms were boarded up and recently compromised.

"Lucille wants me dead, and there's clearly something in here that Eminence doesn't want me to see. I don't want a war. Really, I don't. However, if there's something in here they want, I need to see it and figure out why."

Odette listened to her daughter contemplatively as she said, "I have a box of letters from my sister leading up to my death. You may read them," she gestured to the walk-in closet, which had loose floorboards under the back corner of the carpet.

"Before I begin, the first assassin from Eminence had a gun. Do you know if Eminence possesses any more contraband?" Maria thought it was wise to ask.

"Eminence has weapons up to grade three, that gun only being a second grade assault weapon." Odette replied, recalling something from her memory before she shared it with her daughter. "The worst they will have is a giant 75mm gun, which will give off over a dozen rounds in about a minute. It looks a lot like a canon, from what I can remember."

Maria heard Cienfuegos yell something from outside. Thoman gave a grunt in agreement. Maria was about to jump up from her position, already unsheathing her dagger, when another wispy figure loomed into view. This time though, the figure was a living being.

"Oh," Arabella's eyes went wide as she met Odette's odd appearance. "You're translucent?" she said without thinking.

Odette's eyes squinted in distaste. "I haven't been conscious for seventeen years, sorry if my looks aren't up to par."

"Are you alright? This must be so much on you," Arabella asked Maria as she too entered the closet. "At least you found some letters," she pointed into the hole.

"I'm okay, I think. A little overwhelmed so help make sure I don't miss anything," Maria said with rationality.

The letters were in a wooden box, and then wrapped in parchment. They all were waxed sealed with aesthetically placed dried flowers. Arabella began reading one with her gentle fingers. Maria, on the other hand, was afraid to even hold them with her destructive nature.

Arabella sensed Maria's nerves, and read the letter out loud.

"My dearest sister Odette,
The rumors rage whether Elias will attack soon, yet some believe it is a diversion to get his real target to put their walls down. I need to know if I should prepare myself and my son for the worst. Father is too stubborn, and with

Eugene being so young, I don't want this war to be the beginning of his life. I will forever be sorry for everything I've done, but let me do this one thing right.

> *With genuine love and affection,*
> *Your sister, Lucie"*

The sound of parchment rustled as Arabella sat the letter down by her thigh, pulling a tiny notepad from a pocket in her dress. She jotted down notes as Odette explained.

"This was when Maria was four or five," she told Arabella directly, seeing as she was the organized one. "I did not speak to my sister those years before due to the nature of me and Elias' union."

Arabella looked at Odette with a quizzical brow, but it was Maria who decided to explain that section of the family lore. "She wasn't my father's intended betrothed. My father was supposed to marry Lucille, until my mother slept with him the night before their wedding."

Arabella's mouth fell open as she stared forwards at a blank wall. She folded her hands in her lap, processing a reply to that bit of information.

"Yes," was the only reply from Odette, not wanting to explain further. Arabella failed any and every lesson in reading the room, so she pressed on once she composed her thoughts.

"Why'd you do that?"

Odette rolled her eyes and Maria sighed. Maria didn't know the answer either though, so she kept her ears open. Odette saw her own daughter's curiosity and caved in.

"Elias came to Eminence many times over the years. I met him when I was ten, he was seventeen. I developed a crush instantly. Back then, I wanted to be a designer, and Lucille wanted to be a ballerina." Odette took a seat, as if she was amongst her friends sharing secrets in a little circle. Arabella cut a side eye to Maria upon hearing the age difference between her parents. Maria felt the stare, but did not return it.

"He never noticed me until he returned to court years later, and it truly was such a silly crush. Even when he did come back and I was sixteen, I still didn't necessarily care to be a queen. I wanted to study in Cadence for the art of fashion. Lucille was jealous of my freedom to do so, constantly reminding me that I was a young stupid girl too silly to be a mature dignified royal."

Maria listened attentively. Any trace of her mother was erased in the castle immediately following her death. Honestly, if Maria hadn't seen that portrait at the entrance, she'd likely not have recognized the apparition of her mother.

"The night of Lucille's wedding the bachelor party was ending late, and I was in the garden sowing. My sister didn't invite me to her bachelorette party, saying I was too young for it. In Eminence, you're considered a woman at sixteen. It was a great insult to take away the one exciting thing in the kingdom where we are corralled like a herd of sheep."

The terrain of Eminence was heavily compacted because of the mountain ranges surrounding it, cradling the kingdom like a bowl. It made it near impossible for the country to start any wars or defend itself from them, making the rulers forcibly compliant. There was a narrow pathway as an exit, but no other logical options as a line of defense. The way of life there as a result was less festive than InFiamma was known to be.

"Long story short, he came on to me. Initially teasing about how obvious my crush always was. It got tense and I wanted to spite my sister to show I was more desirable as a woman and queen than she was. It led me to the fate I received. Karma for my vain insolence," Odette explained with a poisonous disdain on the tip of her tongue as she spoke of her youth. Even more so how Elias took it from her.

"Were you scared to marry him?" Arabella asked, pressing her knees to her chest, mimicking Maria's.

"I wasn't scared of Elias, really. I didn't love him once I realized my fairytale would be slain by the presence of mistresses, and Elias' own need to be satisfied. But I never feared that man."

Arabella opened her mouth to ask another question, but Odette gave a polite point to the box of letters. This time Maria took one in hand, telling Arabella to take notes.

The next letter Maria read was sent a year later. This one had another letter stapled to it, written by Elias himself.

"I will not keep going over matters which are none of your business. Wherever my kingdom, my wife, and my heir are concerned, is none of yours.

Maria can hardly remember the incident anyways. I will not put mercy on Odette just because you asked politely. The next time I get correspondence from your country, it better be an admission of defeat, and a promise for three times the minerals.
~ King E. Fiamma"

Maria's eyes widened as her legs shot out forward. "Remember what?"

"It doesn't matter… he just wanted Lucille to feel crazy I'm sure," Odette replied. That convinced Maria, but only because she didn't want to believe something so bad happened that she couldn't remember it.

Maria smoothed her hands over the letter, gathering her thoughts before she resumed.

"My dearest Odette,

Elias will not reason, and his mind seems perfectly set on whatever comes next. I urge you to take Maria and try to run again, before it's too late. She and Eugene can play in the meadows, just as we did when we were young. This time, in a new world. Far away from kings and kingdoms, where we can just be.

I'll wait for you at the Winding Oak, on the date we previously set. If you are not there, I can't do much to stop our father from marching.

With the most love, your sister, Lucille."

Maria flipped the page over, but there was no context on what happened, no date to tell Maria if it was just before her mother died, nothing at all.

Arabella gasped, and when Maria looked up startled, the apparition of her mother was gone. Arabella huffed as she jotted down some more notes, trying to stay focused on what information they received that could help. Maria couldn't think, severely sleep deprived, somehow still hungover from a day ago, and incredibly overstimulated from all the traumatic knowledge dropped on her.

"We came for solutions and all I've been left with are more questions," Maria's eyes narrowed. She peeled herself up from the floor, took in a slow inhale, and then screamed. "Brando you piece of fucking shit! Get over here now!"

Arabella jumped at the sudden noise, then jumped again when Brando appeared right next to her. Before Maria could even begin to drill into him, he began defending himself. "Maria—"

Maria cut him off before he could give his excuses. "Seventeen years," she seethed, her eyes wild with anger. "Since I was a child, I have asked, and asked, and begged to know even a fraction of the information presented to me in the last twenty four hours," her chest was heaving.

Maria began shaking as she grounded out, "Where is she?"

Brando's face looked as if he was a child that broke a vase that carried someone's ashes. He was more red than Arabella thought a ghost could get as he shrunk into himself.

"There are ways that cannot be explained to mortals. I suspect you summoned her when you touched that little tin man—"

"Oh great! So you've been here the whole time and didn't care to weigh in, even when you were mentioned to have stood over my unconscious body as my dead mother looked down on me. Nice!" Maria doubled over and began to chuckle madly.

"Maria-" Brando was cut off again.

"Oh!" Maria said between chuckles, "Let us not forget that before I even stepped foot in here, I learned that my father could see you lot as well!"

"Maria!" Brando bellowed. "I am restricted under more than oaths, and laws, and things petty mortals care for. I am under a rational and cosmic binding to shut the fuck up about these matters."

"By whom?" Arabella invited herself into the conversation, more inquisitively than she'd ever been before.

"Don't you think I'd mention it if I could," Brando snapped, and Maria took a step forward. She'd never seen him hostile, but it felt like she didn't even know him. He was a threat at that moment.

"Your mother wasn't an apparition in a way that has been relevant to you before. Some of us are permanently lucid. Like I, the third tier, Servient. Being summoned, however, is so rare as it takes a multitude of steps that it is rarely ever done," Brando explained.

"This whole time I could have summoned her…" Maria said as she was still laughing between breaths. Arabella got an uneasy feeling that Maria wasn't actually talking about her mother.

"You touched something of hers that was so profoundly personal. Even if you are a proud individual, you must have yearned for her, or something connected to her at that moment. Symbolically, a piece of her soul was in that unfinished piece, and you tapped into it. She received it on her end, and accepted that invitation," Brando paced slightly in Odette's walk-in closet.

"Who could Elias see? Thoman said he spoke to shadows to secure Maria's safety," Arabella asked as she slowly gathered the box of letters.

"He wasn't the only person who gained something the night your mother died…" Brando grimaced. "He got the pleasure of my father's company, the two so suitably paired."

Maria cringed, all instincts to laugh away her grief ceasing immediately. "You don't mean Ares Fiamma, do you?"

"The very same. I think it's partially why your father went mad. My father's soul is an overpowering one to be latched to. The same way you became historically inclined after we met, your father became inclined to war."

"Your souls are connected," Arabella gasped. "Does that mean I'm attached to my sister?" her head reeled, and she could practically feel someone's foreign grip on her very being.

"Hard to say. In theory it should be your sister, but I don't know what will happen when she is put to rest. She isn't going to be Servient, so I'm unsure if your abilities will remain once she is gone," Brando explained, then looked to Maria.

"I cannot interfere in the fate of other wards."

"I want to speak to your Human Resources department," Maria said as she prepared to exit Odette's closet. "Before you go and put that complaint in with God, I'd like to know what can help me in this room against Eminence."

"Before that," Brando added, addressing Arabella, "That row of shoe boxes should be removed as well, as I would hate for any reminiscences of Maria's childhood to be destroyed once the intruders return."

Arabella nodded, calling for Cienfuegos to help her. He gathered boxes into his arms as Arabella vaguely explained the past few minutes, assisting in the task. Once they exited, Brando addressed Maria by herself.

"Something big is coming. I've spent your entire life preparing you for it without ever being able to tell you why. Once it happens, it will be time for me to leave for good. Only then will I be able to find peace, my duty being fulfilled."

"You've known my entire future too?" Maria scoffed, although she was more scared at that moment than offended. She'd never admit it, though. That was partially the reason Brando never told her that fact. Maria knew he could feel out immediate circumstances, but she never suspected he could see beyond closely approaching events. He nodded solemnly.

"The letters you seek are in the bottom of that wooden box. The true meaning of this war will not be clear to you for a long while yet, but to start finding the cause, you must look where you've refused to go. Your father's bedroom. In his own closet, under the portrait."

Arabella strolled back in the room, this time by herself as Cienfuegos was diligently watching over the boxes. When Maria looked over to her, she knew there was no point in looking back. By Arabella's expression she knew Brando was gone.

Chapter 15

The end of August came shortly after that. Maria celebrated her one month as queen with Firenight, the bonfire event the public was notified about before the plague hit. It went as traditionally done in the past, held in the meadow outside the castle. The center bonfire was the biggest, meant to symbolize the current ruler.

Around that giant bonfire was a circle of smaller ones, meant to symbolize the rulers that came before. As everyone danced and enjoyed the revelries around Maria's symbolic bonfire, she stayed hidden by Brando's, wearing a dark brown cloak.

She was too tired to care that everyone seemed to like her more than she'd ever been liked before. She still assumed they talked shit about her behind her back just like the good old days. If anything, the overwhelming sensation of approval, after being outcasted her whole life, made her even more paranoid as the days went on.

As she stared into the fire, she did her best to unpack that there was an assassination attempt at her coronation with a special piece of contraband, a plague, hidden rooms and family secrets, all in the first month of her reign. It was too much.

Arabella was around Maria's symbolic fire with the Island's interns that arrived that same week. Maria watched from afar. Arabella was telling them about all of InFiamma's customs with fire compared to the Island's water-based ones. The interns would be leaving for the village after the party to begin working on their innovations, but Maria observed Arabella's body language and could tell she was not amongst friends. She was, in lack of a nicer term, posturing to gain respect.

That observation had Maria reconsidering Arabella's image, helping her understand that Arabella must too be an outcast amongst her people. Maria always wanted to run away and find where she truly belonged, and it clicked then that when Arabella came to InFiamma, she was doing just that.

Arabella decided to join Maria after a while, the only person able to spot her at the large event. Maria was sharpening a stick as her unbound hair played in the wind. Maria glanced up casually, eyes fixating when she realized it was Arabella who sat before her. Maria kept sharpening as she lowered her gaze. Arabella noticed even under the cloak that her lips twitched upward.

"How are you enjoying Firenight?" Maria asked through the crackle of the flame.

"It is lovely," Arabella said in return, taking in the air that was both hot from the fire, and chill from the breeze.

"Does the flame not scare you?" Maria inquired as the flames roared against the wind. The fires were not the small ones maintained in the castle for survival purposes. Its flames reached the height of the tallest person, threatening whoever was courageous enough to get close.

"No, Your Majesty. I find the fire quite beautiful, actually," was all Arabella gave in return as her cheeks began to heat, a bodily reaction that became something of a nuisance to control when around Maria. She peered upwards through the flames once more, met with Maria's dark eyes studying her features for a moment before returning to her craftwork.

Arabella took a minute to suck in the citrusy and cinnamon smell of the air. Embrace the wind that was promising a storm, and the hardened features of the queen before her working diligently on the wood. Arabella dropped the formalities.

"Do you always sit alone at functions like these?" she questioned as she fiddled with her fingernails.

Not looking up, Maria stated, "I've never been the type to indulge in any functions, unfortunately."

"Me neither," Arabella said, a half-truth. Maria gave her a raised brow, not taking her eyes off the wooden stick as she worked. "Is that why you snuck out to a party?" Maria asked.

"Is that why you were there as well?" Arabella caught herself, remembering to whom she spoke to after her father's past sternness on the matter.

"I still gotta live and more importantly work, but you didn't exactly see me with anyone. Whereas you were with Payje."

"Please, you had women around you, all begging and wanting," Arabella rolled her eyes, folding her arms. This caused Maria to burst into a fit of laughter, the stick falling from her lap as she threw her head back.

"Darling, they could care less about me. They're being political, they're not attracted to me" Maria explained, still coughing out laughs in between the words.

"Why wouldn't they be?" Arabella asked, getting embarrassed by Maria's reaction. Maria subtly stopped laughing and darkened her gaze on Arabella, giving a head tilt as a questioning gesture.

"I had a friend once who was trained in the art of seducing her way into power. I know the signs well," Maria whispered, haunted by a memory.

"Did you fall in love with them, and it ended badly or something?" Arabella questioned, tightening her arms around herself. She didn't foresee the wind being as cold as it was, causing her to gain goosebumps under her mesh sleeves.

"You could say that. She died. Before you ask, no I haven't seen her ghost either." The word *she* rang through Arabella. Nowhere in the modern world cared for specific gendered pairings, but in Arabella's experience, the Island had very few women her age she could meet that weren't already trying to ruin her life. Maria undeniably was strictly into women, Arabella assumed that just upon first glance, but the verbal confirmation gave her foolish hope that she could be a contender.

Yet, Arabella didn't know what to say regarding the devastating topic. She saw Maria putting up a mask of apathy and decided to stop it. "Don't. You can feel your grief around me, I will not judge."

"You mean this time?" Maria inquired sarcastically, slight irritation stemming from their argument at the burning ceremony after the plague. Arabella tensed under the rebuttal.

Maria sighed, tipping her head back. "You would think these women would consider the risk of being fake-loved by me, considering what happens to those who are real-loved by me." A chuckle escaped her lips, but there was no humor or deflection behind it.

Arabella's eyes widened; a creepy sight due to them already being large to begin with. "I dare say the end game, no matter how messy, must have been worth it."

"Why would you say that?" Maria's brows furrowed in confusion. To Maria, nothing seemed worth dying the way Abigail must have. She knew that pain intimately, and even with the power to pull away from it, it lingered after.

"Love will always be worth it," Arabella answered as a few drops of rain began to descend. Nothing serious enough to drown the fires, but enough for some water to fall on Maria's cheek. Arabella could've sworn one of the drops came from Maria's eyes.

"Love is a cunt," was all Maria muttered before standing up, walking into the lush forest to the right. Arabella froze for a minute, scared she offended Maria or pushed her too hard to be vulnerable. Though her mother brought up the manipulative effects of such gifts often, Arabella prided herself on her ability to read others' emotions—and sway them if necessary. Yet now, they seemed to be failing her.

When Arabella began running after Maria, she told herself it was to keep her father from revoking her spot at court and sending her back to Gloucester. At least, the excuse of that position was what masked the real reason she ran after Maria. She was genuinely afraid of being pushed away.

Maria wasn't too far ahead, but her long legs compared to Arabella's average ones had Arabella sprinting through branches to catch up those few feet. "I'm sorry, I'm sorry—" Arabella began before Maria spun around, grasping her chin gently as she usually did when things got too charged between them, tilting Arabella's head to meet her eyes.

"People who get too close to me get very, very hurt, Bella. I'm not upset with you, but because I care about your safety, I must ask you to keep your distance." With that, Maria turned and disappeared into the shadows, leaving Arabella to catch raindrops on her own cheek before the sky began to outright pour.

'♥♥♥'

There was a small council meeting, very brief, to continue discussing safety measures for the people of InFiamma. That was including an evacuation plan, even for the interns, should Eminence make another move. After that meeting, there was a dinner with the entire court, which was pretty informal. Maria did like that dose of social interaction, because she could listen to others without having to respond or perform, just fill her face with food.

Arabella kept looking at Maria, who was intentionally not returning the gaze. Arabella's feelings began to inflate like a lung, stealing her breath and all that she was, causing her to nearly pop from distress.

One of the reasons why she liked Maria was because Maria saw her for who she was and believed in her abilities. For the most part Maria didn't try to tame her unless there was an active threat. Yet, Maria was so busy trying to disguise the wall around her feelings as some bogus power imbalance that Arabella had not acted on her own feelings.

Arabella remembered how Margaret teased her about the sketches she drew of Maria in the first council meeting. The same way the architecture she prized resembled that of ancient cities like the forgotten, fallen Chicago, she saw Maria as a deity to rule over those beautiful sacred places.

After dinner Maria took her leave immediately. Arabella made it seem like she was going to retreat to her own chambers as her father stayed behind to smoke a cigar with Thoman. Instead, she headed in the opposite direction, intimate enough with the route to know it with certainty as her mind wandered, feet leading her up the west wing.

Maria's rooms were repaired in a day, styled to mimic more of a royal's chambers than a forgotten soul. There were now two guards stationed at the foot of the west wing. Even then they did not protest when Arabella slipped by them. Everywhere Maria went, Arabella followed.

Maria was against the usual pillar that she sat on as she took her tea, especially in times of distress. She turned her head towards Arabella hesitantly, knowing she was troubled to some degree. Maria's face looked tired and strained, like she was bracing for an impact she couldn't muster the energy to shield herself from. Arabella took a second to gather her thoughts as she huffed her anxiety into the air.

"Why am I being punished?" Arabella demanded, packed with attitude.

Maria looked her in the eyes and confessed, "I'm protecting you."

This caused Arabella's cheeks to grow red, her temperature rising by the second until her blood was boiling. "I don't need protecting, it's coming across like you're controlling me," she said scoffing in offense.

"Hmm," was all Maria could bring herself to say as she looked Arabella up and down slowly, straining her eyes as she inhaled, in an attempt to reset her brain.

"And what if I am protecting you from me?" Maria said, her mouth turning into a sinister smirk, a coping mechanism of hers when under pressure. That was something Arabella made a mental note of long ago. It took her a moment to process what Maria actually said.

"You wouldn't do anything, please," Arabella scoffed, rolling her eyes. Maria slid over to her, still keeping a few feet distance. At this point she spoke slower, "What. If. I. Did?" It was a sentence that took what felt like years to relay.

Arabella's heart picked up pace, feeling as though it was slowly splitting into two. Her eyes gazed deeply into Maria's, whose pupils grew by the second. "You. Wouldn't," Arabella insisted.

"I'm the daughter of a mad man, who also grew up without a mother's love. Do you want to bet that I won't bite? I'm notoriously known to do so," Maria moved in closer to Arabella, the space between them pulsating.

"You don't scare me one bit," Arabella said with arrogance, taking a step closer, now standing nearly chest to chest with the queen towering over her by a few inches. She refused to let that height difference intimidate her. This made Maria smile again, eyes filling with ego as she fixed her posture. "Yeah?" she retorted in a mocking tone.

This taunt made Arabella put a hand on Maria's chest and push backwards until Maria stumbled against the pillar. Arabella grabbed Maria's chin mocking her signature move, tilting it up so Maria was forced to make eye contact.

Maria leaned back on her hands as Arabella stroked her bottom lip. Infinity passed from the time Arabella leaned over, to the time their lips touched.

Maria snapped forward to wrap her hands around Arabella's waist, pulling her closer. Maria twirled Arabella's corset ribbon in her fingers as she pondered how screwed she was. Kissing Arabella in that moment wasn't just a long-awaited tension being soothed, but confirmation that she was feeling something genuine, and allowing it.

As Maria stood up to carry Arabella into her chambers, she muttered, lips still touching,

"You will be my undoing."

Chapter 16

Their first time was the perfect reflection of Maria's room. Slightly cluttered and worn down, yet Maria let Arabella in anyway. The same way Maria had to toss the book she was reading to the side to lay down Arabella, she had to do the same to her pride. She hesitated more getting on her knees to receive her crown than she did positioning herself between Arabella's legs.

Maria had Arabella placed at the edge of her bed, leaning back so she could have the perfect view of her when glancing up. She didn't want to miss a single frame of Arabella's features, using them as subtitles on a tutorial to learn what turns her on.

After a few questioning licks and twists of the tongue, Maria saw it. As she placed her whole mouth on the top of Arabella's sex and gave a suck, Arabella's mouth opened, emitting the most holy of sounds. While InFiammans confessed to the flames in their homes when particularly troubled, hoping the Sun God would shed its light, Maria was perfectly content having her sorrows drowned as Arabella got progressively more wet. Even when she was soaked, Maria wouldn't stop until she overdosed on it.

Arabella had a minor secret. While she always knew she liked women, she'd only ever been with men sexually. With women, there were passionate kisses and juvenile promises of forever, but nothing that lasted once one of them came to their senses, and they realized that the high came with an ugly, more truthful side as well. Love was messy, at least that's the way Arabella had always experienced it. Of the three people she'd been with before, none of them stayed after seeing her cry. When Arabella looked Maria in her eyes as Arabella's climax came on, she had to tilt her head back to keep the water in her eyes from falling out. She felt so full, so omniscient, like a wave breaking as it crashed onto the north shore of Gloucester.

Maria relished in Arabella's release, pride filling her chest at how undone the girl before her was. Something in her was begging to continue, desperate to chase her own pleasure, as well. Maria slid up Arabella's toned body, lightly grasping her chin for confirmation to continue. If Arabella said the word, if she just wanted a quick orgasm, Maria would allow it. When Arabella nearly died from the plague, Maria vowed she would do anything should Arabella wish it. And when those captivating eyes met Maria's, a lovesick pout gracing Arabella's beautiful face as she whispered, "More," Maria honored that vow.

Arabella reached for the buttons on Maria's shirt. Maria helped her do the unbuttoning, then flung her sports bra off. Arabella leaned down, taking Maria's nipple lightly in her mouth, just as desperate for a taste as Maria had been. Maria usually preferred to be the one worshipping breasts, but the way Arabella looked up at her through those beautiful eyelashes made Maria blush like it was her first time. Arabella gave her a playful nip before pulling away, gauging that while not against it, it wasn't something Maria was particularly into.

Maria let out a breathy chuckle as her eyes lit aflame.

Arabella tensed slightly. "I've never gone this far with another woman before. Do you mind directing me towards what pleases you?" Arabella requested in a much more shy manner than she'd ever been used to. Maria found the formality of the words adorable, a small smile tugging at her lips.

"I am easy to please, as my pleasure comes from touching you and watching you react to it. All I ask from you is that those reactions are genuine, so it is I that requests to be led in the right direction," Maria disclosed, slowly laying Arabella down against the pillows. Color filled Arabella's cheeks as she nodded, agreeing to the request.

"I suggest I be permitted to begin here," Maria requested, taking one of Arabella's nipples in between her pointer and middle fingers. Arabella gave a small hum of approval.

Maria pressed her lips firmly to Arabella's, kissing her so passionately it felt like hours had passed when she finally broke away. Slowly, the kisses traversed down her neck, tracing along her collarbone, then settling on Arabella's breasts.

When Arabella arched, Maria took the opening to wrap her arms around Arabella's back and pull her face in deeper. Arabella began stroking Maria's thigh, awfully close to her center. "If you keep doing that, I'll be finished before I could even begin to get started," Maria warned, pausing to pin Arabella's hands above her head. "Be a good girl and be patient."

Arabella had no choice but to obey as Maria toyed with her body. Light touches and deep kisses tested her patience. It was only when she was reduced to a begging mess, did Maria oblige her with more.

"I'll have to commission a toy later. Are you okay with my fingers?" Maria asked with insecurity laced in her voice. Her dominant hand was riddled with scars, which never bothered her unless intimacy was concerned.

Arabella removed her hands from above her head and grasped Maria's. Guiding Maria's hand into a two-finger position, Arabella took those fingers and placed her lips around them, beginning to suck. Her eyes never left Maria's.

Taking the lead for a bit, Arabella guided Maria onto her back and inserted those two fingers into herself. She started with soft grinding motions on Maria's hand, searching for her rhythm. The fingers reached deep within her, turning her into even more of a wet mess. Her grinding became frantic and sloppy as Maria stimulated Arabella's clit.

Maria held her hand against her own hip bone to give Arabella some stability. Her other hand was gripping Arabella's hip, adding a pinch of pain to the pleasure. Arabella straddled Maria's thigh as she ground her knee in just the right spot to get Maria off. Arabella's breasts swaying in her face played a part as well. Neither woman had experienced a mutual climax before, but it was a time for firsts.

Arabella was forced to grab the headboard to keep from collapsing. Maria's free hand gripped in the middle of the headboard, in between Arabella's, to keep her soul tethered to the earth as she ascended into her own orgasm.

Even then, there was still a hunger between them only beginning to be recognized. They did not stop for a long time yet. It wasn't until the sun kissed the horizon that Maria gave her final kiss to Arabella, succumbing to their exhaustion.

Chapter 17

Steady. Maria wanted to take this thing with Arabella slow and steady. Those plans were foiled immediately. Not just because she spent the night between Arabella's thighs, who was moaning loud enough for the neighboring kingdoms to hear. Though that was to be expected the way they spent weeks dancing around each other.

The issue was that they were discovered immediately the next morning. And if you thought secrets within a court were confined where the ruler wanted, well, you'd be wrong.

Maria was lying on her stomach with her head cradled in her arms, her face smushed into the pillow. On her shoulder blade lay Arabella, who was sleeping completely sprawled out in Maria's shirt. Because of their late night, they didn't consider that there was a council meeting at the exact time they were lounging in bed together.

Maria was the first to awaken when Cienfuegos burst into her room, wondering why his cousin wasn't at the very important meeting to discuss the very real impending threat of war. Maria cracked one eye open and froze when she saw him. "Not. A. Word." she emphasized as she peeled herself up, covering her breasts as Arabella rolled over to the other side of the bed. Cienfuegos gave an amused smile, hiding it by turning his head away.

Maria placed a fur blanket over Arabella. Cienfuegos tossed his cousin a shirt at the same moment causing it to land on her head. "Thanks," she expressed with both grit and gratitude. Her cousin waved her off as he turned around so she could dress. After a few sniffles and adjustments to the morning light, Maria was fully lucid.

Arabella did not initially wake. Until their second intruder, Thoman, barged in with a force that nearly shook the door off its newly enforced hinges.

"God, man. We're coming," groaned Maria, who was more irritated than anything. Arabella jolted awake at that point, blushing with embarrassment and shock as she pulled the covers over her head with a squeaky noise. Maria couldn't tell if it was Arabella, or the bed that made that sound. Considering Maria just got a new bed, she tried not to laugh at what she guessed was a horrified expression on Arabella's face.

Her smile was immediately wiped away when she heard the next set of footsteps coming up the stairs. "Shit," Maria's eyes went cold. Cienfuegos was already on it though, grabbing Thoman and dragging him from the room. Maria slammed the door behind them and locked it.

"All's well Aquilla, they just slept in and will be right out," Cienfuegos promised. Maria heard him kick Thoman in the shin, even from the other side of the door. Arabella threw the covers off and jumped out of bed, scrambling for her clothes. "Shit, shit, fuck, shit," Arabella let out a slew of profanities as she fell over, banging her knees.

"Are they alright?" Aquilla's muffled voice questioned from outside.

"We're fine!" Maria and Arabella shouted in unison.

Maria grabbed Arabella from behind and pulled her back into her chest. Maria bent down and nipped at her throat from behind. "This is not the time," Arabella whispered, trying not to giggle.

"I'm trying to lace up your corset, honey," she alleged. Although, by the time she was finished letting her fingers dance on Arabella's hips, Arabella turned to see a deep desire in Maria's eyes. The tension had her ready to rip both their clothes off and go for another round of it. Until Cienfuegos kicked the door with his foot, leaning against it from the other side.

"Hello, Dad," Arabella greeted calmly as she slipped into the hallway. Maria remained on her side of the threshold. Aquilla analyzed both women before he sighed.

"I don't want to know, you're grown enough. Let's just get to the meeting please."

They gathered in Elias' war museum, a large room next to where they typically held council. The room hadn't been cared for in years, despite Elias using it often in his state of madness. Papers were scattered everywhere, and a thick level of dust covered every surface due to the neglect. Elias had been paranoid about any outsiders entering the war room, and Maria avoided it whenever she wasn't forced into war classes, so it was left in its cluttered state. Even the worn-down war board accumulated dust since Maria ascended the throne.

To begin, they studied and talked over past battles in history. The war board hadn't been out of commission long, as it was well loved especially near Elias' death.

"Your father was taking notes from Ares Fiamma's playbook," Thoman began, dusting off the chess pieces like a delicate maid. "When the War of Invasion happened… you remember, right?" he questioned Maria, who nodded.

"There was a relevant territory to the far east, nestled between Eminence and Cadence. It was called Radiance, and they planned to invade Withelle's land and enslave their people, eradicating what they deemed was weak," Maria recalled as she gestured to the spot marked "ruins" on the war map.

Thoman looked both proud and impressed. "We taught you that when you were eight years old, I'm so glad you were paying attention." Maria rolled her eyes. "Yeah, peanut butter and jelly sandwiches with my genocide lectures. So profound."

"Well, what happened to that lot was deserved. InFiamma banded with Cadence, which was the first time they decided to get involved in anything, because their princess was killed by Radiance," Thoman drawled. Maria flinched when Brando appeared next to her, likely due to the mention of the princess in question. No one noticed though, it could have passed for a mere shiver caused by a draft.

"Long story short, your father wanted to mix ideals. Eminence sided with Radiance, and so he wanted to do to them what they were set to do to Withelle," Thoman finished, unbeknownst to Brando's energy this time. Even Arabella did well at remaining stone-faced.

"That's convenient he saw the opportunity generations later, where no one would have been deserving of that punishment," Aquilla scoffed.

Even Thoman nodded. "It was reckless and unnecessary, but there were things he didn't share even with me. Such as what was found in his chambers."

The room got uncomfortable. Maria recalled what they found when they did as Brando suggested, rummaging through her father's things. In Elias' walk-in closet was a portrait of him, Odette, and Maria, who was sitting on her mother's lap. Below those floorboards held a secondary prophecy from the children of Withelle. Such as how Maria too received a secondary prophecy, it was not customary.

"You will be the king of wars, the champion of Gods. It'll all change when your heir gains odds," the secondary prophecy said. Maria always found them useless, but after reading that one, she started frantically remembering her own.

"When your fate has aligned...when the cycle has been broken and started anew, and the wound bleeds red by the hands of blue, know you did all you could do."

Maria was honest with her confidants, told them about the night of her coronation and how her prophecy was in fact given, just not publicly due to the interruptions.

"The hands of blue have to be Eminence, their colors are dark blue," Cienfuegos pointed out, but that meant nothing considering half of the continent had blue as their signature color, not including Gloucester. If only the child gave the shade of blue. Thoman shoved Cienfuegos' shoulder. "A bunch of bullshit. Believing in fairies and prophecies."

Maria zoned out as she considered what her death would be. She always believed it to be by fire. Every day of her life since she was six years old was consumed by her waiting for the call to be made, ending in her strapped against wood. Anticipating that the last sound she would hear would be her own screams. She always hoped her heart would give out, or she would pass out again like she did the night she got her scars.

"I'd like to see anyone try to touch you with me around. Speaking of, why are you still here Thoman?" Cienfuegos asked. Maria wondered the same. The military city had been unoccupied by a commander for days, and they couldn't risk any more time. "How am I expected to relay word of potential war without giving a plan? It won't be safe for you to send written correspondences; I suspect we still walk amongst the culprits—"

Cienfuegos cut Thoman off, glancing at Maria. "And you won't let us torture anyone either, which is a bit silly."

Maria disregarded her cousin's statement. "I need you to go back after tomorrow's meeting, but my plan is to evade war altogether. I am inviting Lucille to the castle to honor my mother. I'd be surprised if she tried anything then," Maria then turned to Arabella.

"I need you to plan the most fabulous fashion show in the history of fashion history," Maria fumbled out having very little knowledge of what she was even talking about.

"Fashion show. You plan to end a war with corsets?" Thoman gasped absolutely horrified.

"The show will consist of my mother's unreleased clothing. I will be putting my mother to rest and ending this weird squabble with Lucille in the process," Maria said sternly. Everyone nodded in agreement.

"What's the ETA on the interns progress, Arabella?" Aquilla asked his daughter.

"They'll be done with their project before the end of the year," Arabella supplied as she was still mid thought, now planning the fashion show in her mind.

"Excellent," Maria interjected. "They can rest a week or two until the Autumn Festival takes place."

Arabella beamed with excitement, but everyone else turned to Maria with shocked expressions. The Autumn Festival hadn't taken place in eight years, just another InFiamma tradition neglected by her father. He wanted all the resources for war.

"We have the funds. When we invite Cadence to the fashion show, I plan to ask them to bring their circus to the festival as well. It was quite fun last time," Maria said softly. No one wanted to argue with that. She was so good about keeping her life strictly business. With Arabella unwinding all her stress, both privately and professionally, she was given reasons to have fun once more.

Brando was still in the room, silent, forgotten even by Maria as he watched her mutable demeanor. Cataloging the way her shoulders looked lighter, and the way she wasn't so tense in the jaw. He felt so much grief knowing what was to come for her, and that her destiny was his own.

Arabella grasped Maria's hand under the table, running her thumb over Maria's scarred knuckles. Maria thought for the first time in her life that she was deserving of the family before her, free from the weight of her father.

The second half of the meeting was verifying letter drafts. Arabella sent the letters to Cadence asking for their designers to join them in InFiamma's first ever fashion show, to honor the gifted Odette Fiamma, and celebrate her life.

Eminence received somewhat of the same from Thoman, who needed Aquilla to peer review due to his generally threatening tone. Cienfuegos put together notices for his legions in the military district, assigning some of them to be within the castle as Eminence's court arrives. Thoman pocketed Cienfuegos' letters, as he was going to be joining them himself the next day.

Maria dismissed the meeting, and Arabella followed her as they exited the room. Payje was loitering by the great hall with her friends when she saw them depart the hallway where the council room was located, inconspicuously giggling as they ran toward the west wing.

The women of Payje's gossip circle looked at one another with aghast expressions before running off into opposite directions, ready to spread the suspicion. Payje called it though, so she smugly skipped off into the great hall, eating a red apple with great pride in her intuition.

'♥♥♥'

Odette's cottage hadn't been tended to in seventeen years, and it reflected that on the outside. Vines grew up the side of the brick and stone wall. It looked like it was from a fairy tale the way it was slightly deteriorating just as Maria's own wing had in the absence of her mother.

Maria, Arabella, Cienfuegos, and Jessie woke up at the crack of dawn to embark on their journey to the cottage. They decided to skip the council meeting, first making a petty gesture to Thoman for his role in Odette's execution. Before they left, they thought it was only fitting to vandalize the council room with "Thoman sucks" banners everywhere. Even Jessie enthusiastically helped with the prank.

"I can imagine his face red as a cherry when he sees this," Jessie snickered before they closed the door behind them.

They walked through the forest just outside of the west wing for 45 minutes, laughing at everything. From Cienfuegos and Maria playing with every stick that looked like a sword, to Jessie pocketing every flower they passed in the wild woods, idly chatting with Arabella. It felt like no time passed by the time they reached Odette's cottage.

Maria looked across the small lake, close to being a pond truthfully. She almost remembered being taught to swim in those waters as her mother held on to her the whole time. It was a skill she likely had forgotten. She felt a disgusting grief over the fact there were so many memories she did not remember regarding this place, and that she needed to use a map she drew when she was five just to find it.

She refused to make this day about that grief, which would only drag her deeper into herself. For the first time in so long, she had her friends by her side to pull her out of it. She couldn't really be sad, not when Arabella was next to her humming, admiring the lake. Cienfuegos was gearing up to use a crowbar to pry the door open, but halfway through Jessie found the spare key in a fake plant.

Inside had a mildew smell, but was way cleaner than Maria expected it to be. Sure, there was a bit of dust in some places, very scarce water damage from minor leaks in the ceiling after it rained, but other than that it was still habitable.

The carpets were faded blue in the living area, decorated with pink and white. Right off of that was a sitting area with bay windows, like Odette's room, as well as a small kitchen area. There was a quaint hallway that led to the only bedroom, where Maria was leading Arabella.

She was surprised that when she flicked on the light switch, the bulbs powered on. Even the plumbing still worked in the adjoined bathroom. The hydropower used to run InFiamma usually was heavily conserved, meaning any power not used had their source severed. To Maria's understanding, the cottage wasn't even a registered building in the kingdom, making it all the more shocking.

Odette's bedroom was something out of a glamorous fairytale, which didn't surprise Maria. Her mother's rooms were very chic and elegant, which is why she was banking on her mother's collection being as timeless as mahogany wood.

They were halfway through Odette's autumn collection when thunder cracked around the cottage. Pelts of hard rain banged on the roof. "We're going to have to stay here tonight. We don't want to ruin the clothes," Jessie suggested as he smoothed out the bottom of a bright orange dress with rhinestones flowing down one side, meant to mimic a flame.

"Maria and I will take the bedroom then. You and Cienfuegos can take the living area," Arabella proposed, fiddling with her own garment that was made with the spines of old books.

"What if me and Jessie want the bedroom?" Cienfuegos challenged. "You two aren't the only ones on a romantic getaway." Jessie blushed hard, and so did Arabella as her eyes bounced between the two. Cienfuegos only gave her a stare down.

"No one's banging on my dead mom's bed, so maybe, go be horny in the woods," Maria proposed with a tone that gave away she wasn't surprised by Jessie and Cienfuegos' relationship.

Jessie covered his face with embarrassment, but Cienfuegos supplied, "It's raining."

"Shower with the service," Maria shrugged as she pulled out a long, simple rose gold gown. It looked like one that would be practical and comfortable. She put it aside for future use.

"Why are you guys so secretive?" Arabella blushed even deeper. Eyes practically watering with embarrassment.

"It's not a secret, we share a bed at home for Firenze's sake," Cienfuegos began preaching, but Jessie interrupted him. "He keeps everything in his life low key. We don't hide it or anything, but for security reasons we like our business to be between us. We decided not to tell you unless you asked."

"If you two were smart, you'd do the same," Cienfuegos said, eyes darkening with some trauma unspoken. Maria shared the look as they made eye contact. Both were victims of what could happen when secrets are leaked. Those secrets turned fatal.

Abigail was proof of that. Maria pieced together that Abigail and her entire family were killed because Elias saw it as a crime for Maria to be loved. Elias claimed that Abigail and her parents were conspiring against the crown, manipulating Maria's *fragile feelings* to secure Abigail the position of Queen Consort someday.

Maria knew it was bullshit. She refused to let Abigail in for a year before things got romantic due to that very concern. Elias didn't know the way Abigail counted Maria's freckles before bed. He didn't see the way Abigail defended Maria at court, even against teachers. That in itself was proof that Abigail cared more about Maria than her marketable image.

Lastly, Maria definitely wouldn't have proposed to Abigail that night, two weeks before she died, if she wasn't absolutely certain that their love was genuine, and mutually beneficial.

Cienfuegos' parents were on a secret mission at the InFiamma border to spy on Eminence's outposts and report back numbers. The mission was leaked by a traitor conspiring with enemy soldiers. The traitor was on the council at the time, but was now long dead. Cienfuegos' mom was killed by Eminence's arrows first, his father shortly after. Cienfuegos barely had time to mourn before he was recalled to the military as commander. If Elias mourned the death of his sister, he did not show it.

Both events took place the same year. They both lost any shred of innocence and hope they had at the same time. It is why their dark and weary eyes turned to stone as if to tell each other, *"Never again."*

Chapter 18

Maria watched the sun rise while she sipped on her morning tea. She left her door open, and in the hallway the sound of Arabella snoring was like a symphony from heaven. Arabella spent more and more nights by her side, and in turn, she got to sleep earlier in the night. Aquilla gave his blessing to Maria on a hunting trip, which solidified their own relationship dynamic. He was like an uncle she never had.

Aquilla was so understanding towards Maria, even as she was covered in boar's blood. She had been skinning furs for hours around a fire, chatting with Aquilla and Thoman about basic things, survival skills, their cultural customs, etc. Aquilla shared that in Gloucester they usually don't eat red meat, mainly living on a pescatarian diet.

They talked about past loves, in which Maria explained Abigail, and why the threat hit too deeply for her to take it any way but seriously. Thoman opened up about his ex wife and how she used to be Elias' mistress before they got married—a piece of information Maria never knew.

Like Maria's first love Abigail, Jessie's mother was also a member of the Mistress Institution. The institution was no longer a part of InFiamma's court, since Elias' madness was more of a liability than a profit. Jessie's mother heavily advocated for its removal when it was safe to do so, but with Elias around there were few openings.

Maria thought he must have been trying to extend understanding to her situation, as if losing Abigail wasn't a personal fault but rather a condition of her environment. After all, Jessie's mother and Abigail had extremely similar circumstances.

Most kings would have to take offense to Thoman's actions, as to engage in any activity with another man's mistress was seen as a spit to the face. Elias had so many mistresses during his life, that he couldn't even remember the woman's name when he went to give his official blessing.

The issue was that Jessie found out his mother married his father for security, just as they were divorcing when that security was no longer needed. While Thoman loved Jessie's mother, she had just wanted to feel safe for once. Thoman acknowledged this, and never pressed anything until Jessie's mother was willing and ready. Even so, Jessie saw their union as more of a hostage situation than the loving marriage he previously perceived it as.

Aquilla began to talk about Arabella's mother, and how she looked just like her. Arabella's mother's name was Katya. She was a fierce woman who loved being on the water. She died during a category three hurricane when Arabella was eleven.

Maria remembered how Arabella brought up her mother vaguely the first time she was able to see the ghosts throughout the castle. She felt a small guilt that she didn't take the time to ask her more about it, and that in the weeks they'd known each other, she didn't really know much about Arabella at all. Yet, Arabella slept soundly in her bed.

"What ails you child?" Odette asked from the threshold of her un-boarded chambers. She was a bit more solidified in her form, which made Maria jump as she nearly confused Odette for a living being.

"I don't know who I am as a person and it scares me," Maria expressed with blank, tired eyes. Even the extra sleep couldn't hide the exhaustion in her soul.

Odette cocked her head, analyzing her child. "I never liked being a mother," she began. Usually, Maria would scoff and say a snarky retort, but she didn't have it in herself to argue with the universe's sorrowful destiny for her.

"Every time you got in trouble for your outbursts, I thought to myself, 'God, can't someone who gives a damn take care of this? Maybe, the father she mirrors so closely?'" Odette rambled on. Maria put her head on the top of her knees and let out a sigh that sounded an awful lot like a sob.

Odette ignored the distress. "I don't care to hear I am a terrible mother. After all the sacrifices it took to keep your father's temper from you, to keep you alive when I myself was still a child in a way, I don't want to hear of it. But there is one thing I know for certain."

Maria internally scoffed at that, as if being a victim excuses all actions thereon out. Odette took one step out of her room, for the first time since she appeared. Maria picked her head up, tracking her mother's movements. "What I do know is that I was a person. I was a sixteen-year-old girl who had an obsession with fabrics. I was your mother, InFiamma's Queen, your father's wife, Lucille's sister. None of those things I've listed feels like the true definition of my soul."

Maria took a sip of her tea, now cold. "I need to find my soul. I need to do better for the people, and for her," she gestured to Arabella, still sleeping peacefully with one leg hanging off the bed.

"I may not have wanted to be a mother, but at times you were my little best friend sitting by my feet as I designed and sketched. I may not have raised you in any way that has stuck with you, but if I could teach you how to stitch denim with your tiny hands with just my voice, I can teach you to stitch these pieces together all the same.

You are a hot-headed young woman with a tendency to bite when forced to share. You are abrasive and rude.

You do not mask your irritation with etiquette. All these things you know, because you focus on the negatives."

Odette sat beside Maria on the third of the pillar exposed. "You were brave. You bit that poor child once because he threw a block at Cienfuegos. You are loyal. Even as a baby I knew you and Cienfuegos would keep each other alive long after his mother and I left the earth. By the way this wing looks, the way I can see you must have been alone for a very long time until you became queen, is how I know Analise must have died a long time ago."

Analise, Cienfuegos' mother, was a kind woman, and Maria's loving aunt who would bring salted caramels from the Heart of InFiamma on her passage to the castle. With her beautiful dark skin and tight curls, Maria could have sworn she was the Goddess Aphrodite walking the earth. Analise was quite close with Odette. When Odette died, Analise served as a long distance mother to Maria. There were a few times Maria felt the need to call on her Aunt Analise, but when she did, her aunt always came running.

"Cienfuegos has been an orphan since he was sixteen. It was a quick death for Analise, though," Maria replied, recalling the day her cousin was taken from her. How his eyes were broken windows to his soul as he got in the carriage to Inferniana. He did not let go of Maria's hand until they were pried apart by Elias, who was to join Cienfuegos for the blessing of power.

"I take it you've lost more than just your family's company," Odette affirmed.

Maria's face changed as if she thought of something revolutionary. "Hey, did you happen to see a red headed woman named Abigail wherever you've been beyond all this?" Maria made signals to not just the west wing, but the conscious plane they resided in.

Odette's face changed as well, as if she too had learned her own slew of information since she last saw Maria, and wanted to spill what she knew. Brando appeared before Odette could speak, leaning against the wall that separated Maria and Odette's rooms from the hall.

"I'm a fraction away from banishing you. If summoning is the newly added feature, then I'm sure there is an equal and opposite feature," Maria snapped.

Brando pinched his eyebrows before he said, "Maria, you've been dealt a very unfortunate beginning of your reign, but do not mistake me as your enemy."

"I've had a pretty fucked entirety of my life. I had a father who burned people alive, including my mother," Maria pointed to Odette who gave Brando a little wave, even blushing a little. He returned a small smile.

"I had moments where I was too afraid to leave my room because I was scared of what I'd stumble into. I was alone, except for you. I became queen and almost got my brain splattered that same night. There was a plague, there are now infiltrators likely still in the castle, and now I have to plan a fucking fashion show-"

"A fashion show?" Odette cut Maria off with wide eyes. Maria smoothed her hands through her thick hair, which didn't go well, as she hadn't brushed it yet. She went on to explain the idea to save InFiamma with a runway show using Odette's clothing line.

Odette made Maria go over every garment she selected for the show, being sure to give an abundance of tips for styling after each one was mentioned. Maria had to rip her mother back into the imperativeness at hand once shoes were mentioned.

"I don't remember what happens after we leave this place. What I do know, and can feel with a sense that I never had until death, is that Brando here is a good man. He isn't being secretive to hurt you," Odette said calmly, tapping her feet against the stone pillar. It made no noise.

Arabella stirred in the next room, likely from all the voices she too could hear in the hall. Brando glanced back at Arabella with a flattened expression.

"You still have free will despite your specific destiny. I learned a long time ago, in my own life, that nothing is what it seems. People come back to us sometimes and we realize we still need them. Sometimes they come back, and we realize letting them in again may do more damage. Lean into your instincts, but don't forget yourself," Brando sadly offered Maria, extending his hand for Odette to take. She obliged, joining him as they vanished into thin air.

Arabella sneezed so hard in the other room that she jolted out of her sleep. "Maria, I need allergy oils!" she cried. Maria couldn't help but laugh. "I'll run to the med wing and get you some oils, *faccia bella.*"

She threw on her leather jacket and stroked Arabella's cheek before kissing it. She made a joke about Arabella's morning breath, then walked out the door.

'♥♥♥'

"There has to be a way to tell her," Odette protested as she sat on her bed. The air in the castle was now citrusy as the Autumn equinox had come and gone.

Brando sat against the bay windows to her left, drinking his coffee nervously. "There's nothing I want more. She is like my own child. I watched her grow. I knew the plague she could handle fine. I knew she would have to work through your death when she came in here," he referred to the still pristine room around them. "But there's stuff even I don't know. I wasn't told of your arrival, that it was even possible considering…"

"Considering I'm not mother of the year and it seems like I wouldn't have left behind any attachment to our bond?" Odette rhetorically asked.

"Point is," Brando said with a huff. "She shouldn't have been able to do it. It's so rare…" he trailed off.

"Were you able to summon a ghost when you could see them?" Odette asked, laying backwards, smoothing her hands over the silk.

"Yes, once, but I was madly in love and broken inside. That's like, a third of the recipe," he replied, taking a sip of his hot beverage. Odette analyzed him, preferring a good iced coffee herself, she summoned one as well.

"Maria is in love with that Marella girl, whom I approve of. She is the one making most of my dreams happen from beyond the grave," Odette supplied. "Maria's also incredibly angsty, which I assume she got from you?"

Brando did look a lot like a grunge teenager in the twenty-first century, the way he dressed in all black with his ruffled hair, similar to Maria's. "Yeah, well the difference is in our dead lovers."

"Oh please, you were likely angsty before you even met her. All brooding and such, with your legs crossed all regal like," Odette chuckled.

"Yeah, I suppose. Maria knows about her. I used my story as a line to reach Maria after what happened with Abigail. I honestly didn't think she would come back from that, just as I didn't. Obviously, I didn't tell her that. She had the archives for a small time, and history books at least, but until now she's been a shell," Brando confessed.

"My lover, she knew me at every stage of my life. She was the princess of Cadence, yet somehow always around. She was there at every transition. Whether it was medically, or when I lost my brother, once again undergoing a transition from spare to heir. All who I was meant to be… and she waited for me every time to find myself," Brando looked as though he was alive again, even for a fraction of a second. It was as though remembering his love was opening a locket containing a bit of his life.

"Arabella did not know Maria before she became queen. I know the consequences if I talk about what really happened to Abigail, though. I must let it run its course as Maria sees fit with the information presented to her."

Odette sipped her coffee, waiting for Brando to explain. He sighed, "All I'm saying is, Arabella did not see Maria at her worst, or her core, and I don't think she will stay once she does."

"I spent a majority of my time with Maria scolding her for being like her father. Truth is, I was trying to snuff out the fire before it even lit. I look at who she is as a person and know that just because she carried his face, doesn't mean she is him."

Brando nodded solemnly. "I know she is not her father, but she will have to wear his armor again for what is to come. One thing is for certain, When Maria's fate has aligned…when the cycle has been broken and started anew, and the wound bleeds red by the hands of blue…"

"Yeah, I know. How cliché," Odette's features twisted into something protective, and pissed.

<u>Chapter 19</u>

No one likes a gossip, until they need one. Especially if the gossip has an enterprise of information on every juicy social event. There was one person for the job. A blonde woman worth five spies, and worth more than the entirety of a military unit when it came to extravagant foreign affairs. That woman was Payje.

Payje was always aware of what was going on; from the casting of plays in Withelle, to the ballets of Cadence. All in all, she was a lover girl, which made her hyperaware of the drama surrounding Elias and his many mistresses. That put her on Maria's radar when they were young. Maria and Payje would watch each other from afar, respecting each other's game.

Maria needed Payje to help with the basics of assembling the show based on what the people have gone crazy for in the past. Maria very well couldn't have asked Payje's friends for technical help, lest the show look like a Cadencian knock off. Maria would be absolutely mortified. In exchange for Payje's own newspaper empire, she offered her expertise.

Luckily, Payje's friends could help with something that wouldn't impact the integrity of the show, rather elevate it with experience. Most of the female modeling positions were filled within an hour.

They did not get so lucky with the male slots. Cienfuegos volunteered immediately, considering he was built like a war god and knew it. Jessie was shy about the volunteering process, but was sold once he got to pick his outfit. The last male slot would have to go to someone older, wiser, powerful. It was after three weeks straight of begging that Arabella convinced Aquilla to do it.

Even the ghosts were preparing for the fashion show. The ones in the Everyman classification, at least. There were no words from Margaret or Odette since their last appearances. Both Arabella and Maria wandered the castle trying to catch a glimpse of the spirits. Arabella had been getting nervous, wondering if her sister would ever show again. She didn't get to properly say goodbye when she was granted those additional precious moments.

Brando and Maria's relationship had been askew since then as well. He became more distant and cryptic, and Maria became more resentful at the lack of information. All she knew was that whatever bad thing he was afraid of was nearly at her doorstep, and making peace with Lucille was all she could do to try and stop it.

The night before the fashion show, the castle was in complete mayhem. There were two courts arriving simultaneously, Cadence and Withelle.

Maria greeted each of the influential rulers, starting with Cadence's. King Fabian Laurent was notoriously extravagant and already tipsy upon arrival. He was in his mid-thirties, but the makeup he wore made him look five years younger. Cadence's group was just barely directed to their rooms when the next group of arrivals came.

Maria ran back to the front gates to greet the select few members of Withelle's court. Fern Oakland was the head of the kingdom, but never used the official title of king. Maria always thought he ran more of a cult than a kingdom, considering everybody from there was oddly calm and peaceful.

Despite their irregular ruling practices, Withelle followed a standard line of succession, having the new ruler chosen by the current ruler before death. Their government usually contained a central leader—Fern—and an oracle, currently a young girl. The same girl who had given Maria a prophecy at her coronation, had once again been brought to InFiamma. She ran up to Maria and gave her a big hug.

"You're still alive!" she squealed. Maria patted the girl's head, hoping she was only referring to the plague back in August. The Withelle elders gave Maria a smile and shooed the young one away. She could have sworn the girl looked directly at a ghost and yelled, "I told you! They have fairies, too!" Maria chuckled slightly at the use of the Withelle term. Unphased, as children typically gain temporary sight, written off as an overactive imagination.

Maria turned around briefly and gave the ghost a questioning look. The ghost returned it. The ghost wasn't producing a death mark and seemed like a rather casual nobleman. How the child was able to tell he was dead; Maria did not know. They both lightly shrugged their shoulders as she inconspicuously carried on with the greetings.

Arabella was finalizing the preparations for the setup, as well as catering, stressing over the fact that they will be charged for the overuse of power resources. That alone had potential to put them over budget, but she had a plan to resolve it. Arabella befriended many of the servants though, making jokes and trying not to drop equipment as they laughed. Together, they worked towards the finish line of setting up. She lingered by the catering table and tasted the chocolate covered strawberries… multiple times to ensure peak quality.

In keeping with her promise, Maria had raised the wages of the servants who had survived the plague, and a new dorm wing had just recently completed construction. Combined with the interns and the Island's resources, plus war preparations should tomorrow go badly, a lot was at stake financially.

Maria talked to the King of Cadence about selling some of InFiamma's jewels in exchange for resources. Fabian received the offer with a fake contemplation, but both of them knew this conversation would happen before he arrived. Fabian always leaves an event with something, whether through trade or betting.

She also negotiated with Withelle's elders—specifically Fern—bargaining with a rare herb that only grew in the southern region of InFiamma. Unlike Fabian, Fern genuinely contemplated the deal, rubbing his earlobe as he did so.

Late in the evening Maria and Arabella finally made it into the same room together, the packed great hall. InFiammans and foreigners alike shared in casual conversations and finger food. Arabella watched Maria goof around with the King of Cadence, keeping up with the pre-game revelries. Maria made eye contact with Arabella from across the crowded room and gave her a little smirk.

Arabella playfully rolled her eyes before mouthing, "Behave."

Maria put up a hand motion that she understood Arabella's demands. The King of Cadence caught on, bellowing out a laugh, and throwing his arm around Maria. Even in the crowded room Arabella could hear him say, "Don't get in trouble now, that's a pretty one."

At the same time Cienfuegos lingered at the entrance to the castle. He was appreciating the breeze, looking rather relaxed until the most anticipated guests arrived. They were more than fashionably late. He signaled for one of his soldiers, Ignacio, to get Maria at once.

Lucille was at the back of the court's arrival, her opal white carriage standing out obnoxiously amidst the various black ones.

Some of Eminence's higher lords and ladies exited their carriages first, their noses held high. Their expressions twisted as if they could smell the stables, or a remnant of the plague in the air. Lucille exited last. She wore a long sleeve slick black dress that hugged her figure. Cienfuegos guessed that her sneer was a more permanent one.

Her hair was long and black, eyes nearly matching. She looked hungry, not just due to her eerily skeletal figure, but because it showed in her eyes. In a way, she looked just like Eminence's mascot: the wolves. Cienfuegos had never seen such a regal rabid animal before, but here she was, the queen of fangs and minerals.

Maria came sauntering out of the castle with careless ease, also marking Lucille's physical appearance. Maria began throwing her hair into a mid-ponytail as she casually greeted her aunt. "Aunty dearest. Welcome to InFiamma. So happy you made it."

One of the members in Eminence's court stepped forward. "Is there any reason we wouldn't make it?" they demanded with a curled lip. Maria and Cienfuegos looked at each other, nearly laughing at how hard the foreign court was trying to look dangerous. Maria had those sharp teeth too, and a history of biting.

"You had to travel across lands three times the size of your territory. I'm just glad you didn't get lost, or I suppose you could have burrowed underground for a sense of familiarity and comfort," Cienfuegos said with a half-innocent smile.

His comment made Maria's smile falter a bit. She forced herself back to the situation at hand, remembering that this wasn't the time to joke around. The point of the event was to prevent war.

A woman to the left of Lucille took a step forward as if to rock Cienfuegos in the jaw. He felt a deep delight in the prospect. Lucille put her hand out though, stopping the woman from engaging. Cienfuegos' smile widened.

"Thank you. Where will we be staying?" Lucille asked, her face trained with indifference.

Maria's shoulders sagged with relief over Lucille's command for restraint. Embarrassment crept up her spine for not showing that same authority with her cousin. She felt anger at her own immaturity, like she was still a child incapable of conducting herself in a respectable manner. It was one of those rare moments she feared her teachers were right about her.

"Thoman will be showing you. Right this way," Cienfuegos motioned his arm as Thoman lingered in the castle's double doors. Maria gave her aunt a little wave farewell as she explained, "I have some business to attend to, but feel free to roam and mingle."

Lucille looked to Thoman, who had a devious little grin on his face. She rolled her eyes and let out a sigh as she began walking, her group following. There were only about fifteen Eminence nobles aside from Lucille and her guards, which was the average number of first class people in Eminence. Everyone else was subjected to serf status of varying privilege.

It took a minute for Thoman to get with the idea of the fashion show, but when he and Cienfuegos were told to invite a third of InFiamma's military to stay in the barracks—where Eminence will also be housed—they were more than excited to flex their power. Thoman was impressed with Maria's plan and surprised he didn't think of it himself.

Maria knew it was a gamble. All guests were usually housed in the east wing, which took up a majority of the castle. Eminence was sure to find it insulting, but whether they risked voicing it was unforeseeable. The barracks were in the southeast of the castle, separated from the main structure only by the open training pit.

Maria knew they needed to be careful with how far they pushed it though. There was a difference between showing strength and fueling the war she was aiming to avoid. Somehow, she found herself agreeing to let Thoman escort the Eminence ruler, despite knowing that there was a history there. She wanted Lucille to be provoked so she may show her hand and intentions, but not so livid that the offense is considered disrespectful in the eyes of the other kingdoms.

According to Thoman, Lucille couldn't stand him. Their mutual disdain developed long before Elias married Odette. When Elias would be sent to Eminence on Ash Fiamma's orders to prepare a marriage deal, or make trade, Thoman would always follow. Lucille didn't much appreciate the judgment in Thoman's eyes whenever the conversation of marriage came up. Thoman didn't appreciate her constantly acting like he was so far beneath her. Like he was just another serf in the mines.

He offered to escort her though, and came all the way from Inferniana with Cienfuegos' legion just to do so. With Maria entertaining two other courts, her girlfriend coordinating, her cousin preparing his own legion for a pissing contest… too much was happening. Maria had no other choice but to leave Lucille in someone else's hands for the time being.

Thoman escorted Lucille through the dimly lit barracks. There was a large fighting pit in the center of the first floor, with the second, third, and fourth floor balconies looking over it. The dark red doors that accessed individual housing were all in a row, wrapping around the square shaped perimeter. The rooms furthest to the back of the barracks was where Eminence's people would be housed.

Some soldiers were hanging out on the balconies outside of their rooms as Lucille and her people passed, some glanced up from their playing cards to cut the court of Eminence deadly stares. All were cohesive as they wore InFiamma's black leather uniform, like deadly shadows.

Lucille didn't pay them any mind, holding her head high as she was a master in the art of being unbothered. When the people from Eminence arrived at their designated rooms, Ignacio was there, waiting to give a speech about curfew and rules for staying in the barracks. Thoman kept his departure cordial as he bowed slightly toward Lucille, leaving her to settle in. Eminence did not join the rest of the festivities that night.

The pre-show party raged on until three in the morning. The Withelle court was in bed and sleeping by ten, so the festivities were carried on by InFiamma and Cadence's court. Maria wasn't surprised, as the very few times InFiamma received visitors, it would be Elias and Fabian partying for days at a time. Maria stayed in her room back then, never once addressing people from foreign courts. She always told herself it was simply her minding her own business. In reality, she didn't want that glimpse into what could have been a great escape from her father.

Even with a preconceived perception of Fabian, she didn't foresee how overwhelming his company would be. Despite her acclimating to social events since her coronation, she felt like it was her first time being around people all over again. Maria thought that in becoming queen and dealing with a multitude of speeches and social issues, it would be immersion therapy for her.

Maria met her match with the King of Cadence, as his social stamina had no depletion in the hours he dragged her around for drinking games and Cadencian dances. She felt like she'd been hit by an anchor by the time her head hit her pillow that night.

Maria dreamed she couldn't breathe as the ocean overtook her. She had no idea how she was dreaming of the ocean. It was a vast body that she had not been to since she was very young. Even younger than she was when her mother died.

Yet, on the night before her mother's honoring, she found herself dreaming of its raging waters as it pulled her under. There was a riptide keeping her there, suffocating her as she drifted to the ocean floor. For some reason, she didn't feel fear. Sure, while the ocean above was wrathful, underneath was light. Somewhat of a crystalized beauty.

She never expected to die in such an opposite way to what she anticipated, so maybe it was humor, or the jitters from the ice cold water that had her laughing as she took her last breaths. She didn't feel the sharp pain in her lungs as she inhaled, rather, in her heart. It was as if she'd been speared through. As the blood leaked out of her ribs, and things faded to black, the pain turned into a deep guilt. Something of remorse.

Chapter 20

At dawn, Maria startled out of her sleep and reached for Arabella. Her hand was met with the cold satin sheets. Panic set in momentarily before she remembered why her girlfriend was absent. Arabella stayed in her suite with her father, and Thoman, for security reasons.

Laying on Maria's floor by her fireplace was Jessie, who stayed alongside Cienfuegos as Maria's own security measure. Cienfuegos was in the corner of the room preparing a pot of coffee when she jolted up.

"I need my girl back. I tend to sleep like shit without her," Maria groaned as she threw a pillow in front of her eyes.

"I felt the same way, my love," Arabella's voice sounded from the doorway. Her hair was under a baby pink silk bonnet, and she was wearing a bright blue fluffy robe over her nightgown. She jumped into Maria's bed and curled up beside her.

"Maria was just having a scary little nightmare," Cienfuegos pointed to his cousin. He yawned into his freshly brewed cup of black coffee.

"Remember that one time you were sleepwalking, boxing with the clothes in my armoire?" Maria yawned back.

Cienfuegos just gave her a look as if to say, "*Remember the time you had sleep paralysis and refused to sleep again for three days?*"

"No time for arguing," Jessie chimed in with a raspy, sleepy voice. "We have thirteen hours until showtime, that includes set up and the planned events pre-runway."

Everyone groaned in agreement. Maria slipped out of bed and grabbed herself some coffee. Her drink wasn't plain like Cienfuegos', as she always added in at least some hazelnut infused oat milk. "This plan was weeks in the making, so let's not fuck this up," Maria affirmed as she laid out her various outfits, keeping her runway attire a secret from even her closest friends.

'♥♥♥'

Maria decided on all black. Black dress pants, black button up, and for the fun of it all, a homemade black corset under her black dress jacket. She felt appropriately dressed, but typical. Arabella thought the outfit made Maria look anything but average. She was blushing and nearly drooling with every glance she stole towards Maria.

Arabella wasn't hard on the eyes either. She wore an all-white iridescent dress with puffy short sleeves. She looked like an angel, and Maria planned to devote and worship the image later.

Cienfuegos was matching Maria, wearing all black and a corset, while Jessie looked like a junior antiquarian in a multi-shade green suit. Both men held something hidden in their attire. Within Cienfuegos' corset, three daggers and a spray that renders its victims temporarily blind. In Jessie's hidden suit pocket, ibuprofen, a pocket knife, and an assortment of medications.

Maria observed the two remaining members of her council once they made their appearance outside. Thoman looked as though he lost his alcohol weight after returning to his commanding post in Inferniana. The change suited him. He was still bulky, but with accompanying muscle visible through his tan vest and red suit. Aquilla was talking with him, wearing a dark blue velvet suit, embroidered with flowers.

The entirety of Cadence's visiting court was impeccably dressed, clamoring around the outdoor attractions. They specifically took a liking to the ballerina, dancing inside a ring of artificial fire that glowed various colors. It reminded Maria and Cienfuegos of their youth, and the perks that came along with their stations.

One of those perks was having access to special powders that they played with as children that changed the flame's colors. It was usually reserved for holidays in the winter, but Maria considered the event special enough to bring them out, and maybe impress the other kingdoms in the process.

Withelle's court was focusing on an interactive greenhouse filled with bronze flowers. The center of the flowers had little solar panels that would activate fairy lights once the sun went down. Inside the greenhouse were demonstrations on InFiamma's ancient fabric dye techniques, being led by Ember and the rest of the Archival department.

"So far, decent," Cienfuegos complimented Maria after he returned from patrolling around the castle with Jessie.

"Yeah, well, we have a meeting in fifteen minutes. Let's hope it stays decent," Maria stressed. Cienfuegos could tell she was worried by the way she always pressed her thumb and ring finger together. When Maria initially sent out the invitations, there was an offer for all the rulers to meet and casually discuss trading matters. Since sending those invitations, Maria had plenty of time to stress over her first official meeting with the foreign rulers. They were all much more experienced than she.

"I don't think the King of Cadence is familiar with the definition of the word," Jessie quipped from Maria's left.

"Lucille even less so if the meeting goes south," Cienfuegos chimed in. Maria pulled out a blunt that one of the Withelle elders had given her and lit it. She took a ferocious hit before passing it to Cienfuegos, motioning him to follow her so they could prepare.

Arabella watched the interaction from a far, carrying around the new clipboard Maria had made for her. It was painted and sealed to look like the ocean meeting lava rock, rather than a sandy beach. She knew of the meeting, and was cross with Maria for not being invited to sit in on it. Arabella would be lying if she said she didn't want to be in that room. The thrill of that atmosphere gave her goosebumps, then immense irritation that she was being denied the experience.

Arabella had to do the final inspection of the stage before showtime, as well as making sure the models and backstage preparations were running smoothly. Thoman wasn't going to sit in either, as he too had another purpose to serve. Since he was the next in command of the military, he needed to be outside of the meeting should something happen to Cienfuegos.

Aquilla took the hint to follow Maria when she made eye contact with him, signaling with a little head tilt towards the door, wearing a nervous smile. Eminence's representatives, Lucille and her feral bodyguard who looked like she wanted to eat Cienfuegos, were already waiting by the west wing. The west wing and council room were heavily guarded. Fern Oakland from Withelle was accompanied by another elder, as well as the little seer girl. Maria still did not know her name, but had no time to ask.

King Fabian, who insisted Maria call him by his first name only, strutted towards the group with a courtesan by his side. An arrogant smirk adorned his face as he spoke quietly with the woman. She was beautiful, dressed in a layered gown made of silk and lace, but Maria knew she wasn't just any courtesan, as Fabian would like her to think.

Maria had no doubt the woman held various poisons and knowledge on a thousand ways to kill a man with just her fingernail. The Courtesans of Cadence had a reputation, which had always so inspired Abigail. They were warriors in their own right. The woman gave Maria a knowing smirk as she sauntered by.

"Welcome to InFiamma, everyone," Maria greeted, opening the council room door. A special guest Maria invited already waited in the council room, prepared to scout the integrity of the meeting. Leaning against the edge of the fireplace stood Brando.

'♥♥♥'

The meeting was framed around establishing trade, which allowed for a fairly open dialogue as all parties sought to benefit. Maria was on edge as she played the game of give and take, as she wanted to refrain from letting Lucille know what InFiamma needed or where their resources lay. Cadence agreed to take some precious stones such as garnet and rubies from InFiamma in exchange for metals. Withelle agreed that for safflower, they would provide dried rations and lumber.

Theoretically, Maria could have walked away from the meeting then and there and felt satisfied. Yet, Brando's voice was behind her heeding a warning, urging Maria to refrain from making Lucille feel left out. "Lucille, is there anything you're in the business of seeking?" Maria inquired, scribbling around a blank page.

Lucille's stone face gave nothing away, but her eyes did if just for a moment. There was a flicker of silent rage. Everyone assumed she was about to ask for something out of spite. What she requested though, even Maria did not expect. "I want my sister's belongings."

Next to Maria, Cienfuegos' tapping ceased, and Aquilla cut her a quick glance. Maria did not stop her scribbling as she replied, "There appears to be a high demand for your sister's belongings lately. I'm okay with giving you what remains after my team finishes sorting through it."

If the accusation landed, it did not read on Lucille's face. Her eyes lost that fire; exchanged with a blank boredom once more. Instead of insisting on delivery of the belongings immediately, she graciously bowed her head towards her niece.

King Fabian offered to trade Lucille metal as well, in exchange for some amethyst. The metals Cadence were offering to trade would be fit for making mining tools. Fern offered King Fabian their newest decadent wines and cheeses, but their personal luxurious trade had already been withstanding for centuries regarding that matter. Still, as the documents for all the agreements were rolled out and signed, they re-upped their trade then.

As Maria rolled up the signed parchment from her deals, she decided to talk of the newer resources InFiamma had acquired, considering she was aware how scorned Arabella was in being excluded from the meeting. Even if Arabella didn't outwardly express it, Maria read it in the way she sucked in her cheeks at the mention of the meeting, as though she were literally biting her tongue. Maria never talked it out though, hoping to avoid an argument.

"I have recently absorbed the island territory into InFiamma once more. They've been a great help in acquiring a few more delicacies I think you all may be interested in," Maria mentioned. Then, a light bulb went off in her head. That was a great way to carry on to the next part of her plan to address Lucille. When she looked over at Aquilla, it was evident he understood.

"Speaking of delicacies… Aquilla here is from the island Gloucester, where they specialize in pescatarian dishes," Maria proposed. Aquilla smiled and waved for Fern and Fabian to join him, graciously following along with

Maria's undercover plan. The other members of their party then followed suit, but Lucille stayed seated when Maria gave her a sharp headshake, still smiling for appearances.

Maria observed how the courtesan from Cadence took note that she and Lucille stayed put. Once the door closed behind the group led by Aquilla, only four remained. Cienfuegos and Lucille's guard looked appraisingly at each other, ready to leap across the table at any moment. Maria and Lucille sat in silence for a beat. The tension in the atmosphere simmered. Neither wanted to say the wrong thing and risk everything imploding.

It took everything in Maria to remain regal when she really wanted to fold her arms and kick her legs up on the table. When Maria opted to place her elbows on the table instead, Lucille gave a look of judgment. Maria knew then she just had to get the conversation over with, so she never had to see her aunt again.

"Let's not beat around the bush, okay?" Maria suggested, twirling her pen in between her fingers. Lucille made no movements except for her mouth. "Agreed."

"I don't care to go to war with you. I don't care for senseless violence. I'm…" Maria faltered. "I am not Elias."

"In that regard, maybe. Did it ever occur to you that an impending war would be caused by more than just your father's violence? There are more ways a kingdom can threaten another outside of marching, child. There is a legacy here that lives on," Lucille lifted her chin, eyes narrowing. Her neck was long, just like Odette's. As siblings, Maria imagined they were a perfect image of the white swan and black swan from one of Cadence's ballets.

"Look, I have no idea what you want from me. Just say it," Maria gritted with insistence.

"We want expansion outside of the mountain ranges, specifically your forest domain," Lucille acted as if it was no grand request.

"You want me to give you my land?" Maria asked incredulously. She leaned back against her seat and thought to herself that Lucille surely must be baiting her for something else. Brando muttered a shared sentiment, knowing Maria well enough to assume her thoughts.

"My people are crowded and suffering because we were forced into those mountain ranges. We cannot build up the mountains because of the mines underneath, and the liability," Lucille rolled her eyes, as if that was an obvious fact that Maria, being some sort of child, was too novice to understand.

"So build around the mountains?" Maria suggested with a tone of annoyance. She reigned in just how irritating the demand was though. At the end of it all, the point of the talk was to avoid bad blood. As Maria felt her eyes blur, and she began to see red, she questioned how much maturity she had in her. Brando knew that look in her eyes and muttered for her to calm down.

"That leaves civilians out in the open. We want our village to be under the cover of the foliage," Lucille insisted.

"No." Cienfuegos and Maria said at the same time. Maria kicked him under the table. Lucille's guard reached for her pocket for some sort of weapon, and Cienfuegos reached for his. Maria clenched down her jaw as she waited for the blood bath to ensue. Luckily, her aunt had other plans—for now. Lucille put her hand out to stop her bodyguard once more. The guard shot Lucille a pleading look, but the queen's mouth tightened as she shook her head in disapproval.

Lucille then stood, and Maria watched in distaste as her aunt silently exited the council room. Lucille's message was clear. She did not respect Maria or her crown. And she sure as hell was not giving up on her demands.

'♥♥♥'

"What a whore!" Arabella spat as she aggressively fixed the hem of the first dress to walk in the show. The model, Emerson, pressed her lips together to suppress a laugh.

Maria wanted to laugh as well, even though Arabella's reaction was valid. It made Maria feel better to theorize what might happen if Lucille and Arabella were forced into a room together. Maria shook away the thought lest she develop any ideas.

"We will deal with it later," Maria moved on, admiring the gown being prepared while placing the palm of her hand against her jaw. "People are beginning to migrate to the hall for the show. Where do you need me?" Maria asked as she fixed a loose thread on the shoulder of Emerson's gown.

"You can go change and get ready for the opening. Make sure Cienfuegos and my dad get back here soon. Especially my dad, considering how complex his outfit is," Arabella commanded, finishing Emerson's final touches. Emerson then went off to do her hair and makeup.

Maria leaned in and gave Arabella a soft kiss on the cheek. "Thank you for working so hard, my love."

"You can make it up to me tonight," Arabella smiled, grabbing Maria's shirt collar to pull her in for a kiss. They didn't break away until Aquilla rounded the corner and coughed. They separated hastily, blushing and slightly dazed.

"I'll go get Cienfuegos and Jessie," Aquilla slid away again awkwardly. Maria looked at the clock and saw she had less than an hour before she needed to open the show. What she had planned would potentially take longer than that, and a miracle.

"Bella dearest, I need help with my outfit," Maria explained before grabbing a bag previously stored in the corner. In that bag was her outfit, a pair of heels, and an industrial hairbrush. Arabella turned from her station and was instantly hit with a wave of shock, quickly replaced by excitement.

"Make me look pretty?" Maria attempted to mock but had a hint of authenticity behind it. Her mother was a beautiful woman, and she didn't care to match that beauty at all until she was faced with her situation. In her dressing feminine, she was putting on a mask for her mother, to hopefully appease her and not look like such a mistake of a daughter in the process.

Maria's mind went to what her life would have been like with her mother, who grew up in Eminence with something similar to ancient world views. Odette surely would have tried to pair her up with a rich royal to feed Elias' pockets. Maria could practically taste the would-be blood in her mouth from biting her tongue, as her mother would attempt to brush out her thick hair.

Arabella immediately jumped into her makeup box as if it would teleport her to the goddess of beauty. She found a multitude of shades of lip gloss that would go with the dress Maria picked out for herself. Brando appeared soon after Maria was done slipping into the dress, his face regal and composed. "You look nice," he said to Maria as Arabella was dragging her to the vanity, appraising her thick hair.

"Thanks. I take it you have news?" Maria tilted her head. Arabella grabbed her cheeks and centered her face, evening out the front pieces of Maria's hair.

"Yes. Your aunt was talking to her guard. They sent a messenger to take a letter to your cousin Eugene, about your refusal to compromise land," Brando explained, giving every little detail thereafter. From the messenger's appearance, the scent on the paper from Lucille's perfume, to the route the messenger took out of the castle. Maria was surprised Brando didn't count how many cobblestones the messenger stepped on during his departure.

"Why send a letter if they're to return home at dawn?" Arabella's eyes went a bit wider, her face turning pale. Brando matched her worry.

"Unless they weren't planning on leaving… really? Even with me putting a third of my forces in their face…" Maria tapped her fingers to a classic beat as she considered a million strategies.

"I think they plan to leave," Arabella spoke up. "Maybe it's insurance in case we don't let them, or maybe they plan to do something that risks imprisonment. Who is watching her now?"

Brando cringed before giving an ironic chuckle. "Elizabeth is." Maria fell into a fit of laughter, head falling into her own lap with Arabella's hands still tangled in it. Arabella pulled Maria's hair back to make her look upright once more, becoming frustrated.

"Why is that funny?"

"I told you; Elizabeth is obsessed with vanity and beauty. It is what keeps her bitter and tied to the physical world. If she's watching prissy Lucille be vain and bitter… they may have a disdain-off," Maria elaborated, wiping tears from her eyes.

"How many ghosts do you have on duty tonight?" Arabella drawled. Her eyes unfocused as she fiddled with the hairbrush.

"Four," Maria quipped with pride, putting her hands on her hips. "Including me," Brando pivoted, pointing to himself.

Arabella sighed, lightly brushing out Maria's hair and smoothing it over with oils. "Make sure they are trustworthy."

"Yes, because they're able to converse with just anyone," Maria laughed playfully.

Arabella tapped the hairbrush off of Maria's forehead. "We do not know what people in Eminence's court can or cannot do, including who they can and cannot see. Have you considered that?" Arabella expressed with disappointment.

Maria's features dropped as she fell deep into thought. Maria hardly considered the odds that other people would be able to see the ghosts in the castle. There were very few things she carried with her into her reign from before her father died. She suspected her sword, and her gift were the only two things that would keep her alive, but now it felt as though she didn't even have that as a benefit.

Brando tensed next to the doorway. Guilt coated his features as he remembered something that happened during his own reign. Maria caught it, and almost asked him what else he was keeping from her, but her attention was diverted. Arabella let out a muffled scream of frustration before aggressively searching for lip balm. "Idiots," was her only reply.

Maria blushed as Arabella took her chin in between her fingers, something she'd done with the roles reversed many times. "I'm not mad at you, just be more careful please," Arabella softly requested as she smoothed a red color over Maria's bottom lips. Maria gave a gentle moan of approval.

Chapter 21

Maria and Arabella arrived at the fashion show together, analyzing everyone's unfathomably dramatic expressions. Maria locked eyes with Payje, whose mouth was wide open as she scribbled down notes for her newly approved newspaper. Finally, her nosiness would be put to good use. Maria was happy Payje didn't have access to a camera. The last thing Maria needed was for Payje to be running around, fully in charge of what makes the next generation of the archives.

Then again, Maria did consider finding a photographer to work the event. It was nearly a lost art, but there were some wealthy families who cherished their memories. If she would have gone that route, she wondered if pieces of her soul would be trapped in that photograph, frozen in time as she held hands with Arabella.

In the great hall, the throne was now placed at the end of the runway. Next to it was a row of reserved seats. Out of her council, only Thoman would be by her side, as everyone else was walking in the show. Next to Thoman's seat was one that would remain empty. Its card read:

"Reserved: in memory of Margaret Marella."

Arabella froze when she saw the name, tears gathering in her eyes. "If she showed up because of the high energy environment I didn't want her to be scared, rather feel included," Maria whispered nervously. Arabella threw her arms around Maria, careful to mind the hair.

Next to Lucille's assigned seat to the far left, pivoting to be at the side of the runway, *"Reserved: in memory of Odette Chevalier."*

Arabella held onto Maria's forearm as she studied the seat. "You used her maiden name?"

"She was never a Fiamma. Not really," Maria shrugged. They continued the route to the backstage area. It was set up where the raised dais was, shielded by curtains.

"I went with the dimmed lights aside from the spotlight to enhance the storm candles. The original lighting plan they sent us yesterday would have been too pricey, I felt," Arabella pointed to the giant candles lining the runway.

"That's alright. As long as the clothes are visible, they will speak for themselves," Maria encouraged, patting Arabella's head. When they arrived on deck where the models were lining up, Cienfuegos was helping Jessie adjust his outfit. When the two men saw Maria, they stumbled backwards.

Maria's outfit was the elegant rose gold slip dress from her mother's cottage. It had thin straps that showed off her toned arms, its length down to her knees. She was wearing heels which easily threw her over the six foot marker in height. Her hair was still in its natural waves, but oiled back after Arabella spent nearly the last forty minutes on it. She wore mascara, sharp eyeliner, red lipstick, and diamond earrings. By the way Maria was clamping her teeth on the side of the bar, it was evident she put her tongue ring back in again.

"That bad?" Maria raised her brow, earning an elbow in her side by Arabella.

"No, you just actually look like Odette for once," Cienfuegos stammered for possibly the first time in his life. "You look really beautiful," Jessie affirmed to soothe her discomfort. Arabella wore a wide grin at her masterpiece's praise. Maria crossed her arms, and her muscles strained just slightly.

The attention was off of Maria immediately once Aquilla came into view. Since the show was split up into seasons, he was wearing something from the spring collection. Even Maria and Cienfuegos let out a noise that was close to a squeal as they began jumping onto one another. Someone in the group of models proclaimed him a dilf.

"These noises frighten me. I do not understand them," he said in a bland voice, slightly self conscious with his body language as he fidgeted with his wedding band.

Arabella joined her father, patting him on the back as she explained the etymology of the word dilf, and its eternal value. She then called over the models to brief them on the layout of the runway.

Arabella let Aquilla know of the seat dedicated to Margaret, and he too got teary eyed as he hugged Maria. It was short lived as Arabella yelled at him for nearly messing up his eyeliner. Truthfully, she just didn't like seeing her father sad.

It wasn't long until the great hall fell into hushed whispers as the lights dimmed. Gasps and applause sounded throughout the room as Maria entered onto the runway. She looked to Thoman first, who gave her a nod indicating everyone was checked thrice over for contraband before entering.

Maria saw Lucille to the left. Next to Lucille sat Odette with sorrowful eyes as she looked at her sister, then her daughter. If Lucille could for whatever reason see ghosts, she did not indicate any hints as her sister reached for her hand. She never would be able to grasp it. Maria fidgeted with the necklace she had concealed beneath the dress; its charm was the little tin man. Odette mouthed to Maria, "Beautiful."

Maria began her speech for the crowd consisting of some of the most influential people on the continent.

"I'm honored to present to the world a piece of my mother, Odette Chevalier. My people know her in history as Odette Fiamma, as my mother, and as the last queen before myself. I do not see her as any of those things though. I see her as the young woman whose artistic expression had the potential to transcend the fashion industry. She was, without a doubt, one of the best designers of the century.

Yes, she was my mother. Yes, she was a wife, a sister, a queen. Above that, she was an artistic soul who was taken from us too soon, maliciously, before she saw these designs change the world. I know she is here watching, and I hope this gives her peace," Maria finished with tears in her eyes. She would not let them fall though, unlike Odette who was weeping.

More cheers sounded like thunder in a hollow tin can as Maria sat upon her throne. She was closely watched by Thoman while her speech was made, and while he was never good at being warm or comforting, he gave her a gentle pat on the shoulder.

The candles, like magic, all lit down the sides of the runway. They were thick enough that even a draft wouldn't blow them out. That was the cue for the winter collection to begin. Emerson entered the runway, and gasps erupted.

Emerson's gown consisted of a fitted corset, with an arrow protruding from the heart area, leaking a blue to green ombre pattern. More than that, there was a train of feathers standing up, trailing her as she walked. She looked like a human peacock.

"Oh, that's fantastic," Fabian said in awe from three seats down. The courtesan next to him waved herself with her fan, made out of feathers as well. On Fabian's left, Fern sighed. "That's so profoundly sad."

The next dress was a personal favorite of Maria's. The fabric was black with a liquid looking texture, making it look like the model was covered in dark oils. Especially with the way her long black hair was styled with gel. She wore a smokey eye with sharp liner, as Odette insisted in her notes when she last visited Maria. Maria's favorite detail was the pale lips, nearly blue in color, as if the oil was freezing the model to death.

The third look was also a gown, made with fabrics lined with fur. The garment had butterflies sprouting from the rib cage, worn by Viktorie, who had a short blonde bob haircut. Even from the end of the runway Maria could tell she had lip plumper on.

The last look of the winter collection was most personal to Maria's relationship with her mother in a way. It looked like the bottom of the dress was a blue, ancient patterned rug, that was charred on the ends. It faded to black as if the darkness was both protecting, and threatening to consume the model. It was symbolism of living in the castle with someone like Elias on the prowl. Sometimes lingering in the shadows was the only way to keep the flames away.

The winter models did a group walk together before the next season began. Spring.

"So far, pretty dang good kid," Thoman whispered. "Even I didn't know your mother had this much talent. All those requests for sewing kits… I thought she was repairing socks and holes," he confessed solemnly. Odette's ghost shot him a look he could not see, yet he shivered.

Spring wasn't Maria's favorite, but Jessie and Arabella liked the season's line up most. One look was a play on Cadence's most elegant era where they all wore really big wigs, but Odette made her wig entirely out of preserved roses. The model, Mariella, was able to pull it off well. She was the model that studied in Cadence the longest out of Maria's childhood peers, specifically those aspiring to be models at court. Her walk showed that all those years of schooling did her well.

The next look was a relatively simple dress suit that was well tailored. The back of the suit had a cape that trailed after it, with various fake flowers sewn and embroidered into the design.

The next two looks were worn by Maria's star boys. "This should be good," Thoman chuckled as he ate candy from his vest pocket. Old men did have a way of smuggling food anywhere.

Jessie was first, and any smug look on Thoman's face was replaced with pride for his son. His outfit catered towards those from Withelle most, being a love letter to their trippy lore. He wore a vest that looked like fairy wings hugging him from behind, with nothing underneath. His pants were made entirely out of recycled leather in a patch work pattern. Different trinkets dangled from his belt, such as vintage keys. His makeup was dark green eyeshadow smeared on his lids. He continued to wear his round glasses, but Cienfuegos insisted on getting him custom gold frames.

Then there was the heartstopper of spring: Aquilla. The second he was on the runway, even Lucille couldn't help but show her shock. The white wings attached to his forearm spread as he opened his arms, casting shadows onto the crowd.

He had two crossbody rings with giant marble eyes embedded around them. They slowly spun by the use of light weight mechanics. His bottom half wore a flowy white skirt with a belt that matched those spinning hoops, but remained still. Nevertheless, the rings were made from a thin hard material that bounced up and down as he strutted, making the eyes look as though they were blinking.

Aquilla's eyes were lined with a gradient of blue and white eyeliner, his face cool and as beautiful as a Greek statue. He looked like the very biblically accurate angel he embodied as he strutted away. Spring, specifically Aquilla, had the loudest applause yet. Maria was hoping the momentum stayed for summer.

Maria liked summer. She liked one of the models that walked in that collection even more. Before that though, there was a last minute guest appearance.

When rummaging through her mother's collection, she thought the mother/daughter piece was adorable, but couldn't find any children in the castle that would fit in the garment with a parent to walk with them in the accompanying outfit. It reminded Maria what the toll of the plague did to her people. To her own home.

Sure enough, when the excitable seer from Withelle arrived with a variety of companions, Maria asked for them to participate. It would especially keep up morale with the Withelle viewers who were watching a show that was created by a designer devoted to Cadence's abilities. They got to see a piece of themselves outside of just Jessie's outfit.

The little girl walked down the runway with her guardian in hand. The guardian dressed as an avant-garde sunflower, the child an even more ambitious sunflower seed. When they reached the end of the runway the child waved to Maria. The Withelle portion of the crowd cheered while everyone else was awed by the cuteness. The adult and little girl then skipped back down the runway, the little leaf clips in her hair bouncing with her.

Maria's heart caught in her throat when Arabella was the next to walk. The warm light hit the two-piece iridescent liquid chiffon gown just right, making Arabella look like a siren from the deepest parts of Maria's subconscious. Arabella made eye contact with Maria the entire way up the stage, driving her to near insanity when she took her sweet time turning away, glancing back at Maria when she was halfway back to the start.

Maria was not paying attention when the next outfit—inspired by a vulture in the desert—came down the runway. She was more ravenous in that moment than a vulture would ever be in its entire lifetime.

Only Cienfuegos was able to snap her back to reality as he came down the runway wearing no shirt, but very intricately stitched and embroidered baggy pants, paired with a sash of equal intricacy. Its stitching depicted the mythology of Anubis, a dead man's heart being weighed against a feather.

It was all hand stitched. Maria imagined that the piece must have been conceptualized before Odette even moved to InFiamma. Odette yelled out, "That's my nephew!" and to Maria's surprise, three heads turned to see the source of the shout. Maria's heart dropped when she noticed that Lucille's bodyguard flinched ever so slightly. "Shit," Maria mumbled.

That was an issue that would need to be immediately addressed, right after the last collection walked. The last season was Maria's overall favorite, as it highlighted everything she loved about autumn.

The first fall look was a skin tight orange dress. Only one side of the dress had a flow to it, which was adorned with beads to look like fire. It must have taken thousands of beads of varying shades to make it, as it looked strikingly like real flames. It was true to the flame Maria knew so well. Emerson walked in this look as well, but was able to change makeup fast. Her eyeliner was a bold red.

The next dress worn was also fire based. Maria could understand through the look how her mom could find InFiamma beautiful, if just briefly. The silhouette was rather simple, but the print told the story of InFiamma's Firenight. Around the dress were depictions of lit bonfires, the embers climbing up the bodice. Maria felt a knot in her throat when she counted those bonfires, as there should have only been seven when Elias was alive. When designing the print, Odette acknowledged Maria by adding an eighth.

Mariella took the rose wig off from her previous look, showing her natural brown hair as she wore a corset made from recycled leather book spines. There was a white flowy princess dress underneath. The white contrasted with the brown nicely. If Maria had to say, it was probably the cutest ready to wear dress in the bunch.

The very last outfit was worn by Jessie, whose hat was designed to be a mushroom. His outfit was engulfed in vines, to look like anatomical veins, and other smaller mushrooms. It bordered on a soft cottage aesthetic, and a morbid display of decaying.

The models did their last lap, and everyone cheered. Maria looked to her mother with a childlike hope, and felt relief to see her crying with an expression of pure bliss on her face. Odette smiled in her direction, and Maria smiled back until she realized her mother was looking past her, to King Fabian and his group. They were waving themselves off with dramatic gestures of approval while talking about the show they just watched.

Odette looked at her sister and let out a sigh, still smiling. Maria's own smile faded when she watched as her mother disappeared. A hollow feeling filled her chest, but she forced herself to rationalize that Odette was her own person before she was a mother. She deserved to find peace, in whatever way. Even if that way didn't have anything to do with her. Maria knew in her heart that it was for good this time.

Maria had watched people find peace before, and there's always a feeling connected to whatever receptor gives hope. The goal of the fashion show was allowing her mother to find peace as her kingdom does, but Maria couldn't help but feel something familiar in her chest.

Maria could see the words Lucille's guard whispered in her ear. "She's gone now… found peace."

It confirmed it, Eminence knew. Brando must have realized too, appearing beside her throne. "I'll handle it," he said to her. She couldn't openly acknowledge him, so she simply nodded her head, climbing up on the stage as another round of applause sounded.

She gave a fake smile and a little bow, a typical wave as well. She scanned the crowd one more time and saw a small figure sitting next to Thoman. How long Margaret Marella was by Thoman's side, she did not know. Maria exhaled hard and joined the rest of her council out back.

Chapter 22

It was time for Maria to come clean to her cousin about the ghost operation gone wrong. Cienfuegos picked up on her plans immediately though, knowing about her abilities since they manifested when they were children. She felt anxiety over keeping things from him, such as seeing Odette, and Arabella's newfound abilities. Yet, she couldn't shake the habit of keeping everything to herself.

While Cienfuegos and Thoman began preparing the castle for lockdown and other preventative measures, Maria got the picture of unavoidable war in her head. The countless people she was in charge of protecting, dead. Mainly those she loved and had been a rock for her in the months of her reign, gone due to her own ignorance.

Maria slipped away when no one was looking. Even Arabella was too wrapped up in the deconstruction of the event to see Maria walk to the west wing so she could change. She didn't mind the dress she was wearing comfort-wise, but she wouldn't be caught dead in it. Literally.

She threw on her standard brown pants and button up shirt, which had a swirly orange pattern to it. She imagined people thought that's the only type of clothing she owned, and they'd be right. Regardless, she strode right to the military quarters without saying a word to anyone on her council about it.

She passed a few military cadets playing cards, looking at them with initial complex as they sprung from their seats, saluting. The military salute was a weird one, a hand shaped like a teardrop to emulate a fire under the heart, the other hand shielding it as if to protect it from rain. Maria knew its origins were from Ares Fiamma, which was one of the reasons she drew goofy faces over his portrait in her history books. She couldn't help but wonder if he ever saw her do it, knowing what she knows now.

Maria gave them a nod. "Uh, hey," she attempted to say firmly, in hopes of coming off unbothered. Instead, she ended up looking awkward. Maria didn't know the cadets personally, so they were likely recruited from the village. Still, Maria had a hard time exhibiting her power in front of anyone her age, as she always felt transparent. She rather not even try than feel like everyone could see right through her.

They smiled and went back to their cards. Amongst some of the younger cadets were various people she knew growing up, but were still too young to have ever been grouped in with her age class. Growing up in InFiamma's castle was weird like that. There were about twenty people your age, but you never fraternized with those older or younger unless you were aiming for an advantageous marriage, or trade deal on your parents' behalf. Playdates were only ever a good excuse to get in with a crowd.

Finally, Maria reached Lucille's door. Her bodyguard sat outside, filing her nails to be sharp. They made tense eye contact, but Maria wasn't afraid of the woman. Maria took her knuckles to the door, and knocked. "Did I say you could disturb my queen?" the bodyguard bravely sneered.

"That's crazy because I'm pretty sure this door belongs to me, and so does this," Maria pulled the chair out from underneath the guard, forcing her to fall onto the ground.

The guard's face twisted with disgust. As she sprung up to engage in combat, five senior InFiamma officers were on the scene, ready to intervene. Lucille finally opened the door, looking elegant in a cobalt colored nightgown, clearly preparing for bed. The after party was just beginning in the great hall, but Eminence showed they had no desire to engage in anything other than paying Odette respect. They would be gone by first light, if that.

"I need to speak to you in private. You want my mom's things? Let's go then," Maria demanded while leaning on the doorframe. Not many women reached Maria's eye level, but Lucille was maybe even an inch taller than she was. Lucille opened the door fully, and took one step out of the threshold.

"Bring your bitch bodyguard too, but she can't come into my wing. I'll be alone as well because this is between us and no one else." Maria pushed off the wall and began walking.

As Lucille slowly followed, she asked, "How can I trust you?" pausing before they reached the end of the barracks. Maria halted, slowly turning around.

"If you wish to see the monster in me before anything else, know that the monster would have had you killed before you even reached my castle. Should the monster have wished it.""

Everyone, especially those in InFiamma's military who stopped their duties to watch the interaction, knew for absolute certainty that Maria meant it. Lucille resumed her steps until they reached the west wing, her guard in tow.

"Rainie, you are to stay here," Lucille commanded. Rainie, the bodyguard, scrunched her face with both attitude and disappointment, but did not vocally protest. At the side of the west wing's entrance sat Cienfuegos.

How he found out what Maria was up to; she had a few guesses considering she was just in his territory. He, in all his pettiness, brought with him a rocking chair and crochet materials. The ends of his crochet needles were lethally sharp. To anyone else, they looked as though he could rotate them, and they would double as knitting needles. Cienfuegos was smarter than that, though. He and

Rainie appraised each other, so Maria had a hint of threat in her voice as she said, "Play nice you two."

'♥♥♥'

They reached Odette's rooms, and Lucille hesitated upon seeing the damage to the walls, both from the attacks and Maria's personal need for entry. Maria walked into the room, lighting a row of candles as she went. Maria retrieved Odette's letters, then sat on the bed.

"I find it very interesting that there was once a time where you would have graciously allowed me citizenship and amity within your kingdom. Yet here you are trying to begin a war with mine," Maria remarked nonchalantly.

Maria offered Lucille the letters to flip through, the dried flowers still perfectly preserved in the wax sealed stamps despite being opened multiple times throughout the years. Lucille made a face indicating she remembered the day she picked those flowers, and placed them in the blue hot liquid, watching as they dried.

"I'm not giving you any land, but I'm so not interested in whatever hate you have for me and my people. Get over it," Maria said coolly. She was over being polite. If Lucille wouldn't leave InFiamma alone by way of pacifism, it would be by a show of strength.

"I would have taken you in as a child," Lucille whispered, flicking through the correspondences she long ago sent.

"Yet you visited this kingdom when I was a child. After my mother died. Oh, I remember. You took one look at my face and decided I simply was not worth it," Maria recalled with an expression that looked like she tasted something sour. "I get it. You loved your sister and your sister alone. When you looked at me and saw what everyone else saw, and not a drop of your sister reflected through me, you just didn't feel the need to bother."

Lucille crossed her legs and let out a yawn. "Not everything is about you, child."

"Ostensibly," Maria smiled smugly, holding her chin up with the palm of her hand. Lucille read through all the letters in silence. Maria let her, not uttering a word. Maria knew Lucille was done when she neatly folded up the letters and placed her hands in her lap. Maria, still in her contemplative yet carefree mindset, posed the question. "So, what was the incident I clearly do not remember, as speculated?"

Lucille snapped her eyes up and narrowed them as she zeroed in on Maria. "You seriously don't remember *that*?" she spat.

"I take it that by your reaction it was meant to scar me for the rest of my life?" Maria sweetly replied, her words laced with sarcasm.

"You almost died! We couldn't find you for weeks," Lucille continued, letting her feelings take a hold of her as she emoted for the first time since Maria had known her. The display shocked Maria, but she merely arched a brow at her aunt. She didn't let the usage of the word *"we"* slip past her.

Lucille could read that Maria in fact did not remember. "You were five years old. Your father got mad at your mother for failing to produce more heirs. You did not take to him as an authority figure in your early years. Every time he spoke to you, you'd be staring off into some fireplace."

Maria laughed at that, but Lucille shook her head. "Your father started cheating on your mother around then, trying any means necessary to have a spare, maybe even a new heir should you continue being uninterested in his influence. He had competitions where women would compete for his affections, right in front of your mother's face. It was truly dishonorable," Lucille made a grim expression. Maria stopped laughing.

"We all knew he was an official tyrant when he plucked you from your chambers and physically threw you from the castle. He told you that you weren't wanted, that you were too weak and withdrawn to be his heir. He told you if you didn't leave, he'd burn you alive himself," Lucille swallowed. Maria shifted uncomfortably, more unsettled by the fact that Lucille was showing something like care, rather than feeling hurt over Elias' actions.

"How'd I get home? Why didn't he kill me on the spot?" Maria blanched, picking at her fingernails. Suddenly the room that once was both musty and engulfed in the scents of Odette's expired perfumes, felt even more toxic and suffocating.

"Thoman found you three weeks later. I speculate you found your mother's cottage and stayed there. Elias declared she wasn't allowed to go into those woods until your remains were found, so we can't be sure. All I know is Thoman found you in the middle of the woods covered in dirt. He convinced Elias that your survival proved your strength and ability."

Maria didn't want to remember it. Even if she did, when she tried to remember a part of her brain shut down. Maria couldn't afford to black out. She also couldn't afford war.

"So, when my mother died did you consider that my father was already trying to make more heirs, and if he succeeded it would result in my immediate death?" Maria nearly snarled, pissed like she was a teenager all over again.

"It is because of that feral nature right there that I turned around and left you. You were a lone wolf, and you wouldn't fit into a pack. Certainly not mine, certainly not worth the war when you so clearly belonged in the woods."

"The same woods you want to take from me?" Maria scoffed, crossing her legs.

Lucille had to consider that for a moment before she responded. "I'll settle for a trade. Salts, stones, you name it. I just want the promise of protection should we need allies if we expand beyond the mountains. Those roads are free range between Cadence, Withelle and us. March for us if someone tries to take it, as if someone was to take your own woods," Lucille said with sincerity and diplomatic respect.

"Keep your salt and stones. Just promise to leave my kingdom be, and I'll be there to fight for yours," Maria swore.

They talked details for a few hours as they went through Odette's belongings. They agreed on peace, and both of them signed a makeshift contract on a notepad for their recently agreed upon alliance. It wasn't the most professional, but good insurance until the official documents could be written up the next day.

Lucille took some of Odette's personal clothing, jewelry, and sketches. Maria allowed her, the only thing she saw worth keeping was a teal gown with diamonds sewn into the corset. Arabella would look magnificent in it.

While Maria didn't forgive her aunt for leaving her in InFiamma, she wasn't going to dwell on what could have been, not when what could potentially be was infinitely worse. She only knew her aunt during brief snippets of her life, this being yet another one.

There was no telling that being the second in command to Lucille's child, Eugene, wouldn't have been even worse. It made Maria wonder if Cienfuegos was happy in his position, or what he would want if he wasn't stuck to her.

"Your guard dog, Rainie. She could see my mother at the show. She told you," Maria began. That was a very important topic Maria couldn't leave unaddressed. She was careful not to refer to her mother as a ghost, rather let Lucille fill in the language to describe that.

Lucille stiffened but gave a nod. "Is that why you're bordering on odd? You can see the angels too?" The comment made sense to Maria. Brando had confirmed, in one of their less canonized history lessons when she was younger, that the other kingdoms knew ghosts by different names. In Cadence, the ghosts were called angels. In Withelle, they were known as fae.

"Yes. But I want you to know that she is gone now. I think she initially found peace before this room was disturbed, but she found it again seeing the success of her show. She wasn't stuck lingering in the halls or boarded up in the room," Maria comforted. Lucille eased her tension a bit at the hope that her sister wasn't in isolated limbo all those years. Even if her niece couldn't say the same.

After Lucille left the wing, a box filled with the most precious finds of Odette's belongings in arm, she gave Maria a gracious head nod and retreated back to the military barracks with Rainie.

"Call the meeting," Maria said to her cousin, who was halfway done crocheting a winter hat for Jessie.

'♥♥♥'

"It sounds more than fair," Aquilla argued with Thoman as the fireplace in the back of the council room crackled. Maria invited Jessie to sit in on the meeting as well, so he listened diligently as he wiped his makeup off with a washcloth. If anyone could keep Thoman from walloping Maria, it was Jessie. Even if he too was less than thrilled with her impromptu agreement.

"Yeah dad, war," Jessie sarcastically began. "Thought you'd be so excited for double odds in participating. Damned if we do, and damned in the name of protection."

"Her intentions are to prevent war," Arabella stepped in, arms folded.

"I agree with the alliance, but we do need to take it with a grain of salt. Protect them because they need to be protected, but not because they want to start war, or attempt to colonize Withelle again," Cienfuegos amended.

"I have it in writing. We signed that it was protection of their territory in the instance people want to take or terrorize their land, should they expand outside of the mountains, in the neutral zone only," Maria pointed to the signed paper.

"Yeah, signed on a sticky note!" Thoman gritted his teeth, frantically pointing at the paper. The veins in his forehead strained so much Maria thought he was about to pop a blood vessel.

"I believe it won't be an issue anymore," Arabella quipped hopefully. Even she couldn't possibly believe that, but she was supportive of Maria first and foremost. At least, in public. Maria had no doubt in her mind she'd be hearing about it later.

"Keep the third of the army here an additional two weeks and issue a third command. Since I'm constantly hogging you two here in the castle," Maria ordered, biting at her nails, which were splitting due to picking at them earlier. Now chipped and uneven, Arabella grabbed Maria's hand to stop her. Maria leaned into the touch as Arabella ran her thumb over Maria's scarred knuckles.

"I will assign Ignacio to command the third legion. Right now, I have the center and Thoman has the left. Ignacio will take the right, evening us out," Cienfuegos proposed. Maria gave her blessing.

"Everyone can go now except Cienfuegos. We need to speak privately," Maria dismissed with a dramatic sigh. Everyone slid out except Arabella and Jessie, both lingering with curious expressions before Maria gestured for them to hurry and leave.

"Everything alright?" Cienfuegos raised his brows, tapping his fingers on the mahogany wood.

"Do you feel trapped in life? Like you're chained to me?" Maria blurted out. She composed herself quickly, straightening her posture but not bothering to look regal. Cienfuegos would see right through her, as she was sure he already had.

Cienfuegos took a minute to reply, so Maria nodded her head. "Say the word and I'll give you anything you want for whatever life you want. You don't need to be who my father forced you to be-"

"Shut up. I was just caught off guard," Cienfuegos began. He stood up and was face to face with Maria. "I like my position. I like my life, with my family," he pressed a finger below Maria's collar bone. "I'm not forced to do anything. Thank you very much."

"Just asking," Maria said hoarsely. After a beat of silence, she gave a small bow. "Dismissed then." She exited hastily, clutching onto the sticky note Lucille signed for safekeeping. Cienfuegos watched her retreat with deep sorrow. He knew she wasn't going to express more on the issue, or explain what caused the sudden insecurity.

"What's wrong?" Jessie frowned as Cienfuegos exited the council room. Cienfuegos then explained everything on the way back to the barracks. Jessie understood Maria's behavior even if he wasn't as directly exposed to her in their youth. Despite Thoman and Elias being best friends, Maria and Jessie had two different upbringings. Both lingered in the background of court happenings, but Maria could never truly escape it. Jessie was hardly a thought for the other children, making it easy for him to watch Maria, but not for her to reciprocate.

Jessie was a quiet kid who spent most of his time in the stables. He wanted to be a horse veterinarian, but eventually decided to extend his dreams to helping people as well. Truthfully, many of the court's children got pummeled, bitten, or accidentally terrorized by Maria in some way. There was one summer he studied the bacteria within the human bite mark because of it.

When Maria became close with her first love, needing that quality time teenagers regularly sought out, Cienfuegos found himself doing extra training. That training wasn't with his normal sword instructor, but with Thoman, as he was seasoned in the position Cienfuegos would someday take.

Their training landed Cienfuegos in the medical wing often as a young teen. Jessie felt responsible for taking care of him at first. Overall, he needed the practice for his newly appointed medical apprenticeship, which he was given on the condition he would eventually work in the military district as a war surgeon.

When Cienfuegos was sent away to command the military, Jessie went with him. Their relationship blossomed from there. After all, Cienfuegos constantly put himself in situations that required a live-in doctor. He just lucked out that Jessie was cute.

Jessie remembered the first bruises he nurtured for Cienfuegos as they approached their suite. The inside of it was modeled to look like a cozy coffee shop. It was decorated with waterless plants, a red velvet couch, and several paintings. Cienfuegos was the first in the room, plopping his yarn in the basket.

The rest of the castle was still wide awake with Fabian leading the after party, but no one in the council felt the need to participate. Maria would likely have to pop down there at various points to make sure no political parties were left unattended in her home, and Cienfuegos did not envy that of her. Scouting in the forest for hours, in the rain, was not nearly as draining as babysitting Fabian due to his overly sociable nature.

Those festivities would have surpassed the sunrise itself, if it wasn't for the shrill scream that sounded in the barracks just before dawn. The news hit Maria mere minutes after the discovery, but by then the entire barracks knew. Luckily, Cienfuegos was quick to force a lockdown, and everyone's silence. If the news of what happened wasn't given to the foreign courts in the right manner, mayhem would erupt.

Lucille Chevalier was dead.

Chapter 23

Disaster. It was an absolute disaster. Havoc was wreaked in not only the castle amongst the regular citizens, but the guests from each visiting court. Maria had to explain to Fabian and Fern individually what happened when the castle went on lockdown. As orderly as possible, she gave them permission to gather their court and leave in different increments. While she wasn't keen on potentially letting the murderer get away, Maria was determined to maintain the good relationships that had been established.

Lucille Chevalier was found in her bed with a slit throat. The blade was approximately six inches, used by someone right handed. That ruled no one out, save for Jessie and Aquilla, who were left handed.

Withelle left first. Fern was adamant about getting home immediately, while still being neutral with Maria. "The fae whisper of your innocence; I sense your aura is ignorant in this matter," he told Maria solemnly. The little girl from Withelle gave Maria a tight hug even as her council was desperately trying to escape the castle. Nevertheless, Maria hugged her back.

"What is your name, kid?" Maria asked, realizing she was never told. Even when inviting the child to walk in the show, there was so much going on that she never asked. It made her feel like an asshole.

"Oh!" the child said, and Maria realized she must have lost a tooth overnight, as one of her front teeth were gone. "I'm not allowed to have a name. I must be completely neutral as the bridge between the human world and the fae realm," she shrugged, then skipped away to join her elders. Maria just stood there with a feeling she couldn't place in her chest. It was a worse grief than Lucille's death, to be sure.

Fabian's court was too hungover to cause any issues in leaving, luckily. Maria was with Fabian when she received the news of Lucille's death, both of them around five jelly shots in.

The king waved it off as just one of those inconveniences of being a monarch, as if he too had a ruler of an estranged kingdom die on his watch. Still, Maria knew that there would be tensions to come in the following months, not easily fixed. How could anyone trust her? She did not know. He promised he'd be back for their Autumn Festival though, circus in tow.

Eminence was a whole other ballpark in the realm of issues and tribulations. Their queen was dead, and they were all held hostage in the barracks, surrounded by Maria's military. That factor alone made the situation look even worse, but there were little options in the matter. Maria had no clue what to do.

An emergency meeting was called. They had no time to reach the council room, so they held it next to Lucille's corpse. A stone cold Rainie remained in the room, gripping Lucille's hands even though it looked like a blue translucent block of ice.

"You will answer for this," Rainie demanded with a crack in her voice.

"I won't answer for shit. It wasn't one of mine," Maria gritted. She hadn't slept in about thirty eight hours, which was surpassing her usual standards. The bags under her eyes were dark, and she was slightly hungover from running after Fabian for half the night.

"Yes, in the army barracks that belong to your devoted loyalists, it must have been… who? Say what you're insinuating," Rainie snapped.

"I'd bet my sword it was you," Cienfuegos snapped back on Maria's behalf. She began massaging her temples, trying to keep herself awake.

Those were the final fighting words, and Lucille wasn't alive to stop Rainie's lunge for Cienfuegos. Jessie, who was medically examining Lucille just moments prior, launched in front of Cienfuegos. He rocked Rainie so hard in the jaw she twisted as she flew back. Cienfuegos looked at him with a soft expression, like that was the utmost romantic display of love. Maria nearly lost it though.

"Take a walk, you two. Now!"

Cienfuegos and Jessie flinched before they set off into a brisk paced stroll. Maria walked over to Rainie and roughly hauled her up. Luckily, her jaw was still attached to her face.

"I did not order this. I know she told you of our alliance last night. She must have," Maria grounded out.

"That means nothing," Rainie spat, shrugging Maria off. "Just a ploy to get us to let our guard down. Elias always threatened to march if we ever left the mountains, so why now? Why send your little spies?"

"Your people have put holes in my walls to get to my mother's room. Your people have been tasked with trying to put a bullet through my head," Maria gestured to her head using her fingers as the shape of the gun. "That information alone would have been enough to make the other two main kingdoms march on you for possessing contraband. But I. Don't. Want. War," Maria professed passionately.

Rainie considered Maria's words just momentarily before schooling her features into neutrality. "Because you are your father's daughter. Evil is in your blood, his sins are your upbringing. Be righteous, but when you realize how much your people hate you, you will become him all the same.”

“Oh my god! I’m so fucking sick of it!” Maria began hysterically laughing like a madwoman. It certainly did not help her case, as the people listening beyond the room and through the adjacent walls could hear. “Take your court and get the fuck out! I don’t owe you shit.”

Maria grasped Rainie by the back of her neck and dragged her to the door’s threshold. She threw her out so viciously she nearly went over the rail overlooking the indoor pit. InFiamma’s army waited outside, earning a long whistle from multiple soldiers.

“Tell me, does your father’s face reflect in your mirror through you, or beside you? Does he command his reign using you as a vessel?” Rainie sneered with a laugh. Maria knew what she was insinuating. Rainie assumed since Odette was still around, surely Elias must have been too.

Maria kicked Rainie on the bridge of her nose, snapping it sideways. She then turned to face her soldiers as she commanded them, using a tone only Elias would have used, “Evict the Eminence court and do it hastily.” Yet, Maria then added something Elias never would have said. “Make it quick, but be civil about it. Also, disrespect the dead in question and I’ll make you wish that was you.”

Thoman was mute next to her on the balcony, still assessing the situation. He knew better than to be hasty with Maria in the state she was in. Even more cautious not to alert her as to why he felt the need to be cautious. He did not want her to feel like she was a beast being poked at, forced to do a dance she never cared to learn or prepare for until now.

She already knew, could see it in the reflection of the barracks' windows as she walked by them. Her father's evil sneer was what greeted her, just as Rainie said.

"We will do a search. Try to find the knife if we can. You're right though, keeping them here will make things worse," Thoman gruffly agreed as he followed beside her.

Maria nodded her head. With a hoarse voice she agreed, "I'm leaving it all to you then."

'♥♥♥'

There was nothing left to do after Eminence was gone. Every crevice of the castle was scanned. Maria took a nap before she held a court wide meeting with her people, in which she was candid and open about what happened. She was especially honest with what may come next.

Some of Maria's people felt anxiety, knowing what a war this close to winter could mean. Some, the ones who liked living in Elias' depravity, had excitement in their eyes. Maria took mental note of those few that would give anything to see war, and die for it, should the time come. They could be on the front lines for all she cared.

Arabella slipped into Maria's room as she was drafting a statement. The fire was going strong in the fireplace as Maria lounged on the floor in front of the hearth. Her head was leaning against her middle and index finger, elbow resting on her knee. In the ashtray next to her, half a cigarette burned in a graveyard of buds.

"We can cancel the unveiling until later," Arabella said with a small voice as she hung by the door.

Maria exhaled deeply and closed her eyes, making it evident she forgot about the interns and their progress. She picked up her cigarette and motioned for Arabella to come in. She did, and scooted next to Maria in front of the fire. Maria took her free hand and cupped Arabella's face.

"I'm alright to go," Maria insisted, knowing how much the event meant to Arabella. Arabella snatched the cigarette from Maria's hands, who watched in amusement as Arabella inhaled.

"That's disgusting, what is wrong with you?" Arabella gasped, choking on the smoke. Maria let out a smoke-filled chuckle. "I started smoking when I was thirteen. Only when I'm stressed, though. I guess I'm just used to it."

Arabella gave Maria a forehead kiss, "Quit. I can take away your stress just fine."

"Or add to it," Maria said with a fake cough, pretending to conceal the statement. Arabella rolled her eyes and kicked Maria's shoe. "Let's go."

"Wait," Maria requested, placing her correspondence on the coffee table by her couch. Arabella paused, giving Maria a head tilt at the delay. "Tell me something I don't know about you yet."

Arabella considered the question, although odd given the circumstances. It took her a minute to think of something good, and perhaps relevant. "When I first came to InFiamma, I wanted to start over. Not just metaphorically, but rather literally change everything about myself. It was in hopes that people would like me; that I would matter," Arabella confessed, taking the hem of her sleeves in between her fingers.

"Oh," Maria replied, trying to disguise her disappointment due to her knowing that already. Arabella continued on. "I was a freak to everyone on that island. What you don't know is, when I was fifteen, I considered jumping off the highest cliff edge of Gloucester's shore."

Maria sharply inhaled, never suspecting that Arabella could ever be that unhappy. She took a seat on her couch and listened to the rest of what Arabella had to say.

"What talked me down is, if the ocean could be that destructive and all-consuming, yet still be allowed to take up ninety percent of the earth, then so do I. Between you and me, these interns are not my friends. I have made it a point to demand respect as I run this project, just so they will realize that they are fish that can either swim with my current, or get washed up."

Maria nodded, and for the first time in their relationship, she understood that she and Arabella had one powerful thing in common. Spite. Before Maria could give a reply, or an offer to kill everyone who was ever mean to her girlfriend, Arabella flipped the focus onto her. "Your turn."

Maria glanced up to meet Arabella's eyes as she clasped her hands together. "Most of the times when I hurt other kids as a child, it was due to clumsy accidents. There was a novice level sword tournament for twelve-year-olds forever ago that I wanted to participate in. We were to perform for my father, and I wanted so badly to impress him as his heir," Maria cringed. She felt the confession to be embarrassing, the story even more so.

"I spent weeks practicing with my sword instructor. Nonstop, I dedicated myself to this tournament. Well, in the group practice before the event a kid quite literally ran into my wood sword and broke his nose. I was kicked out of the event, and I'll never forget how the coordinator overseeing training yelled at me. He told me all I ever do is hurt people.

I think that was the last time I allowed myself to cry. Brando tried to help but all I could do was scream that everyone hates me until my throat went raw."

Arabella bit her lip and took a seat next to Maria. She put her arm around Maria, resting her head on her shoulder. "I know everyone treated me that way, with such urgent aggression, due to the political climate. It's just heavy sometimes."

Arabella grasped Maria's chin and pulled her in for a kiss. "The freak and the monster, how hot."

"You are so cloy," Maria chuckled, but blushed an even deeper shade of red.

'♥♥♥'

The building wasn't hidden, but Arabella made sure to cover Maria's eyes with her hands so she couldn't see the structure until they left the carriage. Maria looked at the enthusiastic interns before she even looked at the shiny building. With the knowledge she gained, she wanted to gut them all.

However, the building was perfect for a project of that size, completed in only a few weeks with every contractor in InFiamma's help. It created a lot of temporary jobs for other villagers wanting in as well, so a six month project became a six week affair considering they officially began the build well after the plague ended. Maria didn't give the project much thought the entire time it was happening. She wanted Arabella to have her own thing outside of the court's domain.

The budget wasn't too tricky to work out. Elias sat on a lot of public funds he never cared to use after taxing the people most of their income. Thoman and Aquilla gave Maria frequent updates of the polls during her reign, and after significantly reducing those taxes, most people were in her favor. She was then able to afford construction lighting as well, so there could be day, afternoon, night, and dawn shifts. It was an around the clock schedule.

The interns were so happy and unaware about what recently transpired in the castle. That made Maria feel a bit uncomfortable, considering that was the same castle they were about to live in for a few weeks as they prepare for the Autumn Festival. Maria knew she couldn't allow current circumstances to take away from this moment, so she tried to suppress them in her already overflowing vault.

Originally the tour was supposed to be completed by Gregory, one of the interns, but Maria did not protest when Arabella stole his spotlight. Gregory was a little disgruntled at her actions, giving her a look that Maria sensed wasn't new in their dynamic. Arabella dragged Maria around to each sector of the building, explaining how the public would benefit from each resource.

"The gymnasium has a room right off of it that has pipes, bringing back communal shower structures, inspired by those rec center models I went over with Ember," Arabella whispered in order to keep the archives hidden room a secret, showing off the well constructed area. Maria had no idea where Arabella found the time to organize all of that, and meet with people like Ember, while simultaneously always being there for her needs.

"This library will make some of the archived materials public, especially the ones Ember can make replicas of. Some of the interns will be staying behind to work on that project with her," Arabella motioned Maria to follow.

"I'll let Ember know of what must stay private, considering The Accords. She'll have those who participate in the project sign the appropriate documents," Maria informed Arabella as she appreciated the solid wooden bookshelves. The building itself was around 15,000 square feet. The library took up a quarter of that.

"I like this rug, and the colors," Maria complimented as they went back into the hallway.

"Thank you! It reminded me of the castle's grand foyer a bit, so I designed and commissioned the carpet," Arabella beamed with pride, head held high.

The last room was to be used for any programs or meetings the people may have. Maria thought it would be funny if the people planned her coup in that very room. As funny as a coup could possibly be in her personal case scenario. There was also an addition being planned separately for a cafe to be placed off the building's exterior, so patrons could have a treat with their services.

The people who inhabited the village got to see their work before Maria arrived, so there wasn't much of a commotion for the building when she entered. Now, as she and Arabella exited, there was a crowd of people blocked off from the square waiting to get a glimpse of their queen. Maria was dreading that part the most.

Maria asked Ignacio to give them a few minutes so she could let Arabella enjoy the village a little longer. The smell of the food and the sight of the vendors gathered around made Maria's heart warm, and it took her mind off the current circumstances at home. She even considered staying at some inn with Arabella if just to get away for a night.

The two women ate roasted garlic, spinach feta ravioli, and carne asada. They indulged in little red drinks that had vodka, carbonated liquid, and grenadine. To wrap it up they walked around the small showing area, which was just the perimeter of the building. Maria bought Arabella everything in sight.

One thing in particular was a garnet stone necklace, shaped like an anatomical heart. It cost a small fortune in the perspective of the townsfolk, but was worth dust and paper to Maria's standards of troves and custom jewels. Arabella gave a small smile while biting her lip as Maria put it around her neck.

It was when Maria and Arabella began to take their exit, did the events and irritations of the past few weeks come crashing down, on Maria's cheek, in the form of spit.

"Fuck the Fiammas," the villager responsible shouted. Some people in the crowd muttered their agreement.

Maria used her scarred thumb to wipe the saliva from her cheekbone. Her hair slowly fell in front of her face covering her blank expression. First, she felt confused. She thought that her perception amongst the people was getting better. Arabella told her as much, as did the rest of her council. Yet, even with the assurances of those she trusted most, there was the pool of liquid on her face. The second round of spit landed at her feet, serving as a crystal ball for a vision of a past nearly forgotten.

Maria was fifteen. She already made the decision to leave regular classroom instruction to do independent study. Her father hardly cared, seeing as she graduated from his personal war history class already. She still participated in the occasional council meeting with him, where she was hardly permitted to breathe. She did sword training still, but other than that there were no more instructors. No more professors to belittle her, or so she thought.

Maria would have stayed secluded in her wing if it wasn't for Abigail, who was social and alluring; she could not smother the very flame she fell in love with. So, she went to court dinners and parties where she acted like no one else knew her. Her peers did the same.

"It won't kill you to be social before your father dies. You need the support of the next generation. Recruit them if just for their age alone to give fresh perspectives," Abigail pleaded with Maria, who was lingering in the shadows.

Maria couldn't say no, but she couldn't wholeheartedly say yes either. They came to a compromise. Maria devised a plan to have Abigail source information from everyone at court so she could make records of it to be used when she becomes queen. Abigail loved the thrill, but Maria wanted those records to source who should be on her council. Who should work as teachers, like Payje's father, and those who should never be around children because they have power trip problems, like her math teacher.

Maria didn't keep those records in her room. She thought that would be foolish as that's the first place anyone would look. She kept them in one of the office-like rooms in the south wing, near the library. For the first time in her life, she anticipated being a queen, and looked forward to the prospect of making the castle a better place for the next generation. That enthusiasm didn't last long, as the records were found.

Every secret was exposed, such material that even Payje was overwhelmed with the information. Brando gave Maria a five minute warning, but Maria would not leave without Abigail. She forced Cienfuegos to take Abigail and run to Inferniana to hide out with his parents, pretending they were there the entire time.

Naturally, every rich family in the castle didn't take well to their information being exposed, reducing it all to gossip. Maria took the public beating to satisfy the lords and ladies at court whose darkest secrets were now sitting in Elias' office. Elias, of course, was thrilled with her actions and even gave her a birthday gift that year.

That's when she admitted that keeping people's personal information without consent was maybe not the most ethical idea. She refers to that day as her ethics lecture. The professor in question, the brute that carried out Maria's public beating, was Johnny's father. The last thing Maria remembered from that spectacle before she blacked out was her math teacher, whose fetishes became exposed, spat on her.

Maria remembered why she gave up trying in the first place, snapping back into reality just as she landed the blow to the villager's jaw.

Chapter 24

Maria continued in and out of consciousness between punches. Alternating between being the ages of fifteen, and twenty-three, and seventeen, and fifteen again. The realization of what she was doing hit her a few punches too late. The man's nose shattered, and his molar flew onto the floor as he spit the blood into the dirt.

Maria withdrew herself. She held her head down as she walked back to the carriage, well aware everyone's eyes were on her. Fifteen, and twenty-three, and seventeen, and fifteen.

Arabella was on her tail, shoving into the carriage behind her. Her hair was alternating between brown, and orange. Her eyes from being sea-like, to that of a doe. She spoke, but Maria couldn't hear her. Arabella grasped her face with an unfamiliar roughness.

Rough, she needed that right now. Needed to feel some type of pain. Rather, a specific pain that had her hand twitching beneath her glove, now coated in blood. She needed to bathe in the fire, if just to stop fearing it as she did so profoundly deep down. The illusion of safety Arabella provided had crippled her. Weakened her core. She knew Arabella was talking, but she purposefully refrained from listening, retreating to that chasm of her mind. Fifteen, and twenty-three, and seventeen, and fifteen.

Arabella resorted to screaming at Maria for her stonewalling, but still nothing. Not so much as a blink to indicate irritation. When the carriage arrived at the castle, Maria strode out, walking into the forest. Arabella screamed after her until she was hoarse, but Maria did not hear her.

She did not come back for three days.

Arabella found her in the cottage the first day, vaguely making out Maria's figure through the window. Maria did not open the door though. She just sat by the fireplace and watched the flames roar, feeling the heat reach for her palms as she hovered her hands over the fire. Arabella gave up before nightfall, and that's when Maria decided to hunt her food.

Cienfuegos came the next day. Only after he kicked in the door did she hear him out, still not expressing much. She promised after one more day she'd come back and make things right. On that which was the third day, Maria took a long walk in the woods before trudging up the west wing's side entrance.

The interns would be arriving for dinner, which was the only real reason she felt obligated to return. Maria wouldn't disrespect Arabella's hard work or embarrass her in front of her childhood foes any further.

As Maria reached the hallway to her chambers, she was greeted by a dark figure she couldn't register before she was punched in the cheek bone. She partially expected it to be Aquilla, considering she ignored Arabella for three days. She let the person get a few good kicks in. When she swooped her leg and the body above her hit the floor, the groan let her know right away it was Thoman.

"Foolish brat," he wheezed as he clutched his side. The stone floors likely did more damage to his body than his kicks did to Maria's.

"You know everything? Then fix it," Maria said with no emotion. She picked herself off of the ground, then offered to help him up. Thoman reluctantly took her hand.

"Your popularity dropped by fifteen percent amongst the commonfolk, and Eugene's ascension to the throne was yesterday. His terms to prevent war are being written, and if we do not meet those demands, we march," Thoman growled, giving Maria another good slap on the side of her head.

"Is Arabella okay?" Maria asked, disregarding Thoman's spiel.

"Oh, so now you care!" Thoman exclaimed. Maria did not react to that, either. She began her descent back down the stairs. "If you go back into those woods, I will personally burn it to the ground!" Thoman yelled after her, so loud his voice nearly cracked with ferocity.

'♥♥♥'

Margaret's ghost appeared next to Maria as she knocked on the Marella suite's door. If it wasn't for the years of training herself to be cool in situations like such, she would've yelped.

"Hello Majesty, she is in there plotting your demise."

Aquilla answered the front door, but said nothing as he pointed towards the bathroom. Maria swallowed her fear and tiptoed towards the cracked open bathroom door. As she reached for the doorknob, she heard Arabella whisper to Margaret, "Don't vanish, but give us a minute."

Margaret looked uninterested and slightly judgmental of the queen, but obeyed as she swayed from the room. Maria wondered how long Margaret had been conscious, appearing to her seething sister. Maria continued to enter the bathroom further, but just as she creaked open the door, a hand towel hit her chest. Out poured Arabella, fuming.

"You embarrassed me during an event I have spent forever working on! In front of people who have doubted me for my whole life!" Arabella was screeching, steam practically radiating out of her ears with how livid she was.

"I'm so sorry. I'm so—" Maria began, but Arabella cut her off.

"To make matters worse, you then ignore me, and do whatever you were doing in the woods. Making me grab Cienfuegos because I don't know what is wrong with you!"

Maria noticed for the first time that Arabella was accustomed to talking with her hands in a very dramatic fashion while angry. She once again noticed how her eyes, creepily, got rounder as she shouted.

"I'm sorry, Arabella. I was taken back to a bad place. It was wildly inappropriate and disrespectful to everything you've worked on, and I will spend my entire life making it up to you," Maria pleaded. Hesitation still laid behind Arabella's eyes. Needless to say, that would not be enough to rectify the situation.

"I need time. I'll see you at dinner," Arabella replied with a stern tone, dragging Maria out of her family's chambers. Aquilla was sipping his tea while pretending to read the daily paper. Arabella slammed the door on Maria like a dog being thrown outside after ripping furniture.

Aquilla lifted a knowing brow at his daughter, who folded her arms in protest. "You know me, dad. I could have made that way more dramatic given the severity of the situation."

When he didn't reply, resuming reading his newspaper, Arabella rolled her eyes and stormed off. She searched for her sister, who only appeared to her for a fraction of a second prior to Maria's arrival. Margaret did not keep her promise, likely having no say in the matter. She was gone once again.

'♥♥♥'

There was no use hiding it, everyone at court knew Maria was in the doghouse. Arabella certainly made it known as well. At dinner, she appeared wearing the tightest, most delicious looking dress, and walked right past Maria like she had never seen the queen before.

Dinner was in the great hall. The entire court was present and ready to feast on the buffet of assorted foods. Maria's plate was pre-made and tested, so she had to submit her desired portions before the meal took place. Everyone else was chatting idly, which made the hall rather loud.

Arabella took her usual seat next to Maria, but made no effort to interact with her for the entirety of their meal. Maria played the long game, not wanting to rush the deserved groveling process.

Maria watched as the interns, likely terrified of her now, took their seats on Maria's right side. She engaged in conversation about the Island with Gregory, who was visibly shaking the entire time.

"I don't bite or break noses of those I'm engaging in dinner conversations with, no matter how taxing it can be.

Unless you plan on spitting on me as well, you don't need to shake like a leaf."

The boy went pale, eyes bulging with fear. Maria could almost scent it on him. "I- I would never, Your Majesty!"

Maria chuckled lightly before muttering, "That was a joke," which seemed to amuse the other interns, making them chuckle as well. It surely eased the tension. Usually, there were no special customs at regular court dinners on Sundays, but with the interns present, Maria decided to use the opportunity.

She stood from her seat at the head of the long table. Clearing her throat did the job well enough, because within a handful of seconds, the room was dead silent looking at her.

"I'd like to personally welcome our guests, the interns from Gloucester." Cheers and applause filled the table, and Maria let them go on until they tired out.

"I have seen their work first hand, and am extremely impressed by the potential they provide to the mainland. Because of this, I am awarding each of them and their families a living stipend for their time here, as well as granting all eight of them noble titles. Please, welcome the newest Lords and Ladies to the InFiamma court." Everyone from the Island territory, Arabella and Aquilla included, had their mouths wide open. Cheers, naturally, resumed.

Maria added in one last sweetener. "As a gift, if you all will head outside, there should be fireworks starting shortly. It's a surprise in honor of the Lady who made all this happen. My lovely, darling Arabella," Maria gestured to Arabella, who began blushing. There was something wild in her eyes.

The court, including the interns, went crazy for the surprise. People were leaping over each other to get outside. With a distant blast, Maria knew her timing was perfect. Even Aquilla and Thoman gave a synchronized, long whistle, as they walked with each other to the front doors.

Maria and Arabella were the last out of the ballroom, left alone in the hall.

Maria glanced down to see one of the straps of Arabella's high-heeled shoes was loose. It was one of those beautiful opportunities that made her think maybe she was in good graces with the gods after all.

Maria knelt to the ground, taking Arabella's foot into her lap, slowly readjusting the strap. Arabella kept her eyes on Maria, holding her hand in Maria's hair to keep balance. When Maria was done, she leaned in, nipping the inside of Arabella's bare thigh, looking up once more to make eye contact. Maria's eyes darkened as she said, "I always heard it was proper form to take worship on one's knees."

Arabella nearly melted right then and there, ready to let the whole ordeal go hours ago. She planned to make Maria beg tonight just to touch her, but she reevaluated those plans as her lover leaned in for seconds, this time higher.

Arabella placed her other hand in Maria's hair and tugged. "Prove to me that you deserve it," Arabella insisted. Maria chuckled as she slid her tongue higher, nipping at a place where she found a lack of underwear waiting for her. The sensation made Arabella's eyes roll to the back of her head, releasing a groan.

Maria devoured her right there in the middle of the empty hallway as the fireworks released overhead. No one heard Arabella scream as Maria, tongue ring and all, went to work. Arabella was hoisted up against the wall, legs resting on Maria's shoulders as she was feasted on.

Arabella came two times against that wall, and another two times in the west wing's hallway as Maria ravished her in a very unroyal manner. Arabella decided that she was okay being cross with her lover if such repentance was the outcome every time.

She knew that the sacred image of Maria on her knees would stay with her for as long as she lived, the subject of every fantasy, slowly consuming her sanity.

<u>*Chapter 25*</u>

Cienfuegos tried to tell Maria the incident wasn't as bad as she thought it was. Even Thoman, ever blunt, could read the room and see how fragile Maria was at the moment. Everyone was worried about what that meant. That, most of all, made her sick.

"I punched a man, you don't need to worry about me killing your loved ones, everyone. Calm down," she said, taking a generous sip of the vodka she procured in the council room's liquor cabinet.

"Right, no, you simply bashed someone's face in and then disappeared," Thoman replied as he took notes of his battle formations.

"What can I say? Old habits die hard," Maria faked a smile, before taking yet another, large swig of alcohol.

"Not everyone is going to like you, child. You probably lost 20% of favor with the villagers, if the people who were undecided made up their mind and chose negatively," Thoman insisted. Cienfuegos shook his head grimly.

"That's all?" she replied, slightly relieved. She was sure she lost much more than that. Even if Thoman said

15%, she assumed the undecided would make up a much larger addition than 5%.

"That's all it can take to start a coup," Thoman pointed out, aggressively dotting with his ink.

Maria rolled her eyes, cheeks heating with embarrassment. "Yes, because fuck the public library and community building they just received."

Thoman slammed his pen on the table, pointing his finger mere inches from Maria's face. "I stood by and let your father make all the wrong decisions. Let him destroy himself because I loved him. You do NOT get to destroy yourself, or this kingdom."

Maria swallowed the grief in her throat, as well as her rebuttal. She hardly ever saw Thoman act so passionately. "What would you propose I do first to fix this then?" she asked, rolling the sleeves on her shirt up as a distraction, an alleviation of the tension.

"Start by fixing your relationship with Arabella. You're in deep shit," Aquilla replied as he entered the room, delivering Thoman some scrolls and transcripts from past battles.

Maria put her hands in her head muttering, "I'm sorry."

Aquilla put a hand on Maria's shoulder and replied, "Don't worry about me, if anyone's aiming to tear you apart, it's her. When she was three, I watched her gut her first fish—"

Maria blanched, "Thanks for the visual I'm… so happy I made it up to her before it came to that."

"Oh no, you never really make things up to Arabella. I like you though, so I hope she isn't quite as vengeful as her mother," he smiled innocently, giving her a good pat on the back before leaving again.

Maria put her forehead down on the table and groaned into the wood. Arabella then walked into the room with her arms crossed, Ignacio at her side.

"He won't give me the mail," she protested, scouring at Ignacio. Maria didn't blame Ignacio though. His family came from little, being from one of the simpler sectors of the village. He worked extremely hard for his promotion in ways only Cienfuegos would know about. Usually, a promotion that big would go to a royal, or someone in a legacy family within Inferniana. Cienfuegos trusted Ignacio though, and Maria trusted her cousin more than anyone.

"M'lady," Ignacio looked at Arabella with a hint of judgment. "I have told you many times I am to hand this to the queen. Personally."

"Let me see it," Maria said with a sigh, wearily standing from her seat at the head of the council table. She took the envelope in her hand and furrowed her brow. "Thoman, listen to this," Maria said as she read the letter aloud.

"Cousin,

> *My terms to let my mother's death go, despite it occurring in your kingdom, is for there to be peace. My council and I agree this feud is futile, and I will not have either side lose people for our parents' memories. Let us be better.*

~ King Eugene Chevalier"

Everyone looked both shocked and relieved at the letter, except Thoman and Maria, who were weary. "What now?" Maria asked him with a look of distrust. "There's no way it's that easy."

"There's nothing to do now then," Thoman began, scratching at the little scruff on his chin. "At this point, be vigilant as always, and if things change then we adapt in the moment. There's nothing else we can do."

Maria took in a big breath of air, and held it for five seconds just to be sure the universe wasn't going to change its mind, before breathing out. For that fraction in time, she felt free of worry.

It was about time Maria rallied up the gang for some fun, even if that fun was at Brando's expense. At this point, Arabella could see him, Cienfuegos knew about him, so why don't those three just have a silly time impeaching on his privacy?

"When Arabella found the layout of the castle, Brando said not to seek out this hidden room. Therefore, naturally, we are doing that," Maria debriefed her two closest people as she slung a backpack onto her shoulder.

Inside were matches, food, drinks (liquor, which Maria and Cienfuegos decided was more important than water), as well as blankets. They prepared as if the grim reaper awaited them, which would be possible if a bookshelf fell on them when trying to find the hidden room within the library.

Brando protested the entire time they walked through the library, to the very back of the stacks where the ancient atlas section was. "There's no way in. Obviously, a wall and bookshelves were put up," Brando tried to elude, but Maria knew it was a lie.

Cienfuegos studied the shelf, "He's diverting, isn't he?"

"Yep. Try looking at one regarding Cadence, where his lover girl was from," Maria suggested as she zoomed through the titles, focusing on Kingdoms A-C.

"I liked the culture," Brando insisted, turning red and flustered. "My entire life is behind that wall. Everything I hid was to keep it safe. Don't," he attempted to plead. The look in Maria's eyes hinted that she was enjoying his discomfort, intoxicated with the need for revenge.

His pleas were too late though, because Arabella found the book quickly. It was the one atlas specifically dedicated to Cadence's maps, published around Brando's time. Arabella took it into her palm and pulled.

The door, to everyone's surprise, did not groan or make noise as it opened. They were met with a hallway that was pitch black, with stairs leading half a level up. They quickly filed in, and it was Cienfuegos who found something that lit the hallway.

"Woah. I was looking for an exit lever, but that helps," he explained as Maria shut the door behind them, keeping the illumination from seeping into the library.

The lever was easily seen with those white fluorescent lights, different from any other lighting in the castle. "It's so unnaturally bright," Arabella examined as she partially shielded her eyes. Brando wasn't in the hallway with them anymore, but they continued nonetheless.

After climbing the stairs, winding through three different turns, they found a giant arched door. It was Maria who pushed it open.

Everyone's jaws dropped as they entered a large circular room, with a telescope that looked outside a curved window where the ceiling should be. There was a grand display of the planets that were still turning despite no mechanical maintenance being done on them in generations. To the side of the room was a separate nook and a bed similar to Maria's. The comforter was velvet, with a variety of colors and patterns looking like patchwork stars.

"What the fuuuck," Maria breathed out as she explored the room. Everyone went in different directions. "What an asshole, I've known him for seventeen years, never a mention of this place."

Cienfuegos found a magazine on a coffee table near the telescope and began reading. It was so old, it suddenly clicked why they weren't supposed to find this place. "It's all contraband," he said as he took a seat, and read on the world that existed centuries ago.

Arabella found her way to a bookshelf, examining a machine. She did not understand how it worked. "Maria, do you have any idea what this is?"

Arabella knew that Maria had access to a lot of contraband, recalling her nonchalant attitude in InFiamma's archive when they first met. Maria never saw anything like the contents throughout Brando's room though. Where InFiamma's archival knowledge was based on how humans survived, died, and got around, Brando's room was how people lived. How they enjoyed, and criticized, and how their minds worked collectively.

Maria came up behind her, analyzing the contraption. It was a device with a yellow plate in it, and an arm with a needle attached sticking out, pointing down. Brando finally appeared again. "I'd rather tell you how to use it than have you break the last record player on the continent."

He explained how to press the button, and the needle would move. The pair jumped back as the device began playing music as the needle scratched the spinning plate. The melody was haunting, the sound of a variety of instruments coming from the flat disk at the same time. "Holy shit," Arabella breathed, and Cienfuegos paused reading.

When the words started coming out, Maria's eyes went fully wide. She felt awake for the first time in years. The lyrics were from a song not of any tavern ballad or court performance, the genre was foreign to anyone who hadn't been dead since the beginning of InFiamma itself.

"It's from the year 1965," Brando said as the bridge broke out, he fidgeted nervously. When the lyrics talked about falling to one's knees, Maria nearly did as well. Arabella asked, "What is California?" after the lyrics mentioned the name multiple times.

"It was—" Brando began, but Maria cut him off. "It was a state in the western side of the United States, a continent known as North America right before the fall of the last society. It was known to be one of the paradises on earth, with a beach and really wealthy people, but also people who couldn't afford to eat, who had obscure trendy foods, which were expensive. Then again regular food was also expensive."

Arabella studied Maria, causing Maria to fidget under her gaze, "I really like history," she explained. Maria then shot an accusatory finger to Brando, "You knew that but kept all of this hidden."

"You need to understand that this is centuries worth of contraband, powered by a very illegal generator that could start a war based on The Accords if anyone knew I had it. But this is history needing to be preserved."

"For whom? Your wealthy collection and personal benefit? Preserved to be collected but not useful to your people?" Arabella scoffed. Maria clenched her jaw, trying to be neutral. Cienfuegos pretended to go back to his reading.

Brando cut her a look, "You think you know a lot about a lot of things, miss. I was listening to your little reprimanding you gave Maria after the plague." Arabella made a face that was nearly feral. Like a mermaid gearing up to drown a sailor. Brando had been holding onto that snide comment since she made it. Where he was when it was said and how he heard it, Maria did not know.

Maria bobbed her head back and forth in contemplation, "I mean…"

Arabella just cut her off with a wave of the hand. "I said it because I care about her and how she was perceived."

"Go tell yourself that, ignore the double motive of using her as an outlet to get your own sorrow and rage out."

Cienfuegos looked up at the blank space where Brando could be as he tried to grapple with what was going on in that conversation, only hearing it one way. He decided to shake it off and mind his business, resuming an article. He began analyzing something about a board that told people what music was popular that week.

"Nice diversion," Arabella continued, crossing her arms. Maria would be content with jumping in between them, but they couldn't make contact with each other if they tried. "It doesn't change that you probably know a lot of things that could further our society into a better industrial age, different than the last one. More helpful."

"Maybe, but I'm dead. So?" Brando replied, rolling his eyes. "You think I didn't consider it? What was lost in the Secondary Dark Ages? The lack of medical technology that could have been more widely accessible with what we know now? I didn't exactly love having to spend half a trove in expenses to travel to Withelle to get top surgery. Thank you very much," he finished, pacing to the other side of the room.

Maria knew that as rulers they had access to anything they needed, but it wasn't the same for people in the villages. In Elias' time they were taxed nearly forty percent of their overall income for said trove to be spent on the crown. The only thing to keep their displeasure at bay was the lifted poaching laws. To tell starving people that their hunger is the product of their own laziness worked for a generation or so before anyone caught on.

"I just don't think it's right to have a private archive of our, that being a key word here, history. All while no one knows what this place of California is except you, and Maria, and everyone wealthy enough to have the privilege to be told," Arabella finished debating, which had Cienfuegos fully interested.

"We have a comprehensive history in the village library on humanity from the 19th-22nd century before everything fell. That's where we learned about California," Cienfuegos added.

"I wish he could see me so I could tell him he's always been one of my favorites," Brando said with a grin.

Arabella rolled her eyes. "Give me three things to use for the betterment of InFiamma, that isn't against The Accords, and I will use them for good when my interns finish their resting period," she demanded.

Brando rolled his eyes back. "You didn't exactly grow up poor, I'm assuming? Private institutions and tutors, all the finest seafood, you've never been hungry, or really sick even. Never felt like your body was a machine working against your soul, the government working even harder against you?" he pressed as he took a step forward. This time Maria did take a step as well.

"You are the spoiled daughter of a politician, who has these little passion projects that the people out in the fray couldn't even fathom reaching within three generations of their bloodlines. God forbid I harbor some little musical trinkets so they aren't lost to history," Brando spat.

"You were rich too," Maria whispered, still not wanting to get involved. Brando shot her a look as if to remind her that they were two in the same. Children of kings who were rich, but those riches didn't extend to lesser loved children. It wasn't until they came into their own reign were they able to touch generations of blood money. Brando's top surgery happened to be the rare exception due to necessity.

"We still have a moral obligation, Your Highness," Arabella said with sarcasm dripping off her tongue.

"Why do I have the feeling he just collected Arabella? I've never seen such a weak rebuttal from her," Cienfuegos chimed in, flipping through the magazine. He noticed one of the musical artists ranked was named after half a dollar in change, in antique currency.

"This is heated. I just wanted to have fun," Maria murmured, a bit of hurt in her voice.

Brando met her eyes and frowned. "I'm sorry. You've been through so much, and since you're here…" his eyes scanned the room, landing on an instrument. "I know you've always wanted a guitar," he nearly groaned when gesturing to the acoustic leaning against the footboard of his bed.

Maria squealed like a little kid and booked it for the case. "No way, man!" she exclaimed as she began strumming with a pick, as if she studied the art before. It took her a minute to adjust her posture and positioning, as well as finding some sheet music readable by string and fret. Before the day was done, she was playing "Mary Had a Little Lamb."

Arabella pointedly ignored Brando, but was glad to see Maria so happy. She eventually occupied her own time

312

with photographs captured in the sharpest resolution before the collapse of technology. She admired the detail that even the dioramas couldn't provide her with.

She was curious about one box in particular, a photo album the size of a pocket wallet, barely kept together. "Who is this?" Arabella asked Brando as she skimmed over the portraits.

"Firenze Fiamma," he replied hesitantly. Maria plucked the wrong string and Cienfuegos paused his flipping. Both sprung over to Arabella on cue, shoving their faces together to see the photo.

Firenze Fiamma was a young woman, about the same age as the three young adults that looked at her photographs hundreds of years later. She had tan skin and dark brown hair. She wore a sage green tube top, and khaki shorts. She seemed to be posing with a group of friends, eating what looked like the modern-day Fuego, a rolled tortilla chips with chili powder.

"She looks so human," Maria said with surprise.

"You too will one day be regarded as a myth," Brando said with an uncomfortable certainty. "Aren't you just a human girl, trying her best to live life with meaningful connections?"

"I guess I never thought of it," Maria muttered. "How do you know so much about her?"

"You never wondered who my patron was, as I am yours?" he grinned mischievously. At that moment he looked just like Maria, young and smug. His smile quickly faded into a paralyzing stillness, pupils dilating just slightly, enough for Arabella to clock his fear.

"You have guests, in the grand foyer," he swallowed. "Maria, I am sorry I couldn't tell you. It would have changed everything, and we can't afford that," he said before vanishing. Maria had a chill run down her back, but with the guitar in her possession she was too excited to care about all of the things he's withheld. At thirteen years old, she probably would've broken it, or hinted Elias to its whereabouts during her interrogation classes. She decided at that moment he was forgiven, and that it was for the better.

The idea of a guest did intrigue Maria though. She wondered if it was Ember, and he was on edge for fear that Maria would show her the contraband as well. Maria wouldn't. Not all at once, anyways.

The three cleaned up, sure to leave everything the way they found it. They were careful tiptoeing from the hallway and listening for anyone who may be standing on the other side of the bookshelf. Oddly enough, no one was in sight from the time they re-entered the library, to the time they entered the grand foyer.

"Weird," Arabella drawled, scoffing at the idea Brando only said it to get them out of the room, just before they found anything profound.

"Something's wrong," Cienfuegos said coolly, Maria agreeing as her eyes narrowed, senses clearly alerted.

"What?" Arabella nearly whispered.

"Why are there no stragglers in the hall… even now, it's only eleven…" Maria considered before she heard it. Inside the great hall's closed doors someone must have backed into the door.

Maria and Cienfuegos walked up and opened it on cue, seeing half the court's young adults clamored inside. "Did you plan another party? I thought that was for Friday?" Maria asked Arabella as she scratched the back of her head.

The way everyone turned to Maria with bewildered and excited eyes, Maria was afraid Arabella planned some sort of belated birthday party. Or worse, Thoman planned a prank to get back at them for the time they vandalized the council room saying he sucks.

Jessie peeled his way to the front of the crowd and gave Cienfuegos a tense expression, tilting his head toward Maria as if to tell him, *"She's going to need you, watch out for what comes next."*

The crowd slowly parted open a path for another person. It was a curvy red headed woman, who strutted forwards in the midst of applying red lipstick. Cienfuegos staggered backwards, and Maria went dangerously still. Cienfuegos muttered into her ear a much needed affirmation. "I can see her too." His voice was shaky, but sure. Maria wanted to step forwards, but for some reason, did not.

"Your Majesty! How I missed your presence all these years!" the woman exclaimed, heading to the nearest buffet table, popping a cherry with whipped cream into her mouth. She made it a point for it to graze her lips before, just so she can lick them afterwards.

"Abigail," Cienfuegos breathed out, still in shock himself. Jessie went to his side and placed a hand on his back inconspicuously. He rarely comforted Cienfuegos publicly as there were images needing to be kept, but this was an exception.

Arabella couldn't place where she'd heard that name, but she knew it was important. She went through all the royal members of foreign courts, all the archivists in the village, nowhere in public affairs could she find a relevance to an Abigail.

"Cienfuegos!" Abigail turned to him; her arms outstretched. "I missed you too! I heard about your promotion right after I left. I'm sorry about the circumstances, but I'm proud of you," Abigail affirmed, giving him a tight hug. Arabella was surprised to see that he hugged this Abigail woman back.

It wasn't until Maria echoed Cienfuegos that it rang like a bell through Arabella.

"Abigail?" Maria questioned, now looking incredibly pale and withdrawn. The name came back to Arabella then, where she heard that name on multiple occasions. Abigail: the first love to Maria Fiamma.

Maria swayed on her feet, doing a three step stagger before her consciousness left her, and she hit the floor.

Chapter 26

Maria woke up to a circle of her council members surrounding her. Aquilla was saying something with a tone of aggression towards Thoman, but Maria barely made it out. It sounded a lot like he was telling Thoman, *"you let her belief you kilt her louver and shae suffered fort ears."*

None of it made sense, so she groaned in a questioning manner. Arabella flung herself at Maria out of nowhere, and everyone else made a cringed expression. For Maria's throbbing head, or for Arabella being caught in an awkward situation, there was no telling. It was then it all came back to Maria. She curled herself into a ball, dragging Arabella forward as she hung onto Maria's neck.

"Tell me I just woke up from my personal plague-induced fever dream. I am begging you."

"Maria…" Thoman began, but the words couldn't even begin to dissect the implications of Abigail being alive.

"You personally tied them to the pyre," Maria whispered. "You were there. Her necklace was in the ashes," she tried to convince herself, recalling the memory as she avoided thinking of it all the same.

"Her family, yes… but she was sentenced to a different death for what she did," Thoman approached as gently as he could. "I guess her parents must have held onto one of her belongings out of regret, because it was their training that got her charged for treason."

"For loving me," Maria's throat closed and burned from the repressed emotions clawing their way out, like rats that burrowed in her rib cage after years of evading the fire that trapped them there.

"For planning to kill your father, *because* she loved you," Thoman admitted with shame in every word.

Maria lifted her head up at that. "Pardon?"

"Abigail Rossi was charged with treason for attempting to kill the king. When your father found out about you two, he was content paying her future fees and letting you have her… but when she tried to use that advantageous position to slip poison in his cup…" Thoman did not need to explain any further.

"I'd never have let him be alone in a room with her," Maria snapped. Thoman allowed her to express her feelings however she may need to before explaining further.

"Her family was in on it. They wanted you on the throne because your attachment was more personal, the longevity was tempting. They burned for it, and Abigail was to be used as bait for the wolves. She must have found them on the border."

"Eminence," Cienfuegos jumped in, now with cool indifference on his face. As if he'd made peace with whatever logic he learned. "Abigail confirmed she has been in Eminence this entire time. Which means the guards that confirmed her death by wolves were aiding her, and likely who the spies are."

Maria began laughing so hard she twisted to her knees, manically tearing up and screaming between breaths of laughter. Arabella cupped Maria's face in her hands, forcing her to look up.

"Here. You are here, with me, and what happened, happened. You are here, and we will figure out what this means emotionally later. You need to think of the political implications now."

"Oh absolutely fucking not," Cienfuegos snapped with death laced in every word. "I get it, you don't want Maria to think about her first love being a factor and what that means for your relationship, but she can, and she will, feel this. Right now."

Maria heard Brando somewhere off to the side say, "Amen."

Aquilla was on the other side of the room, roughly grunting the command, "Easy."

"I didn't mean it like that," Arabella sprung up, meeting Cienfuegos' cold gaze. Arabella glanced back at Maria once before exiting the council room. That was when Maria realized she had been moved out of the great hall.

"Give us a minute please," Cienfuegos requested from the rest of the room, who obliged. Before Thoman left, he made eye contact with Maria. "I want you to know, I did not know she was alive. When you found whatever belonging of hers in that pile of ash… It was easier to let you think those ashes were hers."

Behind her, Brando approached and confirmed, "He is telling the truth. Everyone genuinely thought Abigail was dead, as well." Maria nodded, rubbing her temple which had stitches in it. "How hard did I fall? Shit," she protested.

"Sorry, I would have caught you," Cienfuegos began to explain, but Maria stopped him. "I don't always need you to catch me. Especially not when you are falling too, in your own way. She meant a lot to both of us."

"Five stitches is a lot," he said with a cringe. Brando muttered an agreement.

Maria took in the council room, eyes gliding across Brando in the process but inevitably scanning past him. She looked forward once again, back turned to Brando as she spoke. "Before I even address you, you better fucking explain. Again. Not even the first time in the past two months. You're a shitty Servient."

"You know the answer. I'm just happy you didn't go mad trying to summon her after your mother," Brando sighed.

"Oddly enough," Maria scoffed, "This time I don't even think I'm mad at you."

Cienfuegos raised his brow. "What?"

"Just Brando explaining why he's an asshole, and built like a nematode," Maria mocked, and both men, living and dead, were worried about how she was joking at a time like this.

"Where is she?" Maria slowly stood up. Cienfuegos jolted forwards to assist her, but she had it handled herself. "Being held in the barracks, with Jessie," Cienfuegos bit the inside of his cheek. "She's wearing the ring."

To that, Maria's face dropped. "Running into the woods isn't an option, I take it?"

"No, but if Arabella kills you, I promise to bury you there," Cienfuegos shrugged, yet there was worry in his eyes.

"I'm going to go, but my advice from the knowledge I have on the matter is… well don't start a war based on truths that sound like lies," Brando lightheartedly suggested. Maria whirled on him, but he had already vanished. Maria almost fell at the sudden whip around. Luckily Cienfuegos caught her this time. "I passed out in front of everyone?" Maria shrunk.

"Yeah," Cienfuegos slightly cringed back.

'♥♥♥'

"Look at you! I would say you look like you've seen a ghost, but I've seen you see a ghost, and it never resulted in THAT," Abigail motioned to Maria's stitches and pale complexion.

"You've *been* dead," Maria said snarkily.

"If I was dead, don't you think you'd have seen me? I'm not your mother—"

Maria's eyes flickered with anger as she cut Abigail off. "Not a word in seven years, Abi. I looked for you everywhere," her voice faltered. "But where exactly were you?"

"Eminence," Abigail's smile deepened. "I was taken into their court on the condition that I never left once I saw the inside. I had no choice. It was that, or the real wolves would have torn me apart in the forest."

Abigail lifted her skirt scandalously high, revealing scars the shape of claw marks going down her hip and thigh.

"I didn't give up on coming home. Knowing your father would die someday, I bid my time to come back to you," Abigail tried to maintain a humorous attitude to the situation, a deflection from the fear she felt regarding being potentially turned away. Especially considering she noticed Arabella's sneers, and what that level of jealousy meant. She felt that same way for Maria more times than she could count, even if Maria was never the unfaithful type.

"What do you really want from me? Let me guess, be my mistress? Live lavishly in my court and pretend to love me, just as my father predicted?" Maria seethed with such hatred, that Abigail dropped her facade, lurching to where Maria was standing.

"I thought it would be a temporary solution. Anyone could've seen your father had a death wish. I didn't let him separate us. It wasn't my choice," Abigail expressed profusely.

"You could have run with me when I proposed to you. Right before you died-" Maria had to recompose herself, and address the situation focusing on the known truths. "When you left. Instead, I hear you tried to kill my father just so I would be on the throne. All I wanted was you, Abigail."

There was a pause while Maria attempted to take it all in. Abigail stood feet away, trying to contain her breathing just as much as Maria was. Everything she had felt since she was sixteen had been a lie. All the grief that consumed Maria's body at every waking moment was for nothing. The corrosion in her heart was all for nothing. Instead, it was replaced with the knowledge that she could have done something– saved Abigail even– the entire time.

Maria couldn't face that double-edged sword just yet. To acknowledge the grief that she was powerless in more ways than one would tip her off the edge, so she suppressed it all. At that moment, her feelings did not exist, and neither did she. She was simply a guest in her body, in her emotions.

"Wanted?" Abigail took a step back, her throat constricting as she swallowed whatever moisture was left in her mouth. "I saw her, the way she looked at you. It's her, isn't it? Why this is so overcomplicated for you? You love her now," Abigail pressed, slightly shaking.

Maria glanced down at the ring on Abigail's finger. It was a gold band with a ruby in the center, surrounded by diamonds. Her jaw moved as she ground down her teeth, remembering the day she proposed to Abigail. It was maybe two weeks before everything fell apart when Maria took Abigail into the garden and got down on her knee. She was young, just sixteen, but she was so sure.

"All I ask is that I am at least allowed to regain my reputation after what that exile did to me. I lost more than just you, but my friends. My life," Abigail insisted, with the fire in her eyes that Maria mourned for so long.

Maria looked her over and noticed how her face became more mature, a woman compared to when they were in their later teens, so naive and full of rebellion. She remembered the last time she saw Abigail. Her auburn hair in a braid, freckles multiplied due to the summer rays.

"You may stay. I will make sure you are taken care of. You have my official pardon." Maria desperately wanted to go back to her room where she knew Arabella was likely waiting, if she wasn't about to barge down the door. She knew that there was one more matter of business with Abigail that she could not let leave the room.

"The ring, Abigail. Take it off please," Maria sighed with an outstretched hand. Abigail choked back her rebuttal with tears in her eyes as she removed the engagement ring, slamming it into Maria's palm.

Maria didn't plan to tell anyone of her and Abigail's old engagement. They didn't exactly announce it back then. She was sure Abigail would bring it up at some point, but now that it was solidified as young love and nothing more, it held no leverage against her and Arabella's relationship.

Maria talked to Thoman next. Never once had she seen that man so remorseful of his actions, that it actually took her aback. Originally, she was going to strip him of his position, as Elias did near the end of his reign. Nothing would have hurt him more, to lose his passions for a second time.

Yet, when Maria saw him double over and throw up upon making eye contact with her, it disturbed her so deeply she reconsidered. That man was anything but a good actor, so he was genuinely unraveling at the guilt. He too was pardoned, out of legal necessity, but not from his guilt. Maria knew what it meant to defy her father. Knew there were no second chances, just death in the most painful way of human comprehension. That didn't change how furious she was.

"The people we had to be to survive my father, and the people we are at our core, are two different things. Despite that, every time you look at yourself in the mirror, I want you to remember what you did to her. When you look at Jessie, it will be Abigail's face you see, before she was forced to run in those woods. I command it. That is your punishment."

Maria left Thoman in the council room pale and sickly, ready to throw up once more at her haunting declaration.

'♥♥♥'

Maria lifted weights with one arm while simultaneously positioned in a plank. Her muscles flexed, but not with a worn out strain. Despite her going at it for half an hour, she was still barely warming up. She had what one might call a sleeper build, as she was rather long and lanky until she was intentionally flexing or working on something. Then, her muscles would ripple out as if ignited.

She needed to get her mind off of the current political state, and it was either an intense workout, or fucking Arabella until the rooster sounded at dawn… three weeks later. Until then, she needed to figure out how a queen could ethically take a vacation.

That would be a long time yet, she pondered as she began doing lateral raises. With Eminence overstepping her gracious mercy after both her coronation, with the wall still barely patched up outside her rooms, and now Abigail living with them all this time, the next step would be war. Eugene claimed not to want that, then her first love showed up from his territory.

A knock sounded at the door, snapping Maria from her thoughts as sweat dripped from her temple. "Come in."

Cienfuegos entered, skirt flowing, cigar in hand, vodka in the other. He stretched the glass bottle to Maria, who took a gracious swig of its contents. "Thank you. I appreciate that."

Cienfuegos looked at her with sad eyes, contemplating a time when his cousin wasn't so withdrawn from him. "You never talk to me anymore, Ria. Don't push me away."

"This whole time I thought my mom and Abigail found peace…" Maria explained softly, "I didn't want them to, not without me."

Cienfuegos understood his cousin. Understood the avoidance, not because of blame, but abandonment. She was mad at them, for not loving her enough in life, nor death, to give her a shred of company or advice. Abigail's assumed death hurt the worst, being the only one Maria truly showed her grief towards. Now, there she was very much alive, and everything was so different.

"With Abigail, I used to wish she would at least come back for a moment to tell me she regretted me, or that I destroyed her future. Obviously, she never did. All this time, it was like she never even cared enough to waste her breath," Maria concluded.

"I know what will cheer you up," Cienfuegos said, running out of Maria's chamber, leaving her to her lateral raises. He took his sweet time, but when he did return to her room, he carried with him an entire chocolate cake, and a duckling for some reason.

"Oh, what the fuck," was all Maria could muster in reply as she laid flat out on the floor.

Cienfuegos studied her before replying, "Some of us have interests beyond war and court. I like throwing birthday parties for farm animals."

Maria let out a hectic laugh as the room began to spin. "Somehow, I think I'm the most fucked up person in the room still."

Maria used her finger to scoop a piece of frosting from the duck's cake. Cienfuegos watched her attentively, waiting for some emotional breakthrough. All she said was, "This is some good cake."

"I bet it's not the best thing you'll be eating this week," Cienfuegos snickered. Arabella may have been keeping a casual distance, but everyone knew from the way she was walking around court that she would be marking her territory. Soon.

"Yeah, it'll be my teeth if I say or do the wrong thing when Arabella decides to grace me with her presence," Maria countered as she threw a couch pillow at Cienfuegos' head, nearly hitting the cake instead, causing chocolate frosting to get on the corner of its tassel.

"I thought you were into that sort of thing," Cienfuegos quipped. Maria gave him a glare as she went back for seconds of cake, this time scooping a fistful into her hand.

She began blushing imagining Arabella getting jealous over her. Maria knew her to be a sweet clumsy mess, but in an endearing way. To think she was capable of making Arabella all vicious, making heat pool to places other than Arabella's cheeks while proving her devotion—

Maria shook the thoughts away as the duck began to quack its approval of the cake. "Should it be eating that? Like, is it safe?" she asked her cousin.

Cienfuegos simply shrugged his shoulders as he replied, "It's gluten free."

'♥♥♥'

"What do you plan to do with her?" Arabella asked in a professional voice, because it was either treating the situation like business, or a planned murder. Her petty game was a fictitious display of maturity.

Maria sighed, summarizing what had happened. "Abigail explained that she was offered an ultimatum at Eminence's borders, and took it. Now that my father is dead, she felt it was finally safe to return."

"Is she safe to return?" Arabella asked, with malice in her voice.

Maria slid a hand down her face in annoyance before continuing, "Yes, she is safe, because I will not burn her alive. And she will be staying at court for a while as she attempts to salvage her social life, which I ruined," Maria finished bitterly, smoothing Arabella's hair then moving to her jaw, tilting up. Looking her in the eyes Maria said, "So behave, okay?"

Arabella nodded. Maria planted a kiss on her lips, pulling her in close. Arabella began to tear up, "How am I sure you'd choose me?" she asked softly.

"Me and her were forever ago, and she let me believe she was dead for years. I only want you." Maria continued to play with Arabella's hair as they lay in Maria's bed. Arabella ended up falling asleep, but Maria could not. The only thing that could keep her at bay from the recent events was listening to Arabella's soft snores.

Maria was still holding onto Arabella when she awoke. The way Arabella sleeps, however, consists of a lot of stirring and nuzzling into things before she becomes lucid enough for a conversation.

When Arabella did come to, sitting up staring at the wall, she remembered the past few hours and the jealousy crept back in even more numbing than before. She turned to Maria, who was already studying her face carefully, waiting to see how they would move forward from the recent events.

Arabella studied her back, looking into Maria's brown eyes and slight frown of the lips. The way her wavy hair was ruffled from her frustration, the way she carried tension in her jaw. It hit Arabella then how much she was emotionally invested in the woman before her. How she would kill everyone in the castle if she was denied Maria's love. No one would take her away, not if she had anything to do with it.

She crawled up to Maria, placing a hand on her chest, pushing her back onto the pillows. Maria looked up to Arabella, eyes darkening with lust as she knew exactly how they were going forward. Arabella reached her hand up, placing it lightly around Maria's throat.

A request lingered in the air between them. Arabella's aura was begging for Maria to take the jealousy and pain away without having to ask. "Don't worry princess, I fully intend to prove my devotion," Maria promised.

Although Maria thought Arabella's attempt at dominance was cute, it was maybe three seconds before she had Arabella flipped onto her stomach. Maria took Arabella's hair in her fist. With her free hand she grabbed Arabella's hips, pushing them upwards to meet her own. Maria towered over Arabella, nuzzling her face into Arabella's neck, leaving love bites at the sweet spot in the nape of her neck.

Arabella rolled her hips backwards while Maria began lapping her tongue over the bite marks she created. Maria let out a moan of her own before she reinforced her grip on Arabella's hair, wrapping her other hand around Arabella's neck.

When Arabella let out a whimper, Maria tutted. "Hush, baby. I got you. Let me prove how much I crave you." Maria pulled Arabella up so her back was flat against Maria's chest. She forced Arabella to tilt her head back far enough so their mouths could meet, yet Arabella wasn't done trying to claim dominance. She rolled her hips back once again. Maria grasped Arabella by the hip and flipped up her skirt.

Arabella premeditatively planned make-up sex, so it was only Maria that was shocked by Arabella already being stripped beneath the silk of her seafoam colored dress. Arabella knew she had Maria where she wanted her, spreading her legs as she raised her hips into an arch once more.

Maria planted a slap to her ass hard enough for it to sting before whispering, "You've been waiting for my attention all day, haven't you? I'm sorry, princess. I should have been more attentive."

"Who said it was for you? Maybe I have secrets too."

Maria thought to herself, *"So that is the game we're going to play?"*

Maria took a singular finger and curved it into a hook as she dragged it lightly through Arabella's folds. She could watch the way her finger glistened with Arabella's wetness forever, making her unopposed to edging Arabella until tears streamed down her face.

She slowly applied more and more pressure as her knuckle grazed the beginning of Arabella's clit. Every time Arabella would moan, Maria would remove her hand, spanking her once more until Arabella would apologize.

"All this torture could've been avoided if you'd just had taken your comfort silently, like a proper Lady," Maria whispered, smirking as she flicked the tip of her finger up just the way Arabella needed.

"Fuck. You," Arabella replied in between sobs.

Maria planted another smack. Then another, for good measure. Maria flipped Arabella onto her back, then ripped her corset downward, breaking the ribbon holding it together in the process.

"Is that any way to speak to your queen?" Maria asked while circling Arabella's nipple with her thumb.

Arabella knew she was losing the unspoken war she declared the second she tried to get a rise out of Maria. Instead of talking back, she arched against the bed, nipples peeking upwards as she spread her bent legs wide, glistening against the light shining in from the windows.

It was a sight that could kill any angel flying by. Luckily, Maria was a devil ready to indulge in glorious sin. Maria tried to stay strong, but that restraint was gone once Arabella chewed on her lip, whimpering the words, "Please, Your Majesty."

Maria snapped with a groan, launching forward to revel in Arabella's breasts, pinning her hands down in the process. Arabella was quite sensitive, so the action nearly threw her over the edge. What truly made her come undone was when Maria kneeled before her, looking her deep in the eyes as she said, "You are mine, as I am all yours." Maria dove in and began feasting. Arabella was moaning as loud as she could, so that everyone in the castle would know just as well.

After Arabella hit her climax, Maria sat back onto her knees. "You feel better?" she asked with a smug smile, anticipating the answer would be an easy 'yes.'

Arabella clumsily sat up and slowly grasped Maria's shirt collar. She leaned in to kiss Maria on the cheek, or so Maria thought. Instead, her lips just barely grazed Maria before she whispered, "You're so cute if you think I'm done with you yet."

Grasping Maria by the cheeks, Arabella placed the queen's mouth on her breasts. "Be a good girl and show me just how devoted you are. You'll stop when I say I'm done. Are you worthy of that?" Arabella asked in a gentle voice.

"Yes," Maria breathed against Arabella's nipple. Still, that answer did not suffice. Arabella grabbed Maria's hair roughly and removed Maria's mouth from her breast. "Yes what?" she demanded.

"Yes, m'lady," Maria whimpered. Her heartbeat was rapid in her chest as her brown eyes looked like that of a begging puppy, doing all the right tricks for a taste of a treat.

"Excellent. Show me that you're my good girl."

Arabella held Maria's head against her breasts as she gently toyed with Maria's core with feather light touches, slowly putting on more pressure. It made Maria come undone even on the most stressful of days, but this time was different. It wasn't just the sounds of Arabella's moans that motivated Maria, but the words of affirmation.

"Just like that, Your Majesty. You're being so good for me," Arabella praised, proceeding to remove her breast from Maria's mouth, telling her to stick her tongue out.

Arabella grazed her nipple over Maria's tongue ring as both of them moaned, which created a vibration that felt like bliss for Arabella. She grasped Maria's jaw and placed her breast back into her lover's mouth.

Arabella straddled Maria's thigh, and began to grind against her hip bone. Those grinds became frantic, desperate attempts to reach her climax. Maria felt like she died and went to heaven at the sight. Maria, still receiving those perfectly pressured touches from Arabella, hit her climax and unintentionally nipped at Arabella's breast in the process. The sensation threw Arabella over the edge as well, arching fully before collapsing on Maria's lap.

<u>*Chapter 27*</u>

When they met, Abigail treated Maria as she would have treated anyone else. It wasn't necessarily kindness, but it was dignity. Something Maria lacked from the adults around her. Abigail could relate to an extent. When they were twelve, Abigail watched Maria seated in the corner of their embroidery elective. She thought it was funny that Maria was sewing her dirty shoelaces with the string, whereas everyone else was trying to perfect their flying doves.

Abigail had to deal with her fair share of problems concerning authority figures, just like Maria. For her, it was either in the form of shame, or exploitation. It was harm under the guise of protection.

Maria and Abigail already had a solidified friendship by the time Abigail found out what her parents had in store for her. They were thirteen years old. Maria let Abigail stay in her rooms for weeks after Abigail ran from her parents, but they swore Abigail was not to be touched by anyone until the bidding when she turned eighteen. Maria planned to run away with her friend long before then. Maria was all political back then, and knew of what went on in the Mistress Institution. She would not watch it happen to Abigail.

They got romantically involved when they were fourteen. Despite the evils that put Abigail there, she was in the right rooms able to hear the right information. She relayed that information to Maria, who was planning to use it for good. After Maria's public beating upon the information being leaked, Abigail came back from Inferniana with the motivation to act against Elias. Those plans were put in motion before Maria proposed, but it all went downhill two weeks after.

Elias wasn't Abigail's parents' first choice for a bidder. As much as their love for their daughter was minimal, they didn't want her to die before a proper cash out. Instead, they were willing to bide their time until Abigail could work her charms on a prince like Eugene, or even a Duke from Cadence. Even if they shot for the moon and landed amongst a lordly star, money was the goal over status. Yet, when Maria and Abigail became official, all Abigail had to do was say the word to her parents. They were already brewing the king's poison.

Some might have looked at their beginning and saw transactional circumstances that didn't result in true feelings, but it was more than their little operations that made them enjoy each other's company. It was the late nights, sneaking around the gardens as they got older.

"Ria, look what I embroidered!" Abigail excitedly showed Maria her latest piece. Maria was already in the

gardens waiting for her when she came running up, her braid bouncing with her movements.

"It's beautiful, I really like the colors you used for the quail, and how its body language is admiring the sunset," Maria replied thoughtfully. Abigail loved that Maria had genuine feedback, not thoughtless compliments like the grown adults trying to manipulate her trust.

They'd always work on their hidden passions by that fountain in the gardens. It was a time when no one could take those things, or each other away. Maria would study her history books, but not the war history Elias shoved down her throat. She studied the history of the twenty-first century, her favorite era.

"How they were living centuries ago, but had such more... automated lives. It's incredible," Maria explained, comparing things like cars to carriages. Explaining how air pollution has been more positively reduced for those in the current times, compared to then, and imagining what breathing must have been like.

"Why didn't they just stop ingesting all the things that caused them harm, and cut off everything polluting the air?" Abigail inquired as she worked on braiding Maria's hair.

"It's hard to cut something off when you're forced to be dependent on it. I'm sure we can understand that,"

Maria shrugged lightly, tipping her head back so Abigail could have better access.

"I'm more intrigued that this week I learned Cadence is a knock off of this old country called France. Brando told me that half of them aren't even French. Some rich people who survived the fall just wanted to bring back Versailles for its indulgence and aesthetic. Ethnically, it's primarily Eminence that carries on the true French line. This was as the initial kingdom that held the entire continent together disbanded," Maria rambled, trying not to alter the inflection of her voice as Abigail pulled on a tangle in her hair.

Abigail could still remember that day vividly as she sat by the fountain once more, now twenty-three years old. She dreamt so long of returning home, and just being in the same building as Maria again. But Maria was walking around with the Marella girl, who didn't just listen to Maria talk about old cities, but was apparently replicating them in a way that improved the town folks' quality of living. It made Abigail sick, but all she could do was aggressively stick her needle into the fabric over, and over, and over again. The picture she depicted now was a dead dove lying next to its own dissected heart.

'♥♥♥'

The castle was getting colder, and everyone was dressing accordingly. Summer dresses were swapped for leggings and long coats as the chill started setting in. To be fair, the summer ended well over a month or so ago, but Maria was far too occupied to notice that life in the castle adapted. She hadn't formally addressed her people since Lucille died, and to give them updates on whether or not there would be war. Today's topic was lighter news.

"As you all know from the newspaper, run by Payje here," Maria pointed to Payje, who gave a raised hand. "There is to be an Autumn Festival on October 31st, three weeks from now."

Approval erupted throughout the hall. Maria smoothed her fingers over the gold armrest of her throne as she continued. "I have, unsurprisingly, given the task of coordinator to Arabella Marella. She has a few words regarding the event."

Maria gave the spotlight to Arabella without ever needing to move off her throne. Arabella beamed up the stage with a stack of papers and clipboard in her hands.

"Now, we have received confirmation from Cadence that they will be returning for the festival with their various performances," Arabella explained, flipping through her notes. "Withelle will not be attending, due to their religious holiday falling on the same day, but will be sending a hefty export of their best cheeses and baked goods," Arabella said with a performative tone of awe and excitement. The people cheered again.

"What of Eminence?" questioned a voice in the crowd. Everyone turned to look at the source, singling Abigail out. Maria scrunched her brows in exhaustion, not wanting to deal with more problems.

Arabella put on a polite smile, but narrowed her eyes. "Haven't heard from them, unless you bear messages? Recently coming from their territory and all." Someone let out a cough. Whispers and mutters broke out. Cienfuegos took a step forward, previously standing behind Maria on the dais.

"There is no telling whether they will show. The invite has been sent with good faith, though. We will keep everyone updated if and when things change." That was a lie. Eminence was never sent an invitation. Maria wanted to keep that distance, hoping it would maintain a silent peace. Considering Withelle wasn't going to be in attendance, Eminence could hardly find it to be impertinent.

Maria mouthed Cienfuegos a silent "*thank you*," suffocating under the underlying tensions. Arabella fell back into form, describing the event and how it would span essentially every acre of the castle's grounds. Even the villagers in the Heart of InFiamma would be celebrating at the castle. There would be a carriage service to transport people back and forth should the lords and ladies, or common folk, wish to intermingle for once.

Maria thought it would be good to bridge that gap, considering she felt most relaxed those few months she spent in the village, interning for Ember as a teen. She went into that internship a shell of a human, but came out of it like most people do when they go on spa retreats. Rejuvenated, in a sense.

She hoped the varying social classes could see the beauty in what each group has to offer. That would be hard though, because what are the nobles if not a group of people who often practice common folk traditions, without ever touching their struggles. While InFiamma prized itself as a great nation during Ash Fiamma's reign, Elias let everything great, including economic equality, slip. While it wasn't yet in total devastation, it caused tension between classes that hadn't been severe until the present.

After that address, which felt like it went on forever yet only thirty minutes, Maria had some rare downtime. She found her way to Brando's hidden room, content as she aimlessly strummed the guitar. Brando graced her presence after an hour.

"I feel like I never see you anymore," Maria admitted in a quiet whisper, not looking up from the instrument.

"You don't need me around that much anymore. You have people now," Brando sat beside her. His black hair had wispy front pieces that fell in front of his face, similar to how Maria's did.

"I'll always need you," Maria confessed, still strumming with no intentional notes. "I was a kid stuck in my room, but with you, I never felt alone."

Brando began to tear up, and that's when Maria knew. "You're going away soon, aren't you?"

Servients were never lifetime companions. They're tasked with a job to lead their wards to the right moment in their lives, and then they leave. Maria assumed if Brando was ever to leave her it wouldn't be until she was decades into her reign. Not so soon, though.

"Eventually, but not yet. We still have some time," he responded, adjusting the sleeves of his black sweater. It almost threw Maria off, considering although always alternative, he would typically appear more regal. Now, he looked just like any other young man. Maria didn't waste any more time asking questions about what happens after life. She knew she would find out eventually.

"You lost the love of your life. Say she came back on your doorstep. What would you do if you were me right now?" Maria inquired instead, ceasing her strumming.

"Melody…" Brando tried to find the words. "I can't answer this for you for the obvious reason that I did not have an Arabella complicating the matter. Not really, at least."

Maria bobbed her head contemplatively before confessing, "I love Arabella, she is my rock. She has kept me from saying fuck all to this kingdom, truthfully."

Brando smiled; his teeth similar to Maria's as well. They could be cousins visually, rather than ancestor and descendant. "I know. If you recall, I hinted at your union the day of your coronation."

"You are so cryptic, but I get it. If you told me I'd feel this way again about someone, I'd likely have avoided her at all costs," Maria leaned back against the footboard of Brando's bed. It made a creaking noise as the wood settled behind her. "Brando… will I see you again after you leave?"

"That depends. The goal is to go into the next life. Hopefully Melody is waiting for me, but I'll find her again even if she is not."

Maria sat straight up again and looked to Brando, who wore a hopeful expression. "You mean, you don't know?"

"Honestly, I don't know much of anything that happens after my job here is done. Since you now are aware that Firenze was my patron, I can at least let you know this.

Everything I know about your life, from the day I met you to the day I will leave you, she told me at the start."

Brando made his hot coffee appear, and Maria could have sworn for the first time ever, she smelt a bit of hazelnut in its contents.

"Then I will find you in the next life, and you better be my parent this time. Melody better be mother material, because you aren't getting rid of me," Maria teased, though she was now hopeful too in the possibility that she could have loving parents next time around.

"For better or worse, I am your parent, Maria. I always will be," his voice broke as the tears began to fall.

Maria began tearing up as well. "I'll be dying soon, won't I? It's why you're leaving, because you did all you could do but it's too late? I'm damned. So, we won't be apart for long," she convinced herself with a sharp nod of her head. Brando went to say something, but it would border on sensitive information that could change the course that was needed. He changed the subject instead.

"I hate that I never got to hug you, not once. That's the first thing I'll do. You deserve a proper hug," Brando stated, quickly drying his eyes just before Cienfuegos entered.

"Dude, are you alright?" he asked concerned, freezing in place. Maria gave a genuine smile. "Just venting to Brando. Show me that thing you were going to though," Maria insisted, standing up to join her cousin. She went to ask Brando if he too had any more cool things to show Maria, but he was gone. He did leave behind a parting gift, pushing a box off the top of a bookshelf.

It startled Maria more than Cienfuegos, as to her knowledge, that was never a possibility. While he didn't physically touch it, it was just another one of those things that Brando likely wouldn't explain to her before he left for good.

They went to investigate the black velvet box that had some sort of magnet inside, keeping it sealed even though it fell. Inside was a locket with a little dove painting inside, handmade. The note next to it read "*Princess Melody's locket: return to Cadence on her birthday.*"

Maria had never seen Brando's handwriting before, but she thought it was elegant, unlike her chicken scratch. Maria said to Cienfuegos, "I hope you have a daughter someday, so I can give her this."

Cienfuegos' facial expression lightened with a smile. "I never heard you say something that was so centered in the future. You think you'll have kids?"

"Yeah, maybe. It depends on what Arabella wants. I'm cool for whatever, or just making your kids my heirs. I don't really care," Maria placed the locket to the side.

"You sound sure of Arabella being the one," Cienfuegos said with hesitation in his voice. He scratched the back of his head with a tight expression.

"Anyways," Maria diverted, smoothing her hand over a green journal with fern leaf engravings. The first page was titled "The History of the Dead: 2181 BCE - 2375 ATF."

"Oh shit! Yes!" Maria jumped up. "I've wanted the historical accounts of this since I was six, but Brando said InFiamma's archive and libraries didn't hold any knowledge outside of the burial practices," Maria explained to Cienfuegos, who was initially startled.

She took the journal to Brando's bed as she plopped down and began reading. The book started with the mythology of the Egyptian deity, Anubis, prior to Osiris' rule in the underworld. Cienfuegos kept digging in the box, finding a rather cool dagger with dragon scale designs adorning the hilt. There was a marble shaped like a dragon as well, made out of some type of resin.

There was also a photograph of Brando with his family, taken when he was much younger. Ares Fiamma looked so horrifically stern and malicious, but growing up with Elias, Cienfuegos thought nothing of it. Brando's mother looked like a tired, worn out, and equally malicious lady with a thick bun on her head.

Next to Brando, around the age of ten, was an older boy. Anyone could deduce that the boy was Blaze "the Burnt." He looked a bit more confident than Brando, and a bit more willing to sit beside his father, whereas Brando was just itching to get away.

After some time, Brando appeared once again. His usual somber demeanor was replaced with an amused one this time around. "Maria," he tried not to laugh. "There's been an incident in the great hall."

'♥♥♥'

"Who did it?" Maria massaged her temples. Just when she thought she could get a break, she entered the great hall to see glass broken everywhere. Arabella and Abigail were mere inches from each other's face, the interns in a corner whispering, *but are we surprised?*" Maria called a meeting to handle it privately, lest the two make the front header of the newspaper. Payje was already starting a fire with how fast she was scribbling down notes.

"Ask the slut from hell," Arabella spat. Her entire dress was soaked with red punch, which was especially unfortunate, seeing as she was wearing all white.

Maria rolled her eyes and groaned. "Cienfuegos, have a bath drawn in my chambers please while I deal with this." Cienfuegos was snickering with Abigail in the back of the council room, who was bone dry. He snapped out of their conversation at the command though, giving a goofy shallow bow.

"Abigail, did you pour punch all over Arabella?" Maria mediated, as if she was talking to children.

"No," Abigail gave the simple, short answer, not elaborating any further. Arabella was losing her mind before Maria could get her next word out. "You saw me at the end of the room and had the table flipped so the punch bowl would fly onto me!"

"I was across the room, talking with Payje," Abigail shrugged. Her body language was relaxed, but there was a twinkle of mischief in her eyes.

"That right there is how you get caught in the lie, because I was talking to Payje. She has punch on her too," Arabella seethed, taking a step forward. Maria put her arm out to stop Arabella from moving any further.

"Oh, that's right," Abigail touched her hand to her forehead, as if recalling the memory. "I was talking to that intern, Gregory, is it?" Abigail's eyes shone with the insult before it left her lips. "He was just telling me how everyone on the Island thinks you are a freaky bitch—"

Arabella launched for Abigail, but Maria hoisted her up and over her shoulder with ease. She didn't care that the punch was seeping into her own white shirt as well, staining it beyond salvation.

"Okay, time for a bath. Thoman, get Abigail's statement," Maria looked to the older gentlemen in the back, who nursed their respective glasses of whiskey.

Thoman was trying not to laugh. Aquilla was looking anywhere but at Arabella, who was banging on Maria's back to be let down. He didn't find the interns' comments funny, and would likely be writing to their families, but the situation itself was unprecedentedly ridiculous.

"Have some fucking dignity you two, in the name of the Sun God. I thought misogyny was left in the old world," Maria muttered horrified.

"Is it misogyny if we aren't fighting over a man?" Abigail jested from the corner. Thoman absolutely lost it, laughing so hard he doubled over. Aquilla had to turn around and put his forehead on the wall. Arabella did a maneuver that allowed her to grab her shoe, and was set to throw it at Abigail. Maria spun at the last second, and the shoe hit Thoman in the face instead.

'♥♥♥'

Maria hopped into the bath with Arabella, who was shaking and tearing up with how upset she was.

"They still think I'm a freak!" Arabella screeched; voice raw. It went beyond the normal definition of the word upset. Arabella hit something that Maria could only describe as a category three meltdown. It worried her, not in the way that made her love Arabella any less, but confirmed what she previously suspected. Arabella gave signals that she felt emotional highs and lows. Maria knew this was one of those lows, but was willing to ride out the storm regardless.

"You're not a freak, sweetie," Maria massaged shampoo into Arabella's brown hair. "If it wasn't for you, your homeland would be rotting off the shoreline. It wasn't me wanting you that saved your people, it was your ambition that got them the resources they needed. Which also factors into why I adore you."

Arabella turned around, putting her head on Maria's shoulder as she sobbed. Maria found herself getting violently enraged that the woman she cared for so deeply, was disrespected in front of her entire court.

"They all laughed," Arabella sniffled. She then explained that when the juice flew all over her, she looked to those she'd known her whole life. All the interns had the same face they always did where Arabella was concerned. *'She's going to be emotional again,'* their expressions read.

Maria pulled her in as close as possible, applying soap to a loofah with her free hand. "I'm understanding how people see my father in me now. I'm tempted to make everyone walk on hot coals while a band plays goofy music in the background."

"Make that bitch do it alone, then I'd feel better."

Maria didn't want to make Arabella recount what happened before the laughs, lest she sounded unsure if she was taking Arabella's side. Instead, she planted many kisses on Arabella's cheeks. "I'm ordering all your favorite food for dinner tonight. We will spend the night in the super cool hidden room that no one knows about, and watch some moving pictures that Cienfuegos found."

That changed Arabella's mood almost instantly. "Moving pictures? Flim?" Arabella perked up, mispronouncing the word film.

"Yes, flim."

Chapter 28

Arabella shot Maria a scorned look when Cienfuegos joined them, considering he was less than discrete over who he liked more between Arabella and Abigail. He was equally irritated by her presence, treating her as if she was a little sister needing to be included or she'd cry to mom.

They all wished they had mothers once the DVD rolled, and they realized they picked a horror movie about thirty minutes into the film. Originally, they thought the premise of the movie was about a woman passionate about archeology and such, trying to find some magic stone. In reality, they were watching *As Above So Below*, which was set in the catacombs of Paris.

"There were six million bones underground?!" Arabella shrieked, thinking of the constructive implications. "No wonder the village fell underground!"

"That's how the city actually went out in the end," Maria explained solemnly. "It collapsed in on itself."

"I thought they reinforced the catacombs so that wouldn't happen?" Cienfuegos began to recall. Maria had a morbid phase when she was younger which included researching all the ways each major city collapsed. The ruins of these cities still existed, but were forbidden to enter due to The Accords.

"Yes but… it's a long history. Anyways…" Maria trailed off, trying to find something else to watch. There were only titles written in marker for hints at the DVDs' contents. Brando luckily came to assist.

"Arabella would like *FernGully* quite a bit. That's the third one from the right. Top shelf. Cienfuegos would like fantasy as well, but live action, which means real people acting with special effects," Brando explained. The DVDs were shelved on a long black bookshelf right below the television. Maria suspected he let them pick a horror movie on purpose after helping them get set up. It was payback for going against his wishes.

"For him, watch *The NeverEnding Story*. I have some films from later eras, but when everything switched to streaming, meaning everything was online and digitized, there was nothing to physically preserve unless you pirated it. Pirating meant downloading it illegally and placing it on a disk like these for repetitive use."

"Who do I need to kill to finally see this guy? I'm sick of being left out," Cienfuegos complained as he shoved calamari into his mouth.

"What about me? Which movie fits me?" Maria asked, tuning out the questions from Cienfuegos, wanting to know his assigned movies as well. Maria relayed Brando's answers to him, before telling him to shut up.

Brando gave a deep laugh before saying, "You're more difficult. I think you wouldn't benefit from a movie, rather a show with multiple seasons and variations. I think I'll leave that for when you need it most."

Maria knew better than to argue, and truthfully, she was too excited to wait a moment longer. The three watched Arabella's movie first, in which Arabella cried, hard. It was good though, because it gave her an opportunity to drain a lot of pent-up feelings she'd been having. Maria could see her going back to normal already. Pre-plague levels of normal.

Cienfuegos needed his movie as well. Being a young warrior himself, yet a sensitive kid with feelings and the ability to articulate that, he often felt split between two realities. Controlling both simultaneously.

To wrap up the night, Maria put on documentaries that were filmed hundreds of years before she was born, content with watching them alone as her cousin and girlfriend slept soundly. She fell asleep in the middle of a documentary on planet Earth, pre-ecological destruction.

The documentary had Maria considering if it was worth seeing what remained out there. After all, the continent had InFiamma in the west, Cadence in the southeast, Eminence in the east, and Withelle in the northeast. The island territory, Gloucester, was as west as the map went. The ruins of Radiance were just as far east, technically.

Beyond that, Maria was told that the other continents such as the ones the Fiamma's came from were still on fire centuries later. The documentary made her question that. Then again, she assumed it must surely be a barren wasteland after the floods and fires, which would have made the soil useless. Who could survive?

'♥♥♥'

Fall in InFiamma highlighted the most beautiful aspects of the culture. Nothing could beat the nights in October, where the majority of the court finds their way outdoors to gaze at the stars. The bonfires were lit three times the size of Maria, without any formal formations like Firenight. They were lit according to need.

Maria was stargazing on a blanket next to Arabella, who was looking at constellations through a telescope, giving descriptions of each one, and their Greek lore.

There were families at court tailgating in the modern way, sharing various roasts and squash-based dishes from large wagons. Maria herself got some soup and kabobs, munching on the meat as her eyes scanned the sky for an airplane. She could have sworn she saw a star slowly move before it blinked out of existence.

"There used to be so much light pollution, people couldn't see stars," Maria told Arabella. Arabella took her eye away from the telescope with an uncomfortable expression.

"That's impossible. They're *stars*," Arabella emphasized. Maria just shrugged, taking another bite from her food. Arabella didn't press further on the topic, but Maria wished she did.

Cienfuegos remained in the castle that night. Not because he didn't feel like going out, although the rest was appreciated. Maria allocated a third of the military to live in the castle permanently, so he could remain indefinitely while still fulfilling his duties.

Thoman was on his way to do his weekly check in with Ignacio in Inferniana, but would be back in the morning once his report was done. Until then, it was business as usual.

Jessie remained with Cienfuegos, steeping some tea that was so fragrant it filled the air in their suite with cinnamon and vanilla, mixed with chamomile, honey, and lemon. They had one more cup of tea than usual, because across from Cienfuegos, Abigail lounged in an armchair by the bookshelf.

"You need to start from the beginning, please," Cienfuegos insisted gently, giving a small smile to Jessie who handed him his hot tea. Jessie then handed Abigail hers with a smile of his own.

"It was the last day I saw you. I went to poison Elias, this is true. I couldn't spend another day watching Maria sneak down to the kitchens at dawn to stock up on meals, because she was too cautious to leave her rooms any other time," Abigail recalled, sipping her tea as she contemplated her old life. Even if Maria couldn't recall her life being so stressful, it was.

"How did he catch you? How'd you even get into the same room as him?" Jessie questioned, slightly impressed.

"When he found out about me and Maria, I was removed from any future drafts in the Mistress Institution. I promise you; it wasn't out of the kindness of his heart. The reason I never told Maria any of this is because I understood I was leverage to be used against her. Any reactions she would have given would play right into Elias' hands. As a gesture of good faith, my parents wanted me to promote my would-be-patron's other mistresses," Abigail's eyes went dark. "They were older, around nineteen—"

Jessie choked on his tea so hard some leaked from his nose. "That old bastard," he scowled. Cienfuegos put a hand on Jessie's knee. The information was not new to him. By the time Elias Fiamma died, his mistresses were younger than his own daughter.

"Yes," Abigail paused to collect her thoughts. "I introduced a variety of women who would soon either die by Elias' hands on faulty charges, or escape to Cadence at the height of his madness. One of the women was Ines, King Fabian's current courtesan. She left for Cadence about three days after her introduction though. The ballerinas at Cadence have an underground program to train…"

"Abigail," Cienfuegos sighed. Abigail knew what he was saying, urging her to get to the point.

"I tried to poison him one night. I rarely had to be there when he met the mistresses, seeing as I was far away from my bidding and promised to Maria, should she still 'desire' me. She never suspected this, of course. I used one of these meetings as an opportunity, claiming I needed a refresher on how it goes on the business end of things. My family was in on it, so they followed along," Abigail recounted as she gripped the cup with white knuckles.

"I was the cupbearer, pouring the drinks while the two talked, promising to just observe. I'll never forget the way he laughed as he sipped the wine, poisoning the mistress instead. That's when I knew I was done for. I didn't have time to run and get Maria before the impromptu burning party was to begin," Abigail took a deep sip of her tea, this time draining the cup.

"As far as how I'm alive, where I've been, and what I've had to do to survive…That is harder to talk about, but I know my options are limited."

Cienfuegos got up from the couch and kneeled in front of her, taking her hand. "I am still your ally, Abi."

Abigail began to tear up and tremble as she continued her story. The burning party was set with about thirty other prisoners, from villagers to court members, they all went out the same. The only reason Abigail did not perish alongside her family was because she spat in Elias' face and let him know every key moment of Maria's life she was there for, when he was not.

Elias decided to parallel her death to the one he would have given Maria, should she have not survived in the woods. This time there would be a spin, for both amusement and insurance.

"As the soldiers chased me through the woods, I ended up on the border of InFiamma and the eastern neutral. Just as I was at the edge of the forest, a wolf appeared out of nowhere and had me pinned. When I thought it was over, an arrow went through its head," Abigail gave visuals with her hand gestures.

"It was Eminence's forces scouting the forest. They wanted that land well before Maria became a queen, and Elias was ready to wipe them out over it. They took me in.

Once I was already in the mountains and in their castle, that's when I was given my ultimatum."

Abigail made a face that could have convinced Cienfuegos the lemon in her drink was too strong. That's when she told the worst part of her story. She was told that her option was to either stay in the castle without ever being able to leave, lest she give the rival court's secrets away as a bargaining chip, or she was to die right then and there. In that regard she understood. She would have used any information to go home.

When her novelty to the people of Eminence's court wore off, she was told it was time for her to pay dues for their gracious safety.

"A year later, after trying to escape twice, their niceties wore off. I was forced into employment under Eugene Chevalier," Abigail turned pale. "I suspect he hasn't been charging into battle because I know every bit of contraband, battle strategies, and warfare Eminence is prepared to use."

"When you say employed under him…" Cienfuegos did not finish the question, and the way Abigail frantically shook her head, he knew that demand alone was the answer.

"I don't want Maria to know the things I've done," Abigail insisted.

"I will keep this between us, out of respect for you, and because Maria has had many surprises the past few months. She is tired, and trying harder than most people in this court deserve after what they did to her," Cienfuegos agreed as he stood. He extended his hand in support, letting Abigail know he would be there every step of the way. Abigail took it.

"I'm proud of Maria, for overcoming such hate shown to her in our youth. For being so good to her court despite it. Lord knows if it was me, I would not be so generous. But I will be winning her back without her sorrows and pities on what has been done to me. You may relay the political information to Maria, but nothing more. Nothing of my duties to Eugene," Abigail asserted as she took her leave, readying to put actions to those words.

'♥♥♥'

Abigail found her way to Maria's chambers two nights later. She didn't need stealth, thus allowing her heels to make loud clunks against the stone floors. She knew that Maria was in the barracks, along with every other soldier preparing for the inevitable use of arms. Maria would probably be sweaty and ready for a bath when she returned. Abigail was banking her entire plan on it.

She slipped past the guards with ease, as some of them were acquaintances and family friends she knew her whole life growing up at court. That was one quality she was lucky to have on Arabella, who was a foreigner from an island hundreds of miles away.

Naturally, Abigail had Maria's bathtub filled, warm, and waiting for her after she entered Maria's chambers, approximately ten minutes before training was to conclude. After letting it cool a bit, she removed all her clothing and dipped herself inside. She allowed her mind to wander, causing her to barely hear anyone enter until she registered the sound of Maria plopping down her swords.

"I wondered why the guards stopped me in the hall, telling me my guest was waiting. Here I was thinking they were referring to my girlfriend." Maria said sarcastically, sweat dripping from her temple, shirt unbuttoned to the part in her cleavage.

Abigail tilted her chin up, showing that courtly arrogance she was well versed in. She partly emerged from the water so the bottom of her full breasts would caress the water. The very clear water, revealing her plump figure.

Maria's eyes almost darted down. Almost. She began to flush, and Abigail knew she was close to having her where she wanted. Abigail saw the way Maria's neck strained while forcing down a swallow and decided to strike; go for the kill.

"My chamber's bathing system wasn't operating," Abigail explained innocently, tilting her head with a clueless look.

"Yeah, I'm sure you had nothing to do with that," Maria rolled her eyes as she strutted to her desk, taking a seat while gazing in a mirror hanging above. "Finish and get out," Maria demanded, gathering her hair in a low ponytail, contemplating if she should cut it shorter as she examined it in the mirror.

Maria heard the water splash as Abigail removed herself from the tub, yet Maria didn't anticipate for Abigail to skip over, body dripping wet. When Abigail reached Maria, she put her knees at either side of the queen, straddling her long torso as she took a seat right at Maria's belt buckle. Water seeped onto Maria's white shirt to the point of it becoming see-through.

Maria refused to give in, to touch, to speak. Abigail moved again, positioning her hand around the back of Maria's head, rubbing the spot that always brought Maria clarity. "Does she know about this? Hmm?" Abigail asked with a soft voice.

"What about this?" she asked innocently, leaning forward, licking the side of Maria's neck in just the right spot, with just the right amount of pressure. One second, Maria was tilting her head back slightly, giving Abigail the impression she had won this round. That was a mistake.

In a matter of a second, Maria lifted Abigail up. Next thing Abigail knew, she was lying flat on the floor, arms being pinned above her head by Maria's right hand. The left hand was pointing a finger, right in Abigail's face.

Maria waited to say what she wanted as Abigail squirmed under her grip, letting out a fake whimper as a secondary trap. Maria stretched her neck, waiting for Abigail to settle down as she replaced the pointed finger with a grasp on Abigail's chin. The roles were now reversed. Maria forced Abigail to look her in the eyes, not in the loving way she usually did when she grasped Arabella's chin, but in a way that promised just how serious she was.

Maria leaned her face into the crook of Abigail's neck, mouth lined up to Abigail's ear as she muttered hatefully, "she reached places I never would have let you near."

With that, Maria pushed herself off the floor, walking towards the exit. "I want you out by the time I get back," Maria said, barely turning her head in Abigail's direction. "If you aren't, I'll see to it that your exile is reinstated."

"That was harsh, Maria," Brando said from the end of the dimly lit hallway. Maria did not give a rebuttal. She already knew he was right. All Maria could think about was the ways Abigail and Eugene talked about her weaknesses, waiting until now to exercise them.

'♥♥♥'

Arabella and Maria spent most of their free time together after that, even if it was just Arabella taking a nap next to Maria, who was typically writing diplomatic letters. At this point, Fabian and Maria were practically pen-pals. It was their dynamic, a celebration of peace, pleasure, and leisure.

"I got you this for the festivities, m'lady," Maria announced, bowing deep in a satirical manner, holding an autumn inferno orange dress. Arabella hated the color orange, causing her to put on a failed attempt at a smile. Maria let out a laugh.

"I'm just kidding, Bella," Maria teased, tossing the dress to the side. She put two fingers in her mouth, smoothly letting out a whistle, inviting a team of designers into the room holding a variety of blue fabrics of all shades and textures.

Maria plopped on her bed, crossed her legs, and opened a letter while obviously faking to read it. Arabella's eyes examined the fabric as the servants set them up on display. Arabella picked up a hand embroidered pillow from the lounge chair, and threw it at Maria's abdomen.

"I would've preferred funding for my housing plan," Arabella insisted.

Maria never looked up from her letter, instead gave a smile and said sweetly, "You can't wear a housing plan, and if you could, I doubt it would do wonders for your breasts like Ontario can."

Arabella turned and looked at the designer, who was adjusting a fabric that looked like the night sky. "If you funded my housing plan, you'd see my boobs without fabrics," Arabella teased, climbing on the bed and snatching the letter.

Maria's hands remained in the same position they were when she was holding the letter, not looking away as she rebutted, "I'll take you up on that when I finish the finances for the educational program."

Arabella knew it was hard on Maria, reallocating funds that her father put into brothels, past mistresses, future mistresses who were really investments for him. It made her heart ache to know Maria grew up in a home where her father invested so much time and energy into anything else but his daughter.

Maria had confided in Arabella scarcely about her past, as it was a wound kept sealed by something stronger than resin. When she did open up, it would be the deep stuff, the stuff they couldn't ignore, such as nightmares of Arabella being hurt and Elias being the culprit.

The recent nightmare emotionally wounded Arabella, and was no doubt what the dress fiasco was truly about. Because the last one was more of a memory than a dream. It was the day Maria lost Abigail, to her previous knowledge, forever. It was the first and last day she really stood up to her father, which was followed by a punishment that Maria refused to mention.

Arabella felt selfish for taking Maria's traumatic memory and making it about their relationship, but she couldn't help but feel an overwhelming insecurity knowing Abigail was roaming the castle. She felt even more on edge considering Maria showed up to the late-night council meeting, wet and agitated over yet another thing she would not mention.

She knew Maria would never cheat; it wasn't in her nature. Maria barely liked to be around one person for an extended period of time, never mind engaging in an emotional juggle between two. Yet, Arabella knew it was weighing on Maria. It showed in her posture.

"I didn't know the Autumn Festival was such a formal event," Arabella inquired, letting Ontario play with draping as she stood like a mannequin.

"It's not, but you always wear such pretty dresses. I wanted you to have something special," Maria offered, crawling to the edge of her bed so she could watch Arabella's fitting.

"Thank you," Arabella said sheepishly. "But I want my funding by January."

Maria laughed, then gave a mocking salute. "It would be my honor to do that for you, m'lady."

Chapter 29

No expenses were spared for the Autumn Festival. Save for the funding for Arabella's housing plan, which Maria had all along. She wanted to give it to her on a special occasion, though.

Naturally, Cadence had their theatrical shows, Withelle their spiritual paraphernalia, but InFiamma had Autumn Festival. The event attracted the most tourism, as much as tourism was normalized at this point in history. It was like the epic high school carnivals that were featured in some of the movies Maria had been watching. There were multiple movies she modeled the festival after; but there were also a lot of attractions that managed to stay the same after all this time.

On October 30th, the work began. Mostly, individuals from Cadence and InFiamma participated in the setup, which would span multiple acres. Fifty of the same villagers that worked on Arabella's public building came to aid in setting up as well. Originally there were meant to be three times that, but after Maria's outburst, many pulled out. That was an issue Maria planned to address later.

There was a row of giant bonfires leading up to the castle. Behind the castle itself, the electric lights shined even brighter. Cadence brought their own sources of energy, which was enough to electrocute whatever was left of humanity. That was another topic Maria planned to investigate, especially considering Brando's tense demeanor towards the subject.

King Fabian was being watched over by Thoman, who would likely be stumbling back to his chambers when Maria relieved him from the duty. The rest of the council held a general meeting while indulging in pumpkin coffee and gingerbread muffins. Cienfuegos wore a pumpkin on his head in an attempt to seem more festive and less threatening to his subordinates. The days surrounding InFiamma's Autumn Festival had deep ties to the old North American version of Halloween.

Arabella wore the dress Maria had commissioned for her, though it was a day earlier than intended. She had a more casual outfit planned for the festival itself. Maria, still in her typical attire, also wore a pumpkin head, making everything that came out of her mouth seem unserious. The meeting was short and rather lighthearted.

"I think we covered everything, I'll see you guys at dinner," Maria smiled to her friends, taking the pumpkin head off.

"Oh, wait, Aquilla. Can I have a word in private?" Maria asked nervously, fiddling with one of the charms on her necklace. It was a new addition to her chain, shaped like a little lighthouse. Aquilla nodded graciously, staying behind as Cienfuegos ushered Arabella out of the room. He sparked conversation to prevent her from becoming nosey.

"Do you and Maria have a set itinerary for the festival?" Cienfuegos politely asked Arabella as they walked towards the great hall.

"She left it to me to make one, but I kept it pretty open so she could see all her favorite childhood attractions," Arabella explained, remaining quiet after that.

Thoman came running down the hall, nearly clashing with Arabella and Cienfuegos. "Guests. Front gate. Now," He blurted, grabbing Cienfuegos by the arm. As Thoman began dragging Cienfuegos away he motioned for Arabella to get Maria. Arabella ran back to the council room where Maria and her father were just exiting. Aquilla was smiling, patting Maria on the back as she blushed.

"People are at the gate. We have to go. Thoman's already with Cienfuegos," Arabella heaved. She only had to run down the hall, but was incredibly winded by just doing that. She made a mental note to take Maria up on her offer of physical training.

Maria and Aquilla's faces turned serious in an instant, sprinting past her to the front doors of the castle. Thoman was already greeting the visitors, standing sternly before a court of twenty people dressed in muted grays and electric blues.

At the head of the pack was a young man with dirty blonde hair, and a stone cold face that had a familiarity to Maria. As previously stated, photographs were rare, but not unheard of. This face Maria saw in a picture before. At the time, the man was much younger, but there was no mistaking he was Maria's maternal cousin, Eugene. He put on a sneer, positively insulted by Thoman's presence.

"Cousin, welcome. We never received confirmation that you would be arriving," Maria greeted with as much nicety as she could muster.

Eugene turned to Maria; leveled two inches shorter than her. He did a shallow bow. "Apologies cousin, our reservation must have gotten lost along the way. Our mail courier never returned."

Maria nodded her head in understanding. Cienfuegos cut Eugene a look, wondering what he was insinuating. Maria adjusted her posture by squaring her shoulders back, as well as consciously fixing her features to be neutral.

"Of course, it is no issue. There is space for all. Rooms are prepared off the east wing, beyond our training centers. I will have my paternal cousin here show your court the way," Maria gestured to Cienfuegos, who was more than thrilled to once again indulge in another military pissing contest.

Eugene nodded with a slight curve of his lip. Cienfuegos gestured towards the hall that led to the barracks. "I look forward to the festivities," Eugene quipped as he followed along, taking his court with him. Maria got an eerie case of deja vu. Then there was the brutal reminder that she never caught whoever killed Lucille. She didn't care who killed her aunt as long as Eugene stayed away. Yet, here he was.

"I want guards on rotation at all times. Make it seem like there's a castle curfew for that wing, say, 11pm. Offer to escort them to the festival grounds. I don't want anyone left unattended on the way to the field," Maria told Thoman as they went back inside.

"I want every single soldier to be aware that acting on anything without my permission, even with good faith towards the crown, will be punished severely," Maria grounded out as she paced back to the council room. She was ready to spend the rest of the night preparing for a coup.

Arabella was by her side, ready to send evacuation orders for the interns who already did drills should something like this occur. "Some of your people will be here tomorrow morning. Their ship is likely already at the ports," Maria told Aquilla, tugging on the front ends of her hair in frustration.

"Breathe. It may be a visit of good faith," Aquilla tried to comfort, but it did little to help. There was no invitation sent to Eminence, so insinuating they had a messenger that got lost RSVPing was a lie in itself. Eugene must have thought Lucille took care of any invitations before her death and went with Maria's lie.

Thoman caught on to her game. Never had he felt so impressed by Maria's abilities to think quickly and act before. He didn't give her enough credit for retaining all those meetings her father made her listen to, of war and the art of succeeding. "Well, fuck them. I'm not letting anyone ruin Autumn Festival," Maria pouted.

Arabella grabbed Cienfuegos' shoulder as she frantically exclaimed, "Abigail was probably sent as the messenger! As some scouting spy!"

Cienfuegos blanched, looking horrified just before bolting out of the room. Everyone could hear his footsteps slamming loudly towards the barracks.

"I'm so happy he finally listens to me," Arabella sighed with relief. That would be nice, except Cienfuegos didn't think Abigail was a spy. It was just the first time he considered Abigail, who was currently sleeping in the very barracks Eugene was heading towards.

When he arrived, Jessie was standing outside the door, blocking Eugene from entering. "She doesn't belong to you, so I advise you to give her back to me. Now,"

Eugene spat. His elegant facade was dropped, replaced with that of a little brat.

Maria was right behind Cienfuegos, knowing anything to warrant that reaction was bound to be a major problem. "She's an InFiamma born citizen, and her exile was abolished by me personally. I'm willing to provide whatever trade you want for her, but she belongs here," Maria calmly insisted.

Eugene put his graceful mask back on as he turned to Maria. "But of course. It's just, you see, Abigail has been in contract to be my… employee. It's just a shame that after all my mother did to protect her from your father, she didn't finish fulfilling her duties."

Maria's blood ran cold as the god of death, and of every black hole, showed through her eyes. "Excuse me?" she spoke lethally. Maria was reaching for her sword Majesty when Abigail flung the door open, tears streaming down her face.

"I couldn't tell you! I just…I'm sorry!"

Maria stalked up to Abigail, not making eye contact with Eugene as she addressed him. "She was mine before she was yours, so find any other woman to replace her, but she is not yours anymore."

Eugene's lip twitched upwards as he gave a small nod, relishing in the lack of care in Maria's words.

Maria led Abigail away, not saying anything until she reached the west wing. "My mother's room is now yours. But please, Abigail, if that was some scheme…"

"It wasn't. I hated him and every day I had to serve that prick. Thank you for not making me go back," Abigail whispered, taking a step away from Maria to prove she wasn't moving in or plotting anything.

Arabella flew up the west wing's stairs. Maria could hear the sound of her flat shoes aggressively slapping on stone as she wound the stairwell. "She probably wants whatever is in this room," Arabella protested, folding her arms as she cut Abigail a snarky look.

"I get it. You're mad about me and Maria's history. However, if you look at a woman trying to find asylum after being held hostage for six years, and claim that it is to my advantage, then you are a witch," Abigail snapped back, eyes red and wet from crying.

Cienfuegos entered a moment later as well, hugging Abigail, stroking her hair. "I'm so sorry, are you okay? I should have gotten you first—"

"You knew?" Maria's eyes filled with betrayal. Cienfuegos loosened his grip on Abigail. "Yes but—"

"How long?" Maria's voice went cold. As cold as she was in the days before her coronation, when she was all alone.

"Not long. I begged him not to tell you," Abigail spoke on his behalf. That didn't make the tension any lighter, or the situation any less dire.

"That's a major security risk," Maria claimed roughly. Even Arabella turned to look at Maria with an uneasy expression. After a moment of consideration, she made a decision. "Thoman can handle your legion. You're suspended until Eminence leaves," Maria commanded dryly, walking out of her mother's room.

"Maria!" Cienfuegos shouted after her, visibly panicked. "That in itself is ten times the security risk!

"It's true. I'm not his biggest fan right now, so I'm being logical with that," Arabella protested as well.

Maria turned around; the coolness replaced with fire in her eyes. "Fine. Meet me in the pit. We'll resolve this there."

Everything about Maria showed she was fuming. Her piercing eyes, clenched jaw, and tense shoulders, all radiated wrath. "Abigail, you aren't to leave this wing without a bag search. If I find out you do, you'll be given back to the wolves."

Arabella went to grab Maria's hand, but she pulled away, straining her fingers as she descended to the training pits.

'♥♥♥'

Eugene didn't get the pleasure of watching Maria and Cienfuegos brawl. Eminence's group was told it was a private event, but that didn't stop Cadence from enjoying the show. King Fabian had bets being placed. Thoman got his wagers in with Aquilla. Sitting on the bench by the pit was Abigail and Arabella, keeping a healthy distance apart. Payje was taking notes by a fountain as Maria and Cienfuegos beat each other to a pulp.

When Maria and Cienfuegos were children, they were aware of what their duties would be from the jump. Every milestone in their development had an equal bit of training regarding their future positions to go with it. At the age of eight, the council found humor in pinning the two against each other in physical fights. Therefore, this was not the first time they pummeled each other in front of an audience.

Their skills were deadly to anyone of lesser build, but both possess similar height, weight, and training. Arabella wished one of them were lesser in any of those departments, so the fight would end quicker. Still, for every jab Maria gave, Cienfuegos gave an equal one. When Cienfuegos slammed Maria onto the dirt floor, she rolled him over into a chokehold with her legs.

Cienfuegos used the back of Maria's kneecap to break free, jumping on top of her to land more vicious hits. Arabella was horrified at the sight. She was ready and willing to jump into the ring to get Cienfuegos off of Maria, if Abigail's chuckle from beside her didn't take her out of the match.

"You find this funny?" Arabella breathed in confusion, running her hands through her hair.

"They did this every time Maria misplaced her sword Majesty and accused him of borrowing it, or whenever Cienfuegos had to beat her ass as a make-up assignment for war council. They'll tire out any second," Abigail insisted, popping some red hot candy into her mouth.

"Are you done yet?" Cienfuegos asked Maria as he climbed off of her. Maria was hoping he'd make that mistake, as she knew there was no way out of his hold unless he let her out of it. "Nope," Maria said when he took a step away from her. She swiped her legs while balancing on her hands, knocking him back onto his ass.

He did not move or attempt to block any of Maria's hits as she jumped up and towered over him. He looked her straight in the eyes as he prepared for her next blow. She surprised him by grabbing the collar of his shirt and whispering in his ear instead. "Never *ever* keep anything like this from me again. It's bad enough I could have protected her then, but to let that man step foot into my home, where he could do it all over…"

Maria released her cousin and stumbled backwards. That was a sign she had all her emotions out of her system.

When she retreated to the bleachers, it signaled that the match was done. Jessie had no idea who he needed to tend to first. Maria had a split eyebrow which would definitely scar. Same for Cienfuegos, but his wound was a gash on his lip. Maria's mouth was bleeding as well, as if she bit the inside of her cheek too hard. Jessie naturally went to Cienfuegos first. He didn't care that Maria was his queen. Not only was Cienfuegos his person, but if you asked anyone, Cienfuegos wasn't the one wrong in this situation.

Arabella grasped Maria by the ends of her hair and dragged her all the way back to the west wing, a trail of Maria's blood following them. By the way Arabella's eyes watered and her chin was held high, Maria knew that she heard the comment about protecting Abigail.

"Idiot asshole!" Arabella called Maria as she placed a cloth on Maria's brow. "Fighting against your cousin…over her," Arabella scoffed to herself.

"Not everything is about your jealousy, Arabella," Maria spat, feeling tired over the entire debate regarding the two women. "It was funny at first, but it's not cute anymore. Cut the shit."

Arabella paused her movements, flaring her nose and smelling the tang of blood. "Excuse me if I have feelings towards your actions," she removed the cloth and slammed it on the floor before walking towards the door.

"Arabella!" Maria yelled after her girlfriend, but she knew Arabella was far too stubborn and wouldn't turn around for anything. Except when it came to having the last word. That she would turn around for.

"So, what? I'm expected to live my life as just one of your mistresses too? Is that what this is?" Arabella scorned. Maria focused on a pile of documents on her desk. "No," was her only reply. Arabella moved in front of the desk, forcing Maria to focus on her instead.

When Maria glanced up, guilt coating her face, Arabella had no choice but to take that as a more definite answer. It had been a deep fear that kept Arabella up at all hours of the night, lest she dreams of Maria running back into Abigail's arms. What did she have in two months over Abigail, who was with Maria during the most vulnerable moments throughout her life? As Maria came more and more into her reign, Arabella felt like she was outliving her use, outliving her place in Maria's heart.

"You don't get me and her. You don't get to emotionally alternate between us like some commodity," Arabella's anger increased. "You don't get to be some entitled bitch like your father and expect me to not see how you still look at her!"

Maria went still, her breath halted in her lungs. Arabella did as well when she realized how deep that insult cut. It was instant guilt that seized her body as the weight of all her recent actions crashed down on her.

In the threshold was Cienfuegos, bloody and battered, but patched up for the most part. His eyes bounced between his cousin, and Arabella, who became very still under his gaze. He brought Jessie to patch Maria up as well. He finished getting his doting on by Jessie moments prior. Sure, Jessie was mad, but never so mad as to remind Cienfuegos of all his darkest fears. Both men stood there in silence, clearly hearing the end of that argument.

When Cienfuegos focused his harsh gaze on Arabella, and Arabella alone, he relished in the fact it made her uncomfortable. She began to bite the inside of her cheek, looking down to avoid eye contact with him. Arabella knew—could feel that shift in the air—that Cienfuegos was no longer her friend.

"I started it," Maria said when she noticed them there. "All of it. So, I'm sorry," she told her cousin.

Cienfuegos pushed past Arabella and gave his cousin a hug. Jessie was content working around their embrace, sewing up the gash in Maria's brow.

"I'll tell you until I'm a corpse in the ground. You aren't him," Cienfuegos whispered into Maria's ear.

Maria didn't care anymore. All she felt she could do was become a walking apology, and hope that it prevents the people she loves from leaving again. Thus starting an internal battle of doing everything she can to keep her life from going back to how it was when her father was alive, to trying to push everyone away because that conclusion is all she could anticipate.

Chapter 30

Maria woke at dawn the next morning. Her head was throbbing, and she felt like she drank half of InFiamma's wine cellar. The sunrise was beautiful though, the way it illuminated into her room through the few stained glass windows mixed in with regular ones. That factor made the morning all right.

She and Arabella hadn't discussed their argument from last night, but they were content enough to sleep beside each other. With everything going on, Maria thought it was best to just let it go. If she worried about her personal relationships while her kingdom's largest threat roamed the halls, she wouldn't be a very good ruler. That's what she told herself to avoid addressing the feeling that lingered in the pit of her stomach.

Maria glanced outside the window by her desk area to see some children laughing, playing in the giant pile of leaves that were raked the night before. That wasn't a common sight back when Elias was king, and the Autumn Festival was just a memory in the hearts of those who resided in the castle.

From dawn until noon, the festival would be aimed at families with young children. That made up a small portion of the court, but a large portion of the villagers that decided to come with little ones. Maria watched as the last of the set-up committee placed out the gourds for the pumpkin patches, and various skipping rocks the children could paint.

Maria got ready for the day silently, allowing Arabella some more time to rest. Instead of a whimsical flowy shirt or some dress pants, she opted for some more casual attire. She went into her mother's closet and found some jeans to wear. Abigail was already settled into Odette's old room, snoozing the entire time Maria sifted through Odette's closet. Abigail only woke just as Maria gathered what she needed.

"How did you find the courage to come in here anyways?" Abigail muttered half awake. She was cocooned in the white floral comforter in the middle of the large bed, laying diagonally across the mattress.

"When Eminence put holes in the walls, I didn't have much of a choice," Maria narrowed her eyes, looking to catch any parts of Abigail that may tense at the statement.

"Hmmph," Abigail shoved her face back into the pillows, falling asleep again in a matter of seconds.

It was set to be a cold day, at least by InFiamma's standards. The people of Eminence would find the weather rather nice. Given it being cooler, the typical white shirt wouldn't do, Maria knew she needed a sweatshirt. She decided, unsure of whatever force inspired her, to slip into her father's abandoned room. The last time she was in his room she found his secondary prophecy in his closet. Before that, she snuck in as part of a dare when she was eleven.

When Elias and his mistress had come barreling in, she hid in a storage compartment of a futon sofa amongst all his sweaters. While she fully anticipated hearing nasty moans and provocative squeaking of furniture, the opposite happened. The mistress and her father were arguing, and Maria knew where that fight was going to lead.

That was yet another thing she forced herself to forget as she riffled through the very same storage compartment. The only distinct feelings regarding the event left were the lack of air in her lungs as the claustrophobia set in, and the brown knit sweater she clung onto as she buried her face deeper into the darkness.

Maria couldn't imagine her father ever wearing it, save for the foggy image of him at the winter solstice when she was four. She had no issue now about slipping it on and claiming it as her own. It was a strange need to have something of her father's that wasn't inherently evil. By the time she got back to her rooms, Arabella was awake with her own jeans and sweater on.

Maria leaned against the door frame, crossing her legs and folding her arms. "Hey," she felt was a good start to whatever reconciliation they needed.

Arabella adjusted the cuffs on her white chunky sweater as she softly replied, "Hello."

Both of them stayed put for a few seconds before Maria headed towards her chair, awkwardly plucking her leather jacket from the armrest. It was big enough that it fit over her father's sweater, and it helped her feel like she was dressed like herself again. They didn't say anything to each other as they left the west wing and headed downstairs.

'♥♥♥'

The tension eased a bit as they began playing small carnival games. Maria won Arabella a stuffed animal after landing three rings over some long neck glass bottles, breaking one accidentally. Arabella didn't mind the minor destruction so long as she could keep her stuffed otter.

"You can make it up to me by both not being mad at me… and being present for the sword fighting tournament," Maria said with a wince.

Arabella stopped in her tracks. "Maria. The next event I'm going to be planning is your funeral."

Maria laughed with flushed cheeks. The cold could have disguised it, but the way she tried to play it off gave her true feelings away. "You're the only person I'd want on the job."

Arabella grabbed Maria's arm and dragged her to the food stand selling funnel cake. "Don't be cute," Arabella rolled her eyes.

"I'll be wearing safety armor, and going against wimps. I'll be fine! Plus, I've been sword fighting since I was young," Maria tried to convince Arabella while circling around her. Arabella ignored her as she ordered her food.

"You've been smoking since you were young. That'll kill you too," Arabella made a sour expression, popping funnel cake into her mouth as if to replace the taste of tobacco.

"If you paid attention, you'd know that I've been trying to quit, despite the stress you cause me," Maria gently nudged her. She waited patiently like a puppy for Arabella's approval.

Arabella grasped Maria's face, squishing her cheeks as she dragged her down to eye level, giving her a kiss. "It's been established I'm the only one who takes away your stress, so maybe hush."

"Speaking of stress…we should talk about last night," Arabella eventually said as Maria nibbled on whatever was left of the funnel cake. Maria tensed, as she wanted to avoid that conversation at all costs. "It's fine, Bella."

"I know it isn't though. There's a reason I was all alone on the Island… no one stays when they see that side of me. What's worse is I know no one should stick through my storms. I'm just afraid, Maria." Arabella picked at her lips.

Maria raised a brow as she set the plate down, to the side. "I'm not going anywhere, sweetie. These aren't exactly normal circumstances we are under at the moment."

"Still, what am I if not the person meant to get you through it?" Arabella inquired, seeing her own blurry reflection through Maria's dark eyes. That's how it always felt for Arabella nowadays.

Maria considered doing what was right, which was squashing their issues then and there. Arabella was dramatic, but could recognize and talk out that toxicity. However, Maria shut down in those moments, preferring to act like nothing was wrong at all, or lying that things were fine to avoid any extra emotional energy.

Truth was, Maria wasn't over it. In the moment, she considered screaming back and telling Arabella to grow the fuck up. She considered telling Arabella that she was acting like a self-victimizing freak, just like everyone on the Island thought her to be, knowing it would sting just as deep as the insult she gave. Maria, however, did love Arabella and knew that if she said that she would be alone for the rest of her life—but then that tempted her even more. It would have cost her a lot more emotional energy to do that, so she took the more mature road and let it go.

That, and Maria could acknowledge even with those petty thoughts, she would never have the stomach to actually hurt Arabella like that. Those thoughts alone made her hate looking at her reflection, made her remember a time when surviving was a war against every other person in the castle. She feared the worst, which was that both of the women she loved became ruined the day they decided to love her, and if her ego was to be let loose, she would be the one doing the ruining.

Maria silently took Arabella's hand, content to hold it the entire time they walked around the minor attractions, which was until noon. They passed by Aquilla who was sitting in a water tank, laughing every time a child hit the target, dunking him in. Most days he was quiet and somber, still mulling over Margaret's death.

"So, Margaret appeared to you again," Maria pointed out, still holding Arabella's hand.

"Took you long enough to bring that up," Arabella smiled. It was a sad smile that didn't quite meet her eyes. "She still doesn't quite believe she is dead. To her, time isn't moving so she isn't understanding, even though she is appearing in different rooms."

Maria nodded. "She likely thinks she was walking around, forgetting where she was going before she arrived. It's foggy."

"How will she find peace then? What happens to my abilities to see ghosts when she does?"

Maria didn't have the answers to that. Her gift was rare, and as far as Maria knew, people had it until they died and joined their ghostly friends. That's because finding peace wasn't as easy as simply deciding to do so.

"I don't know, but the rules still stand. The ghosts will remain to have no effect on you. I know it's an unsettling feeling like they're watching you, but they aren't. Think of how many of them watch you now."

Arabella reflected on how she never really made eye contact with the dead roaming the castle. In fact, only the dramatic ones who show their death marks are the ones who make it obvious they are dead. The ghosts don't usually acknowledge the living other than Brando, and Elizabeth, with her creepy remarks about moisturizer.

"I want apple cider," Maria changed the subject, pulling Arabella to the donut stand. The surrounding area smelt like cinnamon and a chunk of heaven. Maria almost teared up because of the ambience.

For a second, Maria was little again. Her dad held her and handed her some cider in a kiddie cup, as well as a donut hole. It was later in the day then, and the lights of all the attractions illuminated her father. Her mother played with her hair as she took little bites.

Maria took a small sip from her cup to hide the fact she was tearing up. When Arabella asked about it, she said it was the steam.

"It's about that time. Let's go see what Cienfuegos is up to," Maria proposed. She wondered where he was in that memory. Wondered if he was with his parents, missing those little moments of content as well.

Unsurprisingly, he and Thoman were participating in the pie eating contest. At the moment of Maria's arrival, every contestant but those two tapped out. They were going in, pile driving handfuls of filling into their mouth. Their movements were sluggish whilst staring each other down.

Aquilla approached Maria, drying off since finishing his shift in the tank as he chuckled, "Thoman's going to have a heart attack if he doesn't slow down."

Cienfuegos refused to relent as well, mocking Thoman with his mouth full. "Give it up you old geezer. If you get any more bloated, you'll pop."

"I have been eating pies since before you were born, child. I won this contest five years in a row!" Thoman rebutted breathlessly.

Out of nowhere, Cienfuegos turned green. For a second, Maria thought he was silently choking so she jogged forward. Cienfuegos turned to the side, where Maria was approaching, and vomited.

Thoman slammed his hand on the table, shoveling one more good handful of apple pie into his mouth before jumping up in celebration. His face quickly turned to disappointment when he saw Jessie rubbing Cienfuegos' back, rather than celebrating his win. He let out a low cough before accepting his trophy and exiting the stage.

"I dislike you greatly, sir," Maria quipped at Cienfuegos, covered in his vomit.

'♥♥♥'

Maria helped haul Cienfuegos to his chambers before rushing to her own to take a bath. "It's because you wore that ugly sweater," Brando shook his head in disappointment.

"I surely don't own any like this, and neither did my mom. It's like it was the only family knit sweater, now ruined." Maria spoke in a hushed whisper; just in case she was still in earshot of the guards at the base of the wing.

"Thank God, it looks—"

Maria shut her door in his face. He didn't reappear inside as she threw off the ruined clothes and leaped into the bath. Arabella stayed with Aquilla, enjoying some more funnel cake as they bonded. Maria understood that she needed, now more than ever, to spend time with her dad.

Given the impromptu alone time, Maria decided it would be good to crash on her bed and take a nap for once. She got a good three hours of extra sleep in. When she woke, the sun was still out. She dressed in black pants and a flannel from Brando's room, considering she would have to change into her armor within the hour anyways.

As she was preparing to leave her room, Abigail walked in, dressed in the courtly attire that was relevant seven years ago, right around the time she left InFiamma. It made her look like she was a ghost, wearing exactly what she would have back then. Abigail's corset was a blush color lined with gold. Her dress was short, and her sleeves were off the shoulder.

Maria couldn't stomach looking at her first love knowing all the secrets surrounding their relationship. She couldn't face the guilt of never noticing what was happening in private, when she wasn't around.

Abigail read it all on Maria's face. "I do not blame you, Maria. Not for a second." She took a step forward, but

Maria retreated. "I did a lot of things in Eminence for a variety of reasons. However, while you are imagining a very specific scenario that puts me in a devastating light, it was not being Eugene's mistress that has traumatized me."

"I call bullshit," Maria insisted, shaking her head. "As you said, you hated every day you had to serve that prick."

"I promise you, if it was that, I would have ripped out his throat with my teeth and shown him a real wolf," Abigail asserted. "However, my fear of Eugene stems from something deeper that I am not going to talk about."

"Want to talk about the deals you were making with my father then? Taking you out of the Mistress Institution just so you could be given to me like a toy? All the while I was under the assumption we would be married. Were you taking after Jessie's mother?" Maria's eyes lit ablaze.

Abigail thought that Maria surely must have had some audacity to bring up their engagement. "Heard that argument with your new girlfriend last night. Wanna talk about that?" she retorted.

"Want to talk about how juice got all over my girlfriend's dress?" Maria snapped back.

"Obviously, I did it. I don't feel bad about it. Yet, I don't assume you're Elias. So, any form of punishment doesn't scare me. Can Arabella say the same?" Abigail interrogated, jumping onto Maria's bed and crossing her legs.

Maria clenched down her jaw. In the early days, she obviously considered Arabella might presume she was like her father. That was before they got emotionally involved though. All of Maria's emotional wards that aimed to drive Arabella away in the name of self-preservation were dismantled immediately. She assumed Arabella didn't worry about it.

"I'm not going to think myself into a ditch over speculation when I can just ask her about it," Maria remarked, holding a maturity over her inner teen that wanted to self-destruct over the idea.

"You didn't ask her about it last night when she threw your trauma in your face, using it against you. It's almost like that wasn't the first time," Abigail sat up, putting her hands in her lap.

Maria looked Abigail in the eyes and knew she wasn't inquiring because she wanted to scheme, but because she was still Abigail. She still cared. Maria was still Maria, too. Nothing about them changed, except Maria was tired and didn't care to sort through her enemies. She was her own worst one at the end of the day.

Maria walked out of her room, once again leaving Abigail behind.

'♥♥♥'

The carousel was operated by a man cranking a lever the size of two humans. It should have required more than two people considering that, but the man was muscular enough to slam his body weight down on it with ease.

It was also especially easy for the man to operate when just Arabella was on the ride, eating an elote. As the ride was spinning, facing away from the operator, a figure hopped onto the horse next to Arabella.

"What leaves a beautiful maiden like you all alone at such an event?" Eugene asked in his pompous accent.

Arabella took a big bite out of her corn, looking Eugene up and down before swallowing hard. "I enjoy my own company," was her only reply as the ride slowed down. When it came to a halt, she hopped off her horse and casually strode off.

Eugene watched wearily before traipsing after Arabella, leaving the operator wondering where he spawned from. Arabella could sense him behind her, but she did not care to turn around.

"So, where's your threatening queen?" Eugene inquired when he decided to stop being creepy from a distance, catching up to Arabella's side.

"Probably getting some much deserved rest," was all Arabella gave away, immediately regretting the hint that Maria could be in her room.

"I don't doubt you can take care of yourself. I'm happy Maria doesn't worry about you suffocatingly," Eugene supplied, his lip quirking upward. He looked absolutely nothing like Maria or Lucille for that matter, and whoever his father is, was never relevant enough for the council to investigate.

Arabella considered what he said though, and the fact that Maria, especially in the beginning, would've put her on indefinite house arrest if it meant keeping her safe. They've talked about it since then and set the clear boundary that excluding and controlling Arabella would never be tolerated going forward.

"I hope if Maria ever decides to make you an official consort, and if you have an heir, she continues to be that relaxed," Eugene pondered as they walked aimlessly.

"Have an heir?" Arabella scoffed before it dawned on her that it may be expected of her, the way it was expected of Odette, and every woman in the Fiamma line before Maria was born. "But… that's obviously not possible."

"Well, yes, but InFiamma doesn't operate by blood purity like some nations, such as my own. If you adopt the child, it would be recognized as Maria's heir because that child would legally be Maria's," Eugene explained. So far, the rulers of InFiamma haven't had to exact that, but with the decline of fertility with the men on the throne, the clause was an insurance.

Arabella surely wasn't going to drop her project to become a mother, related to her by blood or not. She was sure she'd love an adopted child all the same, but that wasn't the issue. To raise a child instead of chasing her dreams… Arabella got queasy.

She assumed that was Eugene's intention though, to sow discomfort in their relationship for whatever reason. Maria had never mentioned children to her once, which meant she was surely leaving that problem to Cienfuegos.

"What are you playing at?" Arabella sighed, glancing sideward at Eugene.

"I'm not trying anything," he put his hands up. His accent made him so non-threatening, Arabella almost believed him. Almost. When Arabella didn't budge with her assessing glance, he continued. "Truthfully, I wanted to talk to you about Abigail. She isn't what she says she is," he sighed. That piqued her interest. Arabella grabbed his arm and dragged him to the side of the building.

"Spill," Arabella demanded, pinning Eugene against a cobblestone wall.

He put his hand up, commanding someone to hold their fire from above. Arabella looked up to see Rainie, her bow aimed from the top of the castle. Arabella didn't think there was roof access in the castle, which alarmed her. She looked back at Eugene with a cold stare before letting him go.

Eugene smoothed out his jacket as he explained. "Abigail offered to be my mistress when my mother's living stipend wasn't enough for her. I gave her jewels, finery, everything but my heart," he fidgeted as he thought. In that way, he and Maria were similar.

"I fell in love, and she hated that. Before Abigail ran back to Maria, she murdered my lover. I'm afraid that if she doesn't get Maria back, she'll come for you next," he paused, putting his thumbnail in his mouth as he met Arabella's assessing gaze.

Before Arabella could respond, the castle bells rang throughout the grounds. The sword tournament would start soon, and Arabella knew how much it meant to Maria. Arabella dragged Eugene with her.

"You will tell me everything, in detail, but I can't miss this."

Chapter 31

Maria made sure Cienfuegos was done being sick before ripping him out of bed. Jessie was already in the tent outside on medic duty. There were multiple fights happening before Maria's main event, so she took her sweet time getting into her armor, having a coffee, and joking around with Cienfuegos. He wasn't on until right before she was, so they had time to kill.

Naturally, Cienfuegos won fifteen seconds into his match. He knocked down Rainie, who talked a big game when she originally challenged him. She hit the dirt so hard it created a dust cloud around her body. It happened so quick it took the crowd a moment to register Cienfuegos had his sword to Rainie's chest, putting more pressure than would be considered sportsman-like.

The cheers for his victory were Maria's cue to head out into the makeshift sand pit, which was smaller than the one in the castle. She arrived as Cienfuegos took his final bow. He passed Maria, giving her a fist bump before she was to collect her own opponent. Unsurprisingly, Rainie could not handle rejection or failure, as she jumped right back into the pit.

"I'd like to challenge Maria!" Rainie screamed informally, a deliberate outburst of disrespect. Maria rolled her eyes, disappointed that the fight would be over before she could even get a workout in.

Maria scanned the crowd before they began. She saw Aquilla in the third row of the bleachers, but no Arabella. Thoman was sitting next to Aquilla, whispering something in his ear while visibly troubled. Maria decided to ignore it as she unsheathed her sword. Rainie's sword was an ugly looking object, slightly shorter than Majesty, boring Maria even further. "Let's get this over with, storm cloud."

Cienfuegos let out a cheer somewhere off to the side, and the crowd followed suit. There were about five hundred people in attendance, spanning across nationalities and social classes. It was about the same number of people projected to see Cadence's circus.

Maria toyed with Rainie, wearing her out with a cat and mouse tactic. Luckily, Maria did find pleasure in the match, tripping and teasing Rainie for a good two minutes while the Eminence commander got fired up. When Rainie gave a big swing of her sword, Maria ducked, kicking Rainie off balance. Once again, Rainie hit the floor.

"Pathetic," Maria laughed as she looked at the crowd with amusement. At that moment, all joy drained from Maria's face. She spotted Arabella at last, talking intently with Eugene as she rested her hand on his shoulder, the distance in between them too close for comfort.

Maria was so wrapped up in the scene before her, that she forgot all about the match. Rainie had time to get up and shove her blade right through Maria's shoulder. The crowd gasped as Aquilla and Thoman flew out of their seats. It didn't matter though, because even as Maria fell to her knees and Cienfuegos apprehended Rainie, Arabella did not once take her eyes off of Eugene.

'♥♥♥'

Maria was bandaged up by Jessie in the tent, who was not only trying to stop the bleeding, but was also plucking the bits of Maria's armor out of her flesh.

The sound of Cadence's circus could be heard from the tent acres away, mixed with muffled applause. Varying colors of purple, blue, and white illuminated outside. All anyone in the political occupation could wonder, was what natural sourced generator could do that? Faint bits of artificial light occasionally swept through the bottom of the tent.

"How did Rainie's blade do that?" Cienfuegos panicked, pacing the room hyperventilating. "Why weren't you paying attention you asshole?!" he screamed at his cousin.

"The blade… my father is investigating it right now I'm sure," Jessie supplied calmly, working with steady hands.

"Arabella was with Eugene…" Maria didn't need to say more as she bit down on a rag. Jessie found the deepest piece. "Please go get her," Maria begged in agony.

Aquilla walked into the tent, face furious as Arabella followed behind him, tears flooding her eyes when she saw the scene before her.

"We have to move Maria to her chambers," Jessie said, putting his tools down. "Her artery was nicked. I've slowed the bleeding, but we don't have all day. I need to operate somewhere where she won't be moved again while she recovers."

Aquilla and Cienfuegos nodded to each other before rushing to Maria's side. She was going pale.

"Arabella, take the alcohol and saline in my bag and cleanse as much of her room as you can before we get there. I can't operate if it's unsanitary, she'll die for sure," Jessie insisted, keeping pressure on Maria's wound as Aquilla and Cienfuegos hoisted her up.

Arabella quickly obeyed, grabbing the supplies and bolting from the tent. She ran through the crowds of people muttering of their queen's devastating loss. All the rides and their lights blurring together as she sprinted. For a split second, before entering the castle, she looked up at the sky. The sun was gone now, and with all the lights going, she could not see the stars.

When Arabella entered Maria's chambers, she started throwing things off tables and cleansing them to make way for Jessie's medical instruments. She almost didn't notice the lump figure under the covers before she threw them off.

"Ugh, it's cold," said Abigail, sleeping in a short dress barely covering her thighs, or her breasts, for that matter. She sleepily registered Arabella before saying, "I must have knocked out when Maria left."

Arabella staggered back before saying, "Maria is bleeding out as we speak. So get your ass up, they're bringing her here!"

Abigail instantly became alert, throwing the blankets off the bed and removing the sheets. "Clean everything while I change the linen," Abigail said with intense focus. They made good time considering Maria was being hauled in less than a minute later.

"Everyone, out while I operate!" Jessie ordered, excluding the medical team behind him. Arabella was ushered out by her father, Abigail ushered out by Cienfuegos.

They waited in Odette's former chambers for news, but Arabella was never that good at waiting. She slipped out of the room and made her way downstairs.

'♥♥♥'

"Rainie didn't mean it. She accidentally jabbed when she meant to swipe. She hit her head twice," Eugene defended as Arabella wore a face of pure wrath.

"She stabbed my girlfriend with a sword from hell," Arabella recalled as she made to walk away. She didn't intentionally find Eugene, but he was waiting at the base of the west wing for updates on Maria.

"I promise she will be punished when we get home, but she's all I have left in my family. She's my half-sister on my father's side. Please don't let them kill her," Eugene whispered, tears welling in his eyes. Arabella remained still at the mention of someone else having a sibling. In InFiamma, rarely anyone does. Her grief over Margaret was one that couldn't be shared with anyone she'd recently met. They'd never truly understand it.

In some way, Arabella saw Maria's shared loneliness in Eugene. If it was reversed, and someone tried to take Cienfuegos from Maria in those early days of her reign, it would have caused an immediate war.

"I'll talk to my father," was all Arabella promised, using her most diplomatic voice before returning upstairs. The guards let her, but gave tense glares to Eugene. By the time she got back, Maria was out of surgery.

"Brethren, thou art scaring the maidens," Cienfuegos joked in old English while Abigail sat by Maria's side. She was laughing so hard at whatever they were talking about, that she was doubling over. Maria winced with pain in between chuckles. "Brethren, thou can't procure the maidens," she breathed out.

"Fair," Cienfuegos smiled as he surrendered, patting her ankle.

"What about that time we snuck out to the gardens, and the maid caught us, and—" both Abigail and Maria burst into a fit of laughter, causing Maria to arch off the bed. She never laughed like that with Arabella.

Arabella gave a little knock at the threshold of the door, making the room fall silent.

"Oh, hey," Maria said as Arabella walked in, standing off to the side of the bed.

"How are you feeling?" Arabella asked awkwardly.

"Fine," Maria would've shrugged it off, if she wasn't sewn like Frankenstein. "I'm doing a rematch in the morning, so it's all sorted."

"You're in a sling, Maria!" Arabella looked up at the ceiling, to any god as if to accuse them of negligence.

"Well, then that just means it'll be fair this time," Maria laughed, and Cienfuegos covered his mouth trying to suppress his urge to do so. "Rainie will be given one of our swords, so it's fine."

Aquilla entered with some soup for Maria. "It is best if it is done this way. Maria was distracted, but anyone could see that she was going to win that."

Thoman entered behind him, also adding to the conversation. "Maria needs to display strength now more than ever, lest people get any ideas. Payje already published the news in her silly paper." Hours have passed since the incident, but it didn't feel like it to any of them. It felt like mere minutes.

"If this is what it takes to get peace out of the situation, fine. Just don't die," Arabella pinched the bridge of her nose. She then looked at Abigail and gave an irritated expression. First, she waited for her father and Thoman to leave so they could deal with maintaining the court and military, before forcing that expression into neutrality. "Eugene says hello, by the way. He's busy grieving that lover of his, but he sends his best."

Abigail squirmed with unease, and Maria furrowed her brows. "You guys' shared life stories?"

"As much as you likely shared with Abigail while you two were up here getting reacquainted," Arabella smiled. "When I left him a moment ago, he was most troubled by your wounds. He also wishes you quick healing."

Cienfuegos tensed so hard a vein nearly popped from his forehead. "You went to see a political figure of Eminence unannounced, without permission?"

"Do I need your permission to see a friend?" Arabella asked with false confusion. "I do believe that I stated my boundaries on that matter."

"Of course not," Maria smiled back. "By all means, spend as much time around my eerily pale cousin. Getting as close as you were when I saw you at my match. He seems like great company."

"Of course!" Arabella parroted back. "If me and him start fucking, it'll also take out questions of who our donor will be once I'm expected to raise your heirs," she jabbed back with false enthusiasm. Maria sat up too hard for her state, becoming dizzy as she groaned in pain.

"Oh my word," Jessie whispered as he walked in. The poor man looked scandalized by the conversation. He sat next to Maria, checking her stitches. Cienfuegos leaned over and gave him a kiss on his jaw.

"If you insist on fighting one handed tomorrow, maybe stop moving so much tonight. Conserve some strength," Jessie passively suggested.

"I'll stay with you tonight," Abigail told Maria. "Arabella, you can go fuck Eugene. I've got it here. Fair warning, he does have weird interests in bed. You have a weird face though, so it'll work out just fine."

Arabella once again, nearly blacked out from rage. She looked at Maria, who tilted her head back. Maria half laughed, half scoffed with disgust. "Just go."

Abigail gave Arabella a sweet smile. Arabella stormed out of the room, tears forming in her eyes. She waited until she was back in her father's chambers before she let out a scream.

'♥♥♥'

Everyone crowded around the training pit to watch the rematch. Maria was wearing a pair of black sweatpants, and a black loose crop top. Her breasts were bound with bandages instead of a bra, given her injury. Her hair was combed and placed into a loose braid that fell down her spine.

Rainie, on the other hand, was in the same clothes she was apprehended in. Arabella doubted she was given dinner, or the courtesy of a toothbrush before she was shoved into the ring.

Arabella was told the match wasn't going to be until later, around the same time as the night prior. It was Payje who slipped up once again, asking Arabella if she wanted to accompany her. Payje inevitably wandered off to report, taking her new career seriously. That left Arabella watching from the back, still fuming over her and Maria's fight. She was also irate at her father, who let her believe that the rematch was at a different time. It felt like she had no one, as everyone she loved was betraying her.

Eugene, unsurprisingly, joined her.

"I suspect once Maria has had her fun, this pissing contest will be the end of whatever this tension is," Arabella sighed to the King of Eminence. The King of Cadence was, once again, taking his bets at the back of the ring. He made a small fortune visiting InFiamma just on bets alone, fueled by the kingdom's dysfunctionality.

Rainie looked at Eugene with something in her eyes that felt intrusive to watch, like she was sharing a secret with him. Her eyes turned sad as she gave a deep bow. He nodded his head in permission for her to fight back with all she had.

"You are not responsible for the sins of those you love," Eugene confided abruptly, which confused Arabella. His face turned dark and moody as he crossed his arms.

Hardly a second passed before the fight began. Rainie gave her best effort. Maria had multiple advantages, her height, arm reach, and training. Rainie, despite her own skill, still found herself backed into a corner. So, she did something only a wolf would do. She grabbed Maria's hand and pulled, sinking her teeth into Maria's only good arm. Rainie hoped with Maria incapacitated, they truly would become evenly matched. That proved not to be the case.

Maria kicked at Rainie multiple times to get her off. Rainie buckled to the ground as Maria's foot smashed into her hip. Maria had no idea why Rainie was stalling, thinking she could possibly win, but when she made eye contact with Maria from the ground, Maria hesitated. The feral rage in Rainie's eyes, Maria was no stranger to.

She allowed Rainie the dignity of standing and getting a few noble swings in. Unfortunately, Rainie's life swiftly ended when Maria dodged her final hit, and swung Majesty like a bat, cleanly decapitating Rainie at the base of her neck.

Arabella covered her mouth to stifle a scream. Maria had never killed anyone before, to her knowledge. Yet she just did it one handed, like she was chopping wood. Like it was easy.

"I see going for the throat is InFiamma's way," Eugene mumbled. "Very well. Wolves know how to go for the jugular as well," he ominously whispered.

Arabella looked up at him, eyes wide and hand still covering her mouth. Eugene took that hand and held it. "Should you decide to find yourself wanting more, you will always be welcome as an ally. You, and the island of Gloucester. We, unlike InFiamma, would give your culture freedom, while still providing resources in trade."

Arabella rarely heard anyone call the Island by its independent name, but that impression and courtesy stuck with Arabella long after Eugene let her hand go, and left.

Maria took a swig of pumpkin beer as she flicked the blood off her sword with an unimpressed stance. Fabian joined Maria, patting her on her unharmed shoulder, beer flying out of Maria's cup with the impact.

"More circus time!" Fabian yelled, in which everyone from court members, villagers, to Cadence's people, cheered at. Arabella noticed no one from Eminence came to the rematch. They must have been prepared to evacuate at a moment's notice, if they hadn't already.

Arabella strutted up to Maria, tears falling down her face. She never made it though, because before she could reach Maria, Abigail was cupping Maria's face, giving her a quick kiss. Maria jolted back at the surprise, but it didn't seem to offend Abigail. Everyone let out more cheers as the crowd vacated to enjoy the circus. Maria lingered behind.

"I didn't know she was going to kiss me," Maria winced, not making eye contact with Arabella. She must have known Arabella was standing there the entire time.

"I didn't know you planned to become a murderer today," Arabella replied, disgusted.

"Don't," Maria began laughing maniacally. She took a step back, putting her cup down at the edge of the pit.

"You have the nerve to laugh?" Arabella spat, bridging the gap between the two.

"I'm laughing so I don't lose my fucking mind, Bella," Maria chuckled. "I just KILLED somebody! I cut off her fucking head!" Maria grabbed her side, laughs turning to light sobs.

"Whose idea was THAT!?" Arabella enunciated back, forcing Maria to look at her, to see the emotions she laid bare. Maria couldn't stomach the horrified expression on Arabella's face, coated in genuine terror.

"Everybody's," Maria shrugged, trying not to hyperventilate. "Thoman first, then Cienfuegos. Even your dad agreed."

"I'm sure your other girlfriend was on board then? Being a seasoned planner in the homicide department?" Arabella scoffed, letting Maria go.

"I don't understand why this is still a conversation," Maria gritted, taking a step back. "I loved her. Is that a crime? That I was a whole person before I became a shell of a human? Was it the emptiness that you loved?!" Maria yelled, tears welling in her eyes. "How is this, right now, still about her?"

"I need to know that you understand the position I'm in lately. Your ex came back from the dead. Your *first love*. It isn't about her still loving you. I want to know through all of this if you even still see me? Have you seen the agony, or have you only seen the tasks I complete at the end of the day?" Arabella pleaded.

"I see you, Bella! I don't give a shit if this court is entertained or not!" Maria exasperated, throwing her good arm up into the air. That statement sent shock waves through Arabella, the feeling of dread that she truly had already outserved her usefulness. "Why don't my actions speak loud enough? Have I dishonored you at all since her return?" Maria proceeded.

"Yes," Arabella began, holding her arms as if she was cold. "You made me feel like my feelings were childish. I can't be like you, Maria. I need affirmations constantly. I can't compartmentalize like you do. You haven't talked to me about how you're feeling either, so I'm left guessing," she confessed in a more hushed voice, like she had been too afraid to let this argument come this far into the open. Maria was silent, but the way she straightened her posture and adjusted her jaw, her guilt was clear.

"Now, you've kept the true time of this match from me, as well as your plans to take a life. This is more than just that, as everyone in my life, my father, Cienfuegos, and Jessie, have all shut me out, too. I have been alienated, Maria," Arabella finished, smoothing the palm of her hand over her cheekbone.

"What would you have said to this? If this is how we originally addressed our issues, maybe things would have been different. I admit I never voluntarily open up, but you initiated us fucking our issues out. Don't choose methods of coping you're not suited for," Maria said blandly. "With your comments about fucking Eugene, I couldn't trust that you wouldn't go do just that and tell him my plans for today."

"It was *I* you couldn't trust?" Arabella gasped horrified. "I have done *everything* for you since I stepped foot on this fucking continent Maria!" Arabella's voice broke with the force of her sobs as tears flowed from her eyes. Maria never saw Arabella look so hurt, or so broken before. Even when those who have taunted Arabella her entire life made a mockery out of her, it didn't appear to land as hard as Maria's comment did in that moment.

"I'm sorry," Maria said, but Arabella's cries deepened as she hunched over with her head in her hands. "Baby, I'm sorry," Maria whispered.

"I just wish you talked to me," Arabella sobbed. "I know I have been awful to you, if just to invoke a response, and that makes me just as complicit—"

Maria cut Arabella off by pulling her into a deep kiss, placing her good hand on the back of Arabella's head to deepen it. The kiss was one that gave them both nauseatingly intense butterflies they hadn't felt since their first one. It was because there was an equal risk of rejection once again. When they pulled away, Maria kept her hand tangled in Arabella's hair.

"All I know is I love you, Arabella, and saying something so huge with blood on my hands corrupts that very sentiment, but I am a queen and blood will *always* be on my hands. This blood will wash off and be changed out with someone else's, but you alone will consistently be in my heart, until I'm dead. It was never about Abigail, or even this fucked up kingdom. It has always been you."

Arabella started crying again. "That's all I wanted to hear, Maria." She leaned in, giving Maria another kiss. "I love you, too."

Brando watched from the entrance of the pit, tears of his own falling down his face. He turned around, ready to do his last walk through the castle.

"Are you scared?" Margaret Marella asked, appearing at his side.

"No. I'm just really sad to be leaving her behind, and for what I'll have to do to her when the time comes," he replied honestly to the child.

Margaret nodded her head. "I am too, but I find solace knowing my sister will live a long life yet."

Brando gave a deep sigh, wishing he could say the same for Maria. His comfort came in the form of a question. What is death when you can never truly die?

Chapter 32

Arabella and Maria spent the rest of the night together, despite Maria's injury. Because of this, Maria thought it would be amusing to remain on the bottom, while fully planning to make up her tarnished image in the only way she knew how.

Usually, the sex between them was a sport, something they'd be going at for hours until one was ready to pass out. There was a point proven at the end of the climax. It was a dance, a battle, and a gamble.

Tonight was different, and Maria never experienced anything like it before. The need for control always drove her relationships, for better or for worse. But the skin-to-skin bliss recently exchanged wasn't war, it was a prayer. It was giving in to what the self-sabotaging voice in the back of her head told her was a sin. It was surrender.

It was the words that slipped off her tongue as they leveled in their high, looking up at the goddess before her, a breathy whisper,

"I love you."

The white flag her soul needed to end the war that constantly raged inside of her.

Arabella looked down at Maria, who was marveling at the way her chest was heaving as she sat atop her, Maria stroking her side with one hand, gripping her hip. When Arabella uttered no reply, so deep in thought, Maria's eyes met hers.

Arabella leaned forward, placing a soft kiss on Maria's lips.

"I think I'll always love you."

Maria didn't take it as the warning it was, as she had never experienced loved like that before. Not like the way Arabella loved her. She didn't know once obtained, it could have the power to maim from inside the relationship. To kill. So, she cracked a smile, a genuine one.

It was then Arabella noticed Maria's slightly crooked premolar, the bags under her eyes. She wasn't the ruler of a kingdom, infinite and all-consuming. She was just like everyone else.

Chapter 33

Arabella pretended to fall asleep as Maria played with her hair. She knew Maria was unconscious once the motion ceased, which she took her cue to climb out of bed. Slipping on a pale white nightgown, she snuck out of Maria's chambers for some air.

It was cold, but Arabella didn't feel like going back into the room to grab a coat, lest she wake Maria up. The events of the last few months weighed heavy not just on her mind, but her heart. She wasn't sure she was going to find anywhere in the castle that would change that, but she thought it would be good exercise to try.

In the southern wing of the castle, parallel to the library, sat dusty old offices that went down a narrow hallway. That portion of the castle outlived its use centuries ago, remaining unused. Sometimes in the rooms closer to the library, small gatherings and book clubs would take place. Still, the electricity did not extend to the south offices, other than the library, which used up all those resources.

Arabella wandered down the south wing hallway until she reached what she anticipated would be the final office in the hall. She wasn't met with an office door, rather a stone alcove that had intricately designed mahogany double doors. The door handle itself was dusty, evident that no one had used the room for as long as the extra office spaces themselves.

She allowed her curiosity to take the lead, as it was in a much better state than the rest of her consciousness at the moment. The sight she was met with had her breath catch in her throat. It was a church—that much was clear. There were pews in a line, and in front of large stained glass windows, there was a weird looking lowercase *t*. At least, that was how Arabella perceived it.

Assuming it was to worship a deity with a name starting with *t*, when she reached the small dais she knelt, just as Maria had mentioned in the hallway one time.

"I always heard it was proper form to take worship on one's knees."

That was when she allowed herself deep, meditative breaths that fogged the air due to the chill in the room. Her lack of religious knowledge did not help her at that moment, but she gave confessional her best shot.

"Holy God, whose name starts with *t*, I do not know what you represent but if you have a range of authority, it is much needed at the moment. I know little of you, but much of kings and queens. It is said that a royal line is a divine one, so if you love Maria Fiamma, know I love her too," Arabella started off shakily, confessing in more of a whisper, with a tone of uncertainty.

She began to feel a rippling dread as she allowed herself to consider the root of her issues. That would be harder for her to admit, but before this old-world god she knew there was no other hope.

"Truth is, it has been really hard loving someone whose position is so magnificent and all-consuming when I don't have a personal base strong enough to put up a fight. Everything I do is for her name, her reputation, and in the process, I find myself competing with the person I love. I envy her, her position, her ex-girlfriend… When I look inward and try to find something I can give Maria that no one else can, I'm left with no answer. Who am I, God? I don't want to just be the lover of Maria Fiamma. It isn't fair for either of us."

From the top of the dais, there was a podium holding an open book. Arabella wasn't sure where the sudden draft came from, but the air got chillier. The breeze flipped the book pages which piqued Arabella's interest. Not necessarily for the spiritual element, but due to the likeliness that the book was old. She rounded the stage and climbed its steps, approaching the book with caution.

Arabella smoothed her hands over the pages which were still pristine despite their age. Her breath hitched when she saw the entire page was just one giant painting of the sea.

"I always hated religious fanatics," Brando said from behind Arabella, positioned right in front of the cross as he leaned back against it.

Arabella spun around, clutching her chest. "You didn't need to sneak up on me," she whispered. She turned to examine the pages again for any hint on what religion was being presented. "What religion is this?"

"A variation," Brando began, kicking off the cross as he approached. "The church is Catholic, not that you understand what that means, but you are likely wondering about the book anyways."

Arabella looked around, and despite her curiosity about the room she was in, the book felt more relevant. She gave him a nod, flipping some more through its contents.

"In the beginning of the fall, there were many types of disasters, as you already know. That book was the last of a religious group that waited for InFiamma's God, the Sun God, to battle the God of the Sea. It stems from the water taking over entire continents at the same time the sun was scorching bits of the earth," Brando explained as he stood shoulder to shoulder with Arabella, leaning over the podium.

"In later myths, the Sun God and the Sea God fell in love with each other. Destroying the earth was their only way to ensure that nothing would stand in between them again. Some say that they wanted to destroy each other, and insisted that was their love language. Regardless, there is space and matter, so no matter how much gets destroyed, there will always be space keeping them apart," Brando finished, glancing over to assess Arabella's reaction to the information. She was playing with her garnet necklace as she stared into the painting of the sea.

"Why are you here?" Arabella mustered up the courage to ask, disregarding Brando's fairytales.

"You asked for a god, God is busy. I'm here to tell you what I know. If you stay…" Brando hesitated, planning out his words perfectly against a million variations. "You will be the end of Maria, that much is true. You must go home to the Island, as you already suspected was necessary. Stay here, and the sun will swallow the sea."

Arabella felt something drop in her chest as her knees wobbled. It was then she knew she was kidding herself the entire time she was reinventing her image in InFiamma. Above that, submitting Gloucester to the mercy of InFiamma was eradicating not just Arabella's personality, but her homeland's culture in favor of everything that is the exact opposite.

"When?" Arabella demanded the answer dryly. She turned to Brando who regarded her with anticipation, like he saw this play out a thousand times over.

"Tonight," Brando replied with a stone wall behind his eyes. If he was a walking soul, Arabella did not know what lay behind that wall. She felt in her bones she did not want to know.

Brando, for the first time, left Arabella with his own bit of advice. "Fret not, Arabella. You will become a warrior queen in your own right someday."

'♥♥♥'

"You're making the right choice, you know," Margaret Marella encouraged as she spawned behind her sister.

Arabella slowly turned around to face her deceased sibling. "It feels right, but so wrong. My heart breaks but my soul feels like this is what I'm meant to do," Arabella confided. She intended for it to be a small rest. A retreat to gather her thoughts and refine her ambitions.

"Maybe that's because your soul knows Maria is the reason I'm dead," Margaret shrugged. Arabella assessed her sister with wide eyes, like a deer in front of bright lights.

"What?" Arabella asked with disbelief, feeling as though her soul was about to leave her body.

"Maria told Brando to do 'whatever it takes' to save you from the plague. She didn't care for the price, but it was my life," Margaret said as if that was of no consequence. To her, what was done, was done.

Arabella almost threw up at the information, but she honed those feelings into mutable emotions. Affirmation, determination, acceptance.

That information, to be withheld as a secret by Maria, told Arabella that she was making the right choice. Most importantly, that choice needed to be what she knew it had to be all along. Permanent. She couldn't change her mind after a few days. It gave her the confidence to see her plans through. Margaret knew this, knew her sister needed to hear it, to keep Arabella from running back up the west wing into Maria's bed.

"I know you hated Gloucester, but you were always meant to save it. You have to be their leader, their advocate. You have to be your own queen," Margaret professed, walking closer to her sister.

"I know," Arabella sniveled, wiping her tears with the sleeve of the same dress she wore the first day she arrived at court.

"I don't know where I'm going to go now, but I'm not scared anymore. I miss mom, and when I get to her, we'll watch you. I'll always be with you."

Arabella wanted to collapse with despair, but she nodded instead, picking up her storage trunks.

"You should leave now. Dad is opening your letter. I love you," Margaret smiled sadly on her sister's behalf.

With that, Margaret Marella disappeared. Arabella couldn't remember quite what it looked like, her humanity skewing her perception of the metaphysical, but she knew she saw her sister find peace.

Arabella took in the heavenly battle being portrayed on the grand foyer's ceiling one last time. The mahogany walls, the great hall off to the left. While she may have initially needed a compass to find her way when she started, there was only one way out now.

The carriage, for the few islanders who came to visit for the festival, arrived. Arabella heard the castle doors close behind her as she rejoined her people once more.

'♥♥♥'

Maria woke at dawn the next morning to find Arabella's side of the bed cold and empty. Arabella was the type of person to take up the entire bed, throwing her leg around in various positions, yet there wasn't a kernel of warmth to be found within the satin red sheets. Arabella also wasn't the type of person to wake up until noon, making her absence even more unsettling.

Maria found herself in a fight or flight mode out of habit. Especially considering the tensions with Eminence were escalating, to the point that there was talk of them turning around to force a coup. She sprung out of bed, managing to throw on the clothes from the night prior. She sheathed her sword before moving through the hall on a mission. Her hair was a mess, looking as if she had time traveled from the battle that was surely yet to come.

There were no servants out and about to ask about Arabella's disappearance as Maria ran down the west wing, up the east, all in a matter of a minute. It wasn't long before she was pounding on Arabella and Aquilla's suite, panting as sweat dripped from her temple.

Payje opened her door, diagonally across the hall. "She handed this to me before she left. I didn't read it," Payje looked at Maria sympathetically. In her hands was an envelope sealed with a black wax stamp, an InFiamma color representing forces overwhelmed.

Maria's heart sank as she thought of all the possibilities behind the coding. She used the sharp corner of her sword to tear it swiftly, making haste to read the letter.

"To my dearest Maria,

I write to you grieving my decision, even now. I found myself in a position where I have to ask whether it is worth such agony to love so fiercely. I do not mean to make my decision against your favor in an attempt to do harm, but rather, justice. I do not know if I could find a life of a courtesan for Your Majesty to be fulfilling, because I do not know what fulfills someone I cannot recognize when I look into the mirror.

I want to explore who I am and what it means to be an individual with the power to change the world. Therefore, I decided to return to the Island, while my father remains here as your councilman. I beg that you accept him still, with open arms, as it is my dearest wish.

I also desire you to remain put. Do not follow me, but instead be the best ruler you can be. The truth is, when it comes to the choice of loving you, or myself, I choose myself. I anticipate the resources to the Island regardless of this ending and hope our relationship within long distance business can still flourish. Not for my sake, but for my people.

I wish you the best,

Arabella"

Maria read the note three times and begged to be woken from whatever recurring nightmare she was stuck in. The lucidity never came. Not as she crumpled the letter into her pant pocket, not as she ran down to the stables and mounted her stallion, not as she raced towards the port as fast as her horse could take her.

When she did remember that she was a living human being, that she was Maria Fiamma and that her lover had just left her, she was hours into the journey. Nearly to InFiamma's western ports.

'♥♥♥'

The ports were like any seaside town. The paint on the buildings were chipped, and it was busy with sailors getting ready to dock into the unknown. Maria left her horse at the stables, then bought a cloak in one of the little shops, placing Arabella's letter in its pocket. Hopefully no one would recognize their queen as she groveled on the ground for her lover to return. Maria was ready to do just that, and more.

She stopped inside the docking station that kept tabs of where the ships were going and when they were leaving.

"The ship to the Island is—" the man paused, coughing up a slew of mucus. Maria grew impatient, tapping her foot. "Leaving in a few minutes at the western dock," he finished. Maria didn't bother with gratitude as she ran out the door. She thought, if she had any luck, Arabella would get east and west confused again, as she so often did. Just like when the universe dropped her in Maria's life.

Unfortunately, it was the man that got the docks confused, as when she arrived there was no ship to the Island, just a sailor smoking a joint informing her Arabella's ship would've left minutes ago.

Maria ran to the other dock, and watched as the ship in the distance sailed away. Despite not knowing how to swim against the ocean's current, her emotions took over as she removed her cloak, and began to tread the water, screaming after her lover.

"Arabella!" she kept screaming as she went further in, falling to her knees as the waves crashed into her chest. Her clothes soaked, but she kept going, as if she was going to follow the ship all the way to the Island. She would have, if a hand didn't grab her by her good elbow, pulling her back to shore.

Aquilla could tell it wasn't the ocean that initially made her cheeks wet; Maria had been crying by the time he found her screaming in the water. Knew he couldn't say anything to make her feel better, as it would be futile.

"You shouldn't have taken your sling off, it's a miracle your stitches aren't completely ripped," Aquilla said in a fatherly tone. He guided her to his carriage just above them on shore. "Please have Jessie check your wounds," he insisted as he put her in the carriage, and sent her back to the castle.

Aquilla knew Maria's horse, knew the way back to the castle, but above all else he knew the queen would never be the same after this. He respected his daughter's decision to leave and find herself. He is grateful for it, after all the years of watching her adapt her personality to anyone she clung to.

However, he felt more at peace when he saw his daughter with the queen, knowing she was protected, taken care of, and valued. It was refreshing, as Arabella's past lovers alike have never shown that quality to meet his standards.

He knew since Maria's coronation that there would be a spark between his daughter and the queen, but he never quite anticipated that Maria would become a second daughter to him. He felt pride in being Maria's councilman, as she was nothing like Elias. After this, and with an impending war, he wasn't sure everything would remain that way.

'♥♥♥'

Maria arrived back in her room feeling numb. There was nothing but the scratchiness in the back of her throat from her failed attempts to summon the woman she loved so dearly.

Brando appeared before her. "It's time for me to go too, Maria," he hoarsely announced. Maria stumbled in shock.

"Not now. Not you too," Maria frantically shook her head.

"I have to, little princess," Brando's voice shook. He called her that in their early days, but not since she was a pre-teen threatening to gouge his ghostly eyes out.

"I can't lose you too right now. I need you," Maria begged, her own voice giving out from her screaming before.

"Even I learned the painful way that when you love somebody, you have to let them go. It's time for me to let you go, and you must do the same—for me, and Arabella." Brando tried to be strong.

"I don't understand why you have to go. You aren't done yet! You may not be my father, but you're my dad. I need my dad, I can't be alone again!" Maria put her scarred hand to her face, her entire body trembling.

"I'll always be your dad, Maria. In this life, and the next," Brando sobbed. "And I am so, so, sorry."

Then Brando Fiamma, just like Margaret Marella, was gone. This time for as long as Maria shall live.

After breaking down, throwing things, and accepting she may soon die without Arabella, Maria reached her hand in her cloak, and tossed the crumbled paper onto the floor. She just stood there for many minutes doing nothing, being no one. It wasn't until she caught a glimpse of a stack of papers under her history books, that her eyes narrowed into rage.

Her body was consumed by fury and grief like she'd never felt before. She knocked the books away, grabbing the papers that would've legally declared Arabella her queen, and her wife, equal partners in their future together. The same ones she drew up and presented to Aquilla to get his blessing just before the Autumn Festival. The fire was still going strong in her room, tended to by a servant while she was out.

Maria took the documents and shoved them into the fire as she began burning them, burning herself, needing to feel anything else as she gripped those papers, and stuck her entire arm into the flames.

For the first time, since the first time seventeen years ago, she was in agony in so many ways. So much so, she let out an excruciating scream as her arm blistered and bled.

Chapter 34

August 14th, 4 Years Later

The smell of perfume, liquor, and dragon's blood incense filled Maria's chambers as she threw her leather jacket on for comfort. Since the council meeting the night prior, she had been ingesting anything she thought might take the edge off, such as whiskey, and other women. All of these things she put her mouth on regularly since Arabella left. What was different this time is she tripled the intake in hopes it would fill her, numb her, and make her too gone to remember what she was about to do.

Summer was coming to an end. The heat proved to be a nightmare for the troops stationed on the eastern border. A month after Maria killed Rainie, the declaration of war was sent by Eminence. No one was surprised considering Lucille's murderer was still at large. Not that Maria cared. She herself beheaded Rainie in front of everyone and moved on just as swiftly.

Everything went downhill from there, especially the poll ratings on how Maria was perceived as queen. She scoffed when she heard that she was only popular with sixty percent of her people, including those in the military and at court.

It was an accumulation of many things. The war had been ongoing for nearly four years, and had taken resources from everyone associated with the kingdom. Maria wasn't

440

exactly frugal in the beginning of the war either, funding exploration projects that had less than promising results. Not in the way anyone on the continent could have ever anticipated. When you factor in the reminder that Maria was essentially fighting her father's dream war, her reign was less than ideal.

There were three different women she left twisted in her sheets as she stepped out of her chambers, and entered Abigail's next door, lighting a joint.

"Hey, honey," Maria greeted Abigail, who was painting one of the white oak dressers. Abigail did well to make Odette's home her own over the years, using a lot of paint and embroidery skills to do so.

"You smell like smoke and sex," Abigail drawled, still focusing on her work even as Maria planted a kiss on her head. "I mean that with respect and admiration, though," she amended.

Maria gave a sheepish smile, feeling a tinge of guilt deep down. There was no secret that Abigail still loved her, but Maria couldn't find it in herself to form attachments in years. She knew it bothered Abigail; all of the women.

To Abigail, that left a lot of doors open for Maria to fall in love again with anyone other than her. Her sensuality was her only play, and Maria wasn't allowing her to execute it. Maria did fund Abigail's schooling though. She gave

Abigail anything she wanted, really. Just not her heart, as she was working overtime to convince everyone it didn't exist anymore.

"I would like you to stay in and paint while I'm downstairs reducing myself to barbaric power displays," Maria smoothed her hand through Abigail's red hair.

"I was already planning on it," Abigail responded honestly, dipping her paintbrush in some water.

"I understand. If you need anything, let me know," Maria promised, making to leave. Abigail stopped her though, getting some olive green paint on Maria's jacket cuff.

"I think this is going to be harder for you than I. It may not be a contest, but it took us years to convince you this was the right move, even with insurance that no innocents would suffer. Say the word, Ria. I will run with you so far from this hell hole. Cienfuegos and Jessie can come too. We'll never be seen again," Abigail offered for the millionth time that week alone.

Maria wanted to remind Abigail that she never planned to live as long as she had. For the months following Arabella's departure, council meetings were held from the other side of her chamber's solid wood door. With Brando's final warning and apology, she assumed she'd drop dead from despair.

"I have to do this. You know I wouldn't if it wasn't necessary. I tried to bide our time with the excursion project, but there is nowhere to run that isn't occupied. We cannot risk it," Maria explained again, leaving Abigail to her art.

Maria recalled the day the decision was made.

"I cannot," Maria begged at the meeting when it was decided. She tried to exhaust every other option to deal with the rebellion groups in the Heart of InFiamma. Those same groups trickled into the military, which would become even harder to control.

Maria tried to push her council away. She told all of them every wrong thing she'd ever done, including professing to Aquilla her gift, and the bargain that took Margaret's life. She wanted them all to leave just like Arabella did, so their hands wouldn't be scarred by the fire and blood her family's rule was built on. Yet, they all were gathered around that council table anyways.

"This goes against everything I am. When I do this, I'll be proving everyone who has hurt me right. I will be validating decades of abuse," Maria pleaded, breaking down to whatever god could take pity on her. Who needed a god when a devil like Thoman was on her council?

He wasn't new to this. In fact, given the large-scale atrocities he committed under Elias, to him this wasn't even a disgrace in the slightest. "I think you are weak, Maria. You are so soft, you cannot stand on your own two feet and do what needs to be done for your kingdom," he solemnly explained. He didn't want to hurt her, but it was true. The past four years she had marked every action on the hopes Arabella would see she was good, or worth loving again. Maria had either let too much slide, or had not cared enough about ruling to stop it.

"Trust though, if this coup succeeds, everyone in this room will be murdered, brutally. Then those on the Island, who we send resources to. The same resources we aren't giving to the mainland villagers. The Island will face a genocide by the likes we haven't seen since Radiance," Thoman finished, and Aquilla nodded.

Thoman didn't want to leave her with that memory, rather give her a sense of purpose. To specify that point, he held her back when the meeting was over to tell her a story in private.

"I knew your father our whole lives, practically. We didn't get along at first. My father was a known traitor, so I was forced to be in Elias' service as a punishment. I tried to kill your father many times as children before I realized he wasn't the enemy," Thoman opened up. He was hoping to explain to Maria that life has different phases where

perception is concerned, but it became the ramblings of a man past his prime.

Maria swished her glass around as she pondered who the real enemy was. "Don't go on telling me it was actually my grandfather, Ash Fiamma. Because that argument goes up to Firenze herself. The people to blame are the ones who act on their evils."

"Sometimes. But let's just say it was bad enough for me and Elias to kill Ash Fiamma ourselves for what he was doing. If you think your father was a monster, you should have seen Ash," Thoman swore, putting his hands through his hair as he recalled some horrific memory.

"Monsters are monsters. Their actions don't need to be comparable. By tomorrow, my people would agree that I'll be one too," Maria affirmed to herself, swallowing down that sense of dread.

Maria knew there was no turning back now. She grabbed her torch and matches, and headed out into the meadow where three makeshift pyres were built in the night. There were three bodies already tied to them individually. Maria said nothing as she lit her torch, then the pyres.

When the pyres were fully lit, but the outlines of the bodies were clear enough to see through the flames, was when Thoman and Cienfuegos corralled everyone over the age of sixteen to see. There was their ruler, a mere black silhouette as she stood in front of the fires, holding the very torch that lit them.

"I don't do secrets," Maria spoke, solidifying to her people it was in fact her. From the wealthiest families at court, to the servants, all of them gawked at her, frozen in place.

"I'm well aware that this war has cost our people more than just money, but fathers, sisters, children. Before you all are the bodies of three traitors responsible for the attack on unit eleven stationed at the southeast border." Murmuring broke out in the crowd, and when Maria glanced at Thoman he gave a shallow nod to continue.

"If you are worried about it being you or your children on this pyre next, don't. All of these traitors confessed, and were thoroughly investigated before conviction," Maria swore, feeling an intense pang of guilt. She threw the torch into the pyre directly behind her, then repositioned herself to face the crowd.

"This war, this disconnect and disorder in my kingdom, will be over by spring. I swear that on my life. I'll be giving Eminence, and by proxy, the rebellion leaders one last chance to surrender at The Summit. If they decline," Maria sighed, glancing behind her at the pyres again. "Then that will be them, and everyone that supports them. Because I will not send your loved ones to die in this war any longer."

When Maria faced her subjects again, it was dead silent. Through the illumination she could make out their features contemplating, until one man in the crowd slowly began to clap. Maria made him out as Ignacio's father, whose health had declined since Ignacio's unit was stationed in the north. The people followed suit, some even giving exasperated cheers and blessings for the proclamation to get the war over with. It was as if there weren't bodies burning right in front of them.

Maria gave Payje a look on the sidelines. The blonde woman wore a frown on her face, but she did give a gesture to Maria of understanding. No more papers to the Island, and a doubling down of propaganda to be sent in between every gossip log.

Maria returned a gesture of gratitude, relieving her people to spread the news as she knew they would. Yes, there were people who still gave her glares, but they were less directed now that the hope was sowed through her home masses. Even if her actions were fraudulent.

The truth was, those weren't bodies of traitors. The bodies Maria took the torch to were deceased members of unit eleven. That's why Maria had to light that torch before her people arrived, because if anyone looked too closely, they would see the decomposition, hear the lack of screams, and know their ruler was in fact a spineless one.

Thoman went to find something to eat, too desensitized to care. He spent his mealtime alone, remembering the first time he had to burn someone on Elias' orders. He knew he belonged to Elias from the moment he was charged into his service. Maybe even before, when they were boys. But it was at that moment when Thoman had to burn his own father alive, that he made his choice to choose Elias for as long as they lived.

As he reminisced on it with a tuna sandwich in one hand, the onyx necklace he once gifted Elias in the other, he felt a chill run across his back. It was as if someone was rubbing the tension away, as Elias used to when Thoman got especially stressed or remorseful of his actions.

"To think there was a time when I would have rather been caught dead than be seen with that malicious prince," Thoman mumbled to himself, causing some crumbs to fall from his mouth. As he sniffed in the air around him, he swore he could smell Elias' cologne ever so slightly.

'♥♥♥'

Maria was upstairs staring into her fireplace like a cat stares at a bird. Waiting for the flames to strike, and debating whether to be the one to leap into them first to get it over with. She couldn't stand it anymore, so she took a bucket of water and extinguished the flames leaving herself in pitch blackness.

"I get how you lit yourself on fire now, dickhead," Maria cursed her father. Enveloped in the darkness around her, she never imagined that the dickhead in question would answer back.

"Snuffing out your fire is a sign of weakness, child," the voice sounded from both beside her, and everywhere around her, like a cloak in the thick of winter.

"Oh, I'm losing it. You found peace," Maria scoffed with a lighthearted chuckle, trying to find humor in her insanity.

"You have learned about summoning, no?" Elias responded coolly. Maria tensed up every muscle in her body like she was in paralysis.

"I touched nothing that belonged to you, nothing personal to conjure you," Maria insisted, convincing herself.

"It wasn't you who summoned me. I would love to go back to peace though, so get your act together and stop desecrating my legacy before I become more permanent and haunt you," Elias seethed.

"You didn't deserve peace, you bastard. Tell that cunt Ares I said hello as well," Maria demanded, because if anything she was queen now, not him.

She heard her father's chuckle from a bit further away, as if he was pacing in the darkness. Maria moved to her desk to find some matches. "His influence was a hard one to maintain, partially why I went mad. Brando leaving you was the best thing he could have done for you, or you would have mentally declined. Not in war, but in those redundant history books."

"Brando was a better father for me than you ever were. Keep his name out of your mouth." Maria sneered from her desk once she found it in the darkness.

"Maybe so, but to share a soul with someone dead, that is not inconsequential. He knew this moment in your reign would happen and did not prepare you for it. I did," Elias insisted, moving closer to Maria once again.

"By burning your wife! Then letting me believe you killed my first love! How joyous!" Maria mocked like she was fifteen again.

When Maria sparked a match, Elias' face was mere inches from the tiny flame. "There are things in this life more important than love. If that Marella whore never left you wouldn't have realized it, but she is now pen-pals with your enemy as we speak. You'd do well to get that Island in line."

Maria assessed her father's face, and for the first time, couldn't see her own in it. Plus, he was shorter than her, which made her laugh. "You are such a pitiful man, it's humorous. Of course you don't value love, because who could love you?"

Elias' features twisted, not into rage, but something else. "I was loved well enough, but Ares told me that you would grow to hate me more than anyone in the world. Unlike Brando, he didn't withhold his knowledge from me. How was I supposed to know I would be the one to cause it?"

Maria rolled her eyes. "Poor you, having the consequences of your actions coming back to bite you in the ass. Don't blame it on Ares, he's dead. He couldn't force you to do anything."

Maria paced to the fireplace and lit a lantern before flicking the match onto the damp wood. The lantern illuminated her room more, but not as much as the fireplace would have. Even with the minimal firelight, Maria could see her father looked far younger than when he died. Illness aside, he looked even younger than Maria did now at twenty-seven.

"You still don't get it. I commend Brando for not telling you everything, because even I couldn't handle its weight apparently," he confessed, and Maria finally began to listen. She never heard her father admit he was even close to being inadequate.

"Brando knows everything. He knew from the night he met you how you will live, love, fight, kill, and die. He could have told you this would happen, given you time to prepare, but he did not. Ares told me and I made sure you had a model of strength to go off of. That was me, not Brando."

Maria cocked her head. "What do you mean 'Ares told you'? Brando said he never spoke to his father. How would Ares know?"

Elias' eyes turned feral. "You foolish girl. When will you catch on? The Odd One is a liar. He has led you to this very moment, like a sheep to the wolves so you may take his burdens someday. You may think he found peace? He has not. If I could after all I've done, and yet he remains in this liminal space, do you believe there is no reason still?"

"Why are you trying to get into my head?" Maria protested, letting her logic overcome her emotions. "Brando found peace; he told me his job was done once Arabella left me. He told me the day of my coronation to repair old ties and I did. He instructed me the way he needed to until that task was done, then he left," Maria rationalized.

"He may not be here, but his job is far from over. You are too much of a coward to kill the Marella girl, we've all seen it, and so I must watch you oblige by this family's curse until you are the one shackled. Firenze always did have a job for the outcasts in this family."

"What does this have to do with Arabella? She's been gone for years, and she isn't coming back," Maria took a step towards her father. She may not be able to do any damage, but she would throttle the empty air if it meant making a point.

"Even now, you forget yourself where she's concerned. That is when you lose your logic, and your emotions overrule. That is reason enough, take it from me," Elias scoffed, folding his arms in a similar manner Maria always did when on the defense. The flame in the lantern swayed delicately, but the energy in the room was anything but gentle.

"You forget yourself, actually. I'm the reigning monarch of this kingdom now, not you," Maria insisted, feeling pride swell in her chest at the ability to outrank the source of her inferiority growing up.

"Have you ever heard the saying 'kings are small in the presence of a god,' Maria?" Elias insisted, giving her a look that told her she walked into that one.

"When I'm in the presence of a god, then I'll check in with you."

"You will be, soon enough," Elias promised with near devastation in his eyes, which made Maria all the more enraged. He had no right to feel sorrow or profess his familial love for Maria. Yet he stood before her like a fox dressed as a wounded chicken, begging for mercy after killing the flock.

"When you are done here, I want you gone. Disappear into thin air back where you came from. Do. Not. Linger," Maria commanded.

Elias clenched his jaw but nodded, slowly. He fixed his posture and smoothed out the jacket he was wearing, then he took a step back, clasping his hands together.

"Your mother does miss you, by the way. She is apologetic that the applause overtook her before she could say goodbye. I just came to tell you, heaven isn't what you think it is," Elias replied, in a manner more stoic than usual. As if he wasn't allowed to feel anything anymore. That included disdain.

"Am I going where you are?" Maria took advantage of all the talk of secrets. If she wanted to know anything, it was that one major revelation.

"No, you do not belong where I am," his only reply. Before he disappeared, he muttered one last sentiment. "Happy birthday, Maria. It won't be long now."

Elias was gone in an instant, leaving Maria to the weight of what she'd done. She did have one key

distraction. That objective was clear. Find out what Arabella
Marella was up to on her island all those years in solitude.

Acknowledgements

I would first like to thank Kaylee Whitehead for not only supporting me as a friend, but also taking the time to edit this book. Without her, this book never would have seen the light of day (or would have an even more excessive amount of commas, as well as the word serf spelt as surf.) I miss the days of getting email notifications that you were in the beta document editing, as it was the best, and most terrifying time of my life thus far. 154 days since we started those edits to publication, and we've come such a long way.

I'd like to thank Tracy Palmer, who acted as my muse on many occasions. I sat down with her one day stuck on what to do with Odette's character, or if I even wanted her to reappear. Just talking to Tracy gave me such inspiration to make Heart of Arson the finalized version it is today. I'm grateful I could immortalize our time on desk together within this book.

To my mother, if it wasn't for your support, making a safe space and a home for me, I'd never be able to follow my dreams like this. I'm forever grateful for all the sacrifices you make for us children. I love you to the moon and back.

To my friends who listened to me ramble on about this book for hours at a time, such as Laura and Jamesha. You two were with me as I fleshed out my stories in real time. That companionship was the support I needed to keep going, even when the fear of not being a good enough writer constantly plagued my mind.

To anyone who read Heart of Arson to this point, thank you. Being a first time, indie, self-published author I knew that the end project wasn't going to be perfect, but I am so proud of how much I've grown as a writer in the process of creating this story. If it wasn't for the people who read it though, it would forever live in my memory alone. It is because of you that I was able to turn my passion into something so real, that it now lives on outside of myself.

Last, but surely not least, thank you to everyone at PVL. Don't look me in the eyes after reading this, but yeah you guys are the best coworkers, and your support is so personal to me. Very few jobs give an opportunity to write an entire book in between helping patrons on desk, but here we are 100,000+ words later.

Cienfuegos moved to Inferniana immediately following his parents' deaths. He was sixteen, but he was not new blood in the military. He made it a point to gain respect when living with his parents in the military city, which was on and off as he also lived within the castle. Sending Cienfuegos to InFiamma's castle was for more structural training, such as war council.

Analise Fiamma was well loved and respected in the military, not just because she was the sister of Elias Fiamma, but because she was the fiercest, most kind-hearted warrior on the continent. Cienfuegos intended to follow in her footsteps, and everyone knew it. That was likely why he survived his first week as commander, given the hazing that Elias had in mind.

"I demand strength from the commander in charge of my military," Elias emphasized, pushing Cienfuegos into a dirt sparring pit. It was clearly a punishment for holding on to Maria. They needed to be pried away from each other. It made both of them look vulnerable.

"If anyone has the balls to kill him, you can take his place as commander. If he lives after three days, you are to obey him from thereon out," Elias insisted.

Cienfuegos straightened his posture and looked every man in the vicinity right in their eyes, assessing who would strike first. The last pair he landed on were that of Thoman's son, Jessie. There was a glare in Jessie's glasses from the sun as they stood in the dirt pit located outdoors. Even through that glare, Cienfuegos was able to pick up on Jessie's expression which read, *'I'll be seeing you soon, I take it.'*

Cienfuegos gave a small wink to the future war surgeon of Inferniana, having been mended by him multiple times over the past few months. Jessie began to fidget in a way only Cienfuegos had noticed, picking at his fingernails while his hands stayed pressed to the sides of his legs.

InFiamma's military district had a culture of its own. While there were a few groups of people who tried to jump Cienfuegos in the halls, there was more honor in directly challenging him in public. Still, the first day he had to question whether being commander was worth it, or if he could make it back to the castle, and grab Maria before bolting to Withelle without anyone noticing.

"How many men did you take on tonight?" Jessie questioned as he applied tiger balm to Cienfuegos' ribs. Although they were well acquainted in that manner, they still weren't quite out of the small talk stage.

"Seventeen. Why don't you come next time so I don't have to hobble down the hall with a bruised rib?" Cienfuegos grumbled, pressing his face into a pillow as he laid face down on Jessie's medical bed.

Jessie adjusted his glasses before whispering, "I don't want to see the violence."

Cienfuegos snorted, then cringed at the pain it caused him. "You chose a shit profession then, war surgeon." Cienfuegos tried to push himself up, but Jessie pinned him back down. Cienfuegos yelped.

"From how many times I've stitched you up, it should be evident it is only the violent action that bothers me, not the gore."

Cienfuegos rolled his eyes but did not try to leave again. He did attempt to reposition his body, so he wasn't smothering himself. "You blanched the first time you fixed me up. Why did you come here in the first place? You could have gone with the rest of our age group to Cadence to be some fashion model."

"I blanched because- irrelevancy," Jessie shook off the need for a rebuttal. "If you weren't so egotistical, you would be smarter. You know that if you aren't in that pit, you can't be challenged."

Cienfuegos sighed dramatically, but did not waste his breath on explaining the need to show strength. Jessie wasn't ignorant on those matters, especially with having Thoman as a father. Instead, Cienfuegos said just that. "Your intelligence is a direct attribute to your attractiveness. Playing dumb doesn't suit you."

Jessie's face turned red as he threw the balm back into his satchel. "You can go now. I'm sure I'll see you again before dawn," he insisted, leaving Cienfuegos in the medical wing to dress.

Cienfuegos stayed on the bed for a minute. Now alone he had time to process not just the excruciating pain his body was in, but the ache from losing his family less than 48 hours ago. Tears threatened to fall from his eyes. Back when he was younger, that was never allowed. He was told future commanders don't cry. At that moment, if he was to die soon, he would allow himself that liberation. It felt good, even though he felt bad.

He didn't know Jessie was standing behind the door, listening to his soft sobs. Cienfuegos didn't hear the two men at the end of the hall who talked about storming in there and slitting his throat. Jessie did though, reaching into his satchel and grabbing his amputation axe, the one he received that morning for emergencies on the battlefield. He was supposed to do training on how to use it tomorrow, but he was nothing if not an overachiever. He wouldn't be the only one learning a lesson as he rounded the corner, approaching Cienfuegos' would be assailants.

'♥♥♥'

Cienfuegos didn't go to his suite. Although it was the same one he grew up in, he was sure if he smelt his mother's perfume or his father's craft supplies, he wouldn't have the strength to survive the next two days. Instead, he found a broom closet and slept around five hours, which he thought was generous. At dawn he began his first duties as commander. He wondered where Maria was, although he knew he didn't even need to ask. She was on her pillar, drinking her morning tea.

He did his conditioning and drills with the men, who showed him respect even if they were plotting to kill him that night. He did not eat lunch with them though, for fear

461

his food was poisoned. He snuck into the medical wing to purge Jessie's cheese crackers that he always kept in his bag.

After that, he did some more tactical work, assessing formations and strategies. When dinner rolled around, he waited at the pit for his challenges. There were twenty-five opponents that night. The only thing keeping his body working was the hope that if he survived tomorrow, he could take as long of a break as he wanted to on his own authority. He did not make it to the broom closet though.

Cienfuegos luckily did not turn the corner fully when he saw the three men huddled by the door, listening for what Cienfuegos presumed was him. Paranoia from exhaustion set in, making him wonder if Maria wasn't the only one gifted, and if there were ghosts and seers playing their own games within the military district. How else could anyone have known?

He took an alternative route to the medical wing where Jessie worked on him in near silence until the end. "Next time you want some of my crackers, just ask."

"You have no proof it was me," Cienfuegos insisted, halfheartedly claiming innocence. Cienfuegos wasn't offended that Jessie never gave into the argument, or maybe he did, and Cienfuegos just did not hear him considering he fell asleep as Jessie stitched up his cheek.

When he woke up, Jessie was asleep on the recliner to the right of him. He had an axe in his hand, which Cienfuegos thought was odd considering he liked to play

Mr. Pacifism. When Cienfuegos tip-toed out of the room to find a new broom closet for the remainder of the night, this time down the left hall, his heart nearly stopped when he opened one of the broom closets. Two dead bodies were stuffed inside, axe wounds to their necks and chests.

Cienfuegos jogged right back into the medical room and kicked Jessie in the feet. Jessie startled awake and went to swing the axe, but Cienfuegos caught his wrist with one hand. He threw Jessie back against the recliner and climbed atop him, placing his forearm across Jessie's throat. "The weak act was very convincing, I'm impressed. Medical freaks always give off serial killer vibes, so I'm still not quite surprised."

"I'm not a serial killer, Cienfuegos. I heard them say they were going to slit your throat," Jessie said, arching his chest up but Cienfuegos pushed it back down.

"You said you hate violence, but here you are stuffing bodies in a broom closet. Sounds like you secretly love it," Cienfuegos insisted.

"I secretly love a lot of things, but violence isn't amongst them. You have killed before too, assisting in our parents' slaughters. Yet you and your cousin–" Jessie was saying in a whisper before Cienfuegos cut him off, pressing down his entire weight now.

"My. Cousin. What?" Cienfuegos grounded out, his eyes turning feral.

"You and your cousin, you have gentle souls behind your eyes. Even though you two are like rocks with sharp edges, if someone picks the rocks up with firm grasps then gets cut, does that make the rock violent?" Jessie wheezed from the pressure. Cienfuegos did not reply, but his gaze changed to a more assessing one.

"When I said I didn't want to watch the violence, that didn't mean I had no understanding for why there's violence in the first place. Or I would have become one of those models you envisioned me as," Jessie's eyebrow quirked upwards, his glasses slightly tilted to the side.

"It is a reminder that there will always be someone for me to heal. Whether it is people like you, or people like those two. If there must be violence, let it be against those who don't stand for what you do," Jessie fidgeted as Cienfuegos' grip loosened a bit.

"What do I stand for?" Cienfuegos asked. He wanted to know that himself as of late.

"Loyalty, and love."

"Love?" Cienfuegos whispered, eyes subtly flickered down to Jessie's lips, then back up to his eyes as he scrunched his brows. They stayed in that silent moment for mere seconds before someone banged on the door. In protective instinct, Cienfuegos leaped up, ripping the axe from Jessie's hand.

When he flung open the door, some of his fellow high-ranking men, accompanied by a newer cadet, were waiting with stern faces. "Commander!" one of the men said urgently, readying his arm to point down the hall at the dead bodies. He paused when he saw the axe in Cienfuegos' hands, understanding smoothed over his face. "Oh, I see."

"I was being tailed, so I popped in here to grab an amputation axe," Cienfuegos explained. Jessie's mouth parted in confusion, wondering how Cienfuegos knew its exact purpose. It was a last resort tool as far as amputation was concerned. Little did Jessie know; Cienfuegos had been keeping up with his day-to-day itinerary. Half for the necessity, half for reasons even Cienfuegos hasn't admitted to himself.

"Ignacio, dispose of the bodies please," one of the other high-ranking men commanded the younger cadet, maybe fourteen years old. He had a look of cool determination in his eyes as he saluted and carried on to complete the task. Cienfuegos wondered how Ignacio would be able to carry two grown men to their graves, even though the boy was only two years younger than himself. Ignacio looked to still be just a boy, but that didn't stop Cienfuegos from finding admiration in his dedication for getting it done.

"Thank you," Cienfuegos called after Ignacio, who froze at the appreciation. One of the officials tried to cover his sneer. Ignacio turned around with something hesitant in his eyes before bowing to his commander, scurrying away to do his duties after.

The rest of the officials muttered their apologies for wasting Cienfuegos' time, carrying on to play cards in the hall. Cienfuegos stepped out soon after them, not saying a word to Jessie. In order to address that, he needed to first address what he had been putting off.

When he entered his suite, he immediately regretted it. It wasn't his mother's scent or books, nor his father's miniature collection, that made something in him snap with grief. Indeed, people did search the suite for him well before then, as the entire place was ripped to shreds.

It wasn't the destruction of the suite that bothered him. He didn't care for living in Inferniana as a child, where there was so much uniformity and lack of feeling. Most days he stared at the ugly mustard yellow wallpaper and wondered why on earth anyone would prefer staying there, over the castle. In that suite, there was no playing war with his cousin. There were no little league sword competitions—the ones he won every time, but Maria was banned from because she broke some kids' nose. There was just picking at carpet and hearing the soldiers march outside.

What bothered Cienfuegos, is that it was a deliberate attack against Analise Fiamma's memory, from those who likely didn't respect her position as commander either. That, he would have to be violent for. Just as Jessie said, for love, and loyalty.

He knew he couldn't stay in that suite with the way it was. Probably still couldn't even if not, given there were likely different groups of people having similar ideas. He did well at making himself sparse, untraceable. He had one more night of doing that, for by midnight tomorrow, he would be untouchable by law.

He went to sleep in the medical wing again, but quickly noticed it was now in the same state as his parent's suite. Destroyed. It was then he realized his biggest fear. By association, Jessie was under threat.

Cienfuegos ran to where he knew Jessie would be staying. He never approached Jessie's personal chambers before then for the very fear of the reality he now lived in. Banging on the door, Jessie opened after too long of a beat. He saw Cienfuegos preparing to break the door in.

"What is your problem?" Jessie scoffed, taking a step back.

"My problem is the entire medical wing is trashed. I thought they hurt you!" Cienfuegos said frantically. He took a step forward, lingering in the threshold.

"Oh, you worried for your favorite serial killer?" Jessie asked dryly. His glasses weren't on, attributing to his squinting. He kept an extra pair by the entryway table, so he applied those ones instead. The frames were a thicker black compared to his thin round ones.

"They destroyed my suite as well," Cienfuegos evaded the question, a slight blush showing in the torchlight.

"I'm sorry," Jessie frowned, then sighed. "I'm also sorry for not coming to you about those men. I think sometimes it is easier for you to see me as weak."

"Why do you say that?" Cienfuegos inquired, leaning his good side against the door frame.

"Because," Jessie began, smoothing his hair back. "You do the same thing. You act strong when you're secretly a softie. I didn't want to disrupt our dynamic."

"Fuck you, I am not a softie. I took on dozens of men single handedly," Cienfuegos said with offense. "You think you know me, you don't. You think you can see through these eyes? You can barely see through your own."

"Right. So, about a year ago that wasn't you who snuck into the stables, and fed that stray cat an entire birthday cake?" Jessie pinched his lips in between his fingers, looking at Cienfuegos' with a questioning gaze. "We're both liars," he affirmed.

Cienfuegos, caught in the lie, said nothing as he remained as tense as solid wood. Jessie looked him in the eyes and let out a sigh. "I see," he said, taking his glasses off to clean them on his shirt. As he lifted the tank top, revealing a rather fit physique, Cienfuegos swallowed hard.

When Jessie placed his glasses back on, he clasped his hands together for a moment, before grabbing Cienfuegos by the collar of his shirt, and pulling him into a deep kiss. He kicked the door shut behind himself, locking it without looking.

'♥♥♥'

It was the last day Cienfuegos could be challenged, but nobody did. Nobody could hardly eat, either, matching the emptiness of Cienfuegos' own stomach as three of the highest-ranking officials aside from Cienfuegos, now hung decomposing in the cafeteria.

Cienfuegos was an intelligent individual. He knew amongst that group of officials that spoke to him in the medical wing, one of them sent the attack. It took one fourteen-year-old boy, Ignacio, to confirm that. It was Ignacio that enlightened Cienfuegos on every detail from the past few weeks.

From whom the conspirators against his parents were, to who ordered the attack on the wing. Cienfuegos had Ignacio deliver a letter to Elias immediately, telling him who on his own council played a part in his sister's death. Before doing that, Cienfuegos had one question. "Why tell me all of this?"

"My father is a strong man because he is a kind one. Never have I once been thanked for any service I've ever done. My father always told me the first man to thank me is the man to align with. I will happily do what you ask, as long as you never lose that element to yourself," Ignacio said with honesty in his eyes.

Cienfuegos thought for the first time, with comrades like Ignacio, he may be able to build something honorable during his time as commander. He may be able to establish a respectable life, and live long enough to secure his cousin on the throne after all Elias had done, and would do in the years to come.

He hesitantly took Jessie up on his offer to sleep in his room again. "I don't want you to die because of me," Cienfuegos confessed as he laid on Jessie's chest.

"We can worry about the nature of our deaths when we die. Until then, I am rather inspired to live a life with you where we throw weird parties for animals, feeding them cake. I think the horses would like apple pie instead, though," Jessie envisioned with a smile.

"You know, after I am done making renovations to my suite, I may need a live-in doctor. Besides, this room is far too tiny. You need space to put your…axes," Cienfuegos cringed as he botched the request for Jessie to move in with him.

"Can we paint the walls green?" Jessie asked, removing his glasses.

"We can paint the walls green," Cienfuegos yawned.

He was able to sleep peacefully that night.